BETRAYAL OF MERCIA

BOOK 7 THE EAGLE OF MERCIA CHRONICLES

MJ PORTER

Boldwood

First published in Great Britain in 2025 by Boldwood Books Ltd.

Copyright © MJ Porter, 2025

Cover Design by Head Design Ltd.

Cover Images: iStock

Maps designed by Flintlock Covers

The moral right of MJ Porter to be identified as the author of this work has been asserted in accordance with the Copyright, Designs and Patents Act 1988.

All rights reserved. No part of this book may be reproduced in any form or by any electronic or mechanical means, including information storage and retrieval systems, without written permission from the author, except for the use of brief quotations in a book review. This book is a work of fiction and, except in the case of historical fact, any resemblance to actual persons, living or dead, is purely coincidental.

Every effort has been made to obtain the necessary permissions with reference to copyright material, both illustrative and quoted. We apologise for any omissions in this respect and will be pleased to make the appropriate acknowledgements in any future edition.

A CIP catalogue record for this book is available from the British Library.

Paperback ISBN 978-1-83617-486-8

Large Print ISBN 978-1-83617-485-1

Hardback ISBN 978-1-83617-484-4

Ebook ISBN 978-1-83617-487-5

Kindle ISBN 978-1-83617-488-2

Audio CD ISBN 978-1-83617-479-0

MP3 CD ISBN 978-1-83617-480-6

Digital audio download ISBN 978-1-83617-483-7

This book is printed on certified sustainable paper. Boldwood Books is dedicated to putting sustainability at the heart of our business. For more information please visit https://www.boldwoodbooks.com/about-us/sustainability/

Boldwood Books Ltd, 23 Bowerdean Street, London, SW6 3TN

www.boldwoodbooks.com

For my brother, AC, AKA 'Uncle Al,' who taught me all about concussion, and ruined fish pie for two decades. Keep wearing your helmet.

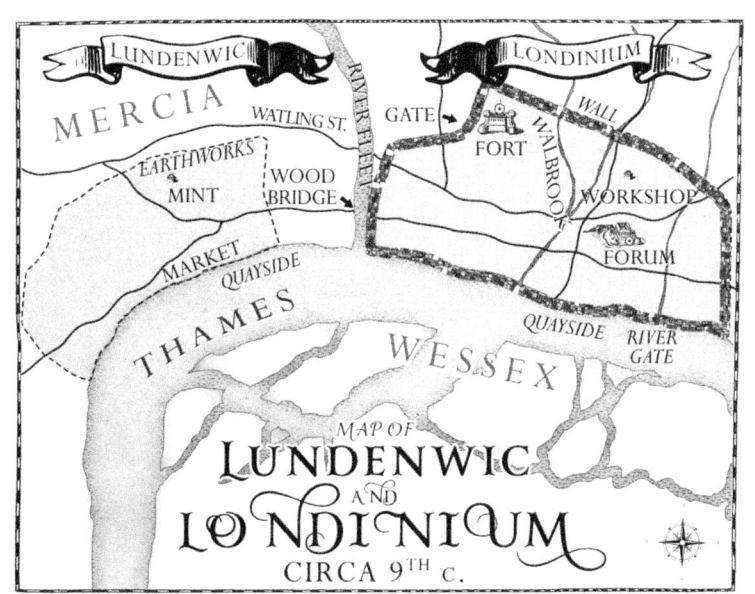

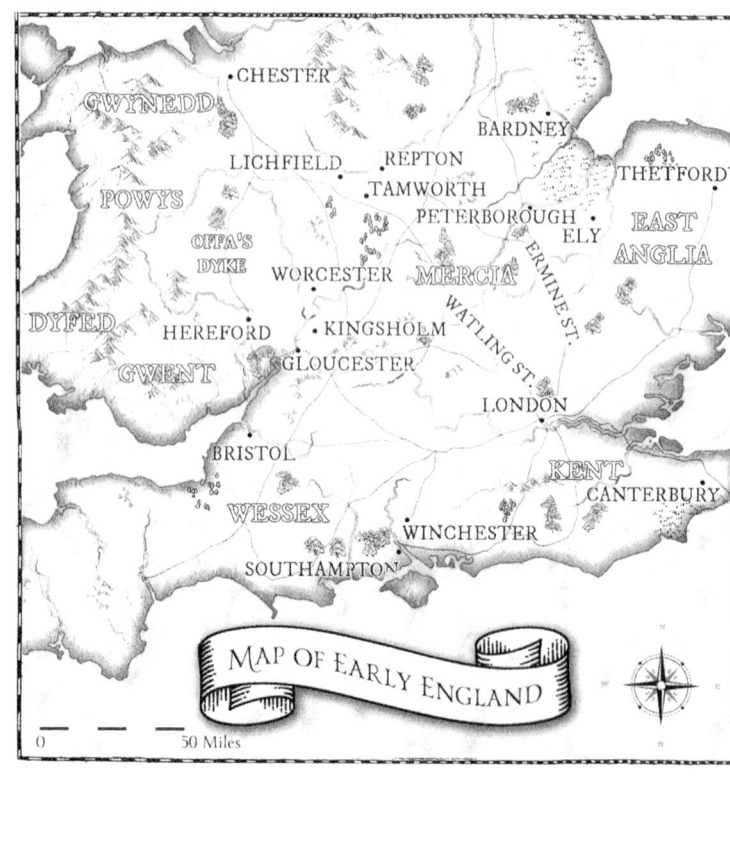

CAST OF CHARACTERS

Brute, Icel's horse
Cenfrith, Icel's uncle, brother of Ceolburh and one of the Mercian king's warriors, who dies in *Son of Mercia*
Edwin, Icel's childhood friend, in exile with Lord Coenwulf
Icel, warrior of Mercia, his mother was Ceolburh, his father a previous king of Mercia, although only he and Wynflæd know this
Wine, Cenfrith's horse, now Icel's alongside Brute
Wynflæd, an old herbwoman at the Mercian king's court at Tamworth

The Kings of Mercia
Coenwulf, king of Mercia r.796–821 (died)
His son, Coenhelm, murdered before his father's death
Coelwulf, king of Mercia r.821–825 (deposed), father of Lord Coenwulf
Beornwulf, king of Mercia r.825–826 (killed)
Lady Cynehild, King Beornwulf's wife before marrying Lord Coenwulf, now dead

Wiglaf, king of Mercia r.827–829 (deposed) r.830–
Queen Cynethryth, Wiglaf's wife
Wigmund, Wiglaf's son, married to Lady Ælflæd, sister of Lord Coenwulf
Wigstan, Wigmund and Lady Ælflæd's young son
Ecgberht, king of Wessex r.802 onwards, r.829 in Mercia

The Ealdormen/Bishops of Mercia
Ælfstan, one of King Wiglaf's supporters, an ally to Icel who is a member of his war band
Ælflæd, Lord Coenwulf's sister, married to Lord Wigmund, the king's son
Ælfred, ally of Lord Wigmund
Æthelweald, bishop of Lichfield
Beornoth, one of King Wiglaf's ealdormen
Beorhtwulf, a lord of Mercia
Ceolbeorht, bishop of Londonia
Ceolnoth, archbishop of Canterbury
Eadwulf, bishop of Hereford
Heahbeorht, bishop of Worcester
Hunbeohrt, bishop of Leicester
Hunberht, an ally of Lord Wigmund
Muca, one of King Wiglaf's ealdormen
Sigegar, Sigered's grandson
Sigered, a long-standing ealdorman who's survived the troubled years of the 820s
Tidwulf, an ally of King Wiglaf
Wicga, ally of Lord Wigmund

Rulers of Other Kingdoms
Æthelwulf, Ecgberht's son, king of Kent, under his father
Athelstan, king of the East Angles

Ealdorman Hereberht, ealdorman of Kent
Ecgberht, king of Wessex

Ealdorman Ælfstan's Warriors
Bada, Wulfheard's horse
Bicwide, Icel's horse
Cenred, Mercian warrior
Fleotan, another horse
Goðeman, Mercian warrior
Kyre, Mercian warrior
Landwine, Mercian warrior
Maneca, Mercian warrior
Ordlaf, Mercian warrior
Oswy, Mercian warrior, once an ally of the queen
Uor, Mercian warrior
Waldhere, Mercian warrior
Wulfgar, Mercian warrior
Wulfheard, Mercian warrior, Ealdorman Ælfstan's oath-sworn man, brother of Wulfnoth

In Kingsholm
Coenwulf and Coelwulf, the sons of Lord Coenwulf and Lady Cynehild
Eadweard, oath-sworn warrior of Lord Wigmund, now dead
Eadburg, living in Kingsholm, protector of the children, her mother was their wet nurse
Eadbald, Mercian warrior
Lady Cynewise, sister of Lord Coenwulf

In Northumbria
Wulfnoth of Eamont, now dead, brother of Wulfheard

In Tamworth
Brother Sampson/Heca, a member of Bishop Æthelweald's community
Cuthred, training to be a healer with Wynflæd
Eahric, commander of the king's household warriors
Gaya, previously a slave woman with a talent for healing, now freed
Theodore, previously a slave man with a talent for healing, now freed

In Winchester
Brihthild, sister of Brihtwulf
Brihtwulf, brother of Brihthild
Heardlulf, Wessex warrior, brother of Heardred
Heardred, Wessex warrior, brother of Heardlulf

Places Mentioned
Canterbury, home of the archbishop in the kingdom of Kent, was Mercian but claimed by the king of Wessex in the 820s. Built on the Roman ruins of *Durovernum*
Eamont, in the north-west, the site of a famous meeting in 927 (if you look at maps of Saxon England, you'll find precious few names on the north-west side of the country)
Hereford, close to the Welsh borders, in Mercia
Isle of Sheppey, part of Kent, where the Viking raiders held Lord Coenwulf captive
Kingdom of Wessex, the area south of the River Thames, including Kent at this time, but not Dumnonia (Cornwall and Devon)
Kingsholm, associated with the ruling family of King Coelwulf, close to Gloucester, home to the exiled Lord Coenwulf. Lady Ælflæd, his sister, is now living there

Lichfield, close to Tamworth and one of the holy sites in Mercia
Londonia, combining the ruins of Roman Londinium and Saxon Lundenwic
Tamworth, the capital of the Mercian kingdom
Winchester, the capital of the Wessex kingdom, built on the Roman ruins of Venta Belgarum

THE STORY SO FAR

The mystery of who was the ultimate instigator in the abduction of the children of Lady Cynehild and Lord Coenwulf of Kingsholm in *Protector of Mercia* nears resolution.

Icel has journeyed to the enemy kingdom of Wessex, particularly Winchester, on King Wiglaf of Mercia's command to determine if Eadbald had truly visited the place. Eadbald was the man whose testimony devastated Lord Coenwulf's cause, ultimately leading to his punishment of seven years' exile, leaving his children behind in the care of his sister, Lady Ælflæd, wed to the king of Mercia's son. King Wiglaf has always doubted Eadbald's testimony, gainsaid by his wife. He demanded the truth.

While in Winchester, with the young healer, Cuthred, Icel discovered the conspiracy against Mercia's kingship ran far deeper than he could have imagined, seeming to involve the king of Wessex, Ecgberht, and his son, Æthelwulf, now king in Kent. Following a journey to Canterbury, part of Kent, to meet up with the rest of Ealdorman Ælfstan's warriors, all of them have managed to return to Mercia having fought clear of Lord Æthelwulf's forces, with their captive, Brihthild, who knows the truth about the West Saxon conspirators.

Brihthild had vowed never to speak of what she knew, but once Icel shared the truth of how her brother met his death within Londinium (in *Wolf of Mercia*), she denounced the queen of Mercia's treasonous actions, as well as Lord Æthelwulf's, revealing the treachery ran deep within Mercia's own ruling family.

Now, King Wiglaf of Mercia must decide the fate of his queen, as well as those who aided her, which might very well include his son, the ætheling Lord Wigmund, and the prominent bishop of Lichfield. Lord Wigmund is wed to the sister of the exiled Lord Coenwulf, known to be in Frankia with his warriors, while his sons remain in Mercia, under her care. Lord Coenwulf's sons, grandsons of a former king, are also both æthelings. Their deaths could have led to Mercia being denuded of her strong ruling line, allowing Wessex to once more take Mercia in her grasp, as aside from Lord Wigmund, only his small, weak son also has a claim to rule after Wiglaf's death.

Not even the queen, or her son, are above the law.

THE MERCIAN REGISTER
AD835

In this year, a synod was convened at Canterbury by Archbishop Ceolnoth, ordering all the bishops from the kingdoms of Mercia, Wessex, Northumbria and the East Angles to attend. After three days, the Mercian bishops were forced to flee the aggression of Lord Æthelwulf, king of Kent and the son of King Ecgberht of Wessex. Archbishop Ceolnoth was most displeased.

1

SUMMER AD835

Londonia, the kingdom of Mercia

'Where is he?' Wynflæd rushes past me and, I confess, a grin tugs my dark-bristled cheeks wide to see the old, wizened healer so hale. I'm far from surprised that her focus is on Cuthred and not me. She moves with a speed that astonishes me, especially considering the dire warning the Wolf Lady gave to me regarding Wynflæd's health at Eastermonað. Wynflæd's more fleet than some of Ealdorman Ælfstan's warriors.

Wynflæd's arrived at Londonia with King Wiglaf and his attendant warriors from Tamworth. His ealdormen and bishops are also accompanying him, and I realise his wife, Queen Cynethryth, will be as well. For a moment, my heart thrums. Will Lord Wigmund's wife, Lady Ælflæd, also be in attendance? But I dismiss the thought. She'll be at Kingsholm with the three children, her son and two nephews. It'll be much safer for them all there. I hope the king has thought to ensure it's well protected from any who might still threaten the young children of Lady Cynehild and Lord Coenwulf.

'It's good to see you as well,' I murmur. I feel the force of Wynflæd's seax-sharp look but incline my head, pointing to where I know Cuthred sits beside the hearth fire within the large hall. There's a cold wind blowing along the River Thames today, raising cloaks and hair within Londonia. At least it's just the wind, though, and not the Viking raiders. That brings me some comfort, even as I shudder inside my cloak. It's the summer. The weather should be much milder than it is. The last few summers have seen my skin sun-baked by this time of the year. I look up and see the heavy clouds overhead, scudding along with the strength of the wind. They remind me of the lambs I've seen in the fields, gambolling over one another. Sometimes, I wish my life were so simple.

'Where's Cuthred?' Wynflæd reiterates, her intent remaining on her young apprentice she insisted I take to Wessex with me. I imagine she didn't consider the risks would be as high as they proved to be.

'He's this way.' And I begin to stride towards the great hall within Londonia beneath whose smoke-blackened rafters Cuthred's sheltering. There's nothing wrong with him. There's nothing wrong with any of us, but we're stuck here, with little to do but argue, drink, fight and train, or wallow about. Cuthred's chosen the latter option. Most of us have chosen the fourth. But I can't encourage Cuthred to train. Not for the first time, I appreciate how different we are. Once, I'd have thanked no one for giving me a blade and encouraging me to battle. I hope Cuthred gets to remain the healer that he is, and that those precious skills aren't dismissed because his strength can be used to drive weapons into our enemies' bodies.

I flex my shoulders and then bend low beneath the low-hanging thatched roof close to the doorway. There's talk it'll need re-thatching when the weather's right for such a task. I think they might be correct. It's covered in green growth, and in some places sunlight occasionally filters through into the hall. And on other, less welcome occasions, rain drums through as well.

Wynflæd doesn't need to duck her head. She's as diminutive as ever. I consider who's had the unhappy task of accompanying her on the journey south. Someone will have needed to help her mount and dismount. Perhaps it was King Wiglaf. I suspect the two are thicker than I've ever presumed. I realise now she's often had the ear of kings, queens and other notable individuals. For someone who's more likely to chastise than offer any encouragement, Wynflæd has managed to become respected by everyone within Mercia from the slaves to the king himself. I admire her afresh, even while she hurries towards Cuthred, as her eyes alight on him, and somehow, her forward gait increases. It's helped by the fact everyone else veers aside from her. No one wants to feel Wynflæd's wrath.

The lad's playing a game or doing something on the table. I saw him earlier. We ate together, but I've been sweating in the training field, testing my skills against Ealdorman Tidwulf's men. I can't say it was much of a fight with the warriors who often protect Londonia. But it's always good to hone skills against men I've never fought before. I learn something from every one of them. Weak warriors can occasionally get lucky. I need to stay alert and not dismiss them immediately.

I hear Wynflæd's cry of greeting and slow my steps, watching how they interact with one another.

Cuthred's much changed from the boy she bid me take to Winchester only a few weeks ago. Equally, he's not changed at all.

His young face broadens into a welcoming smile as he stands, forgetting the bench behind him, only to fall over his growing limbs and land crumpled on the wooden floorboards. A rumble of laughter greets the inelegant movement, quickly stifled as Wynflæd throws his opponent a quelling gaze.

I grin but don't chuckle. Cuthred finds his feet, and soon the pair are embracing. I suppress a pang of jealousy. Wynflæd was never easy with her embraces for me. But then, she's shown the depth of her care in other ways. I won't be surly that she loves Cuthred. I'm pleased they have one another. My guilt for not being the healer's apprentice lessens when I see them together. I can fight for Mercia, knowing that Wynflæd isn't entirely alone, and that the precious knowledge she's accumulated over a long lifetime won't be lost with her.

Wynflæd's shrill complaints reach my ears. I hasten to join them. She's patting Cuthred all over, ensuring he's not wounded. I mean, he's been bruised and cut, but it's his arse that took the brunt of our excursions. For a boy who'd never ridden much, he's spent a considerable part of the last few weeks in the saddle. Admittedly, he knew to take precautions against the inevitable chaffing.

'Tell me everything?' Wynflæd demands as, satisfied he's not wounded, she sits beside him. I notice one of the slaves has hastened to bring Wynflæd food and ale. Wynflæd acknowledges the action and offers a few words. Something changes hands. No doubt some cure for an ailment. Perhaps even a powder to rid the woman of the gentle swell of her belly. I don't know who's been sharing the slave's bed or even if it's been willingly done. I swallow against the unease in my stomach, hoping it's been willingly done. I'd sooner there were no slaves, but I'm a lone voice against the abuse, as I see it. Many have no problem with it, content that others should dig latrine ditches and see to other, less pleasant tasks, as well.

'Um.' Cuthred blanches, seeking me out behind Wynflæd.

'Tell her everything that's befallen you since leaving

Tamworth,' I advise him, sitting beside them, inclining my head towards the two other men who stand, bow and make their excuses to be anywhere but here. 'She'll only find out some other way.' But just as Cuthred opens his mouth to speak, Wynflæd barks another question.

'Where are all those supplies I sent with you? You better still have them.'

I smirk while Cuthred snaps his mouth shut. We might have had occasion to make use of them, but more than anything, that bloody sack of healing supplies was an absolute pain in the arse. I imagine Cuthred's not about to tell her that, though.

'I still have it,' he reassures and then begins to recount our adventures to Wessex.

Sometime later, Cuthred has told Wynflæd everything. During the disclosure, she occasionally cast me a thinly veiled look of anger. I smiled at her in reply. She can berate me all she wants. She was the one who bid me take Cuthred. I'd have happily gone alone, and then he'd never have been in danger.

As he stumbles to the end of the tale, mention of Brihthild causing Wynflæd's eyebrows to arch. I suddenly realise I've not seen the king.

'Where's King Wiglaf?' I manage to interject before Wynflæd can ask any more questions.

'With the ealdormen.' Wynflæd dismisses the king easily, instead turning back to Cuthred, forehead furrowed in thought. She's barely eaten the food brought for her, and I've half a mind to help myself to the cold pottage, but as I snake my hand over the table, she slaps it away without even looking. She has eyes in the back of her head, I'm bloody sure of it.

I go to stand, thinking about finding the king. No doubt he'll want to speak with me – or, at least, I hope he will. He sent me to Winchester, after all, trusting me when he didn't any other. At the thought, I shake my head, realising I'm doing to the king exactly what Wynflæd's doing to me, blaming others for events we happily set in motion.

'He'll wait.' Wynflæd's thin hand rests over my huge one. I startle at the difference between us. I know she's becoming weaker, older and smaller, but the moment reveals it in all its harshness, disabusing me of my earlier thoughts on first seeing her.

I retake my seat. She's not done with me yet, and she's been with the king. She might have information to share with me before I speak with King Wiglaf.

'The queen is with him,' she informs us both. 'She comes with an honour guard, but really, she's his prisoner. He wants her to answer for her crimes.'

I wince to hear this. It would be so much easier to accuse her without her presence and haughty disdain. But then, this must be done correctly and within the laws that King Wiglaf has promulgated during his reign or those laws which have been kept from the reigns of previous kings. Someone, probably a bishop, will know all the correct laws and how they might apply in this case of treachery against the ruling king.

'There'll be a trial, as there was for Lord Coenwulf before his exile,' Wynflæd continues. She's trying to caution me, but without speaking the words aloud. I'm unsure why I need the warning. 'Lord Wigmund will also be attending. And Bishop Æthelweald of Lichfield.'

I groan.

'And Lord Beorhtwulf.'

I groan louder.

'The king's determined to do everything properly, even with the weight of evidence against the queen. Lord Wigmund and Bishop Æthelweald will also be allowed to speak. King Wiglaf intends to discover how deep the treason goes, and how many of his alleged allies have ascribed to allowing the Wessex ruling family to have Mercia to govern.'

'Why would the king invite her allies?' Cuthred queries. 'Surely they'll speak falsehoods, as they did at Lord Coenwulf's trial?' Released from Wynflæd's grilling, Cuthred seems to have recovered his good cheer. I hadn't realised the thought of telling Wynflæd everything that's befallen us was upsetting him so much. I'm sure I used to be more sensitive to such things.

'Because there must be those who can speak for her, her oath-helpers, as well as against her. If King Wiglaf's to set aside his wife of over two decades, everything must be done correctly and within the laws as laid down in the kingdom of Mercia. King Wiglaf's determined no one will have the opportunity to assign bias to the case against her, and in so doing, ensure she isn't found guilty of her crimes.'

'And what does he plan to do about the ambitions of Wessex?'

Wynflæd shrugs her shoulders at my question. 'King Wiglaf has no love for the bastard Wessex ruling family. And neither do I.' That doesn't answer my question, but I don't get time to complain because King Wiglaf finally appears, sweeping into the hall and causing us all to stand and bow. Well, all apart from Wynflæd. From the corner of my eye, I see her stand, but she doesn't bow her head. I consider what it must be like to be an equal, like the king. I suspect it wouldn't be to my taste. But Wynflæd knows her worth. One day, Cuthred will hopefully perform the same service to the men and women who govern Mercia. I can't imagine it. I really can't. He's so young and scrawny.

'Icel, come,' the king calls to me, flanked by the ealdormen and others of his guard. I see Commander Eahric amongst them. He flashes me a smile. He's much kinder to me now. Indeed, everyone offers me their respect. It's a change I'm unsure I appreciate. First, many summers ago when my uncle died, the king made it clear he regarded me highly, gifting me a fine horse, and then he continued to do so, even raising me above others after the events in Peterborough.

I'm uncomfortable with so much attention. Some resent me, and not just the king's son who's accomplished so little in his life. He's no warrior. He's not protected the king from the enemy, as I have done. No, all he's done is marry, produce a child who was sickly but now rallies, and generally make an arse of himself. He's chosen allies poorly, and made connections with people who see him only as a means to their end. No, the king's son, ætheling he might be, has no wisdom to become king, and no warrior prowess. And, worst of all, Wigmund's no fool. He perceives it only too well, which only serves to make him even more petulant.

I hurry to join the king, mindful I don't want to fall as Cuthred did when Wynflæd appeared. Ealdorman Ælfstan beckons me to him.

'The king's keen to hear all you know,' he advises. I seek out the familiar and comforting face of my fellow warrior, Wulfheard, and find him beside the ealdorman, his expression sour.

'Hasn't Wulfheard told him everything?' I mumble. I've already listened to Cuthred tell the tale to Wynflæd. I'm not sure I need to hear it again, and not in my words.

'There's too much at stake. The king sent you south to discover the truth of Eadbald's damning testimony against Lord Coenwulf. It's from your lips he must hear everything that's since been discovered regarding the queen's involvement in the plot to end the Mercian line and subsume the kingdom into Wessex,' the ealdorman informs me. There's no heat to his reply. Our rage at what's been plotted has dampened. It's there, simmering away, but for now, there's no cause to stoke the blacksmith's fire. We need to be calm. We must do this correctly. Perhaps that was the cause of Wynflæd's earlier caution.

'Very well,' I say, and hasten to join the king. He's settled by the hearth, the flames leaping higher as more and more wood is added to it. It's bitter today, even inside the great hall. Not even the smell of the River Thames reaches our noses. It's too cold for the stink to form. I'm grateful for that, if nothing else.

King Wiglaf beckons me closer. I eye him carefully. It's only been a few weeks since I last saw him, but I can see where the weight of his kingship rests on him uneasily. He's always been robust, a warrior and then a king. Well, since he reclaimed the kingship from that snake, Ecgberht of Wessex, six summers ago, when I first came to Wiglaf's attention. Now he seems diminished and I don't like to witness it.

'Icel.' His words are as vigorous as ever, even if his presence isn't.

'My lord king.' I bow and wait for him to tell me to rise. As usual, he does it with an impatient wave, as though I shouldn't have bothered, but I know it would have been poorly received if I hadn't. I suppose kings can be contrary in such ways.

'Tell me of events in Wessex,' he requests. Once more, I look to Ealdorman Ælfstan, but he moves aside, taking with him any other of the king's attendants who shouldn't hear what I have to say while the king and I converse privately.

'I'll do as you bid,' I inform King Wiglaf reluctantly. I'd sooner not be the one to recount this. 'As you know,' I begin, taking the seat beside him so that we appear as equals to any who might enter the building, and not a king and a warrior of Mercia, 'I travelled to Winchester to determine if Eadbald, who denounced Lord Coenwulf at his trial, had indeed visited the place.'

The king nods. I consider if he wishes me to speak more

quickly. But then, he's already been told everything. It's not as though anything I say will be a surprise.

'I discovered that whether Eadbald had visited or not, Wulfnoth, the man who had Lord Coenwulf's two children taken to Eamont, had certainly been there. His name is written in the donation list in one of the churches as Wulfnoth of Eamont. He made a not inconsiderable gift to the church. If that wasn't damning enough, I also heard his name spoken in the market.'

At this, King Wiglaf raises an eyebrow. Perhaps then, he hasn't been informed of everything I discovered.

'And somehow, thanks to the horse I purchased from a trader in Southampton, we became embroiled in a further element of the conspiracy.'

A smirk touches the king's lips. He must find it amusing, as do so many others, that I can draw trouble to myself without even trying.

'By this point, Ealdorman Ælfstan had sent Wulfheard to retrieve me from Winchester, fearing our attempts to discover the truth had been discovered by those loyal to the conspirators. We left Winchester with a woman, Brihthild, and her brother, Brihtwulf. Cuthred promised to heal Brihtwulf when we met, but they became entangled in what was happening to us when we had to leave Winchester immediately, or face being attacked. I didn't know this at the time, but Brihthild's the sister of a man who died inside Londinium when we fought King Ecgberht for Mercia's future all those summer's ago. I didn't kill him,' I hasten to add. 'He was almost my friend, until he realised I was Mercian. But to return to the events of the last few weeks, Brihthild was even more involved in the conspiracy than the man whose horse I'd bought, alongside the saddle and its contents. There was a huge piece of amber and also a written message regarding the plan to incorporate Mercia into Wessex.'

'Indeed,' King Wiglaf muses. He's not enjoying my tale, but he's very interested in all the nuances. I can tell because he's not interrupted me. Not once. But I need to pause to drink and wet my dry mouth.

'We had to kill a few of the Wessex bastards,' I growl when I'm sated, remembering the woodland fight not far from Winchester as we fled in the night from those who wanted that bloody horse and saddle I purchased in good faith from the horse trader in Southampton. 'And then we travelled to Canterbury to see what else we could discover. We intended to join up with the Mercian bishops attending the archbishop's synod and the rest of your warriors, sent to protect them, alongside Commander Eahric. If there were problems, you suggested such action.'

Here, King Wiglaf does interject. 'I would have thought you'd have been keen to return to Mercia, despite my orders to seek out Commander Eahric?'

'I was,' I confirm. 'Wulfheard had other ideas.'

'Ah, Wulfheard. Another one with a penchant for trouble,' King Wiglaf acknowledges, turning his head to seek out Wulfheard in the crowd, sitting away from us while we speak.

'Inside Canterbury, the brother, Brihtwulf, was killed, or rather, he was wounded outside the walls of the settlement, and died within them. Brihthild became separated from us when she took her brother for burial. The next we knew, Lord Æthelwulf was trying to apprehend us, determined to keep Brihthild from us.'

'And this woman, Brihthild, whose brother died, and who you met in Winchester but took to Canterbury, she's our prisoner and the one who'll speak against the queen?'

'Yes. She knows much of the conspiracy between Lord Æthelwulf and Queen Cynethryth. It was no happenstance that we made her acquaintance within Winchester. She was seeking us out.' I snarl while speaking. This part pains me. I travelled in secrecy and by ship, voyaging around Dumnonia, but still, someone knew enough of the king's plans to try and thwart them, and me in the process.

I watch the king carefully, but I can see no visible sign that my words grieve him. No doubt he's reconciled to my discoveries. After all, if he's to present this information to the witan and the church when there's a trial, he must be able to speak of it without showing his true emotions.

'And you believe the woman?'

'She has no true reason to lie. Not now she's our captive with no hope of being released. If she didn't speak the truth, I don't understand why Lord Æthelwulf would be so desperate to keep her in Wessex, and why he followed us all the way back to the River Thames, sending hundreds of warriors against us. It far outweighs what even we would do for a fellow Mercian.'

'A good argument,' King Wiglaf concedes. His hands remain in his lap. He listens more attentively than a child being told a story before sleep. Not that this is a gentle fiction. It's more of a tale of horror and deceit, to keep children awake and not make them sleep at all.

'What will you do?' I question the king, feeling brave enough to do so. After all, he sent me to Winchester. He can't have expected me to accept the task without wanting to know more.

'The way forward is clear. We must' – and by that, I think he means the royal 'we' – 'ensure the queen is denounced using Brihthild's testimony. Our marriage union will then be dissolved. I can't allow her to continue to influence our son, or indeed, our grandson, who are both æthelings, and will rule Mercia one day. She must be removed from the Mercian court, although in doing so, I must also safeguard my son and grandson's future.' Here he looks pensive before continuing. 'However, I can recall Lord

Coenwulf from Frankia, which pleases me. His part in all this has been unravelled and he's an innocent victim. Eadbald never visited Winchester. Or at least, we can be fairly confident he didn't. Eadbald spoke as he did because the queen bid him to do so. He'll be found and made to admit this as well. It'll all add to the growing body of evidence against the queen. And when Lord Coenwulf's returned to Mercia it will free up the armed presence at Kingsholm as the two children will no longer be imperilled.'

'And the king of Wessex's son, Lord Æthelwulf?'

'That's more difficult. He's chosen to work against Mercia, but I expect nothing less from the son of that bastard Ecgberht. They're both too keen to meddle in affairs that don't concern them.' King Wiglaf's words are only just sharp. If anything, resignation thrums within them.

'Will you go to war?' I ask tentatively. We've not known many summers of peace since Wiglaf became king of Mercia. But whether the king will plunge back into hostilities against Wessex, I'm unsure. Wessex has, for the last few years, been the more powerful force. Admittedly, King Ecgberht overextended himself in claiming Mercia and trying to attack the Welsh kingdoms six summers ago. He didn't hold either possession for long. And he's proven himself weak in allowing the Viking raiders to take the Isle of Sheppey. Perhaps his strength is waning, after all.

'It'll depend,' King Wiglaf offers, a quirk of his lips assuring me he knows the answer is a poor one. 'We'll see what more we can discover from the queen about these matters and then make a determination about how Wessex can be punished. I'll keep Mercia secure, Icel, never fear that. But, sometimes, I must do so without threatening the edge of my blade if it's at all within my power.'

I nod. I can understand that. I'd like to know my fellow warriors didn't need to risk their lives again. Yet I can't be reassured of that. There's much at stake for Mercia, if even her queen turns against her. What more could Queen Cynethryth hope to achieve? She's Mercia's queen. Her son will one day rule it, and after him, his son. And yet this hasn't been enough for her. I consider what Lord Æthelwulf has promised her, or what she thinks to achieve. Did she hope to rule Mercia without her husband? Did she wish to be a queen with no king? To my mind, she's risked much to accomplish something I don't believe would have benefitted her. She would surely have lost all influence if Wessex ruled Mercia. And I can't see that the Wessex kingship would have wanted to allow Wigmund to live. Not, of course, that I know much about ruling.

'It seems I must apologise to you once more, young Icel. I placed your life at risk. I didn't appreciate, or truly consider, that the conspiracy would involve so many individuals who would want you dead.'

I grimace at that. 'It seems I'm a magnet for such people,' I offer with a shrug. King Wiglaf nods once more.

'It is surprising. You remind me of someone I once knew. Perhaps you remember King Beornwulf? Or perhaps you don't. He was always getting himself into trouble before becoming king.' The king must not notice the sudden tension through my shoulders at the mention of my father. Of course, he doesn't know Beornwulf was my father. No one does aside from me and Wynflæd. I want to keep it that way. There are few who speak of Beornwulf with any affection. I don't wish to be treated with the same disdain.

King Wiglaf sits back, resting his hands on his belly. I notice the material seems to sag. He's lost weight – perhaps muscle rather than fat. The current situation is causing him disquiet. Although perhaps not as great as my current unease to find myself talking to Wiglaf about Beornwulf, the man who was my father, and through whom I could exert a claim to rule Mercia in Wiglaf's stead.

'You'd have been no more than a boy, if I have your age correct, when Beornwulf was king. Did you live in Tamworth for all of your life?' King Wiglaf questions, forehead furrowed in thought. I try to school my expression to one of mild interest, and not the panic that makes my chest flutter and my breath come too fast.

'I did, my lord king, yes, until King Ecgberht's attack.' A dark cloud momentarily covers King Wiglaf's face at that reminder. He's less alert to the effect such words have on him. But then, it's no secret.

'Indeed. And since then, you've rarely spent more than a summer or a winter in your home.' Now he leans forward, and his words are conspiratorial. 'Wynflæd's a trial, I confess. I'm in awe of how you survived her wrath throughout your years as her apprentice. The new boy, well, he's a brave one as well.'

I narrow my eyes, considering if King Wiglaf realises Cuthred came with me to Winchester. 'He's brave, yes. In time, will he become Tamworth's healer?' For a moment, I think Wiglaf will berate me. His eyes are iron, and his good humour has fled.

'You're a brave one, indeed,' he mumbles. 'And perhaps you're right to be. Cuthred will become the healer eventually. I hope he has the time to grow a beard and a belly before that happens. Wynflæd, a scary as she can be, is a woman of not inconsiderable knowledge and foresight.'

I exhale softly, pleased by my bold stroke and also by redirecting the king from talk of my father. I wouldn't want the similarities between us to spark too much of an interest for the king. For now, he respects me, and I respect him. Long may that continue. I don't wish to become his enemy, as his queen has done. If he knew the truth of my birth, he'd not be so easy with me.

Suddenly, there's a commotion at the doorway, which opens with a creak of iron hinges that need oiling. In the sudden brightness, whoever opened the door is cast into shadow, and I don't know who it is. The king must be unaware as well. I sense his interest and the way his hand fumbles for his weapons belt. I mirror his actions. We're similar in this. Here, we should be safe and protected, but neither of us can quite believe that's possible while conspiracy and turmoil rages all around us.

'My lord king.' I relax at hearing Ealdorman Ælfstan's voice, but his next words are far from reassuring. 'There are reports of Viking raiders on the Isle of Sheppey once more.' The news chills me. Sheppey is in Wessex, not far from the River Thames. Perhaps, when the tide is high, they might be able to make it to Londonia easily. We might have travelled overland to reach it a few summers ago, but my journey to Winchester with the traders has taught me travelling by ship can be quick, with good weather.

'Who reports this?' King Wiglaf demands.

'Some merchants who've just arrived by ship. They've had a terrible time of it.' Instantly, I consider if they might be the men I met in Worcester, but I doubt it. They were to travel to Hedeby to trade for exotic spices from faraway lands which are never as cold as Londonia is today.

For a moment, I anticipate the king calling his warriors together. I think Ealdorman Ælfstan must think the same as he waits, almost bouncing on the balls of his feet with readiness.

'Then the Viking raiders are very far from here,' King Wiglaf finally announces. 'Ensure the fort within Londinium is informed and a watch kept, but we need concern ourselves with the problem of this conspiracy and not of Viking raiders. We'll allow the Wessex king to counter the threat. It's about time he did something other than meddle in the affairs of Mercia.'

Ealdorman Ælfstan bows at the king's command. I'm impressed King Wiglaf doesn't panic and call us out to ride along the River Thames and hunt down our foemen.

'There'll be time for killing the enemy.' King Wiglaf confirms my suspicions. 'But, first, we must somehow make amends with the archbishop of Canterbury for the violence that marred his synod and also contend with the problem of my wife. It would be good if we had Eadbald here, to confirm what you've discovered. But we don't know where he is. However, I'll send word to Lord Coenwulf. He should return as soon as he can, and before winter storms prevent it.'

King Wiglaf glances at me appraisingly, but then shakes his head.

'I imagine you wish to stay here, and not travel to Frankia.'

For the briefest moment, I consider what it would be like to visit another different kingdom, but that's all it is. A momentary thought. 'I'll remain, my lord king. The children could still be in danger until Lord Coenwulf returns, even with so many people alert to the conspiracy these days. If I'm needed at Kingsholm, I'd welcome the opportunity to be summoned quickly.'

'Indeed, Icel, although there are men loyal to me there, now. And they are loyal. I'm sure of it. I've known them much of my life, and every man has had another four as their oath-helpers. I'm aware you made a deathbed oath to Lady Cynehild. You can't always be bound by that oath, although I understand the time to step aside from it hasn't yet come. Men should be honourable, even when it amounts to such an imposition. There are older men who have long abandoned such a task.'

'Then they aren't men who should be considered

honourable,' I murmur. 'Small children must be protected and not seen as a burden.'

King Wiglaf barks a hard laugh at that. 'Indeed, small children will not always be small, and might one day command these men. It would be prudent to heed them.'

With that, the king dismisses me, and his ealdormen hurry back to his side, some repeating the news about the Viking raiders but others more concerned with the problem of Wessex. I watch them, barely suppressing a shudder as King Wiglaf is overwhelmed with demands and querulous opinions. I wish never to be subjected to the whim of other men in such a way. Once more, I appreciate that I could never be king of Mercia, despite my father being King Beornwulf. I must ensure that secret remains mine, and Wynflæd's. When she's no longer here, which I hope will be in many summers' time, only I will carry that burden. And it is a burden. I realise I would sooner have never known. Then, I'd not feel so conflicted by King Wiglaf's failures to control his family and ensure their loyalty to Mercia. Then, in my darkest moments, I'd not consider that I'd do better than he has, and will certainly be a better man than his weak son. Not all of the blame can lie on the shoulders of his conniving wife, the queen of Mercia, a woman who would sooner Mercia was under the command of her ancient enemies, the West Saxons of Wessex.

No. The king's welcome to his responsibilities. Despite my worries, I'd sooner be free to exterminate any who threaten Mercia with blade and shield.

Those who think to betray Mercia must be dealt with harshly.

Better it's done with lethal intent, but the queen will have her trial. The truth will be known. And then Mercia's betrayal will be stopped.

2

When I see Queen Cynethryth, she's sitting haughtily at the front of Londonia's great hall, on a raised dais. She's not bound. She's not even dressed in rags. She presents herself as though attending the king's witan and isn't here to face justice for her involvement in the conspiracy to betray Mercia and her ruling family. She shows no contrition, her chin raised defiantly. The two warriors who guard her are almost unseen in the shadows. How she's accomplished this I'm uncertain. The king should have ensured his wife's involvement in the conspiracy was more obvious.

The queen's appearance is in stark contrast to that of Brihthild's. Not that Brihthild has been poorly used. She's not been beaten. But her hair's lank, and I've been told she refuses to eat once more. Her clothing's not that of a wealthy woman, and it hangs on her thin frame, as though made for a woman twice her width. It's also dank in colour, unlike the queen's bright, thrice-dyed blue dress. That her hands are bound together, and she in turn tied to the chair she sits upon makes it clear Brihthild is a prisoner.

The guard surrounding Brihthild's much more pronounced

than those watching the queen. Every man or woman who speaks with a Wessex accent has been heavily questioned about the purpose of their visit to Londonia, in case they mean harm to Brihthild. Not, I believe, that any attack would be so obvious. No, if Lord Æthelwulf, king of Kent, wishes to silence Brihthild, he'll send a Mercian to kill her. He might know quite a few of them who'd eagerly earn his acclaim and take his coin.

I sit, uneasy, ready to recount my discoveries in Winchester once more. I don't welcome having to speak before so many people, for the hall is filled. The crowd spills out of the doors, opening wide to allow those outside to hear, if not see, the events about to play out.

Ealdorman Ælfstan assures me this is the first time one of Mercia's queens has been called upon to account for her actions before a court. Wynflæd informs me it's not but offers nothing definite, just vague comments concerning marriages with other kingdoms. It's just another tantalising reference to events she's seen that no one else seems to know about, and which have, perhaps, never been correctly recorded.

Wynflæd's seated beside me at the front of the hall. I know a few cast dark looks her way. Many people who don't know her importance must wonder why she has such a position of prominence. Not that any of them are foolish enough to question her, not when I sit beside her, Ealdorman Ælfstan to the other side. Cuthred also sits with me, but somehow his presence is more acceptable. People here know of his adventures to Winchester and Canterbury.

Wynflæd holds one of my hands in her tight grip, preventing me from tracing the line of the eagle scar on my other hand. My heart thuds loudly in my chest. I feel more worried than when fighting Mercia's enemy. I'd sooner face my death than the heated glowers

I'm receiving from Brihthild, where she faces those in attendance. Every so often, I also sense I'm under the cool scrutiny of the queen although, whenever I look at her, she's peering elsewhere.

I wish King Wiglaf would hurry up and arrive. I'd like this to be over and done with.

The bishops already sit to the far side of the hall, alongside the abbots and abbesses. Those who didn't travel to Canterbury have been summoned from their diocese to bear witness and help conduct this trial. It reminds me of how closely bound the king and the church are. In our day-to-day lives, the church always has some impact, of course, but the king relies on the church to govern. It's the holy men and women who can assist with the written tasks that ensure the kingdom is well served.

Those holy men who ventured to Canterbury for the synod haven't had time to return to their diocese. They've been waiting for the king to arrive in Londonia, just as I have. Now they congregate, no doubt as shocked as everyone else by what's about to occur.

I note Bishop Æthelweald of Lichfield hides his unease poorly. He's always been furtive, in my opinion. Now it's reached a whole new level, as he inveigles himself amidst the bishops, abbots and abbesses. It's as though he believes it possible to disappear amongst their number. Bloody fool. I see him, and if I see him then others will also have noted him. I'm sure his name will be mentioned by Brihthild. I'm convinced he'll also have to face the king's wrath for his part in this.

That other snake, the aged and desiccated Ealdorman Sigered, shows no emotion as he sits, not far from Ealdorman Ælfstan. I know he's involved in this as well, and if not him directly, then through his grandson.

Another who I suspect, Lord Beorhtwulf, is also bland of face in his position just to the side of the ealdormen. He's grown in confidence of late, but I suspect he'll soon lose that.

I imagine the queen hopes these three men will speak in her defence, be her oath-helpers: those who'll speak to her good character, and integrity. As Mercia's queen, her word should be accepted far more readily than Brihthild's, who's a West Saxon and already known as a murderer. I don't know who'll speak for Brihthild. I doubt anyone could be her oath-helper because no one knows her. She might even be deemed as not oath-worthy at all because she's not Mercian.

However, Brihthild's integrity could be proven through an ordeal, as prescribed by the king and the holy men and women. What form that might take I fear to think.

There's too much I don't know about how events will proceed. I'd sooner be anywhere but here.

'Sit still,' Wynflæd hisses. I sense Ealdorman Ælfstan's smile at the comment, but his head is turned, seeking out those he knows amongst the crowd. Wulfheard and the rest of his warriors are available if required, but they're busy keeping the peace amongst those invited to witness this momentous event, and also the people of Londonia who believe they have the right to observe it as well. It's important the trial is attested and seen by all, and so the doors are flung wide open, and the press of those from behind is almost stifling. I'm glad I have a space on one of the benches placed before the raised dais of the king's hall.

If the trial of the queen were conducted behind closed doors, people might question the outcome, and rumours could spread about who spoke for whom, and who said what.

Despite all that, I wish I were with the casual bystanders, and able to indulge in such gossip.

And then the king finally arrives. King Wiglaf wears the royal helm, and his clothes shimmer with the eagle emblem of Mercia and threads of gold and silver. His son accompanies him. Lord Wigmund looks uneasy, which doesn't surprise me. I watch him trying not to look at his mother, but still he casts surreptitious glances her way. I consider what's happened between them since my return from Mercia. Has Queen Cynethryth demanded her son's aid, or has she bid him remain silent to protect himself? Have they even spoken?

I expect Lady Ælflæd to be here, but her absence informs me she's decided to remain at Kingsholm. The events about to come under such scrutiny must be hard for her to hear. Her own mother by marriage trying to kill her nephews. I once thought Lady Ælflæd as cold-hearted as the queen, but she's proven me wrong in that. She might temporarily have been hard-hearted and harsh, but I know now it was merely concern for her unwell son. She's far from the young woman who was my friend when my uncle and I were at Kingsholm and her only concern was for her horse. Admittedly, I'm far from being the boy who never wished to become a warrior. I wish times were as simple as then, but they're not. All the same, I'm gratified she's not the terrible self-seeking person I feared she'd become.

Once more, I feel the slap of Wynflæd's hand as I pick at the embroidery on my tunic. It's uncomfortably tight. I've spent the last few weeks training harder than ever. My arms are almost as strong as before I was wounded, and that makes my tunic too tight in the shoulder areas. I should have worn something different, but the king gifted me with it. He's determined we all look our best during the queen's trial.

I don't know how the others survive with such restrictive clothing. It would drive me to distraction. I hope everything runs smoothly and then I can retire from the hall and remove the bloody thing quickly. I don't care that the red dye is so vibrant I look like a tomato. Wynflæd admired it, but I think she did it in spite. She wears her usual clothes. No one's thought to bedeck her in court finery. I wish I were as lucky.

With shuffling and murmured conversation, King Wiglaf settles before us on the dais, but far to the side of the queen and her guards, his son beside him. It's as though an invisible line divides the king from the queen. I notice Commander Eahric orders the queen's guards to stand in a more prominent position, with their hands close to weapons belts. They'll apprehend her if she tries to escape. They might not like it, but they'll do it. I imagine Oswy would like to be the one keeping a careful watch on her.

Queen Cynethryth's posture remains rigid. What she thinks of her husband's actions, I can only imagine.

Ceolbeorht, the bishop of Londonia, steps forward from the collection of holy men and women to begin the proceedings. He has scribes ready to record the details of the events, with pieces of vellum held in place before them, and piles of empty sheets waiting for them if they should be needed. I carefully observe the squint-eyed scribes with ink-stained hands. I admire them for the skills they possess.

'My lord king, ætheling Wigmund.' Bishop Ceolbeorht bows low, speaking respectfully. I wait for him to bow to the queen, but he doesn't. I sense her shift on the hard wooden chair she's been forced to sit upon, whereas the king and his son's are softened with cushions. It's a brave move by Bishop Ceolbeorht. Should it be unfeasible to find against the queen, he'll have to contend with her outrage in the coming years. Not, I reassure myself, that it'll be possible for her to escape this. There's so much evidence against her, but Ealdorman Ælfstan has warned me that having the proof might not be enough, even though Wiglaf is Mercia's king. The bishops and the ealdormen who are to be involved in the trial may have their own interests or refuse to accept the words of Brihthild. The queen might even have those determined to exonerate her. Gaining justice won't be a simple matter. It never is, so I've been assured. The practice of oath-helpers, of ascribing more value to those who hold higher positions within our society, of dismissing those who aren't Mercians, will make it easier for the queen to maintain her innocence by dismissing those who speak against her as having less value, and by implication, less truth.

The king's voice is worth the value of thirty-six common men or women. That of a noble-born man or woman is worth eighteen common voices, and an ealdorman or bishop's is nine. The voice of a king's thegn is valued at six.

'The point of the trial,' Ealdorman Ælfstan informed me with a grimace yesterday, 'is to ensure there's friendship between those affected when a resolution is agreed upon. It'll not be easy. Not when so much is at stake for everyone. It's as though moral right and wrong are irrelevant. What we believe is the right course of action to take may do so much harm to the kingdom the trial must conclude less harm will come from allowing the queen to retain her position.' The words were far from reassuring then, and now I fear even more that ascertaining the queen's guilt will be no easy thing. If too many think to stand for her integrity, or those few who do are ealdormen, bishops and abbesses, it'll be impossible for anyone to doubt her, especially when it's a West Saxon who'll speak against her. It's a pity Wulfnoth of Eamont is dead. If he lived, and could accuse the queen, success might be assured because he was a lord. But, of course, he's dead, and was a traitor as well.

'Men and women of the witan.' Bishop Ceolbeorht faces the swelling crowd, raising his voice so all can hear. 'The people of Mercia. Today, our king has used his jurisdictional rights to convene *sac and soc*, his right to hold a court. It will meditate on a grave matter, that of a conspiracy to irrevocably curtail the ruling line of Mercia, threatening the future and stability of our great kingdom. It's a class of crime known as *botleas* in our law codes.'

His words ring with conviction, even though I won't be alone in not entirely understanding what he means. Not one person shuffles their feet or moves to a more comfortable position. Even I'm mesmerised by this man before me. I've never seen him in such a light before. I've always found him to be just another of the prattling holy men who think their words have more importance than everyone else's. Today, he speaks with gravitas, and conviction. Here, he knows the procedures that must be followed, and he intends to ensure all is done correctly. The king has chosen wisely in asking Bishop Ceolbeorht to officiate.

'The lives of children, mere babes, were put at risk. It's thanks to the king's warriors that the children yet live, and certain peoples are no longer available to meddle further. But alas, the conspiracy didn't end with the deaths of those traitors. It went much further, even involving the kingdom of Wessex.'

A rumble of outraged horror reverberates at this. I consider whether people didn't know or if they're simply being swept along with the bishop's retelling of events. I imagine the latter.

'And not just the involvement of Wessex, but possibly Mercia's queen.' I feel my eyes narrow at this telling admission. Is Bishop Ceolbeorht already hedging his bets? When he didn't bow to the queen, I assumed his opinion was settled, but perhaps it's not. I bite down on my frustration, determined not to show my resurgent unease.

The king has bid me speak against the queen. If this fails and she retains her position, I'll be in danger. Again.

'We'll hear the testimony of Mercia's warriors who've discovered much, Lady Cynethryth, Lord Wigmund, and the woman from Wessex, Brihthild. They'll tell us what they saw with their eyes and heard with their ears, as is the purpose of this court. They'll assert their claim, or *tale*, which is the legal term.'

I'm pleased the bishop thinks to explain all this because I won't be alone in not understanding everything.

'Of course,' and here he offers a small smile, as though determined to include us all and not confuse with strange terms we don't understand, 'we also have the written words retrieved from Wessex and the payment that was to be made for bringing about the death of the children in our grasp.'

Put so simply, this seems like very little to denounce the queen, especially when she's not specifically named in the letter. For a moment, I worry, hoping the king knows what he's doing. He appears serene on the dais, easily able to absorb the attention of all those who watch him. I wouldn't be able to do what he's doing. Lord Wigmund flinched when his name was spoken, but the queen sat as though carved of stone. I didn't think to see what Ealdorman Sigered and Lord Beorhtwulf did. How they hold themselves against the coming onslaught is intriguing. They'll need to abandon the queen, if it proves diplomatic to do so, or they'll lose all.

Instead, Brihthild snags my attention, tugging against her bindings. She's a wild creature. Will she share all she knows about the conspiracy? Will it be believed, if she's not oath-worthy? Must she endure an ordeal to have her testimony taken seriously, provided she survives it? Only if she survives the ordeal will she be deemed, by our Lord God, and therefore the king and holy men and women, to speak the truth, if an ordeal is demanded.

'And we, the men and women of the witan, will have a decision to make, one the king will not be involved in as this is a trial where his wife is the defendant. As a woman cannot denounce her husband in our laws, so the king will also not denounce his wife. This is a grave undertaking. Those called upon to cast their decision must do so on two matters. The question of whether the king can divorce his wife is one of most interest to my fellow religious office-holders. Still, given the extraordinary circumstances, the ealdormen will also have a voice in that decision. The second question will be about the queen's involvement in the conspiracy. Will it be proven or not, and if proven, what will the punishment be? These are not questions to be considered lightly. We'll draw on the righteousness of our Lord God when making our determinations. It's said that it's wrong to murder children. We know our Lord, Jesus Christ, was himself at grave danger of such an abomination. We'll take strength from knowing he was spared, as were the small children of Lord Coenwulf and Lady Cynehild, God rest her soul. But, our decision must also be based on what we deem to be most just, and that which will do the least harm to our king and Mercia. Once the matter is settled, friendships must be mended between all those who felt aggrieved, or Mercia will never know peace again.'

A murmur runs through the crowd at the bishop's words. I'm not alone in anticipating it would be the king who'd reach the decisions on the queen. There's unease that's not the case. It means the queen could have already ensured those loyal to her remain loyal.

However, I also understand King Wiglaf's determination to abide by Mercia's laws. He's united Mercia, not once but twice. He's fought for her against the might of King Ecgberht of Wessex. Now he shows even more wisdom in accepting the determinations of the religious men and women he rules the kingdom alongside, as well as his ealdormen, some of whom I know are suspect in their loyalty and allegiance.

Bishop Ceolbeorht bows towards the king before retiring to a chair beside the other bishops, now he's finished speaking. There are piles of vellum books besides the holy men and women. I consider what they're for, perhaps merely religious texts they might consult, or the law codes the bishop refers to when he mentions specific terms. I don't know. No doubt there must be a precedent for this, or something similar, as the bishop mentioned the story of Jesus.

The quantity of books almost makes me gawp. So much labour went into producing them. I know how hard Ealdorman Tidwulf is finding it to gather the resources he needs for his book of healing. I've heard him complaining to Ealdorman Ælfstan about the cost and the time. This collection of texts is vast compared to anything Ealdorman Tidwulf hopes to accomplish. They've taken men and women many, many years to produce. I hope they'll hold the answer to any questions that might arise.

When the king's the next to arrest the attention of the assembly, I'm surprised. Bishop Ceolbeorht implied the king would distance himself from trying to influence the outcome of the trial. Perhaps he won't.

King Wiglaf smiles, his gaze holding some of those within the crowd, but luckily not mine. When he speaks, his words are soft so that even I, on the front row, feel the need to lean forward to catch them.

'My loyal Mercians,' King Wiglaf begins. 'I implore you to serve your kingdom well. To look to the future of Mercia and how it will best be served by affairs here today. I ask you to forget the more personal nature of my relationship with the queen. This is about much more than just a husband and a wife. This is about the most just resolution for what you'll hear today.' With no fanfare, he sits and settles himself, hands resting lightly on his knees. How he keeps his legs still, I don't know. I struggle to show as much calm as he does, and this doesn't concern my wife. Although, it does my kingdom.

Bishop Ceolbeorht quickly stands once more. 'Icel, lord of

Budworth, and oath-sworn warrior of King Wiglaf, please come forward and freely share your knowledge of events. I ask, as the court does, that you'll tell us what you saw with your eyes and heard with your ears. I already have on record your three oath-helpers, who are Ealdorman Ælfstan, the revered wise woman, Wynflæd, and Lady Ælflæd, the wife of Lord Wigmund. With such honourable oath-helpers, who, due to their status, add almost the weight of the king to your testimony and far exceed what's required, all here should understand your recounting is to be held with the highest regard and your integrity in reporting all you saw and heard isn't to be doubted.'

With a fierce squeeze on my hand, Wynflæd releases me. I find the bishop's words unsettling, but Ealdorman Ælfstan's assured me the bishop must use certain phrases, as preordained in the legal texts. Despite that, I'm astounded Lady Ælflæd is one of my oath-helpers. Yes, I've known her for many years, but for much of that time we've been uneasy with one another, almost enemies since her marriage to Lord Wigmund. Now it seems I've won back her regard. If I weren't about to speak before the king, and the bishops, it would make me joyful.

With heavy legs, I manage to stand. I walk forward, looking directly ahead and not at anyone else, until I turn and take my seat close to the bishops. I see a flicker of sympathy on Bishop Ceolbeorht's face for what I must endure and a swift glower on Bishop Æthelweald's, which reminds me that I've not seen Brother Sampson, or Heca, or whatever his name is. Unquestionably, he should be here to answer for his part in this. But then the bishop's questions begin and I forget all about him.

'My lord.'

Bishop Ceolbeorht startles me with such an address. I thought he merely used it to name me as I should be known. No one calls me 'my lord'. I don't even think I am one. Not really. But, of course, being a lord in my own right means I need fewer oath-helpers to stand as witness to my integrity. It means I'm to be trusted as a reliable and trustworthy voice when I give my testimony.

'The king and we, his advisors, wish to thank you for your endeavours. We're aware you carry serious wounds from protecting the children and imperilled your life. On behalf of Mercia, I extend my humble thanks to you for proving your loyalty by protecting the king's person, and his kingdom. By ensuring such violations were prevented as far as you were able, against the king's *mund*, and by that I use the legal term for his person and the whole of Mercia, you performed a vital task. Be assured, Mercia's monks, nuns and priests pray for you.'

This surprises me. I thought to be questioned about my adventures in Wessex. I wasn't anticipating any thanks. Perhaps this is all part of the trial, to reinforce just how great my integrity is. I confess, it makes me feel apprehensive. I'm not comfortable with praise. Wynflæd ensured that.

Now the bishop looks down, consulting a piece of vellum before speaking. 'They tell me you and Lady Cynehild, the mother of the two boys, weren't close. And yet, she bid you protect her children as she lay dying. Why did she exact such an oath from you, one that most here would expect between a wife and her husband?'

My breath catches at such an opening question. I purposefully avoid looking at Wynflæd as I think of an answer. 'Lady Cynehild was a friend of my uncle, who died protecting Mercia from the ravages of King Ecgberht's attack.' I stumble to a halt, unsure what else to say. Do they speculate as to why Lady Cynehild and I were close, and why she burdened me with such a request? I can't imagine they do. The truth of my birth was always a secret. Not even King Wiglaf suspects the fact of my identity.

'Then that makes more sense,' Bishop Ceolbeorht quickly agrees, as I endeavour to breathe more easily. My chest feels tight. I can hardly take a deep breath, yet I feel more justification is needed.

'I was also trained as a healer by Wynflæd of Tamworth. Lady Cynehild knew she was dying. I'd been instrumental in retrieving Lord Coenwulf from his captivity on the Isle of Sheppey.' Mention of that place, rather than my actions, causes a ripple of unease in the crowd. I should perhaps have been more careful in what I was saying, with the news the Viking raiders once more threaten Sheppey.

'Because of this oath, you became close to the children?' Bishop Ceolbeorht presses.

'I remained at Kingsholm for some time, yes, when they were very small. I was called away at the king's command.'

'Yes, yes,' Bishop Ceolbeorht speaks quickly, cutting me off before I can inform everyone of my summer spent protecting the River Thames. I realise he doesn't want me to recount every little detail, but rather focus on the children and Lady Cynehild. I change direction.

'Lady Cynehild's husband was badly wounded. She knew of this. But, she wished to ensure the child she gave her life to birth would be protected, as well as the older boy, if their father couldn't ensure that. She chose me, I must assume, because of her friendship with my uncle.' I hope that'll be the end of the questions about my connection to Lady Cynehild.

'Thank you for clarifying that, my lord.' Bishop Ceolbeorht's voice is conciliatory. I risk flicking a quick glance towards Wynflæd. She nods sagely, which I take to mean I answered the question well. 'And then you followed the children north, to this Wulfnoth of Eamont's property, when you realised what had befallen them?'

'Eventually,' I confirm unwillingly, focusing on the bishop and not Wulfheard. I don't need to watch him to detect the fury that will be etched into his familiar face at the mention of his traitorous brother. Neither do I wish to labour my delay in going to the aid of the children.

'When the children were thankfully returned to Kingsholm following their capture, you remained once more to protect them?'

'I was wounded. Almost mortally. I carry those scars. I stayed to protect them and to recuperate myself.'

I hear a soft chuckle from amongst the audience and consider whether Oswy laughs at his depiction of a cock pricked into my skin when he sewed my belly wound shut. I should be more grateful to him for that, but I can't always find it in myself to be.

Bishop Ceolbeorht holds my gaze. I consider what more I could tell him to explain how much danger the children were in that I was nearly killed and the children only survived thanks to the aid of the women who also protected them. 'They were lethal warriors, my lord bishop. We're lucky the intention wasn't to harm the children under their care. They were to be handed to someone else, alive, and then their death was to be brought about by these others.'

A shudder of agitation ripples through the crowd, soft murmurs, some shocked. I keep my focus on Bishop Ceolbeorht. Not the king. Not his wife and not his son. After all, many of those warriors I speak about were oath-sworn to Lord Wigmund, and that's no secret.

'After you recovered.' Bishop Ceolbeorht pauses to bend and listen to someone who whispers in his ear. It's one of his monks, with inky hands. I consider what more he believes the bishop should ask me. 'Apologies,' the bishop mutters. 'After you'd recovered, you ventured to Winchester on the king's command to discover whether Eadbald, the man who'd denounced Lord Coenwulf in Kingsholm, leading to his exile, had visited the place.'

'I did, my lord bishop, yes.'

'And you found no proof.'

'None, my lord bishop.'

'But you did find the name Wulfnoth of Eamont in the confraternity book at one of the churches, Saints Peter and Paul? Is that correct?'

'It is, yes.'

The bishop pauses expectantly, waiting for me to explain further.

'I looked over the shoulder of the monk on duty at the doors. I could read the name as he spoke to someone else.'

'A little bit of subterfuge?' Bishop Ceolbeorht chastises.

'All in the name of Mercia, and not, I think, to the detriment of anyone. If the information was to remain private, the monk should have covered it.'

A few chuckles. I consider who might be finding any of this amusing. I'm not. I don't like being under such scrutiny.

'With this information, you returned to Mercia.'

'In the end, my lord bishop. I did have to detour to Canterbury.'

Now his lips form a hard line. He's heard much about events in Canterbury, and I imagine nearly everyone here has. It wasn't our finest attempt to uncover the truth. 'And it was at this time that you discovered "the written message".' The way he says this has me narrowing my eyes, as though he doubts me.

'Yes, it was hidden in the saddle of a horse I purchased from Southampton. Alongside a lump of amber worth many mancuses.' Again, I sense the bishop didn't intend to reveal this. But the sum of money is so outrageously huge I feel no compunction in naming it. A single mancus is worth thousands of pounds.

'And what did you decide about this message?'

'That it was written in a Mercian style and sent to an otherwise unnamed lord of Wessex.'

'Nothing else?'

'No, my lord bishop.'

'So, you don't know who wrote it?'

'I don't, no. Some have suspicions, but I've little experience with writing and those who work in the king's scriptorium.'

'You suspect it was a member of the king's scriptorium?' Bishop Ceolbeorht pounces.

'It was a Mercian hand,' I repeat. 'It would be wise to suspect someone from the scriptorium. Few others have the skills and the resources to be able to write. But as you say, I can only speak to what I've seen.'

But Bishop Ceolbeorht hasn't finished. 'You suspect the involvement of a member of the Mercian church?'

I hesitate, this falls outside the scope of repeating what I've seen and heard.

'An answer, please, my lord.'

'I do, my lord bishop. I do.'

Silence falls as the questions temporarily stop. I risk looking around. The king sits placidly. I'm not convinced the queen remains as calm. Her back's rigid, but there's a flickering movement from beneath her skirts, as though her feet jiggle nervously. And Lord Wigmund offers me a look filled with loathing from beside his father.

I genuinely hope he'll never become king. I don't wish to spend my life avoiding him or being subjected to his ridiculous demands. The ultimate idea of this trial might be to rebuild broken friendships, and to find a means for the kingship of

Mercia to settle without everyone suspecting each other, but there'll be some friendships which are broken, and some hatreds which are formalised. I know what will happen with Lord Wigmund and me.

Brihthild remains entirely still, a faint smile playing on her lips. I've no idea why. I don't believe this is at all enjoyable.

'And this woman, here, Brihthild of Wessex. You became acquainted with her in Winchester?'

'With her and her brother. My young healer friend, Cuthred, found them praying for a miracle within the church in Winchester. He thought it was a simple matter of knowing the correct herbs to treat the ailment and offered his assistance.'

'This meeting was by chance?'

'We thought so. But now suspect it wasn't.'

Bishop Ceolbeorht glowers at Brihthild, and her good humour immediately disappears.

'Indeed. It appears she was somewhat involved in the conspiracy and had, according to your report, been sent to discover the truth of your trip to Winchester?'

'That's correct, my lord bishop. She remained with us throughout the journey to Canterbury and all the way back to Mercia.'

Bishop Ceolbeorht appraises Brihthild. 'And now, we have daily messages from Lord Æthelwulf, king of Kent, demanding her return,' he muses. It's not a question directed at me. I answer it anyway.

'I wouldn't know that, my lord bishop.' I do, but no one else needs to be aware of that. After all, Bishop Ceolbeorht seems to wish to cast doubt on anything Brihthild might say. She is, ultimately, a creature of Lord Æthelwulf's. She's not of Mercia. She will, I'm sure, not be deemed oath-worthy. I must make use of my encounters with her, while not necessarily relying on them. It's a complicated situation.

'She killed her brother within Canterbury?' Bishop Ceolbeorht queries. I wince at the query. Not only is Brihthild not oathworthy, she's openly accused of murdering a member of her family. It's a terrible crime. But, I recall myself, I owe her nothing. My integrity isn't being questioned.

'We believe so, yes. He must not have known about her involvement or wished to distance himself from her objective.'

'What – and again, I appreciate this falls outside what you saw and what you heard – but what do you suspect her intentions were?'

'To ensure the amber and the message were retrieved from the horse's saddle on behalf of Lord Æthelwulf. Those behind the conspiracy wished to make sure we knew little else about it.'

'But when you brought her to Mercia, she confessed to the involvement of others.'

'She informed us that Mercia's queen had sent the amber.' At this, and despite the fact everyone here understands this is the queen's trial, a loud hum of conversation erupts. I wince at some of the sharp words I hear. 'Bitch' being the kindest of them. I hope the king knows what he's doing in ensuring the queen is universally hated.

'Thank you for sharing what you saw and what you heard with us, as well as some of your suspicions from what you've seen and heard.' Bishop Ceolbeorht inclines his head, and I realise I'm being dismissed.

I'm almost standing when he speaks again.

'One more thing, my lord. We understand you'd met Brihthild's brother, another brother, not the one who met his death in Canterbury, within Londinium.'

I flinch at this, evading Brihthild's furious expression. 'Yes, my lord bishop. Brihtwold fought for the enemy when King Ecgberht claimed Londinium and died on the blade of a Mercian. To that, I can tell you I both saw and heard his death.'

'He bloody deserved it, the Wessex bastard,' a voice cries. It could be Oswy, but I don't believe it is. I consider why the bishop feels it necessary to ask me that. Does he mean to imply I'm actually an untrustworthy witness where Brihthild is concerned? Or is it something else? Does he just mean to be thorough?

'My thanks, Lord Budworth.' The bishop dismisses me without further questions. I'm relieved and also considering whether I've helped the queen with my testimony. To those who might not know me, or what I've been through, it could appear as though I've involved myself in affairs that were not my concern, especially regarding another man's children. They might not understand how deeply personal the oath I gave Lady Cynehild was.

Standing, I bow to the king, and his son, even though Lord Wigmund's face is twisted with hatred. I return to Wynflæd and sit heavily. She leans across and grips my hand to show she's pleased with me.

'Well done, Icel. Well done,' she hisses, but her words are loud and carry.

The look of fury I see on Brihthild's face reminds me I've made an implacable enemy of her, as well as the queen. Should Brihthild ever escape from Londonia, I'll need to be wary. She won't let my involvement in her brother's death within Londinium go unpunished.

3

Bishop Ceolbeorht calls others to voice what they know, although not Cuthred, for which I'm grateful. Ealdorman Ælfstan, who has only two oath-helpers, one of whom is the king and the other Ealdorman Tidwulf, which, I determine, means he speaks with more authority than me, tells of retrieving the children from Eamont. Oswy and Cenred, with five oath-helpers each, of which I'm one and Ealdorman Ælfstan another, both recite their part in events in Wessex. Bishop Ceolbeorht informs those in attendance that this means Oswy and Cenred speak with half the value of the king. Then Wulfheard's called forward. Ealdorman Ælfstan told him this would happen, but Wulfheard looks deeply unhappy as he bows to the king and Lord Wigmund and then settles on the chair where all who speak must sit. I observe then that while he wears his usual clothes, his boots have been polished, and his beard and moustache tamed. He's doing his best to look presentable.

'Wulfheard,' Bishop Ceolbeorht begins. I notice the lack of title, but, of course, Wulfheard is a warrior, like Oswy and Cenred. They don't yet have land and can't be termed as lords, unlike me.

'Bishop Ceolbeorht.' Wulfheard's words are softly spoken, his anger banished.

'Wulfheard, you have many who wished to be your oath-helpers, too many in fact. It far exceeded the requirements of this trial. But, I'll tell you we've written down Ealdorman Ælfstan, Lady Ælflæd and Lord Icel of Budworth, as those to whom we believe speak the highest of your integrity. As such, we thank you on behalf of Mercia for all you've done to discover the nature of these attacks on the children.' So far, Bishop Ceolbeorht has thanked everyone. I consider if this is a ploy to make us more likely to speak openly, or to win our regard. 'Now, I understand it's your brother, Wulfnoth of Eamont, who's been so often mentioned this morning.'

'Yes, my lord bishop.' The words are respectful, but they mask a whole host of fury.

'You and your brother weren't close?'

'Not for nearly a decade,' Wulfheard confirms, pleased to be allowed to explain. I hope the bishop moves on to something else, and quickly.

'And you had no prior knowledge of his involvement in this?'

I see the tension return to Wulfheard's face. His answer's sullen. 'No, my lord bishop. We were estranged. In all honesty, I thought him long since dead. I'd have welcomed that.'

'Very good,' Bishop Ceolbeorht confirms, determined to move on to other areas. 'You escorted Ealdorman Ælfstan to Eamont, and also followed Lord Icel to Winchester.' This isn't so much a question as a statement. Looking up from his notes, Bishop Ceolbeorht's next words are deceptively bland. 'It seems you're very involved in this.'

I hold my breath, even as Wynflæd grips my hand ferociously tight with hers. We both know Wulfheard won't like being questioned in such a way. He surprises me with his measured response.

'It's my responsibility as a warrior of Mercia and as that bastard's brother to set this straight.' The answer's surprisingly well spoken and none seem to object to Wulfnoth being termed a bastard. No one can deny the sincerity of Wulfheard's words, either.

'Your brother had meddled in the affairs of Mercia before, I believe?' Bishop Ceolbeorht continues.

'He wished to be closer to the ruling line, certainly. He was, as all here know, instrumental in the usurpation of the kingship from King Coelwulf.'

'King Coelwulf was Lord Coenwulf's father? One of the grandfather's to these two boys who were stolen away.'

'That's correct, my lord bishop.'

'Some would question whether you were implicated in that and, indeed, were still trying to be involved.' Bishop Ceolbeorht's tone is more conciliatory, as though seeking clarity pains him.

'Some might, yes, my lord bishop. Those people wouldn't know me well. They know, as I hope all here do, of my loyalty to the kingship. Icel – sorry, Lord Budworth – Ealdorman Ælfstan and the king, as you've said, and my fellow warriors can attest to my loyalty by revealing the scars that mar my body. They're my oath-helpers. Only my integrity can have earned their high regard.'

Bishop Ceolbeorht inclines his head respectfully. Wulfheard speaks surprisingly well. I think he has a better grip on his temper than I thought he would. He's not usually so reasonable.

'So, if we turn to affairs in Canterbury. This is where everything becomes very confusing. Tell me all you saw and heard.'

'It's not really complicated, my lord bishop. Brihthild there,' and Wulfheard jerks his chin towards her, 'played us for fools.

She murdered her brother outside the walls and then made contact with her true master, Lord Æthelwulf. When things became violent, she attempted to flee. We captured her, eventually, and escorted her to Mercia. While in Mercia, she confessed to her part in the endeavour to murder the children. And she's named those who are involved in the conspiracy.'

'Yes, thank you, Wulfheard.' Again, I suspect the bishop doesn't appreciate Wulfheard saying so much when the question didn't ask for such an outpouring of information. Not that Wulfheard has done more than give a brief account. He's not spoken of the archbishop's involvement in the temporary ceasefire or of the Wessex lord's contempt for it. Neither has he suggested the participation of anyone other than Brihthild. It'll be when Brihthild speaks that the real sparks will fly.

The bishop's next question is intentionally aggressive.

'Your brother, Wulfnoth. How did he come to be a lord in Northumbria?'

I'm unsure why the bishop decides to labour this point when he wanted to know about events in Canterbury only moments ago. Perhaps it's part of the process of testing Wulfheard's integrity further.

'I imagine he killed someone to steal the holding. Or he assisted the king of Northumbria. He'd do anything for coin. And notoriety.' There's no humour to Wulfheard's words.

'Your brother left a will. Do you know of this?'

'No,' Wulfheard responds mildly. I sense Wynflæd stirring beside me again. There's something here that none of us are going to like.

'Your brother makes it very clear you're to inherit his holdings.' Another murmur begins and works its way back through the assembled crowd. 'And that,' Bishop Ceolbeorht beckons for a vellum to be placed in his hands, while raising his voice, '"my brother, Wulfheard, knew of everything I did", those are Wulfnoth's words, as written here, in his will.' Ealdorman Ælfstan's on his feet, but Wulfheard stays remarkably calm, although his hands grip one another.

Unexpectedly, Wulfheard begins to laugh, the sound loud and infectious.

'My brother never wished for me to have anything of his. Now, it seems, he means for me to have something. He means for me to be punished for his actions.' As his words conclude, Wulfheard's tone turns angry. I hear Oswy adding his denial amongst the angry masses. The only reason I don't stand is because Wynflæd holds me still with her strong grip. I don't know how she does it.

The bishop casts an uneasy eye at the crowd. I see him swallow. He didn't expect such an uproar. He named Wulfheard's brother, and then denounced him. I should be furious. The king should be incensed. The uproar only quiets down when King Wiglaf stands.

His posture is imposing. Between him sitting and standing, all eyes swivel to him. He holds his hands to either side of his body.

'Good people,' he begins. 'Wulfheard. My lord bishop.' He inclines his head towards the two men. 'I asked to be one of Wulfheard's oath-helpers but it was deemed he already had enough to attest to his integrity. But, I claim that honour now. I would speak against his brother, for Wulfnoth was a devious bastard. There's no one here who would willingly speak for Wulfnoth. Now, let's have quiet so we can resume. I think it's time we heard from the Wessex woman.'

Bishop Ceolbeorht pauses for a moment, and Oswy's voice ripples through the crowd, the word 'bastard' on his lips, which I hope is directed to Wulfnoth, and not the bishop or king.

'My thanks for your testimony,' Bishop Ceolbeorht concludes.

When Wulfheard stands, he immediately turns and bows

towards the king and his son, entirely ignoring the queen. He stalks from the hall. Ealdorman Ælfstan returns to his seat, but I can sense tension running through his body. It only increases when Brihthild's moved more centrally into the room. Now all can see her, trying to hide beneath her mass of hair. I feel some pity for her, but not enough to denounce what's happening to her. She was deceitful towards me. She murdered her brother. She would also have allowed two small boys to be killed. There's nothing to like about her.

'Brihthild of Wessex,' Bishop Ceolbeorht begins. Her bearing doesn't change. She's not slumped in the chair but neither does she sit as regally as the queen. It's difficult to see her facial expressions beneath her mound of tangled hair. She's much altered from when we met her within Winchester.

'Bishop Ceolbeorht.' Her words, spoken here amongst so many Mercians, mark her as Wessex-born. How, I think, did I expect people not to realise my kingdom of birth when I visited Winchester? It's so obvious to me now.

'You're deemed as not being oath-worthy because you're not Mercian. And yet, we, the bishops of Mercia, believe it's in the best interests of all to listen to what you have to say. Will you faithfully recount, before all and in the eyes of your Lord God, to speak the truth of all you've seen and heard?'

'I will, my lord bishop. All I ask is that I'm not returned to Wessex and the care of Lord Æthelwulf when I'm no longer needed. He'll kill me. I'm certain of that.'

There've been no assurances the Mercians won't kill her, but perhaps Brihthild prefers to die at the hands of a Mercian than in her own kingdom.

Bishop Ceolbeorht makes no pledge. 'We'll hear all you say, and then make a decision,' he states instead. And without further pause, starts his questioning. 'My understanding, Brihthild, is that you were instructed to travel to Winchester and find the Mercians who'd been sent to uncover the truth of the conspiracy against the Mercian kingship.'

'That's correct, my lord bishop. Lord Æthelwulf, the son of King Ecgberht, commanded me to do just that.' Her words are spoken loudly enough all can hear. She's evidently decided to freely share all she knows. I was far from sure she would.

'And Lord Æthelwulf instructed you to wait in the church of Saints Peter and Paul, within Winchester?'

'He was not so specific but I suspected that's where the Mercian would go. Many have heard of Lord Coenwulf's trial, and the man who denounced him. News of it had been shared in Wessex.'

'So, you knew the man who spoke against Lord Coenwulf, Eadbald? He's missing and can't be found.'

'I didn't know Eadbald, no. I understand, from Lord Æthelwulf, that Eadbald never visited Winchester, and so I'd had no opportunity to make his acquaintance.'

This occasions a murmur from amongst the crowd. It seems news of the queen's assistance to Eadbald when describing Winchester at Lord Coenwulf's trial has been shared far beyond Mercia's borders. 'How did you determine who the Mercians were?'

'It was simple, my lord bishop. I was told what the man would look like. Tall, black-bearded, with a warrior's build. It wasn't hard to find him. I did expect him to be alone, however.'

'And you were told he possessed some healing skills?'

'Yes, that as well.' She nods, as though eager to reveal how much Lord Æthelwulf knew. 'I thought to involve my brother for that reason. His illness was a trial, and he didn't bear it with any fortitude. I hoped to accomplish two tasks, not just one.'

'And what were you to do once you found the Mercian?'

'To prevent him leaving Winchester until he could be apprehended by Lord Æthelwulf's warriors.'

'You failed in that?'

'I did, but only because the Mercian – Lord Budworth, as you name him – was already, somehow, ensnared in another problem regarding the horse he bought from Southampton. I wasn't alone in seeking him out. Neither did it help that the other Mercian oafs had been sent to protect him.' Brihthild's words are angrier now, perhaps unhappy at realising how compromised her assignment from Lord Æthelwulf was.

'Ah, yes, Wulfheard, who just spoke.'

'Him, and the two others who gave their testimony before him. They could, admittedly, blend in somewhat better than the dark-haired warrior.'

I can't help feeling stung by that. I cast a dark look at King Wiglaf. He offers me a grimace as though he too realises I was the wrong person to send to Winchester.

'It helped that the youngster was easily led,' Brihthild continues. I notice Bishop Ceolbeorht isn't stopping her from adding incidental details as he did me and Wulfheard.

I feel some sympathy for Cuthred as Brihthild speaks about him. I imagine his face will be burning red with embarrassment. Wynflæd huffs with disgust.

'So, you managed to stay with the two Mercians, despite everything?'

'The boy offered his assistance. And so, yes, we stayed with them. Better to be with them than lose them. One of Lord Æthelwulf's men had already seen me in Winchester. He'd be sure to tell him I'd failed if I didn't keep an eye on the Mercians.'

'So, outside Winchester, you were set upon by these other Wessex warriors, angry about this horse. You decided there was no benefit to helping them overwhelm the Mercians?'

'There was only one reward for taking the Mercians to Lord Æthelwulf. I wanted it, even though events were moving too quickly for me to have complete control over.' Her words are cold. I'm not alone in shuddering at her single-mindedness. 'Anyway, the Mercians were helping my brother, and I recognised the horse as well. It belonged to Heardred, who I knew to be missing.'

'So this brings us to the vellum and the amber.'

'Sent by a lady of Mercia to Lord Æthelwulf to ensure his assistance.' Brihthild shows no concern for her words. The king winces, despite his best attempts to show no emotion, but I focus on Brihthild. I don't look at the queen, even though we all know Brihthild means her when she names a lady. It's evident what the queen will say in her defence. Why should we believe a woman like Brihthild over the queen of Mercia? Mercia's queen has more integrity than a stranger from Wessex.

'And you wanted it?'

'I thought it would help me with Lord Æthelwulf. Prove my loyalty to him. He'd been blaming everyone for the loss of the amber, his payment from this lady of Mercia for his involvement. He'd even sent Heardred's brother to hunt him down.'

'And this is why the horse and the saddle were so important to everyone, aside from Lord Budworth.'

'Yes, my lord bishop.'

'Tell me why you murdered your brother outside Canterbury?' A sharp hiss from the audience greets the question. It's unusual to have a murderess so openly accused amongst us. I would rather the bishop pressed Brihthild to name the queen, but perhaps that will come.

'He suspected my desire to go to Canterbury. He wanted to remain with the Mercians and I can't deny they'd aided him, but he was also suspicious of my intentions. I couldn't let him speak out against me. I was close to Lord Æthelwulf, who I knew to be in Canterbury. A day longer, and all would have been accomplished. I'd have been paid for bringing the Mercians to Lord Æthelwulf, and what happened to the Mercians would no longer be my concern.'

'Yet you say you knew about others, aside from Lord Æthelwulf, who were involved.'

'Lord Æthelwulf liked to brag of his accomplishments. I knew of many implicated in the conspiracy.'

'And are these people within this room?'

'They are, my lord bishop.' The room's grown silent. No one dares move. Few risk breathing in case they draw Brihthild's wrathful eye. King Wiglaf's as immobile as a statue, just like the ones inside the fort of Londinium. The queen is still. Even Wynflæd has stopped gripping my hand and instead sits forward, willing Brihthild to denounce those involved in the conspiracy.

'Can you tell me their names?' Bishop Ceolbeorht prods when she lapses to silence.

'I can, but if I do so, I'll be no more use to you.'

'This is a trial,' the bishop intones. 'The time for bargaining is long past.'

'Then I'll hold my tongue.' Brihthild sits back, crossing her arms over her slim body, hair falling to cover her face, as the entire audience exhales in disappointment.

I sense movement from Queen Cynethryth. A smile touches her cheeks. I narrow my eyes. Brihthild has already told us much of what happened. Why should she be silent now? We know who was involved. Although, of course, we need her testimony spoken before the court and those witnessing it. Has someone made contact with Brihthild and ensured her silence? What could they have said to her? She has no family to benefit from holding her tongue.

Bishop Ceolbeorht continues, showing no sign this abrupt

change has unsettled him. 'Whether you speak now or not, you've already said enough to others that your guilt is assured. You confess to killing your brother. That's a crime of *botleas*. The punishment is to be sentenced to death, even though the murder took place in Canterbury. You know this, as I understand it.'

'I do, my lord bishop,' she replies firmly, but remains otherwise silent.

'This punishment could be changed to one of enslavement,' Bishop Ceolbeorht suggests. I know he means in exchange for denouncing the other accomplices, but Brihthild still doesn't speak.

I look from King Wiglaf to the queen, and then to Bishop Æthelweald, and my eyes narrow. I detect his involvement in this. I also realise Lord Wigmund sits with a satisfied expression on his face. What's he been up to? My suspicions regarding his loyalties remain, although King Wiglaf seems blind to them.

But Bishop Ceolbeorht isn't to be stopped.

'In light of your refusal to answer my questions, I'll call another to speak of all they've heard and seen. Brihthild of Wessex, you have our thanks for the truths you've so far spoken.' He inclines his head. 'Now, I'd request that Brother Sampson speaks to us of all he's heard and seen.'

The smile on Bishop Æthelweald's face disappears as a short man shuffles into view. He's not old. He's not young. He's that strange age in between when he could have twenty-five winters to his name or thirty-five. If he's a scribe, I suspect he's older. His loud breathing fills the air as he waddles into position, skirting around Brihthild with a scowl, bowing to the king and then settling on another chair brought forward for him.

He licks his fat lips and looks to Bishop Ceolbeorht.

I try and recall Brother Sampson. Someone like him should be easy to remember, but I've no recollection of him. None at all.

If I'd seen him at Tamworth, I'm sure my fellow warriors would have made mention of it. Being quite so rotund would be impossible for men who fight and train every day. They'd have wondered how many people's meals he ate each day. I consider it, as well.

'Brother Sampson.' The bishop's tone is chillier than when speaking with me and Wulfheard. That surprises me. Perhaps this is an effort not to be named as biased in his favour.

'My lord bishop.' Sampson's voice is soft, almost impossible to hear. I see the bishop flash him a glance of annoyance, swiftly banished.

'You'll need to speak up so all can hear you,' the bishop informs him, more gently than I suspect.

'I'll do my best.' The words are a little louder. But not much. If someone whispers close by, we won't hear anything he says.

Bishop Ceolbeorht faces the audience. 'As one of Mercia's monks, Brother Sampson is held in high regard by those he serves. But, as all must, he has those who are oath-helpers. One of those is myself, another is the abbot from the monastery he learned within from childhood, and another is Bishop Eadwulf of Hereford.' Bishop Ceolbeorht allows that to be absorbed before continuing. I feel uneasy that the man I think has such a huge part in the conspiracy has not one but two of Mercia's bishops to attest to his integrity. I don't know the abbot, but abbots are men of integrity as well. I wish Brihthild had been more outspoken. 'I have this scrap of vellum here. I've been told you wrote it. Do you recall inking these words?' The monk's eyes scrunch closed as another of the bishop's many adherents walks forward with the small scrap of vellum that's caused us so many problems.

Brother Sampson looks at it, reaching out to take it in his hands, only for the other monk to hold it away from him. It seems he's not to touch it, only to be asked to look at it.

'For those who don't know,' Bishop Ceolbeorht continues, 'the note reads as follows: "My lord of Wessex. The children will be brought to Eamont. Payment to be made on arrival of fifty mancuses."'

A gasp of horror greets those words. I abruptly find a wry smile on my lips. This is almost better than listening to a scop song. The crowd are determined to enjoy the spectacle, although I'm sure some of them are genuinely horrified by what's happened.

'I might have, my lord bishop. It's difficult to know. I send many letters in the name of those who live within Tamworth and other places. Not everyone can write, my lord bishop.'

'Indeed, and do you take payment for these written notes?'

'It depends who asks,' the monk retorts, and now his words are louder. 'I always gift the money to the church or to those poor unfortunates who have so little.'

'So there's no financial gain for you.'

'There's not, my lord bishop.' The monk's outrage seems genuine. But I don't know him, so it might not be.

'This message is very specific.'

'It is, my lord bishop. I confess it does appear to be my writing, but I've no recollection of inking any of the words.'

The furrow on his forehead also seems sincere. I slowly release my breath. I felt sure this would resolve all the questions. But, if Brother Sampson didn't write the note, then who did?

'I do make that very distinctive mark over the "a"s,' he continues. 'But I don't write letters to anyone in Wessex. I have on occasion written to the archbishop of Canterbury.' Wynflæd moves beside me, and her actions remind me of how uncomfortable the seating arrangements are. Indeed, I sense unease amongst everyone within the hall. I risk glancing at the queen. She wears a satisfied smirk on her lips. If she's behind the conspiracy, she's done remarkably well to ensure none of it can be traced back to her. But who would have the stones to use the queen's name in such a way? I wish I knew.

King Wiglaf looks calm but is aware of the unease amongst the crowd. I'm not alone in having my belly growl hungrily.

'Who would know about your writing style?' Bishop Ceolbeorht asks conversationally, as though they're supping wine, and not in the direct sight of at least a hundred people, if not more.

'I imagine anyone who knows me or who's ever had me write something for them. The other members of the scriptorium are obviously aware. It's one of the ways they keep track of who's written what amongst the king's charters and the wills we also write for others.'

'Then, it's not a well-guarded secret?'

'Not at all, my lord bishop. As you know, it has all to do with the angle at which the feather is held, as to how tall or cramped the text is. In this instance, I add a little swirl to my "a". I always have. It's how I was instructed from boyhood.'

Bishop Ceolbeorht smiles, and even I grow still. I've never considered there would be such differences in writing styles. I thought everyone wrote the same, but some were more skilled at it because they practised the art more often.

'Thank you. You may go now.' Bishop Ceolbeorht inclines his head, moving to inspect the next piece of evidence he wishes to examine, but King Wiglaf interjects first as Brother Sampson's shuffling past Brihthild.

'I suggest we allow some time for everyone to stretch their legs,' he offers. 'Or to eat. It's been a long morning.' A sigh of relief rushes through the assembly.

'Indeed, my lord king. I would welcome some sustenance,' Bishop Ceolbeorht announces.

No one waits to be told they can leave. I stand and stretch my back, careful not to bash Wynflæd beside me. While the king's warriors move to encircle Brihthild and the queen, the rest begin to leave the hall. The scent of good food drifts on the air. Outside, it's surprisingly bright. I can glimpse it through the open doorway, but before I can take one step towards it, Ealdorman Ælfstan calls me to his side.

Wynflæd offers me a joyless grin. 'I'll get you some food,' she says, and begins to forge a path through the crowd. She makes good timing, although I wince when she employs her black wooden stick to knock a few people aside. Their cries of outrage are quickly stifled when they realise who inflicted them. Few wish to get on the wrong side of Wynflæd, even here, within Londonia.

Ealdorman Ælfstan walks towards the king. I realise the king's having food brought into the hall for him, and his ealdormen are amassing to hear his opinion on events to date.

I'm not at all convinced it's going as well as we might have thought.

Brihthild hasn't named the queen and now we don't know who wrote the note either, although it seems to have been a Mercian scribe. And while all those who've spoken, aside from Brihthild, have had their integrity reaffirmed by their oathhelpers, Wulfheard's also been closely questioned about his brother, and I've been made to account as to why Lady Cynehild bid me swear an oath to her.

I wish this was simpler. In my mind, I'm assured of the queen's guilt, and perhaps that of her son and certainly Bishop Æthelweald. This desire to ensure the outcome is the best for Mercia and her kingship, as opposed to being all to do with who committed the treason, is perplexing me.

Unhappily, I follow Ealdorman Ælfstan to the king's side.

I hope he's more convinced of the outcome of the trial.

4

'What do you think?' King Wiglaf questions Ealdorman Ælfstan. Ealdorman Tidwulf's already shaking his head.

'Without Brihthild, the evidence isn't as damning as we'd hoped,' Ealdorman Ælfstan admits unhappily. I nod along. Aside from the ealdormen, there's only me and Wulfheard in attendance. Ealdorman Sigered is, thankfully, not included in this select group. I can see him hovering close by, but with two of the king's most loyal warriors effectively barring his entrance to this conclave should he try to gain admittance, he can only witness and not hear the conversation.

'I thought the monk's testimony would be the one,' King Wiglaf admits. 'But if he didn't write the letter, then who did?'

Ealdorman Tidwulf's furious. 'Brihthild spoke to us before. Can't we use that testimony?'

'No, she declares it now, or we have only suspicions. Bishop Ceolbeorht made it clear everything must be spoken before the court. Ealdorman Ælfstan, I understand you doubted her testimony anyway?'

'I did, yes,' Ealdorman Ælfstan admits. 'She's half mad with grief or simply half mad. She'll denounce anyone, which is why the fact she won't speak now to name those involved aside from Lord Æthelwulf is so peculiar, and damaging.'

'Has someone threatened her?' King Wiglaf's holding on to his anxiety well, but I can sense he's unhappy at how events have unfolded this morning. I understand his fears. I'd not want to be forced to live with a woman I suspect has tried to kill small children.

'How? Unless one of the guards is suspect? As Ealdorman Tidwulf says. We got her to speak, and now she won't. I think we have more than enough to prove there's a conspiracy surrounding us. We've nothing to point the finger to who is behind it within Mercia.'

'Perhaps if we had Eadbald?'

'I think Eadbald, who so roundly denounced Lord Coenwulf at Kingsholm, has much less to do with this than we thought. He was known to the queen, admittedly.'

'And we really don't know where he is these days?'

'No, my lord king. He's vanished, just like the man who carried the amber and the vellum in the first place. What was his name? Heardred? Whoever killed Heardred made sure no one knew where he was or where he was buried, and then they sold his horse for good measure.'

I help myself to a bowl of meaty pottage and a hunk of bread brought by bowing servants, and passed over by Wulfheard and Ealdorman Tidwulf. Some of the king's allies have pulled up chairs to help them eat. Others stand because we've been sitting for a long time and as warriors, and men of action, we feel the need to be doing something. King Wiglaf remains on his feet, eating absent-mindedly. I'm going to need to visit the latrines as well before much longer.

The food's redolent of warm spices. I eagerly drink a watered-down ale. I don't want to be inebriated. I also need to quench my thirst from speaking before the king and Bishop Ceolbeorht.

'As ever, we're chasing our tails,' King Wiglaf complains softly. The queen has also been brought food, and two of her servants attend to her. They're escorted outside, the guards keeping a close eye on her. Ealdorman Sigered has given up his efforts to speak to the king. I frown to see him trying to catch the attention of the queen instead while also ensuring he remains inconspicuous to her guards.

There are few within the hall now other than Brihthild, who's in the process of being allowed outside to relieve herself and eat, and us, who surround the king. Two monks keep a careful eye on the bishop's possessions. There are piles of vellums and many bound books containing Mercia's law codes. I'm far from convinced there'll be anything in them that will help us resolve the current problem.

As Bishop Ceolbeorht advised, this trial is about determining what everyone has seen and heard and what that means for the conspiracy. I can't say whether it's enough to ensure the queen is found complicit. I'm furious with Brihthild for refusing to speak, and also concerned. There's something going on of which we're unaware. It makes me itch.

I didn't see Lord Wigmund go, but he's also left the hall. He's such an ineffectual figure.

The sound of rushing hooves reaches our ears, and I'm not alone in reaching for my seax, although no weapons have been allowed within the king's hall. Well, none apart from those the guards are permitted to keep as they protect the queen, or rather, keep her under their surveillance.

We look towards the open doorway, empty now of the crowd from earlier, who've all gone to see to their personal needs. There are shouts, no doubt, between the rider and those who might not want to allow them entry, and then Commander Eahric strides into the king's hall, head down, eyes focused on where he's going. In his hand, he carries a rolled vellum.

'What's all this then?' King Wiglaf questions.

'My lord king.' Commander Eahric sweeps his gaze over the assembled ealdormen, his eyebrows arching when he sees me, although he makes no comment. 'A message from the archbishop of Canterbury.'

King Wiglaf winces and reaches out to take the vellum, only for Ealdorman Tidwulf to intervene.

'I'll open it, my lord king. Better to be safe than sorry.'

The crack of the wax seal rings louder than a church bell. We all watch as the ealdorman unfurls the message, runs his hands along it, and even sniffs it. Such bizarre behaviour.

'I can detect nothing amiss,' he admits and hands the vellum to King Wiglaf with a slight bow. He's not read the message. But King Wiglaf bends to do so, beckoning one of his monks to assist him. It falls to one of those watching the bishop's belongings to scurry to the king's side.

I hear the monk's muffled words as he reads and realise quickly the message is written in church Latin and likely to be incomprehensible to most people within the room, including the king. Even Ealdorman Tidwulf, despite his desire to compile a compendium of herbal law.

'The archbishop sends his warmest greetings and apologises profusely for events in Canterbury. He assures you he knew nothing of Lord Æthelwulf's intentions. He does, though, request the return of Brihthild to his care.'

King Wiglaf smirks, but there's no joy to it. 'Lord Æthelwulf, the bastard, intends to continue involving the archbishop. I wish I had a bloody archbishop to do all I commanded,' he complains.

This is an old argument. But I sense King Wiglaf's unease.

'Does he threaten anything?'

'No, there are no religious overtures to the message, just a request for the woman and the initial apology.'

King Wiglaf nods and dismisses the monk, although he demands the vellum be handed to him.

'Is the messenger to wait for a response?'

'The messenger's to wait for Brihthild to be returned to his care,' Commander Eahric growls. King Wiglaf sighs. I feel my hands form fists beside me. Kyre nearly died to ensure we got Brihthild to Mercia. This was supposed to be a simple matter of having Brihthild denounce the queen. It's not going at all how I thought it would.

'Have the messenger given food and drink. He can watch what happens for the rest of the day. He comes alone, I take it?'

'Yes, via ship across the River Thames. The ship waits for him. I've dispatched men to guard it. And no one else is to be allowed to disembark.'

'Then, it'll just have to wait. I won't be rushed on this,' King Wiglaf announces decisively. Ealdorman Ælfstan and Tidwulf nod their agreement. After all, Tidwulf's role is to protect Londinium and Lundenwic. If trouble comes, it'll fall to him and his warriors, although we're here, as are many of the king's loyal warriors. Commander Eahric would know what to do. And as the message is from the archbishop, we're not about to start a war with Wessex. Not yet.

King Wiglaf finally hands the vellum to Ealdorman Tidwulf, who scours it, grumbling as he does. The king eats hurriedly and then excuses himself. I hasten to follow. Outside, the daylight is bright, and I catch sight of Commander Eahric and the man I assume is the archbishop's messenger. My eyes narrow. I'm sure I know him. As I spent so little time inside the archbishop's complex, I suspect this is one of the Wessex warriors. I sense that Commander Eahric feels the same.

Hastily, I rush to relieve my bladder and then make my way to Commander Eahric.

He acknowledges me with a nod of his head, where he's been joined by six of his warriors. I eye them. They're all armed. The messenger has clearly dismounted, but now rests on his horse once more. It seems he doesn't wish to take advantage of the king's largesse. That surprises me. Most messengers I've ever met are desperate for good food and drink.

'What's his name?' I question Eahric quietly.

'He calls himself Lanfrac.'

'Does he now?' I muse. 'I recognise him. Do you?'

'Yes, he's one of Ealdorman Hereberht's men, I'm sure of it.'

I nod. I suspect the same. 'I thought the archbishop threatened him and Lord Æthelwulf if they didn't give up the chase.'

'He did, but they seem not to care, and anyway, the archbishop has evidently had a change of heart. Whatever they hold over him, the man has been prevailed upon to interfere, whether he wants to or not.'

'Can I speak with him?'

'I don't see why not.'

'Good man,' I begin, stepping through the mass of warriors surrounding the Wessex messenger. He's older than me, not that it's hard to be. His hands rest tightly on the reins, the horse uneasy beneath him. There's some wetness on the horse's long legs. The animal must have been brought with him on the ship, and has walked through the shallows.

'What do you want?' Lanfrac growls angrily. He's tall, and well built. Not at all my idea of a messenger kept by the archbishop of Canterbury. I assume all messengers must be able to defend themselves, but this man looks like he could punch four enemies and not even break a sweat.

'I was being friendly,' I offer. I mean, I wasn't. I'm merely very nosy. 'You know, fellow warrior to fellow warrior.'

'I'm a messenger, not a warrior,' he growls. His long hair is tied neatly back behind his shoulders. The sun glints on the brown mass, and I suspect it contains one or two grey hairs.

His face also carries a few scars, most notably above his right eyebrow. When that wound was healed, the skin was clearly pulled too tightly. Now, one eyebrow appears half as long as the other one.

'I suggest you tell your body that,' I counter. I don't want to start an argument, but pretending to be a messenger is ludicrous. 'I saw you in Canterbury,' I continue, before he can say more.

'What of it? It's my home.'

'But you were with Ealdorman Hereberht, not the archbishop.'

'The archbishop needed a man who knew Lundenwic. I'm that man. I was stationed here when King Ecgberht was also king of Mercia.'

Now I understand why he's been sent. Though it's a good excuse, I doubt it's solely to retrieve Brihthild.

'And, do you find everything to your satisfaction?'

The warrior opens his mouth, no doubt to deny my suggestion, but instead, he grins, sitting back more easily on the horse.

'I can see very little from here,' he offers conversationally. 'The defences have obviously been reinforced. I see the fort remains the final line of defence for Londinium. But, there won't be much to tell the archbishop or Ealdorman Hereberht. As usual, Mercia's content that it won't be attacked.'

Commander Eahric sucks in a harsh breath at the admission,

but I shake my head to stop him from overreacting. I also encourage the man standing next to me to remove his hand from where it rests on his seax hilt.

'King Wiglaf has invited you inside. If you wish to know more, I suggest you take him up on that offer.'

Commander Eahric glowers at me but then shrugs, deciphering my intent.

It's better to have the Wessex warrior where we can restrict what he can learn about Lundenwic. He's already been appraising the defences. We don't want him to see the extent of the reinforced defences that Lundenwic now boasts. Yes, the fort is there, with its high walls and protective embrace, but it's the homes of the traders and the bishop that now boast ditches and ramparts. It's better if our friend from Canterbury doesn't see them.

Lanfrac slides from his horse and hands him over to one of the many squires available to tend to the animal.

'Give him a good rub-down,' I instruct the boy. He nods. The animal's eyes are wild. It's far from exhausted, but has clearly not enjoyed its journey across the River Thames.

With the commotion over for now, I notice people are returning inside, and I hasten to do the same. But first, I speak to Commander Eahric.

'Ensure he has a good view of the proceedings and he's in Brihthild's line of sight.'

Commander Eahric nods, a slow smile on his lips as he inclines his head towards me.

I only then make my way back inside. I'm still unsure how King Wiglaf will make more of the allegations against his wife. It seems impossible to obtain the result we need now Brihthild's shut her mouth tighter than a clam. Perhaps the sight of the man from Canterbury will encourage Brihthild to talk for fear we might just send her back to Lord Æthelwulf. I think it's worth taking a chance.

5

Wynflæd, Cuthred and Ealdorman Ælfstan have beaten me back to our previous place, and they've saved me a seat once more. Wulfheard's also there. The three of us pretend not to notice the loud complaints of those coming from behind. If they want to see better, I'd advise them to go and stand at the back of the hall. It's not as though we can help being so tall. And so wide. Wynflæd has a faint smirk on her face. They wouldn't dare complain to her about it, but then she's not blocking their view.

King Wiglaf and his son reappear after the bishops have returned to the front of the hall. All seem prepared to continue. Not that I truly know what will happen next. Brihthild won't talk. Brother Sampson denies his involvement. The queen won't implicate herself, and now we have a messenger from the archbishop of Canterbury demanding Brihthild's return to his care. This isn't unfolding how I hoped it would. I can't imagine King Wiglaf is pleased either.

But it seems Bishop Ceolbeorht and the king have considered what comes next as the bishop makes a start on proceedings.

'We summon Eadburg, one of the women who was entrusted

with the care of the two children. She was also wounded trying to protect them. Sadly, her mother was killed.'

For a moment, I fear for Eadburg, the woman who has also won Edwin's heart, my erstwhile childhood ally, now in exile with Lord Coenwulf. She's brave to stand before everyone, revealing her scars for all to see. But perhaps that's rather the point, I muse.

I turn to Ealdorman Ælfstan in surprise. He shrugs, which I take to mean he didn't know about this development either.

I look around perplexed, seeking Eadburg, but the cry of young voices explains how she's travelled to Londonia when I thought her at Kingsholm. Eadburg enters the hall, a space forged through the crowd by Commander Eahric's warriors, standing proudly, revealing her scars to a shocked intake of breath from those in attendance. Lady Ælflæd follows on behind Eadburg. The three children, the young æthelings of Mercia, are with the two women. Their eyes are agog as they walk unaided.

I smile to see the children and women, even though the boys look unsettled by so many people. Young Coenwulf, the oldest of the three boys, breaks into a huge grin as he spots me. He rushes towards me and clambers onto my knee without being invited. His speech is clear even though he thinks he whispers.

'My aunt says we need to be quiet. Why are all these people here?' The words occasion a smattering of laughter. I shrug helplessly towards Lady Ælflæd, whose face flushes with embarrassment. But King Wiglaf stands, a smile on his lips, as he beckons for his grandson to be placed in his arms before his father can claim him. Not, I realise, that Lord Wigmund looks keen to do so. If anything, he eyes his wife and Eadburg aghast, and pale faced. Eadburg carries her injuries, as do I. She must also remind him of what his oath-sworn warriors undertook to do.

While young Coenwulf gets comfortable on my lap, I eye Wigstan. He's developed into a fine-looking, chunky child.

Considering all the worry about him, when he was first born, he's hale enough now. King Wiglaf sits proudly with his grandson who, like Coenwulf, is busy absorbing everything around him.

Wigmund's perplexed by his wife's arrival, and almost recoils as Wigstan reaches out with a drool-coated hand to grip his father's shoulder. I don't miss the lack of interest Lady Ælflæd offers her husband. I feel a stirring of hope they'll never be reconciled, no matter what happens here today. That would please me. Lady Ælflæd should never have been forced to marry Lord Wigmund. I doubt anything would have ever happened between us, but I can still hope it might have done.

'My grandson,' King Wiglaf announces proudly, while Eadburg's settling on the chair used by those who must give their testimony. Lady Ælflæd has taken her place to the other side of the king, Coelwulf with her. 'And of course, his cousins, young Coenwulf and Coelwulf, the children of Lord Coenwulf and Lady Cynehild. I felt it important for all to see the children being discussed,' King Wiglaf explains, as though it's needed. It does not clarify why Eadburg's here, but again, perhaps that's self-evident.

Young Coenwulf grips a small wooden toy in his hand. It's in the shape of a horse and is very well crafted. Wynflæd flashes me a genuine look of surprise but holds her tongue, which astounds me.

There's a mumble of greeting for the small children from everyone there now the laughter has died away. I don't miss the look of pride on Eadburg's face either, to see the young boys greeted so warmly by those in attendance. She risked death for those children. I'm pleased she doesn't regret it.

'Apologies, Bishop Ceolbeorht. Please, continue.' King Wiglaf sits, keeping hold of his grandson. Young Coelwulf looks uncertain. I imagine he wishes to sit with Eadburg but senses he shouldn't.

Brihthild purposefully doesn't look at the children, but her gaze is elsewhere, perhaps not really seeing anything, or maybe looking at Lanfrac, a man she must also recognise from Canterbury. Commander Eahric has been as good as his word. Lanfrac's not close to the front, but where he stands, to the side of the hall, with two of Commander Eahric's men watching him in their shimmering byrnies, Brihthild can't help but see him. I wait to observe her response, but find it lacking. She's either not seen him, or doesn't realise why he's here.

Then, because we have new arrivals at the trial, Bishop Ceolbeorht repeats much of what he first said when starting his questioning, stressing how the purpose is to discover all that people have seen and heard. With a faint smile, Bishop Ceolbeorht focuses on Eadburg.

'Now, Eadburg, I ask only that you share with us all you've seen and heard. I understand you're the daughter of the woman who was the boys' wet nurse. Lady Ælflæd is your main oath-helper, although I've been advised that Lord Budworth and Ealdorman Ælfstan will also vouch for you. And that Lord Coenwulf would do the same, were he here.' I smile at Eadburg even though I didn't know about this. Not that I'll argue about it. I'd vouch for Eadburg's integrity no matter what. The terrible scars on her face attest to what she endured for the children. 'With such oath-helpers, I deem it unnecessary to seek more, although usually, a servant would require many more than just three oath-helpers.'

'I am the daughter of the boys' wet nurse, and I'm grateful, my lady and my lords, to you for being my oath-helpers.' Eadburg's words are surprisingly strong. She shows no fear, although she focuses on Bishop Ceolbeorht and not the crowd before her.

Betrayal of Mercia 67

Neither does she show any unease at being close to the queen or Brihthild. Eadburg appears more certain of what will be expected of her, as she sits, hands on her knees, wearing a dress of fine cloth and a cloak rimmed with fur. She's not always been so well dressed. Lady Ælflæd has gifted her with such items and has prepared her well. Much better than I was coached, anyway.

'And you travelled with the children on that fateful journey when they were stolen away to the north.'

'I did, yes. We were told by the men who had command of our cart and baggage that the destination was Tamworth, but it wasn't.'

'They took you far from Tamworth?'

'Yes, into the north. When my mother, God rest her soul, realised the peril we were in, we tried to escape with the children, but the men wounded her and took the children. She died.' The pronouncements are greeted with silence. Bishop Ceolbeorht waits for everyone to absorb that information even though he's already told us as much.

'And you can identify these men?'

'I could, but they're all dead. All of them. They were killed either by Icel, or by the warriors of Ealdorman Ælfstan.'

'Icel is Lord Budworth,' the bishop clarifies, looking at the crowd, but quickly continues his questioning, while Eadburg startles at her mistake. 'Do you recall their names?' Bishop Ceolbeorht questions.

Eadburg speaks with no further prompting. 'Wulfnoth, Eadweard, Mergeat, Frothgar, Deremann and Wulfred, my lord bishop.'

'These men were, I understand, warriors oath-sworn to Lord Wigmund, the king's son?'

'They were, apart from Wulfnoth. He wasn't.'

Lord Wigmund shuffles uncomfortably under the intense

scrutiny of the crowd. I sense he wants to say something but refrains. To the other side of the king, Lady Ælflæd sits as though carved of marble. This must pain her. The queen offers no reaction at all.

'And Lord Budworth rescued you.'

For a moment, Eadburg's confused, but then remembers the bishop's words as she looks at me. 'Oh, yes, Lord Budworth. Apologies.'

I offer her a smile while Coenwulf seems to have fallen asleep in my arms. His soft snores rumble through my body. I glimpse a small smile on Wynflæd's tight lips. She pretends to her severity. She's told me there's no love for the small children, but it's very different seeing them in the flesh. That, I imagine, is why King Wiglaf has ordered the children and their aunt to Londonia.

'Lord Budworth followed the children. He found me, with my mother's body.' She swallows around her sorrow. 'And we continued north to find the children.'

'And you found them?'

'We did, and retrieved them. People within Chester helped us, but on our journey back to Kingsholm, the warriors overtook us and stole the children back again.'

'Thank you. Can you tell me the names of any other people involved or what they intended to do?'

'They were going to take the children to Eamont, far to the north,' Eadburg asserts. 'After that, I believe they meant to end their lives, based on what I saw and heard.' As she says this, my arms tighten on Coenwulf and Eadburg sweeps a look at Coelwulf, who now sits with his aunt.

'So, there was never any suggestion they'd be reunited with their father.'

'No, my lord bishop. There was not.'

Bishop Ceolbeorht nods sagely as though this explains much.

It's very quiet within the hall. Everyone strains to hear Eadburg speak with such composure.

'Prior to the journey, did you have any suspicions about these men?'

'No, my lord bishop. I mean, they had no love for Lord Budworth. They beat him pretty badly.'

'Did they?' Bishop Ceolbeorht fixes me with a look. I can do little with a small child asleep on my lap but nod in agreement. It seems he was ignorant of this fact. 'Did they beat him because the children liked him so much?'

'I don't know why, and the children didn't always like him. They were scared of him when they were younger. He is a warrior.' A murmur of amusement runs through the room. King Wiglaf watches me, a grin on his previously dour lips, where I act as a handy cushion for my young charge. This is doing little for my reputation.

'How did you survive your wounds?' Bishop Ceolbeorht asks softly.

Eadburg looks stricken for a moment, glancing towards Lady Ælflæd. Something passes between them. I confess I understand her reticence about revealing the Wolf Lady. We don't know her story. I wouldn't want to reveal her existence or have her summoned to Londonia. I don't believe she'd come even if the king demanded it.

'I was found by a man in the woodlands, who took me to a healer. She ensured I lived, and then I returned to Kingsholm to care for the children.'

'Then we're most grateful to your healer friend, even if she perhaps works outside the remit of the church.'

Wynflæd stiffens at the downward cast of Bishop Ceolbeorht's face. I can hear her mumbling about 'bloody bishops', but I pretend not to hear.

'Thank you, Eadburg. I'm pleased you're well and I offer my sincere sympathies for the loss of your mother. I assume the wergild was settled for her life?'

'My lord bishop?' she questions.

'Lord Wigmund. The men were his. I presume he settled the wergild for your mother's life being cruelly taken from her.'

Lord Wigmund's face clouds with fury.

'I'll ensure it's done,' King Wiglaf announces, casting a meaningful look at his son. Once more, I can tell the king's disappointed in him. Lady Ælflæd inclines her head, acknowledging she should have thought to see to this.

'Then, Eadburg, we thank you for attending today, and for sharing all you saw and heard. King Wiglaf of Mercia thanks you as do we, the religious men and women of Mercia.'

When Eadburg stands, smoothing down her dress, Coenwulf wakes, and struggles free from my lap.

With a cheeky grin, he dashes towards his nursemaid. Coelwulf and Wigstan also try to win free from the king and Lady Ælflæd. Eadburg beckons them to her side, and with a curtsey for the king, Lord Wigmund, Lady Ælflæd and even the queen, she once more walks through the assembly. I admire her poise, as my eyes once more sweep over Lanfrac. He watches Eadburg with barely disguised contempt.

'Now, Lady Ælflæd, I'll ask you to speak of all you've seen and heard of events that have brought us here today,' Bishop Ceolbeorht announces without delay.

Lady Ælflæd stands smoothly and takes Eadburg's place on the chair, without any sign of unease. As Lady Ælflæd passes the queen, I see her glower of fury.

'Lady Ælflæd, thank you for coming at such short notice,' Bishop Ceolbeorht begins. 'It was important to hear Eadburg speak of all she saw and heard. I understand you're one of her oath-helpers and I ask if you're entirely sure of her integrity in all she recounts. It's not often I must accept the word of a woman of such low status.'

'I do, my lord bishop,' Lady Ælflæd speaks with surety. Her words aren't overly loud. 'She's cared for my brother's children and my son. She's a woman I trust with the most precious people to me. I don't doubt anything she says to me. She may be a servant, but she's honest and good, and I'm grateful to her. She's bled and nearly died in my service and the service of Mercia's royal family. I could ask no more from even the bravest warrior.'

'Thank you, my lady,' Bishop Ceolbeorht offers. 'In that case, I'll inform everyone here that Lady Ælflæd has need of only one oath-helper as the wife of the king's son. That oath-helper is King Wiglaf himself. Thank you, my lord king. Now, Lady Ælflæd, can you please tell us of all you have seen and heard in relation to the apprehension of your nephews, young Coelwulf and Coenwulf, by men oath-sworn to Lord Wigmund.'

'I confess, I knew very little,' Lady Ælflæd admits. She shows no surprise that it's the king who vouches for her. They must have agreed upon this before. It shows the king's regard for Lady Ælflæd. I'm curious as to whether he'll stand as an oath-helper for his son. He won't for his wife, of that there's no question. 'I suspected nothing. It was only when my nephews didn't arrive at Tamworth, as I thought they would, that I grew concerned. I would say here and now that I'm grateful, and entirely unable to compensate those who gave their lives, or risked their lives on behalf of my nephews. Their care was over and above what was required. It should have been me who was with them, to protect them from such terrible malice.' I feel myself exalt a little at the statement, but when Lady Ælflæd looks only at Bishop Ceolbeorht my delight quickly vanishes.

'So, looking back on events, do you now have suspicions? Did you see or hear anything that now makes sense to you but which didn't at the time?'

'I was always unhappy with the men who were subject to my husband's wishes. They were rough and unruly. However, I didn't believe they were capable of concocting such a scheme to squirrel the children away. I didn't fear them, as it were. I didn't believe them a threat to my nephews and myself. I thought they were under my husband's command.'

'But you believe they were instructed by someone else?'

'I do, my lord bishop. Weak-willed men are easily coerced, and they were weak-willed men intent only on violence amongst themselves. After all, they attacked Lord Budworth, as Eadburg has informed you. They were capable of fighting, I won't deny that.'

I'm surprised that Lady Ælflæd knew of the attack upon me. Perhaps, I realise, she's been paying more attention to me than I thought.

'We've heard the name Wulfnoth spoken by Eadburg. Did you know him?'

'I have a faint recollection of him from when I was a child. He wasn't a pleasant man then. He was always uneasy with my family. He was instrumental in taking the kingship from my father.' Rage thrums through her words.

'Did your father, King Coelwulf, the first of his name, respect him?'

'I don't know,' Lady Ælflæd admits after a long pause. 'I was too young. I recall only the outcome of those events, not what led to them.'

'Of course, my lady. You were a child.'

I'm unsure why Bishop Ceolbeorht is pursuing such a line of questioning. Lady Ælflæd can't speak of events when she wasn't much older than her son and nephews. I doubt she can remember anything, and would be even less able to speak the truth of what she saw and heard.

'If you will excuse the next question, my lady. You spoke out against your brother in the trial that had him banished from Mercia?'

Lady Ælflæd shows no emotion at being questioned in such a way. 'I believed all I was told about his treason,' she admits.

'So, you were led by others who convinced you of your brother's guilt?'

'The queen spoke with surety of his culpability. She had Eadbald brought before me to tell of my brother's deceit.'

'Ah, yes, Eadbald, the man who denounced your brother by speaking of his meeting with the West Saxon king. Do you recall Eadbald from your childhood?'

'I do, my lord bishop. I realise now he was often to be found with Wulfnoth.'

This surprises me, but clearly not the bishop. There's much I've not been told. Perhaps I should be grateful, but the more I learn, the more I realise Wulfnoth and Eadbald were involved in this conspiracy long before the children were born. Those births must have upset whatever prior arrangements were in place.

I'm curious as to whether they've been employed by the queen or the Wessex king for a decade and not just a few short months.

'Now, another delicate matter. The men named by Eadburg were your husband's oath-sworn warriors. Did you ask him to remove them from Kingsholm?'

'I didn't – an oversight on my part. Alas, as you know, our son wasn't strong when he was born. My focus was on him, and my nephews. Affairs of the kingdom, I confess, didn't concern me. Neither did the matter of who was guarding Kingsholm. I simply wished to be with my son.'

'Of course, my lady.' Bishop Ceolbeorht oozes sympathy but I feel a spark of anger. That's not entirely how I remember it. The lingering warmth of young Coenwulf sitting in my lap reminds me clearly of that. I almost open my mouth to complain, but Wynflæd grips my arm tightly to distract me. 'My thanks, my lady.' Bishop Ceolbeorht indicates he's finished with his questions. Now I have no idea who'll face him next as Lady Ælflæd returns to her position to the side of the king. She still doesn't make any attempt to speak to her husband, but then they've been living separately for some time. Lady Ælflæd has been at Kingsholm. Lord Wigmund has been with his mother.

Brihthild's gaze follows Lady Ælflæd back to her seat. I'd expect her to despise the Mercian, but it seems to me there's respect on what parts of her face are visible through the tangled mess of her hair.

'It's now time to question Queen Cynethryth.' Bishop Ceolbeorht half bows, but his eyes watch the king. King Wiglaf nods encouragingly. This won't be easy. I'm sure of it.

The queen labours upright, taking her sweet time, beckoning the two women to assist her, while her guards glower and endeavour to stay close. The dress the queen wears has a long trail. It's as though she's wearing her bedding and not a dress. Why has she done such a thing? She appears strangely elongated, almost serpent-like. Eventually, after much arranging, rearranging and whispered commands to her women, and angry looks at the guards, the two women curtsey and leave the queen to sit alone at the front of the hall, facing the holy men and women, her husband behind her on the dais.

I try to observe the queen without my growing hatred colouring my perceptions.

She's an older woman. Her hair, beneath the shimmering veil on her head, is entirely grey. Her eyes are lined, and her lips thin and pursed. Her forehead is high, eyes bright with fury, but her chin reveals a tendency to rotundness. She sits proudly, hands clasped together in her lap. Whether she was a beautiful woman or not in her youth, she's now merely arrogant and likes food too much, while exercising too little.

'My lady,' Bishop Ceolbeorht begins.

'Your queen,' she corrects him immediately. The bishop's eyes narrow. Queen Cynethryth means to be difficult. A brief look of pure loathing crosses Brihthild's face. King Wiglaf, despite his words to the contrary, is far from impassive. This will be interesting.

'My lady, Queen Cynethryth,' Bishop Ceolbeorht corrects himself. 'You're here to answer my questions about the attempt to kill the children of Lord Coenwulf, and to speak truthfully about all you've seen and heard about this affair. In this, there are, alas, surprisingly few who will be your oath-helpers. The king is, of course, unable to do so. It would be wrong to cast discord between a husband and his wife. And as a woman can't denounce her husband, so a husband can't denounce his wife. However, your son, Lord Wigmund and Ealdorman Sigered have determined to be your oath-helpers. I would like all those here to know that although she's queen, in this regard, we would have liked more people to support her integrity. Lady Ælflæd needed only the king to stand as her surety. It's not the same for a queen implicated in such terrible crimes. As such, all here are warned to listen carefully. What Queen Cynethryth has to say isn't to be accepted as truthful unless more will be her oath-helpers. Those who are her oath-helpers are also suspected of being involved.'

'Preposterous,' Queen Cynethryth complains angrily. She eyes Lanfrac with interest. I consider if she knows his identity.

'There's also the matter of your perjury to address with regards to Lord Coenwulf,' Bishop Ceolbeorht continues, as though this also explains why her testimony isn't to be given as much credence even with the king's son and an ealdorman as her oath-helpers.

'Outrageous,' she interjects once more.

'My lady, Queen Cynethryth,' the bishop interrupts, 'please only speak when called upon to answer a question.' She grimaces but thins her lips even further, an attempt to hold her peace. Ealdorman Sigered and his nephew watch the queen carefully from their position to the other side of the holy men and women. The king, his son and Lady Ælflæd sit on the dais, visible to all. The ealdormen and king's thegns are to my left. Lord Beorhtwulf's also showing too much interest. Lord Wigmund fidgets in his chair, but whether he's uncomfortable at also being called into question, or whether he fears for his mother, I don't know. Certainly, he shows his wife no warmth, and his son even less.

'So, to begin, why did you support Eadbald when he denounced Lord Coenwulf, and in doing so, commit perjury and damage the king's *mund*?'

'I didn't,' the queen denies.

'My lady, Queen Cynethryth, there's a record of your words. It's clear you offered him the name of a church in Winchester when he was unsure.'

'I did no such thing,' she interjects.

Bishop Ceolbeorht's heavy sigh is audible. 'I can read the transcript, if you so desire.'

'And why should we believe the words that were written down? I was never asked to confirm them.'

'My lady, Queen Cynethryth, I'd ask you not to denounce the work of a member of the king's scriptorium. They well know only to record what was said. It is, as ever, always important to be able to refer back to these things. I'm sure you can understand.'

A heavy silence falls. I think Queen Cynethryth will offer nothing further. But, now she's been given the opportunity to speak, she seems to welcome it.

'Eadbald was known to me. He seemed overwhelmed by the questions levelled at him by the king. I didn't mean to prompt him, only to offer reassurance that he could speak honestly about Lord Coenwulf. It's hard for those who aren't lords to speak their mind when matters become so formal as to require a court to be convened.'

I narrow my eyes at her outrageous lie. After all, we've all just heard Eadburg. She needed no one to aid her.

'And you knew of this church in Winchester because you've visited there?'

'I've never been to Winchester,' she clarifies. 'I'm the queen of Mercia. Why should I venture to an enemy kingdom?'

'But you've not always been the queen of Mercia?'

'Before I was queen, I was a wife and mother of a Mercian lord. I've never been to Winchester.' Now she speaks more forcefully. Bishop Ceolbeorht nods, but he's not alone in suspecting the queen's answer as a murmur ripples through the crowd.

'What do you say about the allegations against you? That you provided this expensive piece of amber as payment to ensure the children were murdered. It's a gem worthy of Mercia's queen, is it not?'

Bishop Ceolbeorht holds the large piece of amber before him. It glistens from the reflected candles and sunlight that illuminate the hall. A gasp of astonishment runs through those assembled. It truly appears priceless with its fiery heart and huge size.

'I've never seen that before,' Queen Cynethryth quickly replies, barely looking at it.

'Here, have a closer look,' Bishop Ceolbeorht suggests, moving to hand her the piece of amber. I watch the queen as she reluctantly takes it into her hand. I notice how she tenses for the weight of the stone and how her hand cups it easily. I'm sure she's held the amber before. A brief look of triumph touches the bishop's face. He sees it, too. It's unfortunate only those close by will have been able to witness the ease with which the queen claimed the amber. It might be a small thing, but it reveals much.

'It's heavy,' she offers, belatedly lowering her hand as though to absorb an unexpected weight.

'It is, yes. Some would say priceless. Where do you think someone would get something like this from?' Bishop Ceolbeorht questions.

The queen shrugs, hand extended as though the amber burns her, and she wants it back in the hand of the bishop. 'It would need to be a gift from someone or purchased from one of the gem traders. But I think it's more likely a gift. Who would dare travel with something so valuable? Anyone who saw it would covet it.'

'Indeed. It was found inside a saddle, just a normal saddle, but cleverly hidden.'

'If it were mine, I would also hide it in such a place. Or bury it, as our ancestors did. Bury it somewhere that no one can find it.'

I gasp at her response. It's as though she speaks of her intentions towards the children. She wanted them buried, far from Mercia, where no one would ever think to look for them. She wanted their bones to be undiscovered.

Wynflæd's gaze turns to mine. Briefly, she doesn't understand my reaction, only then she does. I sense Ealdorman Ælfstan also appraising me.

'How much do you think it's worth?'

'I wouldn't know,' the queen gabbles, clearly not anticipating such a question. 'About fifty mancuses, as you said earlier.'

'About fifty mancuses,' Bishop Ceolbeorht repeats. 'So many, many thousands of pounds.' He finally takes back the amber, and hands it carefully to one of his monks. They make a great show of returning it to a highly polished and gleaming wooden box. That then is where an amber stone of such value should be stored. Not in a saddle, and not buried in the ground. 'Now, I would question you about a friendship you have with the king of Wessex, Ecgberht.' Bishop Ceolbeorht's tone has hardened.

'There's no friendship,' the queen retorts.

'There is, and we know about it. Indeed, before you were queen, you were open about your friendship with King Ecgberht. I understand you know his wife well. I've been shown your correspondence, and your messenger informs me of the many times he's travelled between your home and Wessex. Admittedly, that friendship has suffered since you became queen, and as he understands it, has entirely failed since King Wiglaf was usurped, and forced to take back his kingship of Mercia from King Ecgberht.'

As Bishop Ceolbeorht explains, the queen's furious face settles. 'As you say. I was once friendly. But no more.' She believes this is enough.

'Indeed, and yet, it's suspected you still communicate, only using more official channels, abusing the trust of your kingdom, not to mention that of your husband, the king.'

'That's not true,' the queen rejects. 'My friend is dead. How could I still be in contact with her?'

'I understand it's now her son you carry out a correspondence with.'

For a moment, I believe the queen will deny it, but then she juts out her chin. 'As you say, it's a political necessity. I knew his mother, and so now I attempt to guide him, as I know she would try and do with my son if I were dead.'

I look to Wynflæd. I don't think I even know the name of the woman who was married to Ecgberht. I confess I've never given it much thought. She shakes her head, assuring me she doesn't know either.

'I don't believe that's treason or a crime against the king,' Queen Cynethryth hisses. It probably isn't, and yet it's building an image of a woman who's content to be friends with Mercia's enemies. And, indeed, a man who now rules in Kent when it was once Mercian. That, added to the lack of noble born and well-placed people willing to be her oath-helpers, isn't helping the queen.

'She doesn't send him words of wisdom.' Unexpectedly, Brihthild speaks. Her words are laced with delight. 'Unless it's wisdom to tell him of the whereabouts of Mercia's æthelings.'

'And you know this?' Bishop Ceolbeorht pounces. He berated the queen for speaking out of turn, but he doesn't do the same to Brihthild. If anything, he's eager for her to respond.

'Of course. Who do you think delivered those messages?'

I find myself leaning forward in surprise, eyes flashing between the two women and occasionally Bishop Ceolbeorht. I sense Lanfrac shifting in his position nearby. We've managed to discover much less than I hoped. Perhaps, though, this was intentional.

'How did you receive these letters?'

'Through official channels. But I was tasked with extracting a certain letter every time. I then delivered it to Lord Æthelwulf.'

'So, you saw the amber?'

'No, the messenger, Heardred, went missing,' Brihthild announces. 'It was his horse that great oaf purchased in Southampton.'

My heart beats a little faster. At last, we're starting to get somewhere.

'You'd believe the words of this whore? This woman who isn't even deemed oath-worthy by this court?' Queen Cynethryth demands. I know how Brihthild will respond to that. But she surprises me.

'I'm not the whore here,' she taunts. The entire audience gasps. Queen Cynethryth surges to her feet. I already know what she'll do even before she steps towards Brihthild.

I'm pitching to my feet, determined to stop Queen Cynethryth from attacking her accuser. But I'm not alone. Ealdorman Ælfstan also rushes forwards, as do others. I notice Bishop Ceolbeorht standing, his mouth falling open in shock at the queen's unexpected response. Briefly, I see Lord Wigmund's smirking face. But my focus is on Brihthild. She's bound to the chair. The queen has greater movement, and the two guards are caught entirely unprepared.

Hands outstretched, I aim for Brihthild, determined to knock her out of the queen's path. The queen holds something flashing in her hand. I don't know how. She should have no weapons. Why would she need them? Yet it's evident she's resolved to one course of action. To silence Brihthild, for the allegations can never be proven if she can't name those involved, as she's refused to do today. If Brihthild is dead, the queen will gain more oath-helpers, regardless of whether they believe her integrity or not. That is the way politics works in the Mercian court. After all, if there wasn't some corruption, Ealdorman Sigered would never have been able to retain his position when he refuses to fight in the king's name. King Wiglaf will be stuck with his traitorous wife forever.

No. I must stop that from happening.

Events move too slowly. The queen will get to Brihthild before me or Ealdorman Ælfstan can stop her. All we've endured will have been for nothing.

The blade flashes. Brihthild's screech of rage sounds more akin to an eagle after its prey, but my hands close on her chair, knocking it aside.

Brihthild falls, just out of the queen's reach, as I see the flash of metal coming unimaginably close to my face.

I'll be struck. There's no chance I won't be. I can't arrest my forward momentum.

I try to hold my head backwards to avoid the seax the queen shouldn't have in her hands, but the next thing I'm aware of is the cold heat of metal cutting into my cheek. Then I know nothing else.

6

'Icel.' It's Wynflæd's voice that brings me back. She sounds furious and insistent. I open my eyes to gaze into her lined face. She harrumphs and then leans back on her knees from where she's been leaning over me. 'He'll live,' she announces decisively.

I can feel her hand on my face, holding a piece of linen. A delayed stab of pain makes itself known, as I reach up to touch it.

'Leave it,' she snaps. 'Leave it well alone. Cuthred will return momentarily with my healing supplies.'

'Where is everyone?' I realise then that while I'm in Lundenwic's great hall, I can't hear the press of others.

'The king concluded events for today. The queen's under guard, as is Brihthild. Bishop Ceolbeorht's demanding action be taken against the queen for her attack, on you, and in the presence of the king. As furious as he was, he could still recite whatever laws the queen has broken.' Even she seems impressed by this feat.

'And the Wessex warrior?' Cuthred's returned. For a moment, he looks concerned, but seeing me awake, he merely concentrates on the task. I hear the familiar thrum of pig's gut being threaded.

The cut I took is deep enough to need stitches, then. I don't know how I feel. A bit sick. Very perplexed. As Wynflæd says, I'll live.

'The Wessex messenger is still here. Understandably the king refuses to allow him to leave with Brihthild.'

I allow myself to relax at the news. Cuthred tends to me, while Wynflæd watches on. I can tell she tries not to direct him, allowing him to decide what needs doing. His touch is firm but gentle. When he stitches my right cheek back together, I close my eyes. No man needs to see a sharp needle that close to his eye.

'You can get up now,' Cuthred informs me when he's done. The smell of healing herbs floods my nose. He's applied a poultice over the stitches.

Wulfheard helps me sit upright, Oswy with him. I watch them both, but they swerve in and out of focus, and every so often there are four of them, not two.

'Take your time,' Wynflæd cautions from above. She's already standing. 'You took a nasty blow to the head. Any moment now, I imagine you'll be sick.'

I think she might be right. I feel my belly gurgling, and try to hold it in, but there's no chance. Luckily, it seems Cuthred's thought of this. A bucket appears before me, and it's quickly filled with my vomit. Oswy or Wulfheard, I'm unsure which of them it is, grumbles at the sharp stink of it. I'd apologise, but I concentrate on not vomiting again. Now I'm upright, it's difficult to risk opening my mouth for fear of violently emptying my belly.

'Get him sitting on a chair,' Wynflæd orders those surrounding me. I'm assisted onto a chair, but I'm still slumped, as Wulfheard, I think, ensures I stay upright by holding my shoulders from behind. I'd chuckle, but I think I might be sick again. Oswy looks less than pleased to be forced to stand before me. 'Now, just wait for the nausea to pass before you start haring around. Help him by telling him what's happened,' Wynflæd instructs Wulfheard and Oswy. They jump to do as they're told, Wynflæd's commands more quickly obeyed than even Ealdorman Ælfstan's would be.

'The king and the ealdormen are discussing matters,' Wulfheard informs me quickly.

'What matters?' I mumble, risking speaking although I have to swallow quickly.

'What will happen next with the queen? She did, after all, try to kill someone in front of everyone else. There's not any need for the trial to continue, is there? She can't say it wasn't her when so many witnessed it. Her oath-helpers won't vouch for her integrity now.' I'm startled that Wulfheard knows the legal terms, but perhaps, like me, his morning has been filled with learning all this new information.

'Depends if we want to make sure it's really over, and the children will be safe from now on,' I counter, again wishing I didn't need to speak.

'Well, yes, apart from that,' Wulfheard admits. 'For now, she's being taken to Londinium's fort. There's a room with a big lock on the door to keep her within in the fortress proper.'

'Bloody hell.' I vent all my frustration, head spinning, unable to decide whether it's better to keep my eyes shut or open. 'Why couldn't Brihthild have spoken when she had the chance? It didn't need to descend into this chaos.'

'It's probably better like this. Everything we knew about the queen's involvement was circumstantial. No one had truly seen everything she'd seen and done. We have many suspicions. Now there's proof she meant to kill Brihthild. It hardly matters why. I don't believe even Ealdorman Sigered and Lord Wigmund will be able to prevail upon the king now to be more amenable towards the queen, even if they're foolish enough to make the attempt.'

'I'd hope not,' I counter, swallowing down another urge to

vomit. 'Can I have some water?' I ask, and a wooden beaker appears in my hand.

'Drink slowly,' Wynflæd cautions.

I do as she suggests. I want to drink it all in one gulp. I'm thirsty, but I know enough about head wounds not to do so. I've seen the after-effects before. I've skipped out of the way many times before when people didn't heed Wynflæd's directives, and they needed the use of a bucket.

'If you can stand, that would be good,' she suggests when I've drunk enough. 'Carefully,' she cautions, as I attempt to surge to my feet. I totter alarmingly, pleased Wulfheard's alert enough to grip my shoulders when I sway forward.

'Come on.' Wulfheard's words are filled with sympathy. 'We'll get you outside, and then you can walk it off. Are you ever going to stop involving yourself in other people's business?'

'It appears not,' I offer wryly, taking one step and then another, the thought of getting away from the stink of my vomit driving me onwards. The room wobbles alarmingly around me, but I make it outside. Only then, I wish I hadn't. The sunlight's too bright, and I wince against its glare.

To shield myself, I look at Wulfheard, noting how the sun illuminates the fine lines around his eyes and lips. I've always thought Wulfheard a young man – after all, he was younger than my uncle when I met him – but suddenly, he's older than my uncle. The passage of time is strange.

'But,' I start, my thoughts tripping over one another as they coalesce. Something doesn't feel right.

'But what?' Wulfheard questions.

'The Wessex messenger, Lanfrac. Where is he?'

'With the men Commander Eahric had watch him, I suspect.' I see Wulfheard's forehead furrow. Abruptly, he understands my unease. 'Bollocks,' he exclaims, hastening to a run before the 's' has fled his lips. 'Bollocks,' he repeats.

I want to follow him, but nausea wells once more, my head pounding, my cheek throbbing.

'Oswy, Cenred.' I listen to Wulfheard call for his fellow warriors. Commander Eahric's no doubt already involved in moving the queen. I bend and place my hands on my thighs, trying to recover. Cuthred hastens to my side. Wynflæd has hurried away, more quickly than I'd expect. No doubt she expects me to stay here, and not embroil myself in this.

'Are you well?' he asks, perhaps concerned he missed something while tending to my wound.

'Yes, yes. Get me my byrnie, shield and weapons belt,' I huff through tight lips. I don't want to join my fellow warriors but know there's no choice. We thought the Wessex messenger came here to release Brihthild, but I fear it's something else. I worry he's no longer alone. How this has been coordinated is beyond me, but it has certainly been.

'Icel, you can't fight?' Cuthred chastises, although he sounds perplexed. 'There's no one to fight.'

I turn to him and grip his arms, trying to fasten on his face, which wavers in and out of focus. 'I must. Do as I say, or Wessex will steal away Mercia's queen, and then there can only be war once more.' The colour drains from his face, as he too realises what I suspect. He shrugs loose from my grip and, without further questions, hastens to do as I ask. I detect the cries of Ealdormen Ælfstan and Tidwulf as they muster their men. I can also hear King Wiglaf's outraged shout as he too is informed of what's about to unfurl. I strain to hear, knowing there'll be more of this to come.

Lord Æthelwulf, the king of Kent, has played this remarkably well. He's distracted us all by having us think about Brihthild, but his target was someone else. If he can get his hands on the queen, he'll have a powerful prisoner on his hands. It doesn't help that Queen Cynethryth won't truly be a prisoner. She'll welcome being away from Mercia and somewhere she can cause even more problems for King Wiglaf, while Wiglaf will need to do all he can to recover her.

'Here.' Cuthred returns more quickly than I expected, bowed under the weight of my byrnie, shield and weapons belt. 'I'll get Bicwide, now.' I wish it were Brute, but Brute remains in Kingsholm. If I'd known Lady Ælflæd was journeying to Londonia, I'd have asked her to bring my faster horse. But I didn't know, and Bicwide will have to do.

Dropping my weapons belt, I bend to force my byrnie over my head. Nausea once more threatens to undo me, but I force the protection into place, mindful of the bandage stuck to my cheek. I don't want to dislodge it, or my wound will become infected with the sweat and blood of the men I mean to kill.

Peripherally, I'm aware of the thunder of hooves, whether Mercian or Wessex, I don't know. With a final heave of effort, I have my byrnie in place and then bend to retrieve my weapons belt. This part of the process leaves me weak. I watch my hand waver, thinking the belt is in one place when it's in another. The blow to my head is severe. I should, perhaps, relent and refuse to join the coming battle. Where the Wessex warriors have been hiding, I don't know. But they're coming. I sense it. It's clear Wulfheard does as well, or he wouldn't have run off or involved the ealdormen and the king. Even Wynflæd must realise my suspicions are correct as she's hurried to add her voice to those informing the king of what's about to happen.

A shriek fills the air. It's a terrible sound, speaking of abject terror. I stand, weapons belt finally in hand, and look to where the cry originates. A ship's emerged from along the River Thames.

I don't know whether from up or downstream, but as I get a clear view of the river, stumbling over my feet, I see warriors jumping onto the open waterfront. They wear the black and white colours of the king of Wessex. I peer left and right, blinking ferociously to clear my vision. People run hither and thither, panic making them unsure what to do. Mothers and fathers grab small children. Dogs bark. Horses neigh, and above it all, I hear the too familiar crash of wood on iron.

The bastards mean to attack Londonia. Was this the plan all along?

Cuthred rushes to me, Bicwide saddled and ready. It takes me three attempts to mount. As I finally place my feet in both stirrups, the world spins again, the ground veering alarmingly up and down. I blink and then blink again. I need my vision to clear and my nausea to pass.

The cries of Ealdorman Tidwulf's warriors encourage people to take shelter within Lundenwic's great hall. I look down at Cuthred as he passes me my shield. My thoughts are consumed with how foolish we've been and also with Wynflæd.

'Find Wynflæd and get yourselves inside the hall. The Wessex warriors won't prevail,' I reassure him, wishing my young friend didn't look so frightened. 'Do it,' I urge him, ramming my helm on my head and managing to only hurt my cut a little in the process. I convince myself that with my helm in place, the swaying has reduced.

'Icel.' I turn at the sound of my name, recognising the king's voice.

'Go,' I urge Cuthred. He finally leaps away and hurries to assist Wynflæd, who's moving far too slowly towards the main hall, no doubt sent there by the king, while Ealdorman Tidwulf's warriors protect it. Already, I see mounted warriors surrounding the new defences and hastening towards the fort of Londinium.

We should be able to withstand the assault, but if not, I hope Ealdorman Tidwulf will know to take everyone from inside the settlement to Londinium. The fort can be much better protected with its high stone walls, few entrances and lack of a full and open quayside.

King Wiglaf calls my name again. I gather the reins and kick Bicwide to a slow trot, avoiding people still running for shelter. King Wiglaf's mounted and commands the force meeting the enemy emerging from the river. I see there are two ships now. I bite my lips. That's not nearly enough for what they intend to do. I doubt that's all of them. If there are only a hundred Wessex warriors, they'll be quickly overwhelmed.

'What is this?' King Wiglaf queries, his lips downturned beneath his helm. His eyes are everywhere. In that moment, I appreciate how the years have changed him. Not long ago, Wiglaf fled from the attack of the Wessex king. He's not going to this time.

'They mean to take your wife, I'm sure of it,' I explain. The last vestiges of nausea are leaving me. Still, I'd sooner not be sick all over the king.

'What?' His voice is whip-sharp at my determination.

'They sent the messenger to distract us into thinking they wanted Brihthild, but it's not her. It's the queen.'

'She's inside Londinium.'

'Not yet. That's where they're taking her.' My eyes are busy spotting those meeting the attack. The king's personal warriors are all good men. I don't want them to die on Wessex blades.

'Go, go,' the king urges me. He'd call his warriors back if he could, but they've been deployed and must continue their intentions.

Turning Bicwide, I aim him towards the closest exit to leave Lundenwic and rush for Londinium. I need to get across the River

Fleet. I hope Wulfheard, Oswy and Ealdorman Ælfstan are already there. But I can't deny we've been caught unprepared. Queen Cynethryth might already be captured by the enemy.

Bicwide's heavy hooves kick up the mud from along the road, but we make good progress. People have been quick to hasten to the king's hall. I don't need to pull him aside to stop him from running into others. But I do hear the sound of other hooves above those of Bicwide's and turn horrified to find King Wiglaf catching me. I want to tell him to go back to protect the people of Lundenwic, but a cry of outrage arrests my attention. Ahead, the view opens up, and I see what's unfolding.

Commander Eahric and his warriors, alongside those of Ealdorman Ælfstan, are beleaguered. They've not yet made it to the River Fleet, and already a collection of mounted enemy warriors bar their way. How, I consider, have the Wessex warriors made it so far onto Mercian land without being noticed? Not that it matters. All that concerns me is ensuring they don't get their hands on the queen. And she's there, amidst the fighting. It's impossible to miss her grey hair and fine dress.

'Hurry,' I urge King Wiglaf. I bend low over Bicwide's wide shoulders to spur him to greater speed. The view before me continues to flicker, as his speed increases. I almost close my eyes to stop the uncomfortable swaying, but realise that'll only make it worse. I need to keep focused. I must watch what's happening.

I witness Ealdorman Ælfstan call back his warriors, preventing them from trying to forge a path through the enemy and instead protect the queen. Commander Eahric's warriors do the same. Men already lie bleeding and wounded. A riderless horse races back towards Lundenwic, a weeping bloody gash on its front leg. I hope his rider lives.

Then I'm too close to see more. I hurry to reinforce the rear of Commander Eahric's men. I want to get to the queen and ensure her safety. Although, if I can't, I'd sooner she died on the edge of a Wessex blade than was taken to Wessex. I consider whether King Wiglaf thinks the same.

I've not seen his son, Ealdorman Sigered, or Lord Beorhtwulf. Whatever they're doing, it's not safeguarding the queen. No doubt Ealdorman Tidwulf's men inside Lundenwic are protecting them. I force my way into the mass of horsemen. The Wessex force is equal to ours, I'm certain of that. If we'd been warned of their presence, they'd have been overwhelmed already.

'Get the queen,' I hear a Wessex accent urging the other warriors.

'Protect the queen,' King Wiglaf counters. I don't know what the queen thinks of all this. No doubt, she'd welcome being taken to Wessex rather than facing justice for her actions against the king's *mund*. We can't allow that to happen.

'Icel.' The gruff voice of Wulfheard beckons me to his side. It's still a fight between horses. The queen's encircled, but the Wessex warriors keep trying to attack into her protectors. Commander Eahric's men have made it to the bridge over the River Fleet. Now some of the riders are over the bridge, but the Wessex warriors have urged their horses through the thigh-high water and now stand to the west of the river so some Wessex warriors are much closer to the queen than others. We can't quite retreat because the queen is stuck between the two forces. 'Get here and help me. We need to reach the queen.'

I growl low at such an obvious statement. Wulfheard doesn't hear or doesn't care. I spare a thought for the king. He's embroiled in the battle as well. If the Wessex warriors realise the king is involved, they could change their objective.

'We need to protect the king,' I murmur to Wulfheard, low enough that others won't hear.

'We can do that by getting the queen. Then, we can get the

pair locked up tight inside Londinium and defeat the bastard enemy.'

It's a lofty plan. I'm not convinced it'll work. We need to focus on one thing, not two.

'No, we need to get to the king,' I assert. Wulfheard rounds on me, his face twisted in fury, but immediately I hear a shout that tells me I'm correct.

'The king,' one of the enemy cries. Regardless of Wulfheard's command, I direct Bicwide to where King Wiglaf fights. He has his warriors with him, but their focus is on helping him get to the queen and not on protecting him.

While my eyes swim and I swallow another sudden urge to be sick, I shout for others to help me, 'Cenred, Maneca, get here,' as Bicwide races behind them. I don't direct Bicwide around the enemy. Instead, their horses rear back, startled by the thundering sound of his heavy hoofbeats.

More and more of the Mercians sense the danger. Even Wulfheard's ordering the men now. The queen's no longer the objective. If Mercia loses her king to the Wessex bastards, they'll have scored a greater triumph.

'Wiglaf,' I roar, Bicwide coming to a halt in a splattering of kicked-up mud. The king turns to me, fury evident in the cast of his lips and resolve of his chin. 'You're in danger,' I urge him before he can berate me for not speaking to him with more respect.

'What?' he glowers, but the Wessex warriors are quickly forming up. Ahead, I see the queen's been sprung free from the enemy. The Wessex warriors, sensing a greater prize in King Wiglaf, have abandoned her, and now Commander Eahric's men hasten to get her to the safety of Londinium and the huge wooden gate. And, of course, the room with its solid lock.

'The enemy know you're here,' I shout, turning Bicwide to

protect King Wiglaf's back from the probing spear of one of the enemy. They've made quick work of changing tactic. Already, the Wessex force have made their way through the river and surged up the bank. Wiglaf's cut off from the safety of the fort. We can only go back towards Lundenwic. And we must do it quickly because that will be blocked soon as well. The Wessex warriors who thought to stop us from getting to the queen have redirected their purpose. Damn the bastards.

I have the king, but only four of his warriors have stopped their efforts to keep hold of the queen. The rest of the fools have forged a path across the bridge, not realising why the gap's suddenly opened up for them. I'll have a few choice words to say to them when this is over.

'To the king,' Wulfheard orders, the time for keeping his presence a secret long past. We must protect Wiglaf.

The king meets my gaze. 'Bollocks,' he mouths, sensing the danger himself now.

'We need to get you back,' I inform him. 'And quickly.'

'The queen?' he questions.

'Is almost inside Londinium's gate, even as we speak. The enemy have determined their king would welcome another prisoner.'

King Wiglaf growls, his face thunderous, as he turns his horse in a tight circle. His four warriors watch his back, facing towards the River Fleet. I turn Bicwide as well, my heart sinking as I appreciate the strength of the Wessex force we need to evade. I look left and right, up the hill, and also down, towards the River Thames. It's there the Wessex ships wait to take the warriors, and Mercia's queen, to the Wessex side of the River Thames. I notice the ships are poorly defended. The mounted warriors are all here, by the bridge. I open my mouth to direct the king that way, but abruptly, the path is impassable. A Wessex warrior, wearing a much-dented helm, blocks my path. His horse is huge, taller and wider even than Bicwide. The animal's encased in more battle gear than the warrior, his saddle and harness gleaming with leather and metal.

'Bollocks,' I exclaim, turning the other way. I bat aside the spear trying to reach the king with my shield. If the warrior wants Mercia's king, he's going to have to get closer than that. 'North,' I urge the king, gathering Bicwide beneath me and directing the king the way I want him to go. 'Hurry,' I shout, and then, when he still doesn't move quickly enough, and before my vision can sway once more, I reach out and slap his horse's rump. The animal whinnies with surprise and pain, almost unseating the king, but at least he hurries to a gallop. I follow the beast. It doesn't pause for the Wessex warriors belatedly understanding they've left a gap. Indeed, it knocks one of the animals aside, the thud of horseflesh meeting almost as loud as wood on iron. I kick the animal for good measure, wincing at another shrill whinny. The king's warriors follow on behind, or so I assume, for I've lifted myself out of the saddle, bending low over Bicwide's neck to allow him to rush even more quickly.

The king's recovered himself, and now he does the same. Behind us, the angry cries of the Wessex warriors ring loudly, as can their attempts to chase us.

In no time, we're close to where King Wiglaf once raised his camp when we retook Londonia from the Wessex enemy. From there, I'm unsure where to go, but the king continues before veering towards Lundenwic. The River Fleet's too deep here to attempt the crossing to Londinium's fort, but we can reach Lundenwic through another gate. I hope.

'Ware.' Wulfheard's cry assures me the enemy hasn't given up the chase. I duck low as the sound of a thrown spear reaches my ears. I'll not be skewered in the back by these arseholes. I turn at the cry of one of the king's warriors. His horse has been wounded, and the animal veers aside. My eyes struggle to focus, and my belly feels hollow, but the three other Mercian warriors are there. Wulfheard, Oswy and Cenred also trade blows with the enemy.

I encourage Bicwide to greater speed. I need to speak with the king. I can't spare a look for anything other than where we're going. I'm worried it's not where the king will find safety. There were Wessex warriors within Lundenwic, I recall, on the quayside. We can't ride from one disaster right into another.

'Wiglaf,' I call. The thunder of hooves is loud. Inside my helm, it feels as though my head's being bashed all over the place. A piercing headache has started, and once more, I fear I'll be sick. The enemy won't appreciate a face full of vomit, but they might get one. It would be an unusual weapon to employ. 'Lundenwic was overwhelmed,' I shout, not taking my eyes off the uneven path we're forging. We're not on a roadway. The road curls down along the River Fleet and then into the trading settlement. We're on an animal track, I suspect, north of it.

'I know. Follow me,' King Wiglaf urges. I hurry to do as he suggests as he directs his horse along what might be a sheep track and is even narrower than the animal track we were on. It's not wide enough for a cart, that's for sure. I don't know what he plans, but I vow to follow Wiglaf wherever he goes. The shouts of those chasing sound too close, but we've not had any other spears flung at us, or arrows, or even a stone. I hope Wulfheard, Oswy and Cenred are overwhelming the bastards.

I can't believe how quickly and how badly today's events have unfolded. I hoped it would be a simple matter to find the queen complicit alongside Brihthild. I never suspected this.

Ahead, a sudden covering of trees emerges. I detect the king's intent. Easier to be lost in the woods. That way, the ealdormen and the rest of Mercia's warriors should have the time to track down the enemy. Bowing my head along Bicwide's neck to avoid being knocked off by low-hanging boughs, I surge into the trees, allowing Wiglaf to lead. I consider if there are charcoal burners ahead, or perhaps a hunting lodge. I don't know the area well enough. My focus has always been on the River Thames, with its access to the sea, and never on the land slightly north of the Thames.

I hear shouts from behind and appreciate whatever my fellow warriors are attempting; the Wessex warriors are managing to keep pace with the king's escape. The further inland the king tempts the enemy, the more cut off they'll be. Provided Ealdormen Tidwulf and Ælfstan can secure Lundenwic, they'll be able to stake out the enemy and cut them down. I can't imagine the Wessex warriors have thought enough to bring reinforcements. They planned on a quick attack, securing the queen and then leaving. That's not at all what's happened.

The trees are in full leaf. Branches smack into my helm, and the sun floods through in dappled patches, making me feel uncertain as to where the ground is. If I wasn't mounted, I'm sure I'd have fallen by now. I have to rely on Bicwide to keep pace with the king and his horse.

Again, I hear the crash and snap of other mounted warriors flooding into the woodlands from behind. I wish I knew if they were Wessex warriors or Mercians. Well, I suppose I do. The Mercians would tell the king it was safe to cease his headlong dash. As that's not happened, we must still be being chased by the enemy.

I sense Bicwide faltering. He can't keep up the pace beneath the trees. The branches are low in places, and in others there are roots that he hits his hooves on, sending up hollow thuds as though a woodsman cutting the trees. I still see the king, but his animal is fleeter-footed, and we'll lose him if we're not careful. I can't allow that to happen.

Bending low so my body stretches over Bicwide's, I encourage my horse, keeping my eyes focused on where the sleek black tail of the king's steed flashes with the sunlight. Sweat drips into my eyes, stinging them and adding to my general misery, as it slithers down my cheek and stings my wound. Bloody hell. This day is getting more and more difficult.

Bicwide stumbles. I release my feet from the stirrups as though I'll jump from his back should he falter, but he regains his footing. I hope he's not wounded himself. While I pat his long neck and encourage him onwards, I suddenly realise I've lost track of the king.

'Arse,' I exclaim. I'm not going to shout for the king. I don't want the enemy to know I've lost him. Instead, I pull Bicwide up short and strain to hear. My heart's thudding in my chest, my ears filled with the thrum of my body. Bicwide's breath is laboured, and my head pounds with each beat of my heart. I hold my breath, hoping to hear above my breathing, but it's impossible. The king has disappeared on my watch.

I turn my head one way and then another, hoping to detect the sound of his advance somehow, but I can't. I can hear almost nothing, not those behind and not the king ahead. I close my eyes, trying to ignore the way I sway. I grip Bicwide's reins almost too tightly, and still I can't decide which way to go. The king was ahead. I'm sure of it.

'This way,' I encourage Bicwide, trusting I aim in the direction the king's horse was last seen cantering. I curse myself for a bloody fool. I told the king to avoid Lundenwic, and now I've lost him. There are none of his warriors. They've also fallen behind, the thick branches and trees making it almost impossible to make any headway. I'd been doing well, keeping up. But no more.

I duck low to avoid another low-hanging branch and feel my hair that snakes below my helm snag on a smaller branch. I pull it free, wincing at the uncomfortably tight feeling of losing some of my hair, while my head pounds and my cheek throbs. I sense there's some brightness ahead, perhaps a break in the denseness of the trees.

I urge Bicwide onwards. But there's no sign of the king. None at all, as we emerge into the widest space so far. Here, the trees press less tightly together. The ground's covered in a thick mat of shimmering green grasses and bright blue flowers. It's a beautiful spot. But there's one thing missing. One really important thing.

How the hell, I think, will I explain losing Mercia's king to my fellow warriors?

I must bloody find him, before they find me.

7

I urge Bicwide on through the clearing, bending to either side trying to banish my nausea from the action, hoping there'll be hoof marks to show where the king has gone. I can scarcely breathe. My chest feels tight. My heart thuds too loudly. Only Bicwide beneath me keeps me grounded. I know what I need to do, but how I'm going to do it is beyond me. I look up. If Cenred were close, he could climb one of the tall trees and perhaps find the king. But he's not here. I don't know where Cenred or King Wiglaf are.

I consider whether I should clamber up the thick branches myself. One of the trees even seems to extend a warm welcome, the gap between the lower branches eminently climbable for those fleet-footed enough. But that's not me. Not at the moment. Riding is a problem. I know I'll fall and injure myself if I even attempt it.

I pull Bicwide to a stop. The air's filled with the trill of birdsong, the rustle of animals through the undergrowth, but little else. I can't even hear if we're being followed. But then, it's the summer. The undergrowth is rich and lush, absorbing much of the passage of hooves other than when a hidden root is kicked.

I look up once more, biting my lip, fighting back the persistent nausea. I need to drink, but I don't have anything with me. Perhaps there's a stream close by. But my eyes alight on something else. Far above my head, I see a black image against the shape of the sun. It's been a long day, but the sun's always loath to set at this time of the year. I recognise the eagle, flying high, circling above me. I consider it for a moment. An eagle. It's Mercia's emblem. It's the very shape I have scored into my hand. I rub my gloved hand over the other one. The scar's faded, admittedly, but I know it's there. And when I'm hot or cold, it makes itself known, the outline easy to see when my flesh is too pale, or reddened.

There are no crows or ravens alongside the eagle, no creatures come to feast, and a feeling stirs within me. It's foolish and farfetched, yet I've nothing else to guide me.

With a soft click of my tongue, I encourage Bicwide onwards, glancing to the sky to see if the bird's moved. It hasn't. It appears to urge me northwards. Bicwide trots through the stunning glade opening up before us, his hooves releasing the verdant smell of rich soil, flooding the air with pollen. I wince as he tramples the beautiful blue flowers, but I can't have him avoid them all. It's a carpet of magnificent azure, almost a mirror of the sky above my head.

I give the eagle a final clear look, swallowing down my nausea from moving my head so high, and slip once more into the trees to the north of the gap. I won't see the eagle again unless the canopy opens up above me. I shouldn't be letting it guide my steps, but perhaps, just perhaps, it's pointing me in the direction of the king. What a story that would be. One for the scops to conjure their tales with, that's a certainty.

Here, the trees are even more closely bound together. I consider whether some of them need felling to allow their neighbours to grow taller and thicker. Mercian wood is good. It's one of our greatest assets, but here the trunks are thin and narrow, branches almost too heavy to be supported by them. I shake my head, and immediately regret it. I'm here to find the king, not consider what work the woodspeople need to undertake when they're next engaged in coppicing.

Bicwide picks out our path. His steps are sure, his nose focusing on the northern route. I feel enclosed, almost cocooned beneath the canopy. The events taking place within Londonia. The treachery of the queen. The fact Wessex riders might be following me. All of that fades away to nothing. I'm lulled by the serenity of it all. A woodpecker's noisy about his task, the sharp sound reverberating without malice even though it clatters so loudly, echoing beneath the trees. The scampering of small animals occasionally reaches my ears. The call of the many small birds sheltering in the trees, chattering one to another, swells as I get deeper and deeper into the tightly packed woodlands. I could be going anywhere. I've certainly seen nothing to indicate the king came this way. Not one snapped-off twig. Not one piece of torn cloth, handily sighted for me to see. I should turn and go the other way, dismissing my decision to follow the eagle's trail as foolish, but I don't. I keep thinking, *Just a few moments longer.* I trust my instinct. My breathing calms. My head slowly stops spinning. My nausea fades away, as my chest swells with the rich smell of the woods.

I shouldn't feel so calm, so rested. I should be alert to every small sound, to every uneven snap of a twig. But I sense I'm alone. There's no one following me. Not here. No one would dare break this peaceful moment. I'm tempted to slip from Bicwide's back and sleep. It's been a long day. I've been wound tight as a bowstring, and now all that tension leaves me. I don't think I've ever felt so at one with nature, not even when Wynflæd sent me to hunt for honey, mushrooms or other herbs she might have wanted. I smell garlic close by, the scent making my belly rumble, even while my thirst seems to have been banished.

Bicwide abruptly stops. It takes me a moment to realise why. I look around and see a resplendent stag ahead, his magnificent antlers gleaming with health. He watches me. I don't move. I don't want to scare the beast. What a special moment, I consider. I'm here. The stag is here. There's no one else but Bicwide. The stag needn't fear me. I'm not here to intrude on his place of sanctuary. He watches me and then makes some infinitesimal movement, and more deer step free from where they've been hiding. Small does and even smaller fawns. They eye me and then walk past. I must be on one of their woodland trackways. I see then where the grasses are bowed low. In the distance, I hear the familiar sound of water over stones. They must be going to drink. I lick my lips. I could do with following.

I hold Bicwide steady. The magnificent stag never takes his eyes from me, and then, when all the other deer have gone, he turns his head as though directing me along the path they've just taken. Overhead, I hear the harsh shriek of the eagle and the cry I've been dreading. That of warriors clashing violently, and it's coming from further north.

I incline my head towards the stag as he hastens to a run, keen to be away from the fight. I bend low over Bicwide. We resume our path more quickly, the eagle's shriek assuring me time is critical.

Bicwide's hooves pound over the spongy surface of the woodland floor, but even so, I still hear the shriek of the eagle. And above it all, the crash of men fighting. Sweat once more beads down my face, stinging my wounded cheek. I reach for my seax and, assured it remains on my weapons belt, focus on keeping my seat, ducking and weaving through the branches that threaten to snag me and smack my wound.

I sense an opening once more, up ahead, and it's there, as Bicwide thunders to a halt, that I find King Wiglaf, surrounded by three Wessex warriors.

The evening sunlight glints from the king's byrnie and weapons. His horse noses the ground behind him, oblivious to the fight to the death taking place. I kick Bicwide to a quick gallop, releasing my feet from the stirrups so I can jump onto the men who attack King Wiglaf at the last possible moment. Overhead, the shrill cry of the eagle's even louder. It seems to thrum through my blood. All I can hear is its shriek. Not my breathing. Not the sound of Bicwide's hooves. Just the cry of the eagle.

I jump free from Bicwide, having first tied his reins high so he won't tangle his legs in them. I land with a heavy thud, my knees not absorbing the fall as I'd hoped so I stumble, curling into a ball, rolling into the back of one of the enemy warriors instead of springing forward to take him down from behind. Their horses are to the far side of the clearing. They've dismounted to face the king.

The enemy warrior tumbles as I bowl his legs from beneath him, wincing at the stab of pain from knocking my wound. I unfurl, seax drawn, risking cutting my chin with the motion, and stab into his side. He shrieks, but not as loud as the eagle, who's relentless up above. I veer backwards as King Wiglaf stamps down with his foot on the man's head. I stab again and then again, breathing heavily, feeling the body still beneath me. I wobble upwards onto my hands, knees and feet, wishing the ground would keep still. My sense of serenity is gone, and with it, my nausea has returned in force. The two Wessex warriors appear unaware of what's happened to their fellow countryman, too intent on attacking the king, but Wiglaf flashes me a quick look, conveying much. I lash into one of the two remaining warriors.

The man turns, lips glistening with blood and spit, his front tooth hanging by a thread, tangling with his short beard. I grimace at the mad fury in his eyes. He's a big bugger. His body is encased in a thickly padded byrnie. Sweat streams down his exposed throat.

'Bastard Mercian,' he hollers into my face, his hot air mingling with mine, as he raises his shield to counter my attack. I spare a look to King Wiglaf. With only one warrior left, he's fighting well, but I can see a drip of blood on his chin. He's wounded. His movements are precise but not as quick as the foeman he faces. I need to kill my enemy and aid the king.

Without my shield, I dart around the other man. He jabs his shield towards me, his foot knocking into the lifeless man so he jumps back, startled. He doesn't realise one of his numbers is dead.

I offer him a grin, taking responsibility for the kill. I imagine the three Wessex warriors were dreaming of the renown they'd win for beating Mercia's king rather than concentrating on their surroundings. I hope there are no more of them close by.

I raise my seax to slice the man's unprotected side. But his movements are quick and succinct. He evades my reach, skipping closer to the king. I growl. I want to angle him away from Wiglaf. Not towards him.

I rush my enemy, ensuring my strike seeks the left side of his body. He holds his shield before me, protecting himself, even as he moves the way I want him to go. It's better to separate him from his fellow warrior. My movements are small and sharp, changing direction as often as possible. I think of my shield, but it remains on Bicwide. Not that I'm sure it would do more than protect me from his attack, and here I want to overwhelm him quickly, not extend the assault.

King Wiglaf roars as he fights – the sound revealing his fury and tiredness. Wiglaf's not fought like this for some summers. In that time, his waistline's expanded and he's become more used to wrestling in his witan, not on the slaughter field. I must reach him.

My enemy lowers his shield, realising my thoughts, and slashes at me with his sword. The edge is burnished golden in the dulling sunlight. I must get this done before the sun sinks beneath the trees, and I can see too little to fell my foeman.

I rush forward, my seax striking the shield, running from side to side as though there's no other way to get to him. In its wake, a trail of paint shards fill the air. They're smaller than dust motes. The shield moves along with my blows, keeping pace with my actions. We could continue like this until we both tire too much to continue. The man's sword is almost ineffectual while he relies exclusively on his shield in such a way. He won't move his shield aside to take a swipe at me. He won't chance that I'll wound him before he can land a blow on me. My breath burns in my throat, my thudding head making me wince, as every so often I misstep, my eyes telling me the ground bucks even though it doesn't. But I'm wearing him down. I need only continue the onslaught. Any moment now, I'll land a killing blow.

I don't risk gazing at King Wiglaf. I can tell that he's weakening. His defence against the foeman is good, but nothing too challenging. He holds against him as my enemy holds against me. I need to bring this to an end. I'm hardly in a fit state for a prolonged fight, and if the king's roars bring other Wessex warriors close, then I'll strain to defend him. I'm struggling with just two enemies.

I work to lull my opponent into a sense of rhythm and regularity, striking his shield in the same set pattern four times in a row. He moves his shield, predicting I'll do the same again, but I don't. Instead, I dart closer, bringing my seax around the left side of his body, finally getting through to him. His screech brings a smile to my face as his shield butts into my back, but it's too late. I stab and slash, opening up the side of his byrnie and piercing deep into his chest. Blood bursts forth, hot and bright. I lean forward, using my elbow to knock his nose, which explodes with even more blood. He goes down with barely a whimper.

'Right, you bastard.' I gaze towards King Wiglaf and the man who fights him. The warrior he labours against is tall and well built, encased in a thick byrnie, a helm covering his head, and a wide shoulder guard also in evidence. He's a good fighter, I note dispassionately. The king holds his shield firm against him, and the enemy warrior is ensuring his strokes against it use as little strength as possible even while trapping the king.

I suck in a hot breath, spit aside the coppery tang of my dead enemy's blood, and grab the shield from his still body. Only then do I launch myself at the remaining warrior. My blows impact his back, just above his shoulders, two quick jabbing motions that have no chance of piercing his byrnie. It would be good if they did, but I'm more concerned with freeing the king from the attack.

Confident in his byrnie, my blows don't distract the warrior. I bend lower then, aiming for his legs, below where his byrnie finishes. He wears thick cloth on his legs, but it's not padded. All the same, momentarily, it holds against my seax blade. Forcing my shield above my head, I slash with more force, finally opening up a gap in the material, a line of blood welling on his left leg.

Still, my foeman focuses on King Wiglaf. My breath grows hotter, nausea again threatening to undo me. I try once more, ripping open his right leg, but the bastard either doesn't feel it or refuses to notice. Instead, I feel his attack against the king becoming ever more savage. He means to kill him with violent blow after violent strike. King Wiglaf can do little but hold his shield before him.

I stand back, frustrated, and catch sight of the king's flushed face. I know I need to do something else. Taking ten steps back, mindful of the dead bodies, I hasten to a run, shield before me, aiming for the enemy warrior's side, not his back. We meet in a cacophony of wood on wood, the sound drowning out even the continual shriek of the eagle overhead.

My shield hits his chin guard, and we tumble to the ground in a collection of twisted limbs, my shield between us. I feel a thousand hurts along my already bruised body, my wounded cheek throbbing, but I veer upwards, squirming along the length of the round shield, wincing as the boss gets in my way, determined to get to the man's head before he can regain his feet.

'Go,' I huff to King Wiglaf, hoping he can hear me. I need him gone from here.

'No,' the king replies, but his breath's laboured. He has nothing left to give.

'Get on your bloody horse, my lord king, and get the hell away from here,' I manage to huff as I finally get to where I want to be. My enemy's fallen poorly, his head knocked to the side, exposing a small gap between his helm and shoulder guard. I must reach it. But while he sways, perhaps fighting a concussion as I am, his arms know what to do. A seax jabs against my back, even as I surge upwards to stab him through the small gap, where the brown of a thick beard assures me his throat waits for me to pierce it.

I almost get to him, finally aware of running footsteps. I don't look, but my enemy cries out in fury, still trapped, redoubling his efforts to get free from me. My blow glances off his shoulder guard, my aim disturbed by the thud of something hitting my back.

This bastard is really starting to try my patience.

I lift to strike again, but he's turning, more concerned with fighting off the weight of me and my shield and continuing his attack on King Wiglaf. I can't let him get away from me, but I'm almost as spent as the king. As the shield bucks upwards, I'm forced to veer backwards to avoid a glancing blow to my chin. A sound reaches my ears. I'm aware I growl like a bear in heat. I always thought I was silent when I fought, but apparently not. Like a man who denies he snores at night, I grunt and growl.

My arms are exhausted, but still, I cling on, grabbing my foeman's byrnie and holding tight. As he moves, I slide with him, and despite the ache in my arms and the pain in my fingers from holding so tight, I don't let go.

I hear the sound of hooves hurrying to a gallop and pray it's the king and not more of the Wessex warriors. With my right hand, I stab and jab at my enemy, desperate to pierce his byrnie, to break through his reinforced defence, even as he surges to his knees. I'm also on mine, moving forward as quickly as possible, kicking aside the shields. Both of them are useless now.

'Will you let go, you Mercian scum,' he growls, attempting to swipe me with his sword. But it clatters uselessly against my back, and I'm on my feet, just as he is. My grip finally fails me, but I'm upright. He takes three steps, trying to run from me. I match his pace. His eyes are on the king, while mine are on him. Neither of us sees the hole in the ground. His foot slips into it first.

He falls, his arms windmilling around him, his grip on the sword he wields failing. I think I finally have him. But he's not given up yet. I hear the crack of bone, but he continues to fight. Frantically, he paws at the ground, determined to reach his sword.

I straddle him, landing on his back, holding him in place, even though he bucks and claws for his weapon.

'Will you just bloody die,' I howl, stabbing into his back time and time again, forging a path through his thick byrnie, and then repeatedly jabbing into it. His blood fills my nostrils, and the scent of his sweat is disgusting. He fights on and on. I think he's the strongest man I've ever met. He bellows in pain, the sound echoing in the clearing. I hear the unhappy answering whinny from the horses.

I stab and stab, all my strength focused on that one thing, as slowly, slowly, his fight ceases, his body stops bucking, and his reaching hand becomes immobile.

Still, I stab. I need to know he's dead. I must be sure he's dead.

Finally, having expelled all of my strength, I look down into the hollow I've made of his back, his innards visible to my eyes, his blood soaking into his byrnie and into my trews.

Almost too tired, I stagger upright, kicking his body, assuring myself he's truly dead, as I focus on sucking in much-needed air. I look around, noting with some satisfaction the three corpses. Once more, I've killed for Mercia. I feel the ground sway alarmingly and spit aside fluid that rises in my throat. It lands wetly, flecked with blood. I grimace at the sight of it.

Sweat drips down my nose. I'm keen to remove my helm, drink water, and be still for a moment. The daylight's leaching from the sky, and with that comes the realisation I'm not done yet. I've sent the king away, but I don't know where.

Trusting more to luck than skill, I whistle for Bicwide. He lifts his head and comes towards me. I offer him a smack of welcome as I pull myself into his saddle. It takes what remains of my strength. I look at the shields abandoned on the ground, stained now with the blood of my enemy, but I don't need them. I leave them where they are. I direct Bicwide to the Wessex horses. The animals eye me uneasily. I'm pleased to see they've been tied to a tree, the men knowing enough not to leave their reins dangling.

I move Bicwide closer, and with the last of the day's light, I release them, tying their reins high in a complicated arrangement of knots so they won't come loose and trip the animals. As I direct Bicwide to where I think the king has gone, I offer a soft smack to the rumps of the animals.

'Go,' I direct them. 'Go.' But I don't wait to see that they do. As the world turns sepia, I need to find the king. While the eagle overhead has finally stilled its angry cry, I know King Wiglaf remains in danger. And without any chance of my fellow warriors finding me, I must do all I can to find the king.

I hope the eagle of Mercia will aid me in that.

8

Exhausted, I allow Bicwide to follow his instincts. First, he brings us to a small stream, where both of us take our fill of the cool water as I remove my gloves. It pains me to dismount and mount again, but my thirst drives me. I spit aside the salt of my exertions, remove my helm painfully, and plunge my head into the cold water. The shock of the water keeps me awake, banishing the dizziness that continues to plague me, although I forget about my wound and have to abruptly place my hand over it, as I feel the sharp bite of cold on my severed flesh. Overhead, thin clouds ensure the moon is bright. I need whatever light it has as a soft breeze ruffles the leaves on the trees.

But quickly, I can't see past the end of my nose, and I know continuing to hunt for the king is foolish. I carry on all the same, head turning time and time again when I hear something. But it's the animals who inhabit this woodland. I hear the hoots of owls and the shuffle of other denizens. I pray no wolves are keen to feast, for I've little left to give. I can't even risk finding something to eat because I can't see well enough to detect if the berries are safe. My belly growls. I've vomited what little I've consumed today and probably yesterday's food as well. As the night advances, I shiver. It's summer, but beneath the spreading branches and without the sun, I quickly become cold. I pull my gloves back on. My drying sweat makes me itchy and chilled. I wince at the memory of all the day has brought me.

'Bloody bollocks,' I exclaim softly. Perhaps we should have realised the Wessex lord wouldn't take kindly to our plans. Maybe a little more alertness would have prevented what's happened. But I don't know. They must have been sneaky to get across the River Thames without being seen. If those on watch duty inside Londinium's fort didn't see the ships, they could have been planning this for days, taking advantage of a moonless night to cross and then hiding out somewhere. Or perhaps the river was running low at Laleham Gulls or Lechlade, and they didn't come via ship after all, and those ships came later, only today. I wish I knew.

My thoughts keep me awake for a while, but soon I sense I'm starting to nod off in the saddle. I wake sometime later, the world around me darker than pitch. I'm still mounted, but Bicwide has succumbed to sleep as well, somehow finding a tree stump to rest against, or at least that's what I assume. I wince. What's woken me is the tingling in my leg, trapped between Bicwide's huge body and the wood. I scrunch my toes together, and when that doesn't work, I unwillingly try to wake him. But my horse is as tired as I am. With the pain increasing, I have to slide my foot back, along his body, gasping with relief when it finally comes free. I dismount but regret it immediately. My trapped leg has little or no strength in it. I tumble to the ground, my hands landing in a steaming pile of horse shit. I growl low, and then my rage gets the better of me.

'Bollocks to this crap,' I shout, forcing myself upwards, my words ringing in the enclosed space of the canopy overhead. I'm aware of the sudden silence my outburst occasions, but I don't care.

Stamping the life back into my feet, I bend again and wipe my gloved hands on the ground hoping it will clear away the worst of the horse shit, checking first that there's no more horse shit to add to that already there. I stand, breath rasping in my throat, and yanking my gloves free. I can either rage or sob. I decide to rage. Bicwide doesn't stir as I stamp around in the space he's found amongst the trees.

'Bollocks, bollocks, bollocks,' I continue to shout, the single word conveying all I feel about this current situation. I've been in some terrible positions before, but this really takes the oat biscuit. I don't know where the king is. I don't know which way Lundenwic is. I don't know where the damn enemy is.

I kick a large branch with my foot that doesn't tingle, and hobble on both feet, shouting my fury and pain. I feel about four hundred winters old, not the twenty-one I have to my name. If I could see, I imagine I'd be horrified by my state.

Limping, licking my thick lips as though they'll conjure up some fluid for my parched mouth, I continue to stamp and stomp, working through my rage, but with the sense not to get too far from Bicwide. I need him to take me from here and find the bloody king when it's light.

The night-time sounds resume. I listen to the sharp flap of bat wings, the hooting of owls and the scrabbling of other animals, and I again hope there are no wolves out there.

I run my hand over the bandage covering the wound on my cheek. I wince, expecting to feel blood on my hand, but there's none. I shiver again. It's bloody cold, as well as impenetrably black. Eventually, both feet stop hurting, but it does nothing for my thirst, if anything, making me realise just how thirsty I am. I feel I could drink the bloody River Thames dry. Although, perhaps not. I've seen what goes into the River Thames. I've swum it enough times. No, it's better to think of drinking something else.

Cold and unable to see, shivering ever more violently, I return to Bicwide's side. The animal still sleeps, standing up. I wish I could. I lean against him, allowing the warmth of his gently rising belly to seep into my back. I hold my hands behind me, between his belly and my back, and close my eyes. I don't think I'll sleep, but I must; the night-time sounds lull me. When I wake again, I'm lying on my back, and Bicwide's huge face peers down at me.

My eyes itch with exhaustion, but immediately I realise it's light enough to see, at least here. The sepia of dusk and the black of night have given way to the grey half-light of false dawn.

'Good to see you're awake,' I say.

He nods as though understanding my words and begins to move off. I hasten to my feet, following him. I imagine he can smell water or sense where there's something to eat. I stay close, walking beside him. His tail swishes as he disappears into the dark beneath the trees. I follow him, eyes alert, but I'm convinced there's no one here but us. Wherever the king is, I hope he's had a more peaceful night than I have. Bicwide walks on without stopping. I lick my lips again, regretting it as a fresh burst of salt dries my throat and tongue.

'Is there water?' I ask my horse. He makes no reply. I shadow him as the area beneath the trees grows ever lighter. I'm just about to announce my horse has no idea what he's doing when I hear the unmistakable sound of running water once more. Whether Bicwide knew it was here or not, and I suspect not, I'm grateful as I rush towards it and, taking to my knees, wash them clear of the horse shit that adheres despite my gloves, watching it flow downstream, before drinking deeply from my cupped hands, wincing every time because my cheek wound has been stitched together tightly. Bicwide does the same, although not using his hands.

Eventually, I sit back on my knees, and peer around me. My head pounds. I reach up and feel a lump on the back of my head as well as the cut on my cheek. I wash my hands again and then do the same. This time, my hand comes away slicked in pale pink. I suspected my cut bled afresh, now I know it does. But I leave the bandage in place. It's better than nothing, and it will at least stop it from being fouled by whatever scrape I find myself in next.

'Now, what the hell are we going to do?' I turn to Bicwide, wincing as I replace my helm and stand. He makes no reply, of course. I close my eyes, wishing the world still didn't sway when I did so, and then open them to look directly upwards. Yesterday, the shrieking eagle brought me to the king. Since I ensured he escaped the three Wessex warriors, now dead, I've seen no one, and I've not even heard the sound of another person in the woodlands who didn't have four feet or wings to aid it.

'I might suggest you head south,' a voice calls. I startle, and then a smile breaks out on my face.

'My lord king.' I half bow with relief.

'I think, here, you can just name me as Wiglaf, after all,' the king offers. I eye him. He looks bruised and battered. His horse has developed a limp on its right hoof, which appears sore even from where I stand.

'It's good to see you, Wiglaf.' I hesitate before I name him as such, and his eyebrows lift as he removes his helm, and staggers towards me. 'You're wounded?' I question, already determining what ails him.

'Bruised all over. My chest took a real pounding from that big bastard in the woodland. I take it you killed them?'

'I did, my... Wiglaf,' I correct myself quickly.

'Good, and you're wounded?'

'I am, but mostly it's from the queen's blade and when I hit my head falling to the ground in Lundenwic's hall.'

'It seems to be a little more than that,' the king counters, flinching slightly as I name the queen and what she tried to do.

'I'll live,' I offer, so relieved to see the king alive and well that I could be almost cut in two, and I'd probably not feel any pain.

'And do you know where you are?' the king questions, indicating the trees that surround us.

'I've no idea. You?'

'No. I hoped to find a better path today, but so far, I've failed, and then I heard your angry cries earlier, and found you here. I recognised your voice. I think there might be some safety in numbers, even if it's just me and you.'

'I agree. But, we should probably remain helmed.'

'When I've drunk, yes. I assume you have no food?' The king walks towards me. I see how he hobbles, and his horse does the same beside him. It's going to take us a long time to get anywhere. Neither of us is exactly in good condition, and nor are the horses. Bicwide's not limping, but he's hungry. I can tell from how he keeps testing any piece of grass he finds with his long tongue.

'No food. I might be able to find something: some berries or mushrooms. I didn't want to risk it during the night. The last thing I needed was a bad belly to go with my sore head.'

King Wiglaf nods but bends tiredly to drink. I move to his horse and inspect its leg just above the hoof. It's certainly red and inflamed, and his mount nickers unhappily as I press my hands around it. I know much less about horse care than I might like, but I know enough to understand the horse can't be ridden.

It probably can't even be walked very far either, not in a single day.

I let the animal drink. Bicwide takes comfort in having another horse with him. I smirk, pulling my bandage tight on my face. I grimace and then realise I need to neither smile nor grimace. Indeed, talking is uncomfortable, as it pulls my cheek tight.

'What now?' King Wiglaf questions when he's drunk his fill. I can hear his belly rumbling. I consider when the last time was that he missed a meal.

'Do you know which way is south?' I peer upwards as I speak, trying to see the sun through the dense canopy of bright green leaves. It's not easy. One of us should climb high to get a good look, but neither of us can do that without risking falling.

'I think it's this way.' The king points, but I shake my head.

'I came from that way. I think it's this way.'

We're not at cross purposes; it's not as though I point one way and him exactly the opposite, but we don't agree, either.

'We're not that far apart,' I admit with a shrug, regretting the movement immediately as it activates all my aches and pains.

'Somewhere in the middle,' Wiglaf suggests with a smirk.

'Probably the best plan,' I grudgingly admit.

'I can't help feeling I should know where I am,' King Wiglaf mutters unhappily.

'I suppose you can be king of somewhere without knowing every single hide of it.'

'Yes.' We lapse into silence. The thought of continuing our journey, for the time being, saps what strength remains to me.

'You should ride,' I inform Wiglaf.

'No, neither of us should ride. Rest the horses, as best we can.'

'And try and find some food.'

'Indeed,' Wiglaf agrees, bending to drink again. In the

absence of anything that looks edible, I do the same. It's the summer, but it's too early for any fruit to be edible, and even if it wasn't, here, in the woodlands, I don't expect to find an apple or pear tree waiting to be harvested.

When I stand, I get a good look at the king. His hair is threaded with grey, his beard and moustache shimmering in the pale sunlight. He walks with slightly bowed legs, as though he's spent all of his life in the saddle, but what concerns me most is the lack of thick muscles along his arms and legs, and his protruding belly. Whether I like it or not, the king isn't a young man any more. He's grown somewhat fat and indolent of late.

Not that it's my problem. I just need to return him to Londonia and hope Mercia hasn't fallen to Wessex blades. Again.

Wiglaf's next words surprise me.

'You look like her, you know.' I startle and meet his appraising gaze.

'Who?'

'Your mother, of course. I knew her. We were younger then. Bloody hell, everyone was younger then,' he mutters, wincing at some reawakened hurt.

I feel my heart beating too fast. I thought no one knew my father's identity, but if Wiglaf knew my mother, then surely he must know my father was Beornwulf.

King Wiglaf offers me a pain-tinged smile.

'She was a beautiful young woman. I knew her from when we were both around six or seven winters. Our families were close. Then.'

My mouth's dry once more, despite how much I've drunk. I can't have this discussion here. Panic threatens to undo me. I feel my hand clenching, reminding me of my eagle scar.

'You look like your uncle, too. He was younger than your mother. He had fire in his belly, just as you do. It was, alas, eventually, somewhat misplaced.' Wiglaf scowls once more, stretching his back by sticking out his hips.

I lick my still dry lips.

'We lost track. My family lost all alongside King Coelwulf, the first of his name. My father was determined to keep out of the eye of those playing with power. He knew he had a claim to the kingship.'

Slowly, I start to breathe evenly. This isn't what I'm expecting it to be. Not at all.

'When you first appeared before me, at Bardney, I confess, I didn't recognise you. I should have done. Icel, you've saved my life more often than Commander Eahric and his warriors. I would thank you, once more. You helped restore my kingship. You rescued me when we faced the Wessex warriors in Wales, and also outside the fort of Londinium. And, I've rewarded you poorly. I should have sent someone else to Winchester. Will you accept my apology?' I startle at that. Wiglaf stands before me, hand extended, seeming to want me to shake it.

I extend my hand, mindful of my grubby fingers, suddenly realising I've mislaid my gloves somewhere. His grip is firm, unfaltering. I don't squeeze as hard as I might. Wiglaf's as old as my uncle should have been. That makes him older than most men I know, aside from Ealdorman Sigered, and I know Sigered only lives because he runs from any fight with his tail between his legs. He's lived a long time because of his cowardice. I wonder that no one else sees it.

'Your father had a claim to the kingship?' I question, curious, despite myself, and wanting to break the strangely tense atmosphere that's developed between us. I hope the king's reminiscing hasn't reminded him of my father's identity, or rather, the lack of knowledge about it. It does need to remain a secret.

'Yes, he and, obviously, I, and my son and grandson, are

descended from Wærmund, king of Mercia before even Penda. You must have heard the scops tell the linking tale? It goes something like Woden begot Watholgeot, begot Waga, begot Wihtlaed, begot Waermund, begot Offa, begot Angengeot, begot Eomer, begot Icel, begot Cnebba, begot Cynewald, begot Creoda, begot Pybba. I muddle the names. It's something like that. My father and his father before him could trace their lineage to Wærmund. Alas, our ancestor didn't become king, and the line descended through a different branch. With the royal line so denuded, that's all that was needed. It's written in one of the holy books somewhere. Bishop Ceolbeorht will know where.'

The names Wiglaf recites are tales from a bygone age. I find it astounding that his father and his father before him held so tight to such an ancient claim. And yet I also startle at the sound of my name included amongst them all.

'Icel.' Wiglaf pauses, his forehead furrowed in thought, as he too makes the connection. 'It seems you were named for a king as well. Your mother named you?'

'I don't believe she did.'

'Then who determined on your name?'

I shrug my shoulders, unsure how to answer that. I've never considered it.

'You were no bastard, were you?'

'My uncle assures me I wasn't. But wouldn't name my father. I doubt he knew.' I shrug again. Wiglaf's busy tending to his wounded horse. He doesn't look at me as I reply. I hope my voice sounds even. I wouldn't want to be caught in a lie.

'Indeed. He worshipped his sister. Her death was a terrible tragedy. I can't imagine your uncle took it well, but then, I didn't know him during those years. When I returned to the witan, your uncle was there, his sister was gone, and all knew he cared for his nephew.'

I swallow a sudden sadness. As a child, I knew I was different. As an adult, I realise I'm not so different. And yet I wish I'd had a mother to sing me lullabies. I'm sure young Coenwulf and Coelwulf will one day think the same.

'But, I was talking of her living, not dead. She had the voice of a songbird. She would sing wherever she went. Often, she'd forget and even walk into church singing some tune or other. The bishop didn't approve of her lightness of spirit. It made her bold. She did things I'd never have dreamed of doing. She said it was her duty to misbehave, for soon the duties of motherhood would be placed on her, and if she couldn't tell her children of such mischief, she'd be no fun at all.'

The silly story brings a smile to my tight face. My uncle would never speak of my mother. Wynflæd too has memories that are more sorrowful than joyful. It brings me untold joy to know she wasn't always a staid woman who'd lose her life birthing me.

'She was also quite well versed in how to fight. I can assure you that while many didn't approve of her desire to defend herself, your grandfather thought it was entirely acceptable. He taught her to protect herself. A pity he and your grandmother died before you were born.'

I nod along. It's strange to realise Wiglaf knows more about my family than I do. Again, I never thought to ask. My uncle didn't offer any information about them. He was a taciturn man. Perhaps, when this is over, it'll be time for me to return to Budworth and learn more about my heritage.

'The queen was a childhood acquaintance of your mother as well. We were a close-knit group, for a while. There were rifts long before King Coelwulf had his position stolen from him. We kept our distance then. None thought it would last. All believed Coelwulf would reclaim the kingship and then his son, the current Lord Coenwulf, would be king in his place.'

'And then it would be his son, Coenwulf.'

'Yes, it would,' King Wiglaf muses, his eyes flashing darkly. 'Come to think of it, perhaps the spark of this movement against my kingship began long ago, even before then.' His eyebrows furrow, and he seems lost in thought. His mouth opens and closes. I believe he'll say more, but he lapses into silence. My eyes alight on a cluster of very early berries, and I move towards them, unsure whether they'll be edible until I get closer.

Bicwide follows me, his lips already curling back as though he'll eat them himself. I snatch them away, seeing early gooseberries that can be eaten. The small plant is entirely out of place here, amongst the trees, but of course, wherever the birds shit the seeds, the plants will grow. I offer a few of the gooseberries to Bicwide, having first checked them and found them to be neither bitter nor sweet. Tasteless is fine as long as it's food, and I can perhaps taste nothing because chewing is painful. I return to the king and hold out my hand. He eyes the hairy fruits, takes some and offers his horse the same as Bicwide. I feel the harsh hairs on my hand, know enough not to wipe them down my clothes. I'll need to use some more water to remove them or my hands will feel their bite.

'Talking of your mother has reminded me of when I first encountered Wulfnoth of Eamont.' I bite my tongue as King Wiglaf speaks, astounded that, perhaps, I might finally receive my answers here. 'His family once shared land close to my family. They were all brutish boys, even Wulfheard. Wulfheard puts his skills to better use than his brother. All the same, the family were always ambitious. Wulfnoth held a grudge against everyone at Mercia's court, for his father died fighting in the Welsh kingdoms. He blamed King Coenwulf for that. And then he blamed King Coelwulf as well, for no matter how many Mercians you throw against the Welsh, the Welsh will always bloody recover, and the battle must be won all over again. I believe that's why Wulfnoth was complicit in removing King Coelwulf from power. The new king, Beornwulf, promised once and for all to overwhelm the Welsh.'

'He lied then,' I answer blandly, finding it strange I'm talking of King Beornwulf, my father, with King Wiglaf.

'He did. He did great damage. Wulfnoth, I seem to recall, was most displeased.'

'But you don't fight the Welsh?' I object because his argument seems incomplete.

'I don't, no. But when a man believes he can overthrow one king, why not another? And then another. Wulfnoth's family lost much when King Beornwulf died. It didn't affect Wulfheard who was already with Ealdorman Ælfstan. Wulfnoth wasn't then in a position like Wulfheard. Instead, he decided to exact his revenge on the Welsh and those dwelling in the borderlands.'

I nod, absorbing all this. It doesn't answer all of my questions, but slowly, more and more of it makes sense.

'We should get on,' I inform Wiglaf. The few early gooseberries have done little to ease my hunger, and the horse still limps. We have a long way to go. If we're not careful, it'll be dark again and we'll be trapped once more.

'Of course, excuse an old man for talking of the past. It's too easy to do.'

I'm not sure talking about ten years ago is really so unforgivable, but I hold my tongue. The more King Wiglaf peers into his past, the more connections he's making. I have to hope he doesn't gaze too far and realise he knows the identity of my father. Then, not even having saved his life on multiple occasions is likely to prevent him from wanting me out of the way so his son, and then grandson, can become kings of Mercia. I consider just how angry Queen Cynethryth would be to know there are others, aside from the two young boys she tried to have killed, who could rule Mercia.

Without further discussion, I direct Bicwide towards the space between where I want to go, and where the king thinks we should go. Hopefully, we'll soon be back in Londonia. And then, I'll work to distance myself from the king before he remembers something about my beginnings I don't want him to know.

9

The going's hard. I'm hungry. Bicwide's found little to sustain him besides water and a few tall green grasses. The woodland floor's muddy, not grassy. We need to redirect our steps to where I killed the three Wessex warriors to feed the horses, but I'm not sure I want to go there. What if their allies have found them and are now hunting for us? What if they haven't found them and track us anyway?

I'm wary of every step and every loud thwack from Bicwide's hooves hitting against a hollow tree trunk or large branch. We're not exactly being quiet. We're not being loud either, but with all four of us moving, it's hard to hear above the noises we make. The enemy could be just around the next tree, and none of us would notice. The animals and birds are also raucous. I can't help thinking that if even the birds and denizens of the woodland aren't scared of us, then why would the Wessex warriors be?

When we next find a stream, I also find some thick dock leaves to wet and wrap around the inflamed leg of the lame horse. The knee joint is swollen. The cool water will stop it from becoming more tender. I wince as I secure them in place, but he doesn't. I take that to be a good sign. I need the horse to keep on going. Admittedly, if I must, I can send the king away with Bicwide. I'm not sure either of them would appreciate that, however.

'Do you think we're going in the correct direction?' I eventually question Wiglaf. I wish I'd paid more attention to some of the other warriors. Maneca always seems to know where we're going. He tried to teach me once. I wasn't overly interested. I saw no need when others took on the position of making sure we went where we intended.

Wiglaf, his face drawn and tired, shrugs his shoulders. I feel the same. With only the sound of slurping and water pooling over our hands, all four of us drink deeply. I'd welcome something else, but we won't satisfy our hunger until we find someone with bread for us and oats for the horses. Once more, I check my wounded cheek. The bandage is filthy when I hold it in my hands, having winced on pulling at my cheek. I thought it time to see how badly it still bled. I'm not going to replace it. It'll only encourage dirt at this stage, now I see how filthy my nails are, and I know better than to do that. I also run my hand over the lump on my head. It feels huge, but my nausea has passed. I no longer look at a swaying world. I'll take that as progress.

'We should carry on,' I eventually announce. Wiglaf looks like he could sleep, and now isn't the time for that. We must continue while we can see and there's light with which to see.

I consign myself to more time trudging through the strange half-lit world beneath the dense canopy overhead, but just as I'm getting into a steady rhythm, one where I hardly need to think about what I'm doing, I pick up an unwelcome sound. Looking up, I catch sight of a lessening in the dense camouflage. We've returned to the grassy opening where I rescued the king, even though I wasn't intending to do so.

'Bugger,' I exclaim. Wiglaf is also alert. The voices that shout one to another don't ring with the Mercian dialect. Almost too late, I grab hold of Bicwide and steer him away from the clearing. He can sense the damp and luxuriant grass. Even I can smell the grass, and my belly rumbles. 'This way,' I whisper to Wiglaf. He nods, wincing as he steps on the only twig to be seen for a fair distance. I grimace but don't wait to see if we've been detected. I don't want to return the way we've just laboriously walked, but it's the only option for now. Behind me, the voices never come any closer, and I hope that means we've evaded them. I doubt they've heard us over the clamour they're making. It's as though they're doing their best to ensure no one comes close to them. Perhaps they don't wish to find Mercia's king after all.

When I'm content we're out of sight amongst the densely packed trees, I start to navigate around the clearing in the direction I believe is south. From there, I feel we have more chance of reaching some Mercian warriors. They must surely be searching for the king. They won't have given him up as lost. Or me, I acknowledge. I hope my warrior friends are also seeking me. I'm unsure whether they think I'm with the king or not. No doubt, they suspect I've got myself caught up in some fresh problem. I'd really like to bloody stop doing that.

Wiglaf lumbers on behind. Neither of us speaks. Every so often, the horses falter slightly, but even Wiglaf's wounded mount keeps going. We're all sweating, the heat becoming oppressive as the day advances. I suspected the opposite would happen. It's frustrating that the weather has been so cool of late, until, of course, I'd welcome it being so.

I find myself clenching my hands to stop myself rubbing at the itchy wound on my right cheek. I lick my lips repeatedly. I feel I might never be sated again. I've done little but crave water. I know a man can survive for longer without eating than he can without drinking. It's hardly been long, though. It's just the heat and dreariness of our slow progress, or so I convince myself.

Eventually, darkness descends once more. I'd have hoped to make better headway. Surely, we can't have galloped and cantered so far? But, of course, neither of us truly knows the route back.

'We should stop,' I whisper to Wiglaf, allowing his horse to draw level with Bicwide. The king's hardly visibly in the gloaming. We could be walking right past a way out of the woodlands and not even realise.

'No, we carry on. It can't be much further.' He's exhausted but stubborn. I nod unwillingly. We found the grassy vista at nearly noon; we've been walking ever since. It would be so much easier if we could ride, but we can't risk his horse. At least the enemy haven't found us.

Bowing my head, acceding to the inevitable resolve of the king, I continue to put one foot in front of the other. I'm grateful we've not had to fight the Wessex warriors today, but I remain furious with them and their bloody king and his son. Mercia has done nothing to interfere in the Wessex kingship in my lifetime. Why, then, are they so determined to meddle in ours? If this is all because of something King Offa once did to King Ecgberht over thirty years ago, then I wish Ecgberht's memory was shorter. Offa has been dead for nearly forty winters, as has his son. Mercia's current king has no connection to Offa.

On and on we go, our footsteps more and more laboured, the horses growing increasingly tired. When I hear running water, I direct Bicwide that way, hopeful the king will follow us. It's almost impossible to see anything. It's so dark I could walk into a tree and not notice. I have my hand out, directing our steps. It's already bruised from contact with thick tree trunks, but I'm starting to sense the way ahead, using the gentle breeze on my forehead to guide my steps. At least it's not as hot as it was during the day.

I step into the water before I realise we've reached it. Wincing at the dampness spreading through my booted foot, I pull the king to my side. We drink deeply, unable to see if the water has been fouled but too thirsty to care. It tastes pleasant enough. I strain to listen and, on the periphery of my hearing, detect something out of place. Wiglaf must catch it as well, as I sense him turning his head to seek out the source of the noise.

I peer all around me. No one can be looking for us in this darkness. It's impossible to see anything, not even the tip of my nose. Wiglaf and I are visible to one another because of the whites of our eyes and nothing else. I sense him moving, and his hand reaches out, inadvertently knocking my cut cheek, to have me looking where he does.

There's something there, the glimmer of a light against the blackness of the trees and the night. I struggle to my feet, gripping Bicwide and reaching for my seax. Wiglaf quickly mirrors my actions, but what should we do then? We've made it here by chance.

I shuffle backwards until there's a thick branch at my back, Wiglaf beside me. I scarcely dare breathe as the light seems to bloom and then grows closer and closer. It's painful to look at and also impossible not to look at. The promise of being able to see has its grip on me. Neither the king nor I make any attempt to move further. We need to know who it is. If it's the enemy, then we require their light to see by. If it's our allies, then we must have it as well.

The light draws ever closer, and finally I hear the rumble of voices, and then I detect the most welcome sound I've ever heard.

'Wulfheard,' I murmur to the king. I don't know what his reaction is. I open my mouth to call out, but the king grabs my arm, cautioning me with his finger on my lips. I hold my tongue. He's right. The Wessex warriors might have been drawn by the light as well. They could be waiting to attack us when we give ourselves away. I'm not sure how Wulfheard and whoever escorts him is to find us. Admittedly, we could follow the light if they don't come to the water, but I hope they come this way.

'Bloody things,' I hear Landwine complain. A loud thwack of something hitting a branch brings a smile to my face. I know exactly how he feels.

'You'll wake the bloody dead with that racket,' Wulfheard protests.

'Or bring the bastard enemy to our side,' Cenred murmurs.

'If we had more brands,' Landwine continues.

'You'd be setting the place alight.' Oswy adds his comment to the general bitching and moaning.

'Can we not wait for daylight?' This voice comes from further back. Godeman. It appears they're all looking for us.

'Are you even sure they're here?' Landwine's voice is a low moan.

'Where else would they be? I'm sure if they'd run to Lundenwic someone would have thought to tell us.'

'Trust bloody Icel.'

'He's not the only one we're seeking,' Wulfheard offers, his patience slipping. 'What about the king?'

'King Wiglaf wouldn't get himself lost out here,' Landwine huffs. I smirk as I sense Wiglaf stiffen beside me. I feel that I should inform my fellow warriors that the king can hear everything they say, but mindful of the enemy we nearly encountered earlier, I don't. I offer a swift prayer my allies won't say something entirely inappropriate.

'He could be wounded,' Wulfheard resumes. 'And unable to get back. His horse might be lame. Anything could have befallen them. Ealdorman Ælfstan was adamant we look for them tonight. We'll find them before Ealdorman Sigered's men can get anywhere near because we don't trust his intentions.'

The light glows brighter, almost too bright, and even though I do nothing to give myself away, it moves unerringly towards where the king and I stand with the two horses.

'Hiding in the dark, are we?' Wulfheard asks conversationally from the back of his horse, the brand too bright before my eyes. I blink away the searing illumination, even as Wulfheard dismounts and bows towards the king, holding the brand to the side so I can see some of the other warriors, including Oswy and Landwine. Whether Oswy's pleased to see me or not, I don't know. His expression is strangely difficult to read in the yellow glow, even though I wear a huge grin of pleasure at seeing him, which tugs on my wounded cheek. 'My lord king, it's good to see you. Thank you for keeping our young friend safe. It's gratifying to see him in one piece, for once,' Wulfheard continues, his eyes piercing as he views me. I'm sure he winces at the mark on my face, but doesn't offer any praise.

I open my mouth to deny that, but again, I feel the king's hand on my arm. It's evidently best these are the words heard by anyone close by if, indeed, the enemy is near. I can't deny how relieved I feel to have been found, and by Wulfheard and my other friends amongst Ealdorman Ælfstan's warriors. Immediately, I sag. I'm no longer entirely responsible for the king. But, I would have appreciated not being thought the incompetent one here. I've killed the king's enemies. I've kept him safe when they were all somewhere else doing something else.

'We've a fresh mount for you, my lord king.' Wulfheard's busy organising everything. His focus is on the king. I'd appreciate a wink or something to assure me he knows I've been the one accountable for keeping the king safe, but he offers nothing after his assessing glance.

I look around in the flickering glow from the flames. Ealdorman Ælfstan has sent his entire warrior band to look for King Wiglaf, aside from Maneca and Kyre who are too wounded to ride, not just Wulfheard, Oswy and Landwine. And perhaps to seek me out as well, I try and console myself with that thought.

'We'll bring back your horse more slowly. Give them the food we brought,' Wulfheard instructs as my belly growls angrily. A piece of bread materialises before my nose.

The king eats more eagerly than I do because my cheek pains me with each bite. Quickly, he's mounted on the fresh horse.

'Take the king back under heavy guard. Be alert for the enemy, although we've evaded them so far. Oswy, you have the command. Cenred and I will escort the animals and Icel.'

'Tell me,' King Wiglaf asks, as I realise the brand is to go with the king held aloft by Oswy, and we're to remain in darkness. 'Is the queen still under guard?'

'Events in Lundenwic are difficult to explain,' Wulfheard murmurs respectfully. 'But the queen is inside the fort of Londinium. Your son, alas, is determined to free her. We hear he's determined that as you must be dead, he's now Mercia's king, or at least, that's what his messenger said when he came to demand the return of the queen. Ealdormen Ælfstan and Tidwulf ordered the messenger away, stating you still lived, and refusing to open the gates to anyone.'

'Does he now?' Wiglaf murmurs unhappily, his voice filled with a combination of fury and unease as he considers what his son has done in his absence. It's been all of two days.

Lord Wigmund lacks all the skills required to lead Mercia, especially with a persistent enemy on her borders. I know the kingship would need to be secured quickly in light of the death of the king, but surely Lord Wigmund should have made more effort to find his father before declaring himself king in his place. Wulfheard's words about Ealdorman Sigered make sense now. Ealdorman Sigered's intentions towards Wiglaf might not have been to ensure his survival even if found alive.

'Never fear. Ealdorman Tidwulf has command of Londinium's fort and the queen. The Wessex warriors are, unfortunately, maintaining a hold on the land close to the Thames. There are unconfirmed reports King Ecgberht will shortly cross to Mercia to reinforce his warriors, and take back Londonia before securing the whole of Mercia under his control once more. We don't know the truth of that, but the ealdormen – well, apart from Sigered – are preparing to counter any attempt on Londonia. Ealdorman Ælfstan has sent us to protect you, but the other ealdormen are busy organising Mercia's defence. Muca holds Lundenwic.'

I can't see the king's response as his back is turned to me, but I can imagine it.

'Now, go with the majority of Ealdorman Ælfstan's force. Cenred and I will chaperon Icel and your horses back in the daylight, my lord king.'

I think the king will leave then, but instead, he reaches for me in the darkness from his horse's saddle and grasps my arm firmly in his tight grip. When he speaks, his words are only loud enough for me to hear.

'My thanks, Icel. Once more, you prove yourself the best and most loyal of men. I won't forget that. You have more integrity than my own son who thinks to declare himself king, and cares little for whether I live or die.'

I don't know how to reply to that. I'm grateful to hear the thunder of horses' hooves on the move and to know the king has gone, leaving me to make sense of the uncomfortable sensation his praise has inflicted on me. Only then does Wulfheard round on me. I think he might embrace me, but as with Wynflæd, Wulfheard shows his concern by berating me.

'Bloody hell, Icel. You need to stop doing this. I can't deny, however, that it's good to see you in one piece, as well as the king. No doubt you'll earn yourself some new reward to infuriate the king's son.' His words are flecked with barely concealed concern. 'You make allies and enemies far too easily.'

I nod, but he can't see the movement now the brand's gone with Oswy, Landwine and the others. I feel mollified to hear his pleasure in finding me.

'My thanks, Wulfheard, it's good to see you too,' I mutter, and now he turns to face me, gripping my chin but not too tightly.

'It is good to see you, Icel. It really is,' he murmurs.

'I really bloody do need to stop doing this,' I admit, sagging with relief at his steadying presence. I don't like the news from Londonia, though. Lord Wigmund really is a bloody arse. And King Ecgberht? How I'd love to put an end to his life.

10

We remain where we are even as the sound of the king, Oswy, Landwine and the others fades away. Wulfheard and Cenred tell me all they can about events since I disappeared after the king, as the darkness of night closes in around us.

'The queen was quickly taken into Londinium's fort,' Wulfheard assures me. 'She screamed like a vixen in heat but we still have her, thank God, in one of the cell-like rooms with no access to the outside world aside from a heavily guarded door.'

'And Brihthild?' She's key to this. Not even the king has thought to ask about her, but I risked my life to protect her. I'd like to know she's still in Mercian hands.

I sense hesitation in my fellow warriors.

'Does she live?'

'Yes, but Lord Wigmund, or rather Ealdorman Sigered was quick to take control of her. Those loyal to King Wiglaf can't get near her.'

I grimace and then remember they can't see me.

'That's not going to help any of this.'

'It's not, no. I heard reports that Lord Wigmund intended to give her to the Wessex lord in return for being acknowledged as Mercia's king. But we've heard many whispers. Not all of them can be true. Ealdorman Ælfstan awaits the king with more of the king's warriors close to Londinium. They'll protect the king, and ensure everyone knows he lives, but it might still be war. Alliances are no doubt being built on the belief King Wiglaf is dead.'

'He's only been absent for two days.'

'A lot can happen in two bloody days,' Cenred murmurs morosely.

Another piece of bread appears before me, and I eat hungrily, although it remains painful to do so. The horses are also being fed. Good oats to restore their strength. Their chewing is rhythmic and filled with soft noises of appreciation. I wish eating could bring me such pleasure.

'Did Lady Ælflæd get away, with Eadburg and the three children?' I question, remembering how all this began.

'They're safe. They escaped Lundenwic, as far as I understand it,' Wulfheard offers. 'We've no reports of them being captive or stuck inside Lundenwic with either Ealdorman Muca or Lord Wigmund.'

'How did the Wessex warriors get across the River Thames without being seen?'

'That's being looked into,' Wulfheard growls. I mirror his fury. The queen's trial would have been a damn sight easier to accomplish without the bastards getting involved.

'Is Lord Wigmund or the queen implicated, other than the rumour you've heard that Wigmund will give Brihthild to Lord Æthelwulf of Kent?'

'Not at the moment, but it's possible. It wasn't exactly a secret that there'd be a trial in Lundenwic. We should have taken

Brihthild to Tamworth, far from the border with Wessex, where it would have been much more difficult to get to her.'

'Then the enemy would have claimed Tamworth again. We didn't want that to happen.'

'No, we didn't, you're right. Bad enough they're here, so close to Londonia. Have you killed all those searching for the king?'

'I've killed three. They'd surrounded the king in a clearing, deep within the woodlands. But there are more of them now. We saw them in the same place at about noon. Was that yesterday? I've lost track of time.'

'Will you ever stop being the one to protect the king's life?' Wulfheard questions. I can sense him shaking his head, whether in dismay or disbelief I keep finding myself in such a predicament, I don't know.

'It doesn't seem that way,' I comment with downcast lips, while Cenred chuckles darkly.

'For the time being that task falls to Oswy and the others. We need to keep the guard heavy around the king, in case they encounter more Wessex warriors, or Ealdorman Sigered.' His tone is sour as he says the Mercian ealdorman's name. 'But, of course, we're here to protect you,' Wulfheard offers, as though me having two warriors, while the king has at least five times that number, should please me.

'What, you two useless turds? The king gets everyone else, and I get you two to protect me?'

Cenred snarls as I try to make light of the situation.

'Indeed, just us two, and you, and two exhausted horses, this could be a most enjoyable day,' Wulfheard tries to jest.

'How far are we from Londonia?'

'A good day's journey. You've turned on yourself. You'd have come in from the south, but now you're towards the west. It's a bloody miracle we found you when we did. We followed a river here. I was convinced you'd be close to water.'

'It's very disorientating with the tree canopy overhead,' I try to explain.

'It doesn't matter. All that's of concern is that we found you, and the king, before the enemy could. And of course, the enemy won't know the king's been rescued.'

'No, they won't,' I agree. I'm not entirely sure where Wulfheard's thoughts have taken him. 'We're not going after them?' I question, but I hope it sounds more like a statement. I'm exhausted. I've kept the king safe on my own. I can't be expected to find the enemy. Can I?

'No, no, not yet. But, if they don't appear soon, we'll have to return to the woodlands. The ealdorman's adamant they're to be hunted down. We can't have Wessex warriors so deeply within Mercia again.'

We lapse into silence. I stifle a yawn.

'You can sleep until daybreak,' Wulfheard suggests, and rather than arguing, I sink to the ground, mindful of the nearby stream, and close my eyes.

Not that I get long to sleep. I'm kicked awake, not unkindly. I wince at the bright daylight. My eyes burn with exhaustion and my head aches all over again.

Wulfheard offers me his hand to stand, flinching at me as he finally gets a good look at my face.

'Your wound looks bad. You need to clean it and cover it, or it'll get the wound rot.' His assessment is probably fair. My cheek feels really tight, as though swollen. Three days beneath the trees, avoiding the enemy, and I'm also encrusted in sweat.

I snap my hand away from running it over my cheek, grimacing at the state of my nails once more. I look for Cenred, but he's not visible, although I can hear him taking a long piss close by, the sound even managing to overwhelm that of the stream. I look at Bicwide. He offers me a sated look. He's full and happy. Perhaps he'll allow me to ride him rather than the slightly too small animal they've brought for me. My legs will drag on the ground if I ride that horse.

I follow Cenred and piss as well and then clean my face carefully, wincing at the chill of the water, while Wulfheard offers me a piece of linen to place over my cut. It'll hold until it becomes too dry, but I've nothing else with which to secure it. Only then do I seek out Wiglaf's horse. I'm surprised to see the animal already has a linen wrapped around its swollen leg rather than the dock leaves I used yesterday.

'I know how to treat a limping horse,' Wulfheard growls at my shocked look. I smirk, pleased to be with my fellow warriors once more, even if there are only three of us in total.

I mount Bicwide and settle in the saddle, and only then do I hear the voices of the Wessex warriors we've been evading since yesterday.

'It looks like we need to hurry,' Cenred grumbles, already mounted, while Wulfheard fiddles with lead ropes and generally slows us down.

'We can't leave the king's bloody horse,' he explains, no doubt sensing our frustration. I reach for my seax. It comes free from my weapons belt after a struggle. I need to clean the blood from it, but not now. At the moment, I only need to focus on following Wulfheard, who leads the way. I hope he knows the route. Other than the path of the stream, I can't differentiate any walking routes or even pathways used by the animals who make the woodland their home, or others who might venture here to coppice the trees. I'm entirely reliant on Wulfheard to take us south.

Cenred's behind, unencumbered by a spare horse, as Wulfheard and I have one each. Wiglaf's horse, who I lead, picks his way over the collection of sticks and protruding roots with more skill than Bicwide. Bicwide clunks his hooves on them time and time again. Cenred huffs with annoyance. I don't blame him. With the sound of the Wessex warriors appearing to come closer, I wouldn't want to be at the rear either.

For a while, I listen and don't talk. I've replaced my seax, and ride with both hands on the reins, but eventually the sound fades away. Wulfheard slows his speed. He looks over his shoulder at us.

'The fools are lost,' he offers with a wide grin. 'They don't know their arse from their elbows.'

I think we should be pleased about that, but I hold my tongue. I'm starting to feel nauseous again. My cheek's burning unpleasantly, and the bread I've eaten hasn't satisfied me enough to stop my belly from rumbling. I don't know if it's hunger or my pulsing head wound that makes me feel sick. The heat of the day's building as well. Sweat drips down my forehead. At least, I reason, it's keeping my bandage in place.

Eventually, Wulfheard calls a halt, and I clamber from the saddle to drink deeply from the welcoming stream. It's not the same one as earlier. At some point, Wulfheard's veered aside, perhaps to the south.

'How exactly did you find us?' I find myself asking, sitting back on my knees and looking up through a small gap in the covering overhead. I know they said they followed the water, but all the same, we were far from where we should have been.

'We didn't know where to find you. We were told to come in from the west. Ealdorman Tidwulf sent a force east as well. They might find the Wessex warriors and kill them.' Wulfheard speaks with more optimism than I'm feeling. 'We were very lucky.'

'Ealdorman Sigered sent men from the south as well. But their intentions, we suspect, were not to find the king alive.'

'Do you truly believe Lord Wigmund would have the support of the witan?' I question. I'm really struggling to believe anyone would support Wigmund to replace his father.

'Wigmund thinks so, as does Ealdorman Sigered. Who else would there be to name as king if Wiglaf was dead? His grandson's a child. Mercia needs an adult male to lead her, especially with Wessex on the offensive once more.'

'I notice you didn't say a warrior king,' Cenred comments.

Wulfheard scowls. 'Wigmund doesn't know his arse from his elbow either. But, perhaps he doesn't need to do so. Desperate times, and all that. He could be a figure head, but little else.'

'That's hardly the foundation for a good kingship.'

'It's not, no. But, others have done just as well.'

I eye him then. He's stretching out his back from too much time in the saddle, his greying hair and beard illuminated by the bright sun.

'The king spoke of your brother,' I comment lightly, surprising myself by sharing that information.

'Did he now?' Wulfheard muses, his tone deceptively bland.

'He remembers his involvement in previous plots.'

'He's not alone in doing so.' Wulfheard frowns, although whether it's because he's relieved a sore spot on his back, or because I talk about his brother, I'm unsure.

'The king suggests Wulfnoth's aggression towards the current king and his line could extend back to the usurpation of Coelwulf's kingship.'

'He could be correct. Wulfnoth was always a surly cock. He thought much more was owed to him than his birth allowed.'

'He wished to be king?' My voice rises at the thought.

Wulfheard's answering laughter shocks me. 'No, young Icel.

But there are more ways to rule than by being declared Mercia's king. Wulfnoth knew that well enough. Kings Coenwulf and Coelwulf were powerful and influential, but there were always those standing behind them, ensuring things were done as they wanted them to be done. Even now, the ealdormen point the king in the direction they wish to go. Mercia's kings don't make all their decisions alone. You should learn that. In time, when you no longer ride to war or fight every one of Mercia's battles, you'll be regarded well by the witan. You're the lord of Budworth. You'll have a position of responsibility and a voice when the witan convenes.'

Now I laugh.

'I've no wisdom to offer,' I counter.

Cenred chuckles. 'We know that well enough, Icel, but others won't.'

I glower at him. He laughs louder.

'Better to be a warrior than a lord forced to attend the witan. I can't be doing with all that bloody talking. Ealdorman Sigered and his weaselling ways have shown me enough times that I don't wish to be the sort of man he is. I don't understand why he's not lost his ealdordom?' I huff with annoyance. Sigered has been ineffectual for as long as I can remember, and he was an old man when I first realised who he was.

'He's as persistent as a boil,' Wulfheard mutters. I hear the tight fury in his voice. 'Enough debate, come on. I want to be out of this woodland before night falls again. As much as I like you, Icel, you stink and need to bathe. And I want more than day-old bread to eat for my meals this day.'

I haul myself back into the saddle. As Bicwide resumes his steady gait, my cheek and head start to pulse in time with his movements. I wince.

It's already been a bloody long day, and if Wulfheard's correct, we still have the same distance to go.

It's going to take much of my resolve not to bitch and moan.

11

We break free from the cover of the trees when it's growing dark once more. This time, however, the lack of thick branch cover overhead allows the remaining daylight to illuminate the landscape. I take a deep, shuddering breath, forgetting my injured cheek and wincing, even as I absorb the sense of freedom that floods through my body. I could have been lost in the woodland forever, if not for Wulfheard and Cenred. Or worse, we might have been found by Ealdorman Sigered, or rather his warriors. Then I think I'd have needed to fight more of the enemy, only this time Mercians, no doubt content to return the king's corpse as a means of ensuring Lord Wigmund becomes king. Ealdorman Sigered thinks only of himself and how he'll gain from the events that befall Mercia.

I confess my thoughts have turned violent.

Why am I the only one risking my life to save the king? It should be the job of Ealdorman Sigered and Wiglaf's son. And his bloody wife. I'm astounded they're so blinded by ambition they can't see they risk the kingdom with their desire to create fresh upheaval beneath the royal helm. I mean, to think about

Wigmund wearing it has me entirely reconsidering my absolute determination not to be Mercia's king. I've no problem with King Wiglaf. His son? I don't believe I could ever serve him. And his grandson is still a small child. This isn't the time for more strife.

Wulfheard and Cenred also grow more sullen, the further south we come. I eye the twin settlement of Londonia before me. And then I turn to Wulfheard in surprise.

In the far distance, the moon shimmers over the obvious divide separating Mercia and Wessex, the River Thames, but that's not what holds my attention.

'What the hell?' I growl. Wulfheard's snarling as well. He doesn't even speak, but spurs Bada onwards, forgetting I lead the king's lame horse, while Wulfheard has the more lithe spare mount they brought. Cenred hurries onwards as well. 'Bloody wonderful,' I grumble, fear making a knot of my belly.

Beneath us, the ground slopes towards the River Thames, and the sound of the River Fleet can be heard clearly as it murmurs its way to join the River Thames to our left. Turning backwards, I see its obvious path through the woodland with a downturned grimace. I should have had the sense to find the river's source beneath the trees and follow it from there.

But what's caused Wulfheard and Cenred to leave me is the strong smell of smoke in the air, the collection of robust fires burning close to Lundenwic. They're not bloody cook fires, not at this time of the day, and not with the flames leaping high into the air, fuelled by more than just prudent use of wood. Indeed, it's so bright I have to blink dots from my eyes and keep my head low, focusing on where I want Bicwide to step, as darkness begins to close in tightly. Wiglaf's horse initially gave a nicker of joy at finally smelling freedom on the wind, but the scent of smoke has replaced that. I doubt the two horses are as happy now.

The fires are so vast I can hear the crackle of wood snapping under the onslaught. No matter where I turn my head as I gaze at Lundenwic, I see leaping flames and the wall of smoke is growing thicker, the grey visible against the black of night. If the moon should appear tonight, I doubt many will see it with the pall of thick smoke.

We thought we were home. It seems we're riding into something that's far from welcoming.

Bicwide ambles to a canter, Wiglaf's horse managing to do the same. I don't push either of them. We've been on this journey for days. Neither they nor I have been well fed, other than the oats they were given last night. We may have drunk so much water, we might sink in the river, but I need good food. I imagine they do as well. I've half a mind to release my grip on the king's horse, but I worry it'll run back into the woods, and then we'll never find it again.

Not that I need fear unduly, Wulfheard and Cenred haven't left me. Instead, they wait on an outcropping, surveying Londonia in its entirety, Londinium to the left, Lundenwic to the right.

'What the hell?' I repeat.

Wulfheard snarls. 'The bastard Wessex warriors,' he decides. I imagine he's correct. It seems they've launched a new attack. They'd sooner burn all of Lundenwic than have it stand in opposition to King Ecgberht of Wessex.

'Couldn't Ealdorman Muca, or even Lord Wigmund, hold against the advance? If it was only a few ships filled with warriors, even if they're mounted, the new defences surrounding Lundenwic should have held.'

'They should, yes,' Wulfheard unwillingly admits.

'What are you thinking?'

'I don't know, but I don't bloody like it.'

'The fort of Londinium appears to be secure.' Cenred tries to sound optimistic.

'I agree. We were going there anyway, but now we need to discover what's happened in our absence.'

'Do we risk the bridge over the Fleet?' Cenred questions.

'No, we'll return to the woodland and cross where the river's shallower and wider. Come on.'

Although every part of my body aches, I turn Bicwide and the king's horse to follow Wulfheard. It's easier to look north than south, the firelight not obscuring my vision. All the same, I check my seax. We're directing our horses back to where Wessex warriors seek the king.

Making use of the growing moonlight and dismounting so water rushes up to my waist, we lead the exhausted animals across the wide river not wanting to risk them slipping with our added weights on their backs. It's not deep enough to swim it. I'm grateful because the water's bloody cold. On the far bank, we mount again, dripping with water. I'm wet all over now. It'll probably help drive the smell of stale sweat from my body. We pick a path towards Londinium. I see the shades of the king's past encampment in the darkness. This was where I first brought the healers Theodore and Gaya when I rescued them from inside Londinium when they were slaves and I was trapped inside with only Wessex warriors for companions. They've been free ever since. The ghost of a smile touches my lips at that. I've accomplished much, even if there always seems to be more to do.

'Remain alert,' Wulfheard huffs. I hardly think he needs to remind us of that, but I don't argue. We draw closer and closer to Londinium's huge walls, menacing in the darkness. I focus on the fires close to Lundenwic, trying to make sense of them. The flames lick where defences have been put in place to protect the market settlement, a deep ditch, a high rampart and guard towers to the east of the settlement. Those defences are not as spectacular as Londinium's stone walls, but were supposed to be a deterrent. I can't see the effort put into constructing them has been worth it.

As we get close enough for our horses' hooves to be heard, I become aware of heads over the side of Londinium's walls, looking down at us, peering into the dark to determine how many riders pass by. They call one to another, sharing their thoughts.

Wulfheard rides straight to the huge door blocking the gateway, knocking on the heavy wood.

'Who is it?' a recognisable if gruff Mercian voice calls from inside.

'Wulfheard, you damn arse, now let us inside.'

'Wulfheard, Ealdorman Ælfstan's man?' the faceless man questions, and I try not to smirk at Oswy's delay in allowing us within, even though I'm relieved to find him here. That means the king is also safe.

'Open the damn door, Oswy, or so help me, I'll scalp your arse.'

'Are you alone?' Oswy demands more aggressively.

'Yes, we're bloody alone,' Wulfheard huffs, although I risk looking behind to ensure we are truly alone and some Wessex warrior hasn't risen from the muddy banks of the River Fleet to join us.

Oswy doesn't speak further, but we can clearly hear him chuckling as the door bars are lifted clear, and a small crack opens to allow us and the horses inside.

'Wulfheard, Cenred, Icel, good of you to finally get yourselves here,' Oswy offers with a wink, his face visible thanks to the sentry fires. Inside, the fort is as I remember it, lit by braziers so we can see what we're doing.

'What's happening over there?' Wulfheard demands, jerking his head towards the fires, while Oswy closes the door and, with the help of Maneca, shoves the huge wooden bars back into place to secure them against our enemy. I cast a professional eye over Maneca. He's on the mend but remains pale. Undoubtedly, guard duty is the only thing he can be tasked with. Riding his horse will be too painful. I'll ask Cuthred to make him a healing pottage when I've had some sleep. Provided Cuthred's here, of course. I open my mouth to ask the question I should have voiced during the last day, but Oswy's speaking.

'It's a bloody mess,' Oswy confirms. 'Ealdormen Ælfstan and Tidwulf, as well as King Wiglaf, are inside. Go and see them. They'll be pleased to know you're here. Although, Icel, get the king to stop singing your bloody praises. It's starting to get annoying. Even Wynflæd tires of hearing about you.' He slaps me on the shoulder as I dismount, almost knocking me sideways because I'm not expecting it. Hastily, he holds me upright as my wet boots squelch on the ground. 'Well, you might want to get dry first,' Oswy cautions, wiping his hands on his trews. 'Good to see you, mind,' he offers, returning to his guard duty. I can see he and Maneca are really struggling. Before them, they have a table laid out with ale and food. My belly growls, and I reach across and help myself to a slice of seared fish, no doubt from the River Thames. It tastes amazing to my tongue, used only to a few gooseberries, bread and water for the last few days.

Oswy mutters something uncomplimentary.

'Is Cuthred here?' I ask through the heat of the fish. Not only are they being fed, but even at this time of night, they're being served with freshly cooked food.

'Yes, with Wynflæd,' Oswy responds, slapping at my hand when I reach for more food. 'Leave it,' he complains.

'Sod off,' I glower. 'I've not eaten for days.'

We hold the gaze of one another, and then, just before I step away, I snatch another piece of fish. I skip away from Oswy.

The horses are led away by squires roused from their beds by Maneca.

'They need drying and warming. Good food, and plenty of water. Cover them in blankets for the night and watch the king's animal. It's lame. Treat it, if you can, or leave it until there's daylight.' The sleep-tousled youths hasten to carry out Wulfheard's bidding, and we slink through the open doorway, a fire lighting our path and the smell of a meaty pottage making my belly growl again. 'Icel. It sounds like you've not eaten for a month, not a few days. In future, I suggest you add some oatcakes to your saddlebags. After all, you have a tendency to get caught up in such unexpected expeditions. And your ability to find food in the woodlands is really very poor. I'm embarrassed for you.'

A servant greets us, eyes the dripping mess we leave on the wooden boards, and departs again. She returns with a collection of dry tunics, trews and some cloths to dry ourselves with. While some of the men sleep around the hearth, the room's surprisingly devoid of people. We strip there, and only then seek out the king and Ealdorman Ælfstan.

I'm grateful for the dry clothes as we crest the steep steps to the battlements. It's easy to find the ealdorman and the king. They're not arguing, but their voices are raised in a heated debate. I'm surprised to find Wynflæd beside them. How she's managed the steps is beyond me. She offers me a cursory glance in the yellow glow of the flames where she leans on her walking stick. I'd tell her it was good to see her, but Wulfheard's speaking.

'My lord king, ealdorman, Wynflæd.' Wulfheard inclines his head, and we follow suit.

King Wiglaf appraises me and offers me a smile. The ealdorman notes my seeping cheek with a wince. It must be bad if he can see it in the flickering lamplight. The fact Wynflæd makes no comment assures me she thinks it'll heal despite the ealdorman's worry.

'What's happening?'

'Lundenwic burns,' King Wiglaf announces, directing our attention towards it, even though it's bloody obvious as flames dance in the sky, almost providing enough light to illuminate those standing on the walls.

'At whose hands?' Wulfheard asks, not put off by the king's aggravated tone.

'We don't rightly know, but the Wessex warriors are close to the River Thames, to the east of the River Fleet. They should retreat to their ships, but they won't. It has to be my son,' King Wiglaf decides despondently. 'It can be no one else. King Athelstan of the East Angles has made no move against Mercia. And, we know the Viking raiders are at Sheppey. They couldn't have slipped along the River Thames without being seen.'

'Why would Wigmund burn Lundenwic?'

'Because he's a damn fool,' Wiglaf huffs angrily. I recoil at his tone. When we spoke of his son within the woodlands, he was determined to make him king after his death. It doesn't sound like that's still Wiglaf's intention. He's been betrayed by all who should be loyal to him. I feel some sympathy for him. He's in a truly unenviable position. At least his warriors and ealdormen are loyal – well, all apart from Ealdorman Sigered.

'We suspect,' Ealdorman Ælfstan speaks with less heat, 'he means for us to rush to the aid of the settlement, suspecting it's the work of the Wessex warriors and in that way, he can assume control of Londinium and his mother.'

'But you haven't?' I direct to the king.

'No, and we've no intention of doing so. Ealdorman Tidwulf and Ælfstan have their warriors within Londinium, protecting me

Betrayal of Mercia

and the queen. We also have a good number of people from Lundenwic who sought shelter here.'

'But not everyone?' I look to Wynflæd. She nods.

'No, alas. There are always those who wish to stay behind to protect their homes and businesses. Ealdorman Muca also remained, although we don't know his part in this.'

'What do you plan?' Wulfheard questions.

'That, Wulfheard, is why you find me and Ealdorman Ælfstan here, enjoying a discussion. As well as Wynflæd.'

I consider why she's there. What does she know about the conspiracies around the king she's never shared with me?

'We can't allow Lundenwic to burn?' I question, just to be sure this isn't the king's intention.

'No, we can't. But neither will we risk my warriors fighting whoever supports Lord Wigmund as well as the Wessex force, who hold the ground close to the riverbank. I'm entirely convinced they're in this together. They just wanted the opportunity when King Wiglaf would be in Londonia with his wife, and son, to make this attack a reality. Admittedly, it helps that they believe the king's dead.' Ealdorman Ælfstan announces succinctly. He offers no leeway for us to argue with his deductions. 'The intention has always been to steal Mercia from King Wiglaf. Perhaps this was the point of the conspiracy and their attempts to keep hold of Brihthild. It could all have been intended to bring us to this moment. A few years ago, King Wiglaf escaped from Londonia. The Wessex force means to ensure that doesn't happen this time.'

Once more, I consider why Wynflæd's here. She knows nothing of military actions, other than how to stitch men back together again. As if sensing my interest, she speaks.

'The king invited me to see the view.' She smirks. 'And to tell him all I learned about King Ecgberht and the Wessex warriors when they held Tamworth. The queen, alas, is reluctant to share what she knows about the plans of her allies.' Wynflæd's tone has me considering just what the queen's response to this has been.

'And what is it that you know?' I question, considering how much force might have been used against the queen. I don't think the king would countenance violence against her, but, as I focus on his pensive face, I consider whether necessity might make it inevitable. The queen knows much more than we do, and the king has only recently returned to Londinium. In his absence, the queen might have been prevailed upon by Ealdorman Ælfstan.

'I know more than any of you suspect. Whether King Ecgberht is in the Wessex encampment or it's his son leading the attack, I can tell you he's a man chasing his shadows. He believes in portents and the ancient ways. Some might call them magic, but they're not. He holds much store by charms and their implied power.'

I'm astounded. King Ecgberht presents himself as a good Christian. I've seen the many churches within Winchester, and Canterbury, although admittedly Canterbury has had its churches since the first days of Christianity amongst the Saxons.

'How would that help us?' Wulfheard asks gruffly.

Wynflæd shrugs her narrow shoulders. 'I was asked for my thoughts, not my determination as to how that knowledge can be exploited.'

Wulfheard grumbles, but King Wiglaf holds his hand towards him, cautioning him in how he might respond.

'We should know all we can about our enemy,' Ealdorman Ælfstan confirms. His lips are pensive. The king's uneasy as well.

'Damn bastards,' Cenred complains. He voices what we're all thinking.

I've never liked the queen. She always despised my childhood friend, Edwin, and me for that matter. Perhaps she never liked her husband either. No doubt, she plans to rule through Lord Wigmund. She's held this hope for many years, although it's only just become apparent. Why she'd then welcome interference from Wessex is more difficult to understand. I don't trust anyone from Wessex. Why she would is beyond me. The way I see it, she's risking herself and her son by involving Wessex.

The air's thick with the smell of smoke. I strain, but I can't hear the shrieks of our fellow Mercians. But, if I squint against the brightness, it seems the fires have yet to be controlled. The exterior of Lundenwic burns. At least, I realise, Londinium will struggle to do the same. There's much stone but little wood inside the great walls. Although, the wooden gates are a weakness.

'What does Ealdorman Tidwulf suggest?' Wulfheard breaks the heavy silence.

'He's sleeping,' Ealdorman Ælfstan informs us. I note his unease, and turn to Wynflæd.

'He has a wound to his belly. It'll heal. In time.'

'Bollocks,' Wulfheard expels.

'We have his men. Their loyalty isn't doubted.'

All the same, I'm not alone in turning my eyes back towards the flames outside Lundenwic. What will we find come the morning? I sigh unhappily.

I thought my task was to keep King Wiglaf safe from Wessex, but in the meantime, other enemies have made themselves known and now we fight more than just the Wessex warriors. We must, it seems, fight our fellow Mercians as well.

I shake my head, unhappy and uneasy.

It's such a bloody waste.

It's a dark day for Mercia. She's betrayed from within as well as without.

12

Cuthred wakes me in the morning, from where I've slept in the hall, his young face filled with concern. I sit upright, eyes wincing against the brightness, something tickling my nose unpleasantly. I lift my hand to bat it aside, but Cuthred's there first.

'Leave it,' he orders. I drop my hand, seeing he has his pots and unguents. 'I need to clean it and restitch it,' he offers compassionately, for all he appraises me as though I'm a fine specimen.

'It doesn't hurt,' I mutter, and then regret it as hot water removes the filth and muck. I'm left without an itchy nose and with a piece of my skin flapping just within sight.

'What did you do? Roll in the pigsty?' Cuthred questions.

'I was in the woodlands, nothing else.'

'Well, are there wild boar in there?'

'No. I've hardly slept.'

'Keep still,' he instructs. I'd shrug, but I can feel his fingers prodding my cut, and it bloody hurts.

'Wynflæd said it looked a mess, but wasn't in danger of getting the wound rot. I agree with her. But if we don't do this properly, there's still the possibility.'

'Then do it properly,' I say through tight lips.

'Hold still,' he growls. Around me, I see people busy with their daily tasks. Warriors eat at tables, and the king prowls in and out of my vision. I'm unsure what task he's performing.

No resolution was reached on Londinium's battlements last night other than to see what daylight brought. It felt like the correct decision at the time, but now I itch to do something. Is this what Wulfnoth hoped to accomplish with his meddling, I consider. Complete chaos. It's a pity his death didn't bring such scheming to an end.

'There,' Cuthred announces, later. I've tried not to wince my way through his ministrations. They've certainly been more gentle than Oswy's. Indeed, I'm grateful Oswy hasn't had this task. With what he did to my belly, I dread to think what he'd do to my face, and everyone would see it. It wouldn't just be a joke between him, me and the rest of my fellow warriors.

'Tell me how you got here?' I ask my young friend. Considering what's happening, he seems remarkably unaffected, but then, he has healing to occupy his mind. That will keep other worries from him.

'Ealdormen Tidwulf and Ælfstan ordered us here. We came with what we could carry. We didn't know you'd disappeared with the king, but the path was clear of the enemy, the bridge over the Fleet still in Mercian hands, and so it was thought best to use the stone walls as opposed to the wooden battlements and ditches.'

'You saw the Wessex warriors?'

'Only the back of them. They rushed into the woodland, chasing you, I now know. The rest were kept in position by the king's guards close to the Thames.'

'Is Eahric in command there?'

'No, I'm not, Icel,' and Eahric appears before me. He sports a bruised eye, and can only see through a narrow slit with his left eye, his cheek puffed up and purple and green. I wince in sympathy, as he offers me his hand. I stand. I could do with a piss, but that'll have to wait.

'Who has the command then?'

'At the moment, it's a mix of the king's men and Ealdorman Tidwulf's. Ealdorman Tidwulf's directing affairs from his sickbed.'

Eahric sounds exhausted. I consider if he's just come from night-watch duty, although I didn't see him when we arrived last night.

Cuthred remains, listening to our conversation as he slowly clears away his pots and unguents. I know he could do it much more quickly, but he deserves to hear what's happening.

'At daybreak, ten of the enemy tried to break through. They're dead now.'

'Good,' I reply, pleased to hear there are fewer and fewer Wessex warriors in Mercia.

'Have you seen the king?' Eahric questions.

'He's been in and out of here while Cuthred's been tending to me.'

'He's checking on his horse,' one of the servants offers with a bob. Eahric grins on hearing that, and I confess to being surprised. I expected him to have left the horse to someone else's care with everything happening.

'With me, Icel.'

I follow Eahric to the stables, pretending not to notice Cuthred's attendance. He carries his sack of supplies. I admit he could be going to help the horse, but I doubt it.

The king's voice can be heard before we see him. He might have gone to check on his horse, but something else has angered him now. 'Then find who did it and bring them to me.'

We watch as two of his warriors scamper from the stables, not even speaking to Eahric, their commander, in their haste to be away.

'Bloody fools,' King Wiglaf complains, erupting from where the animals are stabled before we can enter.

'My lord king.' Commander Eahric bows respectfully. Wiglaf must catch sight of me, for he winces in sympathy at whatever Cuthred's done to my face.

'Ah, Eahric,' the king begins. 'Two of your fool men say they've lost the key to the room the queen's being kept within.'

'What?' Eahric startles.

'Yes, they say it's not where it should be.'

'Is the queen contained?'

'They don't know. They've called for her, but there's no reply. I assure you, the stubborn bitch wouldn't say even if she were there.' Any remaining affection the king might have had for his wife has evaporated.

'What will you do?'

'With me,' King Wiglaf instructs us all. 'I'm yet to decide.' He hurries onwards. I follow on, unsure if I'm needed but concerned by this news. We had the queen. She's an important prisoner, even though she won't speak about the plans with Wessex. It must be remembered she tried to kill Brihthild in full sight of everyone.

Has someone enabled her to escape? If she joins with her son, the king will face an even more difficult decision than the one he currently does.

We retrace our steps back to the fort, and I'm almost running to keep up with King Wiglaf, his anger etched into every line of his face, and every movement he makes. Wulfheard eyes me as we sweep past him and joins the grouping, without asking further questions.

We go through the great hall and into the open courtyard, the warriors on guard duty calling to one another so their voices echo between the tall stone walls. The king enters another door – one I'm not sure I've seen before – and hastens down some uneven stone steps. Torchlight gutters smokily on the walls, and the smell of dampness pervades everything. I wrinkle my nose and then regret it because it makes whatever Cuthred's done to my cheek hurt once more.

Light floods a passageway. I turn, startled to find a collection of ancient wooden doors barring other rooms. The wood on some is stained and buckled, and the hinges are decaying, although they're holding for now.

'The storerooms,' Cuthred whispers to me. 'And the prison,' he adds with trepidation.

The space opens up. I see two long benches and a table before them on which a smoking tallow candle sits, pooling over the saucer it sits upon. It offers a glow of yellow light, but it feels as though we're entirely cut off from the daylight.

The guards scamper here and there. There are four of them. Two of them reported to the king. The other two are on all fours, running their hands over the aged and cracked stone floor, questing their fingers in and out of the crevices.

King Wiglaf stamps to one of the doors, the one that's most complete, and bangs on it with his fists.

'Cynethryth, are you in there?' he bellows. 'Answer me, you damn conniving bitch.' But there's no reply. It's too noisy with so many people to determine if anyone breathes on the other side.

King Wiglaf stands back, his features etched into shadows and troughs, and then suddenly Wulfheard appears from behind me, hefting a huge war axe, which he directs towards the door while I scamper out of the way.

There's a loud bang as the blade bounces off the surface of the barred door. Not that Wulfheard stops. His next blow is more successful. A chunk of wood flies into the air, and I'm not alone in ducking to avoid it.

With a huff of frustration, Wulfheard redirects his actions towards the ancient hinges. He hits them with a metallic twang, once, twice, three times, and first the top one springs loose, and then the bottom one. He goes to work on the middle one. There are now so many people within the small space it feels congested. I'm forced to brace myself against the wall to avoid getting in Wulfheard's way.

Eventually, the final hinge falls to the floor. I rush forward to help Wulfheard move the impossibly heavy door aside. The only glimpse I see is of a dark room, rank with the smell of piss and shit, but the king rushes inside, the candle from the guard table in his hand, and then he groans.

'She's not here, and this poor woman is dead in her place.'

For a long moment, no one moves. King Wiglaf's illuminated by the halo from the candle. I see blood on his hands from where he must have checked the woman to see if she breathed.

'When did she enter the room?' Commander Eahric breaks the heavy silence. The four men who were on guard duty stand proudly. They're brave to do so when the king's so wrathful. The four will be on some horrible duty for the rest of their lives after this.

'Her servant was escorted within to tend to the queen's needs and bring her some food.' One of the men is compelled to speak. I look at him, even as my hand reaches for my seax. For a flickering moment, I consider if the queen is here, with us. Could she be hiding somewhere?

Wulfheard stamps to the king's side, and runs his hand over the woman, grief on his rough face. 'She's still warm. This didn't happen long ago.'

I meet his eyes, and immediately I'm pushing my way back

through the press of bodies and up the long stairs. I sense others following on behind. I hear Wulfheard's gruff command that the king should be protected, and then his heavy footsteps echo mine, as do others. Abruptly, Commander Eahric and the king have realised what this means.

'Wait, Icel,' Wulfheard orders me, but I don't, dashing back up the stairs to emerge, blinking into the light. I look into the corners of the open courtyard around the high fort, but she isn't there.

Hastily, I rush back inside the main building, through the great hall to emerge, blinking once more, close to the gateway.

Oswy and Maneca are no longer on guard duty, but others of Ealdorman Ælfstan's men are.

'Goðemon, Waldhere,' I huff. 'Has anyone come this way?'

'What?' They turn surprised eyes to look at me. I quickly realise why. The gate's locked up tight. After all, why would they open it when, even from here, I can smell the smoke from the fires burning close to Lundenwic and hear the Wessex encampment?

'No one?' I ask, just to be sure. 'The queen has killed her servant and escaped. Be on your guard.'

Goðemon looks shocked. 'Those warriors will be in the shit up to their arseholes,' he offers, tightening his hand into a fist. I know he's not alone in considering what he'd do to the queen if she were unfortunate enough to find us now.

'Where will she go?' I think aloud. Goðemon and Waldhere are correct. She won't be getting out of this doorway. Londinium, as I appreciate well enough, is hardly bursting with easy ways to escape. Of course, there's the hole in the drainage system I once used, but I can't see the queen even knowing where that is. And it's been filled, as far as I know, to ensure the enemy can't use that to steal Londinium away from under our noses.

That leaves only one place.

'The river gate,' I growl. Wulfheard's joined me, as has Oswy, sleep-tousled and roused from his bed. He has a face that could kill a fart, let alone the damn queen.

'Get the horses,' Wulfheard orders, running towards the stables.

Godemon and Waldhere startle forward as though they'll be coming with us.

'Stay here, and keep those damn gates shut,' Wulfheard orders over his shoulder. More and more of Ealdorman Ælfstan's warriors and those of Commander Eahric stream through the small gateway. I shake my head at the sight of two men trying to fit through the narrow doorway at the same time – bloody fools.

'One at a time,' I urge them, hurrying to follow Wulfheard to Bicwide.

I hope the horse has recovered. He's only had as much rest as I have. Already, my limbs feel heavy. They've not had time to rejuvenate. I need to eat more and sleep. The bloody treacherous queen is determined that won't happen.

'Come on, boy,' I encourage Bicwide, grateful to see his saddle close by. I slip it on and quickly tighten the buckles, mindful he was asleep when I ran inside the building. He eyes me drowsily, the soft brush of his hay-scented breath over my aching cheek. 'I know. We rescued the king. But now we need to hunt the bloody queen.'

And then my eyes fall on Wiglaf's horse. Or rather, where it should be.

'Where's the king's horse?' I call, suddenly frantic. 'Has the queen taken it?'

From the fort, the shouts and cries of men being informed about what's happened are easily heard. I also detect shrieks from some of the women, no doubt being rudely searched to ensure they're not the queen, hiding in plain sight.

'The king's horse?' I roar over the ruckus. 'Where is it? Has the queen taken it?'

'Bollocks,' Wulfheard explodes, finally hearing me. 'She'll be ahead of us. Perhaps there's a ship waiting for her at the river gate. We need to hurry.'

Wulfheard directs Bada towards the entrance, and quickly thunders to a gallop. I'm just about to follow when Cuthred erupts before me. He reaches for one of the horses as well, moving with far more ease around the animal than when we first journeyed to Worcester, what feels like years ago but was barely a few weeks past.

I don't order Cuthred to remain behind. We need everyone looking for the queen. But then, I spare a thought for Wynflæd. Cuthred's quick to reassure me.

'Don't worry, Icel. King Wiglaf's beaten you to it. Wynflæd's with him, Ealdorman Tidwulf and the king's guards. Nothing will happen to her.'

'My thanks,' I call, emerging into the daylight. I leap into the saddle, wincing at the burn in the back of my calves from such a movement, and hasten to follow Wulfheard. I spare a glance behind me. Men and women rush everywhere. No one's exempt from searching or being searched. It's chaos. Bicwide ploughs through a collection of clucking hens, and then I'm on the old roadway that leads towards the ruined stone building, where the forest of defaced and broken statues are a stark testament to the death of the Romans, or Giants, as Wulfheard would have me believe.

The treasonous queen might have gone there, but I can't think what she'd hope to accomplish by doing so. No one could come to her assistance. Ealdorman Sigered and her son are in Lundenwic. No, she'll be trying to find a means of escape, and the only place that could be possible is at the quayside, I'm sure of it.

I bend low over Bicwide. Other, faster horses quickly overtake us, Oswy's amongst them.

'Hurry up, Icel. You'll miss it all,' he calls, but I don't encourage Bicwide to go faster. Oswy's horse has had more rest, and he's foolish to push the animal. There are any number of disturbed cobbles and gaping holes in the long-abandoned road. I'm not going to allow Bicwide to wound himself. The fleeing queen will be there. I can't see where else she could go.

I consider whether she means to swim the River Thames. Will she escape Mercia for Wessex? There may even be a ship waiting for her. Although, how they'd know to rescue her today, I'm unsure. There are guards on the quayside; I remember Oswy telling me last night. The buildings might have almost all burned to ash when we reclaimed Londinium from the Wessex warriors, but the opening to the river must still be protected. There's no point in maintaining the fort inside Londinium, with its huge wooden gate protecting those within, if there are other means of gaining entry.

Bicwide's sure-footed as he ambles on. Here, the smell is dank with the River Walbrook that courses through the interior of Londinium. Once more, I'm struck by how few trees there are and also by the ruin of the place. Considering what's happened with Lundenwic, perhaps it would be better for the people to live here. Maybe they should even open up access to the quayside. Not that it's my concern for today.

Today, we hunt Mercia's poisonous queen, who thinks only of endangering her kingdom, happy to involve its ancient enemy, Wessex, in that. What a bitch she's turned out to be.

Not that I haven't always suspected it ever since the day she laughed at Edwin. As a queen, she has always lacked the very elements that make men and women loyal to King Wiglaf. She has no compassion, and no bloody loyalty.

13

By the time Bicwide and I reach the river gate, pushing our way through the heavily guarded gateway and onto the wooden and stone quays, the place is filled with Mercian warriors. Four of the guards on duty there stand shocked as someone explains what we're doing. Even Cuthred's caught up with me. I seek out Wiglaf's horse, but can't see it.

'Have you seen a mounted rider?' I demand from the confused men, but they shrug. 'Order others to look for the king's horse. I believe the queen took it. If we find the horse, we might find her,' I instruct the guards.

Oswy and Wulfheard have abandoned their horses, reins tied high, to make their way onto what remains of the stone quayside, running along the foreshore of Londinium, to almost where the River Fleet joins the Thames, if not for the huge walls encircling the interior. I turn to Cuthred. He nods with resignation as I hand him Bicwide's reins.

'Take care of the horses,' I urge him. 'Do you have your seax?' I'm fearful the queen might slip through the melee unheeded, if she's bold enough to take the risk.

'I do, yes.' He shows it to me. I also note he wears his cloak.

'If she comes at you, don't engage her. Shout to us. Protect yourself and the horses,' I command him, already bounding away to follow where the Mercian warriors have gone. My exhaustion has disappeared in the wake of my fury.

The entranceway to the quayside has been filled with a heavy-looking set of wooden doors since my time inside the settlement, when I had to cast aside my Mercian heritage and pretend to be a Wessex warrior. They've been swung open on one side to allow us through, but the other side remains closed. I glance around. There are no women here. If the queen comes this way, she'll be easy to see. Unless, of course, she's traded clothes with someone else. Having seen the results of her attack on the servant sent to tend to her, I suspect the queen is capable of anything. I don't yet know what killed the servant, but whatever it was, the attack was brutal and fatal. It appears that having attacked Brihthild so violently, the queen has no compunction about her actions any more.

I step through the gateway and, instantly, I'm buffeted by a strong breeze that the huge walls of Londinium have been repulsing on my flight through the centre of the settlement. I twist so my back faces the wind, gasping to breathe deeply, and only then turn back to where I can see Oswy, Wulfheard and others striding along the remains of the mostly heavily worn stones of the quayside. There are one or two wooden stumps, sticking up from the opaque mass of the River Thames. Once upon a time, they must have supported huge lengths of wood, extending the reach even further along the walls and, indeed, into the river itself. I duck my chin low, holding my hand before my mouth so I can breathe, while also shielding my wounded cheek. My cloak streams behind me, my long hair falling into my eyes. I'm grateful for my thick beard. It's supposed to be summer, but the wind holds the threat of rain.

My eyes water with the force of the wind. More than once I blink away what I assume are pieces of ash from the fires. I stride onwards, determined to find Mercia's treasonous queen.

Not content with wounding me when she attacked Brihthild, she's killed another as well. I fear she'll stop at nothing to achieve her ends of betraying Mercia. A slither of worry worms its way down my back that the king's warriors are all here, seeking his wife, only to remember Cuthred's assurance that Wynflæd's with the king and Ealdorman Tidwulf. They're all being protected by Commander Eahric's loyal warriors, oath-sworn directly to the king.

Still, as I move along the remains of the stone wall, being careful not to let the wind tumble me backwards into the river, I see no sight of the queen. No one else calls to say they've found her either. I don't know where she'll hide, if she makes it this far. The queen of Mercia isn't going to be used to hiding in muddy holes, exposed to the wind, and rain. The dark clouds are descending, making it difficult to see, as the River Thames turns from a menacing grey to a dank black, mirroring what lies above it.

'This is bloody useless,' I hear Oswy shout against the wind, as he catches me. The spring in his step from hunting the queen has long since evaporated.

'She has to be here, somewhere,' I urge. Admittedly, she could be hiding anywhere within the ruins of Londinium. But if she's doing that, how does she hope to escape? The walls are too high for anyone to risk climbing them alone. Even those areas where they might be slightly ruined have, I've been told before, been rebuilt, even if haphazardly. Maintaining the height of the walls was what was important, not how it was brought about.

Even taking the king's lame horse wouldn't necessarily aid her unless she's made it to the foreshore in advance of us. Not, of course, that she'd know the animal was lame. I gaze around, seeking out gaps in the walls, other than those guarded by the new doorway. I squint, and consider where they might be. It's possible she might have found another way to escape. The walls are certainly taller from the outside than within.

'Where?' Oswy huffs angrily. He's turned to peer back the way we've come, his face almost blue with the cold. He's standing right in my way, as I sweep the exterior of the tall defences, and further round, to where the western wall projects into the river itself. My eyes narrow. Something catches my attention.

'There.' I point. He turns, squinting where I'm looking, but shakes his head.

'It's a bloody big bird, nothing else,' he states, seeing what I do but dismissing it quickly.

But I'm not so convinced. Carefully, for what remains of the foreshore is precarious at best, I continue onwards, trying to see if it is a bird, a flapping cloak or even hair. It doesn't help that the further along I step, the closer and closer I come to the Wessex encampment on the far side of the projecting wall. I can't reach it. I'm sure of that because the remains of the wall extend into the river, but I can smell their cook fires, the wind bringing fitful smoke towards me, as well as the scent of pottage being cooked.

Does the queen think to escape that way? Surely not. Does she not know the walls of Londinium spread out into where the river runs deep? There's no way around it, not unless she risks slipping into the water. Would she swim? Can she swim? I wouldn't want to swim it, and I have swum the Thames before. It's not as though she could bring the king's horse here and use it to aid her, as we've done. It would never make it over the uneven stones. And the guards at the gateway would have surely seen her.

'Icel,' Oswy barks, his intention to call me back obvious in the censure in his voice. But I beckon him towards me. I sense his huff of frustration. He comes all the same. 'What?' His word is flecked with fury at my stubbornness.

'Over there.' Once more, he looks to where I point. I don't take my eyes from what I've seen. It's not a bird. I'm sure of that. It's something flapping in the stiff breeze.

'Bloody hell,' he huffs, striding onwards, not looking where he steps. I suppress a smirk that he's changed his opinion so quickly. But the riverbank path grows even more narrow and perilous. I wish I wore my byrnie, but equally, I'm pleased I don't. If I lose my balance here, on the slick rocks we're forced to step onto, festooned with green slippery muck, I'll tumble into the water. I don't think I'd make it back to the surface again if I had slipped my byrnie over my head.

Oswy's in front. Belatedly realising the peril he's in, he assesses each step carefully, making sure not to fall. For all he's older, and bulkier than me, he seems to jump onwards. My progress is much slower. My arms windmill around me more than once as I struggle for balance. I curse myself for seeing what I saw, even as we draw nearer.

How, I consider, could the queen, a woman old enough to be my mother, have made it so far along slippery rocks and treacherous footings? Perhaps only sheer stubbornness has forced her to this. And desperation.

What Oswy thought was a bird is nothing of the sort. It's a cloak trapped between rocks close to the wall jutting into the river. The swirl of the water below my feet is dark and impenetrable, the rain making our passage even more perilous as it's hard to see and the rocks are becoming even more slippery. Oswy reaches the strip of cloth first and bends to collect it into his hands. I join him, huffing heavily, my toes spread as wide as possible in my boots to keep my balance. They're still wet from yesterday's crossing of the Fleet.

The stink here is overpowering. The water hasn't been high enough to carry away all the detritus thrown from behind Londinium's walls, or just wedged in the crevices of protruding stones. The wall's stained with the white shit of birds sitting atop it and the dead who've fallen from their perches. The odour is worse than the tanners' pits.

'It is a cloak,' Oswy confirms, unable to cover his surprise. I swallow. It's a good cloak, no doubt worn by one of the queen's special servants.

'Where is she?' I huff, reaching out to run my hand along the twice-dyed fabric as dark as day-old blood.

'She must be close,' Oswy confirms, squinting into the gloom. He turns back the way we've come, beckoning others to join us. I don't risk it. I know I'll fall, and I don't much want a bruised knee or, worse, another crack for my battered head. I've not long since stopped seeing double from my last injury. 'Although, how the hell she made it so far, I just don't know. She should have slipped into the river. Perhaps she has,' he says hopefully, peering down.

Recovering my breath, I don't answer him. For now, it's just me and him, some bloody slippery rocks, the smell of bird shit, and an abandoned cloak. But, I sense eyes watching me. The queen, wherever she is, is close. I'm sure of it. Like Wulfheard, I'm astounded by the risks she's taken, but she was prepared to imperil all to endanger Mercia's kingship. Perhaps this is nothing in comparison.

Slowly, I scan the area, turning my head, not my body. The day turns even darker. I have to squint to see anything aside from the dirty white of the standing stone wall, jutting into the River Thames. The sound of the rain drumming on the water, the wind rushing through my hair, it all serves to make it impossible to hear anything else.

'Why would she remove her cloak?' I murmur. Oswy's not moved on. We stand together. I imagine we look like some strange two-headed bird from a distance.

'She needs to stay hidden,' Oswy announces. 'Or she didn't mean to, and it's slipped away from her back and she's not thought to retrieve it.'

My thoughts are a tumbling riot in my mind. The queen is here, somewhere. How does she mean to escape? Who could even know she'd make it here? It's so ill-thought-out. She risks her life again, or perhaps that's her intention. Does she mean to die at her own hand, and not that of the king and his justice?

'What's she doing here?' I muse softly.

At the same time, Wulfheard and I make the connection.

Above the thrum of the increasing rain, the slurping sounds of the river, the heavy slap of a poorly timed oar over the river draws my eye.

'There.' I point again. Where the river wall protruding into the Thames ends, almost in the middle of the river, I see a figure dressed in a pale dress, one so pale it's almost impossible to see against the dirty white of the wall. The figure's huddled against the stone, gripping tightly, keen to stay hidden. I know then why she discarded the cloak. It would have flapped in the strong wind, attracting the eyes of those who pursue her. Better if the dress she wore blended into the wall.

I can't see the queen's face, because her back is to us, but I know it's her all the same. No one else would be here.

The boat the oar belongs to wallows in the current. It's not too far from her, but she's stopped moving, evidently determined not to draw our attention. That's failed. The boat's arrival has given her away.

'Be careful,' I call to Oswy as he sprints away from me, seemingly ambivalent to the real threat that he might slip or fall into the river, tumbling from the slick rocks. 'Bloody hell,' I glower, overbalancing just looking at him. From behind, other voices come closer, but they won't make it before the boat reaches the queen.

With a swift prayer that I won't fall into the river fully dressed, I hurry to follow Oswy. If he reaches the queen first, I can only imagine what he'll do to her. He served her for many years, and his memories of that time aren't fond.

My eyes firmly on where I need to place my feet, I stumble and correct myself and then manage to keep upright for a good few paces. The stone footings of the wall here are thankfully clear of the slippery green slime. I sense I'm gaining. I don't look at the boat. I focus only on where Oswy has gone on ahead. We need to reach the queen before she gets in that boat. I don't know who's sent it but we must retain our hold on her. Only then can we find out who within Londinium has betrayed the king by aiding the queen.

With my seax slapping against my thigh, my feet finding some bounce in them, I scurry as quickly as I dare. I follow Oswy. His movements have gone from tottering from one foot to another, to almost leaping as he descends closer to the river, and the perilous ledge on which the queen stands. I wince, fearing he'll fall into the water, even while hurrying to follow him.

The boat now emerges fully from the gloom of the rain clouds. I fear I'm not going to reach the queen before the boat gets to her. But Oswy will.

Queen Cynethryth's voice carries to me on the wind. Now she's been sighted, there's no need to hide. 'Hurry up,' she calls frantically, but the reply's snatched on the wind.

It's getting more and more dangerous. The few pieces of stone

Oswy and I try to balance on are becoming so widely spaced I almost can't leap to reach them, and I'm a tall man. Water coats those rocks that remain. Any moment now, I fear I'll fall. I stamp down on that thought. To think it is to have it happen.

'Hurry up,' the queen repeats more frantically. Oswy's almost close enough to clasp her in his arms. But there are four men on that small boat. Two of them are in control of the oars, powering their way through the slurping river water. Another stands, beckoning the queen onwards towards them. Yet another holds a blade in his hand. Of everything here, it catches a stray blast of sunlight, illuminating it. These men mean to kill to protect Mercia's disgraced queen.

I don't know if they're Mercians or from Wessex.

'Grab her,' I huff, wishing I could shout louder, but my breath burns in my throat. And then I mistime my next step. I plunge into the water, arms windmilling all around me. The vile green tendrils of rank-smelling seaweed cover me as I'm sucked beneath the deep water. I'm almost in the middle of the River Thames, so of course it's bloody deep.

My mouth fills with foul-tasting water. I feel myself struggling against the current and the weight of my clothes. My boots are filled with water, dragging me down. I kick out, once, twice. My head surfaces. I gasp for breath. My arms reach around me, attempting to find something to grip hold of, but my hands, so cold I can hardly feel them, slip off the stone I grip, and I'm floundering again.

My head goes under once more. The shock of the cold water running over my cut cheek makes me want to cry out with pain. I keep my mouth clamped shut, wishing the horrible sensation of water running up my nose wasn't muddling my thoughts.

I need to get out of the water fast. My feet kick something solid behind me. I use it to rear upwards again. This time, my right hand manages to grab something. I can't make sense of what it is, but I'm grateful for it. I pull and pull, bringing my left hand to it and surging out of the water to lie, half of my body out of the water, the other half in it. I look like a bloody seal taking its ease, as I gasp in much-needed air.

I lift my head, but I'm too low to see how Oswy's doing. My ears are filled with water. I can hear little. Gritting my teeth, muttering to myself beneath my breath, I bring my knees beneath me. The rock I'm perched on is exposed and yet seems to have been placed here purposefully. There's even the remnants of some water-fouled chain, more orange with rust than silver, which has allowed me to escape from the embrace of the frigid River Thames.

Oswy's cries finally permeate my hearing. I struggle to my feet, gasping and shivering, the rain heavier, but it's not as though I can get bloody wetter.

Oswy's engaged in a struggle with the bladed man. He shoves the queen behind him, to ensure she can't reach the violently rocking boat, but two men fight him. He can't continue like this forever.

'Bloody hell, Icel,' Cenred huffs, appearing beside me, eyes wild with shock.

'Help him,' I pant while pointing. He struggles onwards, leaving me. I concentrate on breathing, calming my thudding heart, and only then continue, keeping as close to the ledge of the bottom of the wall as possible.

Cenred joins Oswy, but neither man is safe. I shiver, so cold I bite my lower lip without realising until I taste blood. The queen remains behind Oswy, but she's fighting as well. In her hands, she carries something that flashes redly, the damn bitch. Did she use that to kill her servant? And if she did, where did she get it from?

I don't look behind. My gaze is only on the queen and those

who mean to rescue her from Londinium. Who intend to release her from the king's incarceration. Who don't wish her to have to answer for her crimes against Mercia. And against Brihthild and me.

I eye the boat as I get close enough to see the two men within it. I blink away the rain's deluge and recognise them as allies of Ealdorman Sigered. Damn the arsehole. They're standing, as though to aid their collaborators fighting Oswy and Cenred, and with absolutely no thought for my safety, I launch myself into the boat, unbalancing it so that it lurches alarmingly from side to side, threatening to dunk me again, and also to knock them into the water. One of the oars slides into the river; the boat bounces on the rope being used to keep it close to where the other two men fight. Seax in my hand, I point at both of my enemies.

'This isn't your fight, you bumbling bastard,' one of them shrieks. He's not only one of Ealdorman Sigered's men, he's his bloody nephew, Sigegar. I whip my seax blade before him. He rears backwards, knocking into the backside of the other man who's desperately trying to claw back the sinking oar. Losing his balance, he lands with a wet splash in the water, his scream of terror cut off with a watery gurgle. I slice open Sigegar's tunic with my seax. He shrieks like a child. I move to press the point, determined to end this, but Oswy's commanding voice stays my hand.

'We've got her, Icel. No need to kill any more of the bloody arseholes.'

I grimace, shivering, and retract my blade. But Sigegar comes at me, a seax blade in his hand, panic on his cold face. I dodge the sweeping cut he tries to land on me, but it sends the boat wobbling once more, as I skip to the side of Sigegar. The next I know, Cenred's landed a heavy blow to Sigegar's head with his fist. Sigegar drops into the bilge water, and I face Cenred, blowing hard, trying to stay upright as the boat wobbles ever more precariously as the man who fell into the water attempts to clamber back on board.

'You really do make these things difficult for yourself,' Cenred mutters, bending to tie Sigegar's unresponsive hands together with a handy piece of rough rope.

'My thanks,' I gasp, but the only reply is a huff as he also leans over and grabs the other man, pulling him onto the boat with much speed and no care for his person. Perhaps I shouldn't be surprised to recognise Eadbald, the man who denounced Lord Coenwulf with the queen's connivance. It appears Eadbald was being kept hidden, until needed by the queen.

'Come on then, you bastards,' Oswy growls, the queen unceremoniously dumped in the bilge water alongside Sigegar and Eadbald. She strains against the rope binding her. I look for the final man, but he's unmoving. He's clearly dead, as is the other man who first faced Oswy. 'Now, how are we to get back to the quayside?' Oswy calls, grimacing, realising we only have one bloody oar, as the other one is caught by the current out of reach unless we fancy another swim, which I don't.

I shake from the cold and wet of my clothes, scowling at the surviving men who thought to rescue the queen. She shrieks like a vixen, defiant even though she's been captured once more. I scowl at the noise which makes my head pound again.

'We need another oar,' I complain through clenched teeth. Pushed away from the river wall by Oswy, the boat swirls around uselessly.

'Then someone better find the other one,' Oswy glowers. Cenred huffs, stands and slides into the water, six powerful strokes taking him to where the oar is spinning.

'Here,' he calls, throwing it within the boat, so that it lands on Sigegar's head. If he was conscious, it would probably have hurt. I stand unsteadily and pull Cenred within the boat. As Oswy still refuses to row, the pair of us settle on the rowing bench, and slowly, agonisingly slowly, as I shiver and shudder, the exercise doing nothing to warm me, we begin to make our way back to the quayside.

Damn the bloody queen of Mercia.

14

It takes longer to return to the quayside than it did to reach the queen. My arms strain with the unfamiliar motion, not assisted by the less-than-helpful comments from those who line the haphazard path along the riverbank we wove to reach her. They cheer us on. Well, perhaps cheer isn't quite the right word for what they're doing. Taunting is perhaps better. They're watching us make a mess of it.

'Row together, you arseholes.' Commander Eahric's voice reaches me over the sound of everyone else, where he stands on the riverbank, but too far away to help us. 'Not like that,' he continues, as Cenred's oar dips low while mine is out of the water, causing us to spin in a nauseating circle, despite having two oars. 'Together, one two, one two, in out, in out.' Cenred glowers at me, and I scowl at him.

'Arsehole,' Cenred mutters. I'd say something a little less pleasant, but I'm trying to keep to the rhythm Eahric's shouting, and it's bloody hard. We don't want to dash ourselves against the rocky outcroppings making this part of the riverfront so inhospitable to boats, although birds love them. Neither do we want to be caught by the river's surging current which would take us towards the far-distant sea. I'd sooner be taking my chance with the perilous passage we took to reach the queen than wobbling along in the small boat. Not, I appreciate, that it would have been possible with our prisoners.

Sitting in the bilge water, we're greeted with sullen eyes. Sigegar's still somewhat out of it, his eyes closed although he's groaning. Queen Cynethryth strains against her bindings, her hair dishevelled, her pale dress sodden with rain and river water. Oswy sits on the other bench, watching the queen so closely he's almost leering into her face. None of us mean to lose her again. She's caused more than enough problems. All the same, I'm amazed by her bravery – or perhaps desperation. I'd expect her to be crying, or sobbing, but instead, her face is filled with hatred, and her eyes glower at those who were meant to protect her. She mutters at them, but I don't listen to her complaints, which fall heavier than the rain. At least she's stopped shrieking.

The boat shudders unpleasantly beneath our feet.

'This is bloody impossible,' I huff with frustration. I've rowed before, towards the Isle of Sheppey and the Viking raiders there. Why this is so difficult, I don't know. The river's being a contrary bastard today. The boat sits low in the water with so many inside it, threatening to sink lower every time it moves. Water occasionally laps over the side, adding to the weight, and dampness stretches along my feet and lower legs, adding to the misery of my waterlogged and too-tight tunic.

'The boat's too heavy. We should throw two of them overboard,' Oswy calls, occasioning shrieks of terror from the men. Eahric continues to shout from the riverbank, his advice aiding me, although I'll never tell him that.

My hands are aching, and I'm cold from my dip in the water, while hot from my exertions. I really have had enough. We're not out of trouble yet, even if we've managed to recapture the queen, and will be feted by the king. That moment of triumph seems far away, almost impossible. My wounded cheek itches, almost to distraction. I grip the oar tight to stop myself scratching it.

A sharp crack draws my attention. The boat veers alarmingly, and Cenred offers me a sickly smile, with only half an oar still in his hands.

'Bollocks,' he offers in dismay.

'Bloody wonderful.' I redouble my efforts now we only have one oar once more, but all that happens is that we drift further into the centre of the river, caught by the current, spinning lazily.

There's a cry from the quayside, where the single wooden jetty juts out into the wide river, offering the opportunity for many ships to be tied there. Commander Eahric pushes his way through to the front of those waiting for our arrival. A heavy thud hits the boat, only just missing the queen's head. Oswy stands to grab the rope, wrapping his hands around it and bracing himself to pull, while the boat wobbles. Quickly, I join him, abandoning my oar. It won't get us back to dry land. We hold tight as everyone on the quayside is tasked with pulling us in.

Eventually, we get close enough that Commander Eahric and his warriors reach across and hold us steady against the quayside, so we can extract our prisoners from the interior of the small boat. Cenred forces the queen upright. She stands haughtily, hands bound before her, face white with cold, eyes blazing with fury. Commander Eahric and Wulfheard take control of her, one to either side so she can't try and escape, risking her death in the river.

King Wiglaf watches her, disgust on his soaked face, the drumming of this unseasonal rain loud on the surrounding water. He's been forced to confront what she is, but this is a fresh betrayal. She's tried to kill, and now she has killed. What else, I shudder with cold, is she capable of doing? It's a sign of how long it's taken us to row back that the king has been summoned from the fort.

'Take her back to a locked room,' King Wiglaf orders. 'Ensure she has dry clothes. She'll live to account for her crimes. Let no one inside without four armed guards.' Commander Eahric nods at the king, as those on the jetty move aside to let the procession through.

I turn back to the task of handing over the prisoners. Eadbald's lifted upwards to stand on shaking legs, and a flash of recognition on the king's face assures me he knows who he is. The king's eyes have fallen on Ealdorman Sigered's nephew, Sigegar.

'I assume your uncle is involved in this,' the king spits angrily, although he stands back to allow more of Commander Eahric's men to do their work in taking the prisoners away. 'Take him to another of the locked rooms. Separate him from the queen, and his ally,' he orders.

Finally, with our prisoners dispatched towards the fort, Oswy, Cenred and I are helped ashore by the strong arms of those who've not been rowing so fiercely.

'What do we do with the boat?' one of the men questions.

'You can sink it for all I care,' Oswy counters aggressively, but Ealdorman Ælfstan has other ideas.

'Tie it up, closer to the riverbank. We might need it. Well done,' he offers the three of us. 'We found the king's horse. It was abandoned close to where the Walbrook joins the Thames. There's a small gap in the wall. She must have fled through it. But, by the time we found it, you already had the queen. The animal's been returned to the stables. The king rides my horse instead.'

I shiver, and Ealdorman Ælfstan must see it.

'Get yourselves indoors and warmed up. No one's going anywhere at the moment.'

On feet so cold I can hardly feel them, I trudge through the even more heavily guarded gate and meet my horse. Bicwide eyes me aghast, but I clamber onto his back anyway. Cuthred's filled with questions, but I see him bite his tongue.

He's learning, for which I'm also grateful.

Once more, we're greeted with a rippling cheer from those who didn't leave the fort to hunt out the queen as we return to the stables. The king has already gone on ahead.

I slide from Bicwide's back, grateful Cuthred offers to tend to him, and hurry inside. This unseasonably cold summer is doing me no favours. The fire has been built high inside the hall, and heat washes over me. Immediately, my face starts to itch even more, and I'm desperate to remove my clothes. I lift my hand to scratch my cheek, but Wynflæd appears, her firm grip stopping it.

'There's enough Thames water in there to give you the yellow disease and wound rot,' she grumbles. She comes close but then moves aside. 'You stink like it, as well.' She doesn't offer any other sympathy.

Aware I'm not going to get any warmer in my wet clothes, I look around for something with which to cover my body. A servant hurries towards me, a cloak in her hand. I wrap it around my neck, and then with hands grown so cold as to almost not move, I remove my weapons belt, trews and boots. A swell of cold water rushes over the floor. Wynflæd moves aside with a scowl, although Oswy and Cenred are not in a much better condition.

'You could have done that outside,' she mutters. But I'm too busy shivering to argue with her. I lower the cloak and wrap it around my waist before removing my tunic and then lift it around my chest as well. I'm aware that as cold as I am, the cock-pricked shape on my belly will be visible to all. I hurry to cover it, and then accept another cloak from the servant, who gathers my wet clothes together with a grimace.

'Apologies,' I call. She shakes her head but says nothing else. Beneath both cloaks I'm naked but I am starting to warm up.

'I've laid the dead woman out. She didn't deserve such a death,' Wynflæd comments when I settle. I'm reminded of how the queen managed to escape.

'She shouldn't have done that,' I growl.

'I never knew her to be so keen to murder,' Wynflæd agrees, voice rich with dismay. A hot bowl of pottage is placed into my hands, Wynflæd sneaking one as well. 'No one will stand as her oath-helper now. All have seen her crimes for what they are. Her ambitions, and desperation to see them fulfilled, have placed her on a path from which there's no return. The king will not see her executed for such crimes, but he should.'

I listen to the sounds of the fort, aware of heavy doors slamming below ground. The queen and her erstwhile allies have been imprisoned. I hope the locks and hinges are good enough to keep everyone contained.

'The king wants an attack on the Wessex force in the morning,' Wynflæd informs us. 'He ordered it as soon as he returned to the fort.'

'The encampment or Lundenwic?' Oswy questions.

'Both,' Cuthred pipes up. He's also been given a bowl of pottage and eats it with the same relish as Wynflæd. If he gets any taller, he won't be able to enter any building within Tamworth without knocking himself out on the wooden supports.

'It's for the best,' Ealdorman Ælfstan confirms, entering the room alone. He glances around, notes who's there and who isn't, and sits with us. He holds his hands towards the fire. The sound of the heavy rainfall is clearly audible, and the room seems to be filled with steam as we all dry off after our forays outside.

'What's happening with the queen?' Oswy questions.

'Nothing yet. She's been found a new prison, with a strong lock and decent hinges. And five men standing guard outside it. For now, the king's more interested in Ealdorman Sigered's nephew and Eadbald, although Sigegar is the most weak-willed. He's been singing like a bird, blaming the rescue attempt on his uncle. Says he was told to get the queen or his uncle would disinherit him.'

'And how did the queen get word to them that she intended to escape?'

'Eadbald's been here all along, masquerading as one of the king's warriors, and therefore, able to move with more freedom than anyone else. He made his way to Lundenwic as soon as he'd spoken to the queen when she was captured, and the king still missing. He sought out Ealdorman Sigered, his oath-sworn lord, with news of how the queen intended to escape, or at least that's what Sigegar's saying. Eadbald's shut his mouth tighter than a clam.'

'So what happened to the key to the room?' I muse. Although it seems the least of our problems, it's annoying me that we've not found it.

'The queen had it. She pocketed it on escaping, forgetting it needed to be left behind so as to not arouse suspicion until she was next due to be fed.'

'And the guards?'

'They saw a woman leaving the queen's prison, just as they expected to do. They didn't look more closely than that.'

Silence falls between us all. I'm exhausted and itchy. I might have warm clothes, and the feeling might have been restored to my feet, but my cheek wound is pulsing in pain.

'So, now what?' Oswy eventually questions.

'As Wynflæd said, tomorrow we beat back the Wessex

warriors to their side of the River Thames. Once that's accomplished, the king will turn his attention to his queen, his son, and Ealdorman Sigered's involvement in all this.' The words are ominous, but of course, we need to triumph against the Wessex warriors before the queen's trial can be resumed. That's never as easy as we'd like.

15

'Bloody hell, it's cold,' Oswy moans beside me. It's still dark outside. King Wiglaf has ordered his warriors to be prepared for a dawn attack. Beneath me, Bicwide's as sleep-addled as I am. I'm not at all sure I'll be able to accomplish a great deal. I shake my head. Not even the bite of the bitter wind is waking me up, or the complaint from my newly bandaged cheek following yesterday's exertions and dip in the River Thames.

'Stop your bitching,' Kyre calls. He shouldn't be here, preparing to fight, not after the wounds he took only a few weeks ago battling his way out of Canterbury, but Kyre wasn't allowing anyone to stop him after he was denied the opportunity to join the hunt for me and King Wiglaf. Not even Wynflæd's dire warnings about doing too much too soon would keep him in his bed. And they were very dire.

'You stop your bloody bitching,' Oswy counters aggressively.

'Both of you stop your bitching,' Wulfheard orders in a tight voice.

Everyone's grumpy and, no doubt, fearful of what the day will bring. We need to win two battles today. I'm not convinced we have the men for it, but the king has determined we must strike, and soon. If the Wessex warriors are allowed to remain on Mercian land for much longer, I imagine he sees a repeat of events from six summers ago. King Ecgberht will not have the chance to declare himself as Mercia's king once more.

'Quiet, all of you,' Commander Eahric commands, his voice floating to us from where he waits, closest to the sealed gate. He'll lead his forces across the bridge that spans the River Fleet towards Lundenwic. We'll be attacking the encampment close to the River Thames on this side of the River Fleet, with the aid of Ealdorman Tidwulf's warriors.

I hardly think we've been quiet. If the Wessex warriors have half a thought in their heads, they'll know our intentions by now. It's not as though braziers and sentry fires don't light the space behind Londinium's barred gates, throwing up flickering shapes that cast people in and out of light and shadow.

King Wiglaf has been denied the chance to join us. It took a great deal of persuasion from Ealdorman Ælfstan and then an order from Ealdorman Tidwulf's sickbed. Instead, he has command of the garrison inside Londinium, at the fort and down at the quayside. The gap in the wall where the Walbrook joins the River Thames the queen used to escape has been blocked with available pieces of wood and stone. I've not seen it, but I've been assured it's now impassable. There are only two ways in and out of Londinium, and they're heavily guarded. When we leave here, the gates will be barred behind us. The Wessex warriors will not be allowed inside Londinium. Those within Londinium will be safe, but we must aid those trapped in Lundenwic.

I bend and rub a comforting hand along Bicwide's wide neck, flexing my fingers in the new gloves that have been found for me. He's a good horse, but I don't welcome riding him into this fight. I hope to dismount as soon as possible, but speed is important. We need to crash into the Wessex encampment close to the Thames before they can attempt to escape across the river, or rush to their allies we know are attacking Lundenwic. We'll cut off the warriors from one another. The only thing I can see that could go wrong is if the warriors seeking King Wiglaf in the woodlands remain close. We don't know if they've been caught. We don't know if they yet live. We don't know how many of them there are.

'Not long now,' King Wiglaf calls the instruction. He's standing close to the fort, fully garbed in his warrior's gear, although he'll not join us. All the same, it's comforting to know he wants to do so.

'Bollocks, it's cold,' Oswy huffs once more. We've discarded our cloaks in favour of our battle gear, and it is cold. It should be warmer. It's summer, but the accompanying weather is late to arrive, cold winds and heavy rain making it miserable conditions in which to be fighting.

Oswy's been cold since our boat ride yesterday. He's not been able to warm up, as I did. That worries the part of my mind not consumed with the coming battle.

'Shut up,' Landwine directs towards him. 'It's only cold because you've been roasting your arse before the hearth all night long. You should have been on guard duty, you soft git.' A murmur of laughter greets the words. I don't look at Oswy; I look ahead. That way, he won't see the smirk on my lips. I'm sure the daylight's starting to grow on the grey-tinged horizon. It won't be long, and we'll be released to battle the enemy.

I lick my lips, feeling the need to drink and piss. I've fought for the king on many occasions. I've fought for myself as well. This feels different, somehow. Is there more at stake here? I don't know. Maybe it's just this situation has unfolded so bloody quickly. One moment, we were attending the queen's trial, convinced Brihthild would speak against her and the king would be divorced from his wife so she could face her punishment. The next, we were locked up inside Londinium. I hope it's not a portent of things to come.

'You're quiet?' Wulfheard growls at me.

'Just thinking,' I reply, because it's the truth.

'Well, don't do too much of that. It's what gets you into bloody trouble every time.'

Ahead, I see hands hurrying to remove the bars on the gates. I swallow and collect myself. I'm riding into battle once more without trusty Brute or the even trustier Wine, but I think Bicwide will do well enough. It's not as if this is his first fight.

'Stay alive,' Wulfheard orders me. I offer him a smile, and he returns the grin, eyes bright with something. I don't look too closely.

'The same to you, old man.' I break the sudden tension. And we're released, Wulfheard's reply lost in the clatter of hooves over the stone road. It's better that way. We can argue about it later when the Wessex warriors are dead.

Beyond the gates, what daylight there is seems muted. I glance behind me, but daybreak's little more than a smudge on the horizon. It's light enough to ride. Is it light enough to fight? We're going to find out.

Bicwide ambles to a canter and then a gallop. Ahead, Wulfheard leads us, and I turn to see Oswy beside me. His face is pale in the grey light. I hope he's not really sickening with something. Landwine and Cenred are close to Wulfheard. Ealdorman Tidwulf's men are with us. Between us, there are about twenty-two or -three. I've not taken the time to count. It's not a huge force. That's directed at Lundenwic, with Commander Eahric leading it. If this is all the king has thought to send to tackle the Wessex warriors close to the River Thames, it must be enough to overwhelm them.

I watched their military camp from the battlements last night, wrapped tightly in my cloak against the wind and rain. It was hardly large or bristling with warriors.

Wulfheard will lead us towards the encampment, which abuts the ancient wall of Londinium on the exterior. Ealdorman Tidwulf's men will head towards the west. The only way the enemy can escape is to either rush into the River Thames or risk running uphill, deeper into Mercia to disappear in the woodland I was lost in only a day or two ago. That can't be allowed to happen.

The encampment's sentry lights quickly materialise from the riverside mist. In no time, I jump clear from Bicwide, retrieving my shield. We don't need the animals to fight the enemy, only to get us in position quickly.

Shouts of anger greet our appearance, the roll of Wessex voices easy to hear in the chill of dawn. We've not made a quiet approach with the thunder of horses' hooves and the jangle of iron on wood.

'With me,' Wulfheard urges. I rush to join the shield wall, slotting between Oswy and Cenred, all tall men. It's better to keep those of a similar height together. 'Advance.' As one, we step forward. The Wessex warriors have dug a small ditch around their encampment, and it's filled with sharpened wooden stakes, but Wulfheard's not directed us there. We intend to slide close to the stone wall they think's protecting them.

I glance at Oswy, concerned by the sweat streaming down his face, but it's not as if I can send him away now.

Wulfheard directs our steps. We're a shield wall moving sideways, to slide between the wall and the enemy camp, rather than forwards. The Wessex warriors scramble to meet our approach. Someone shouts orders in their distinctive accent, as Ealdorman Tidwulf's warriors rush to strike from the west. The shrieks and cries of fighting men fill the air, but no one has met our attack so far.

'Keep up,' Oswy huffs from beside me. I hurry to join my shield with his, hopping over the small ditch surrounding the encampment. That's when I feel the first blow against my shield.

I look around, confused. There's no one facing us, but I've been hit.

'Ware,' I call, redoubling the grip on my shield, seeking the enemy in the greyness.

'Heads,' Wulfheard shouts, and now I understand. I duck, bringing my eyes almost level with my shield. Being tall is suddenly a curse.

Something else hits me, oozing down my helm and landing on my byrnie.

'Bloody hell,' I all but gag. They're throwing mud at us from above. It also stinks of the River Thames, as I know only too well. A sharp ting on my helm assures me there's also something heavier mixed in with the foul-smelling mud.

'Heads,' Wulfheard roars again. I thought to face iron and shields face to face, not mud and stones from above us.

I feel the rough stone of Londinium's wall at my back as I raise the shield over my head. In the growing daylight, I see a handful of Wessex warriors have roped themselves to the wall. They have their shields with them, suspended and lying flat to hold whatever it is they're pelting us with from above. I'd like to know how they managed that, and all without us being able to see them do it.

'Take them down, Landwine,' Wulfheard menaces. Landwine's good with a spear. He steps free from the shield wall and aims. I think he'll hit one of the men, but instead, it's the shield and rope which holds them aloft.

'Ware,' Landwine bellows while we crouch below our shields.

I wrinkle my nose as more disgusting mud hits my shield, and then falls to the ground.

'Shields,' I call, suspecting no one else has seen the oncoming line of Wessex warriors, with their shields pulled tight to their heads to stop the disgusting mud from landing on them.

'The crafty bastards,' Cenred offers with a modicum of respect.

Landwine rushes to retrieve his spear from where it's fallen in front of us, and flings it upwards once more. But then there's no more time. He collects his shield and retakes his position because we face an enemy from above and one that's coming towards us through their camp. I count the number of shields. They outnumber us. I consider if they've been sent reinforcement by ship from Wessex? Only, surely, if that were the case, the men watching the quayside last night should have seen them. Admittedly, there's been a lot of river mist to obscure the dank view of our foes.

I growl, clutching my seax as the enemy crash against us. We're pinned. Londinium's exterior wall is no longer our ally. We can't go backwards. We can't go forward. And over us, more mud and stones thunder down onto our helmed heads. How bloody delightful.

Enemy shields crash against ours. Wulfheard's voice rises. 'Advance,' he bellows.

'Chance would be a bloody fine thing,' Cenred complains, but as one, we try and move against our opponents. Inside the enemy encampment, we're unencumbered by the ditch that ended at Londinium's wall. Their tents have been placed much closer to the river. There's open ground we can exploit.

Head down, I surge against my foes, left shoulder pressed into my shield. My friends and allies do the same. The enemy is strong. I wince as yet another stone impacts my helm, and then smirk as I see a foul-smelling pile of mud hit my foeman in the face, temporarily blinding him, and not me.

'Keep it up,' I bellow to those dangling above us, grinning despite the smell and press of our adversary. 'Bloody keep it up,' I holler, realising if we keep close to the wall, those above will struggle to target us with direct throws. They'll hit their allies instead. That can only aid us. 'Keep back,' I urge my fellow warriors. I hear Wulfheard start to shout something, but then he echoes my cry.

'Mercian scum,' rumbles from the mouth of the man opposite me.

'Wessex arsehole,' I counter, enjoying his discomfort. He stinks. I sense his hold on the shield falter as he wipes the mud from his face. I take advantage of his distraction to kick against his shield. The shield holds firm, but not because my enemy's gripping it. A shriek and cry of dismay, and I know he's tripped over the foot I thrust beneath his shield, using the wall at my back to keep me upright. I snatch back my foot and thrust my seax over my shield. I stab the enemy to my left. My blade comes away bloody. The enemy shield wall falters with both men temporarily distracted, but then my original foeman is back on his feet. Furious blows aim for my helmed head. I duck low, enjoying his vehemence, when another lump of something foul-smelling lands on his helm with a thud.

'You arseholes,' he bellows. 'Hit the enemy, not your allies.'

Oswy barks in laughter. I press onwards. We need to overwhelm them quickly. We must secure this encampment and then help those riding on Lundenwic and relieve them from the besieging Wessex force.

Projectiles from above rain down on us all as though the Wessex warriors suspended above us have decided to throw everything at once. Perhaps they'll join the fight. We're not going to want that.

A blade snakes over my shield, its edge glistening with muck. The smell has me rearing backwards, almost hitting my head on the wall behind. I growl and redouble my attack. Our line of men is having some success. I can't see much other than Oswy and Cenred. But the shield wall's still intact. That tells me a great deal.

'Advance,' Wulfheard bawls again.

As one we surge forward one step. Sweat beads my face. It's a cool day, but here, I'm feeling hot. The press of bodies is overwhelming, the stench of the thrown mud and the River Thames making it difficult to take a deep breath. I can feel my heart thundering in my chest, and my lips are crusted with the salt of my exertions. We need to finish this.

'Advance,' Wulfheard repeats. I sense something change in the shield wall with the sharp slap of iron on stone. Landwine's once more aiming at the men who dangle above us, his rear protected by us. Our force pushes the enemy to retreat and then to retreat again. I don't know if their warriors are dying or if we're just the stronger force. Perhaps they mean for us to reach so far and then stumble on another of their hidden defences. I can't see my feet. With each step, I feel my way, hoping there are no weapons or ditches for us to fall into, or stakes to impale ourselves on.

My foeman slices at my face. This time, when I evade the blade, I don't have to worry about a wall at my back. There's enough room between us and it for me to move with more freedom. I lift my seax, and land a heavy blow on his helmed head. My hand vibrates, but I've not cut him yet. Using the hilt of my seax, I bash him repeatedly, the sound like a stone falling from a great height. I notice his eyes lose focus, but he doesn't move, instead pressing his advantage against me. His seax comes closer. I grit my teeth, trying not to watch the blade but focus on my attack. Beside me, Cenred lands a blow on his foeman, and a splatter of blood slaps onto my helm.

'Die, you bastard,' Cenred huffs. I sense the shield wall give as the man relaxes his grip. I'm not sure whether he's dead. I redouble my efforts to overwhelm my enemy, finally landing a slicing blow to his chin. His beard shears away, revealing a sagging cut, almost to the bone. Not that I have time to enjoy the victory, as his blade pokes against my shield. The sharp stab of something else hitting my cheek makes me cry out in pain. My helm protects the higher cut delivered by the queen, but not all of my cheek. By the time this is over, my face will look as ragged as the Wolf Lady's.

'Bollocks,' I mutter, tasting the iron of my blood over parched lips. The blade continues on its way, lowering as though to stab through my shoulder.

With my seax hand, I grip his hand, holding it firm, feeling his strength, even as the shield that separates us threatens to fall. He's wavering but bloody determined. I'm even more resolved. His shield slips lower again. I fear for my feet but not enough to stop pulling on him. His shoulder's almost entirely over the shield wall now, my left hand which holds my shield warring with my right, which grips my foeman's hand, although both hold.

'Do it,' I urge Cenred. He turns, seax poised, and stabs upwards and into the man's underarm. A flood of blood coats my boots. I growl at the sharp stink of his bowels giving way. He's dying. He knows it. His arm remains over my shield, so I fling it backwards. He thuds from view as though a taut sail snapped by the wind. 'My thanks,' I mutter, but where before we confronted one enemy, two have replaced him, fear etched into their faces we can see beneath their helms.

'Mercian bastard,' the one menaces.

'Wessex arsehole,' I counter, and so begins the dance once more.

My face pulses with pain. When I move my head from side to side, I can sense the edges of my helm moving the flesh of my cut cheek from the corner of my eye. It's uncomfortable, but I try to ignore it in the thrust and stab of the fight. We move forward, my foot questing over the dead man until I can find somewhere firm to stand. I give him a good kick, all the same, keen to reassure myself he's not going to be getting up any time soon.

Now Oswy threatens to be overwhelmed. His opponent is tall, even taller than him, able to easily lean over Oswy's shield. I don't think we'll be able to stab his underarm. I attempt it, but my blade hits something solid. He wears protection from such an action. Cool eyes appraise me, a mouth of cracked teeth opening in a leering smirk as he clatters his war axe against Oswy's shield. Oswy's had to raise it high. It means he's protected, but the shield wall's weakened. If the tall man can bend down that far, then his feet might be in peril.

With a slanting blow, I dismiss the man who fights me. He shrieks in pain, my blade piercing the top of his byrnie, close to his neck. He doesn't have the defensive armour that Oswy's foe does.

I glance to Cenred. He's holding his own against the enemy. It's Oswy who needs my help. About now, I'd appreciate having another line to our shield wall – someone small or armed with a spear to stab the other man's legs through Oswy's. But that's not going to happen – not unless Landwine finishes killing those dangling from the wall behind us.

I can't scamper to the ground either. That would disturb the shield wall.

Oswy huffs as he batters against his enemy. His blows are good, but I can smell his rankness, as well as see the sweat beading his face and into his byrnie. He's not well. I must help him.

With a count to three, I puff out my cheeks, wincing at the reminder of the twin cuts, and lower my shield to dance into our giant enemy.

I sense Oswy and Cenred temporarily falter, but they correct themselves and I'm stabbing into the side of Oswy's foeman. Short, sharp actions, my elbow going backwards and forward almost too fast for me to notice, while I thrust my shield against him as well. I hear his growl of fury. All I need is for him to turn to face me, and then Oswy can finish him. But he's reticent to do as I want. I can sense Cenred's enemy sensing an easy strike against my back.

'Bollocks,' I exclaim. This isn't working. All the same, I continue, pounding into his byrnie, thrusting my shield upwards to where I hope his face might be. If I could land a blow beneath his chin, that might stun him. He's stubborn, though. Even facing an attack on two fronts, his focus remains on Oswy, and not on me.

My blade doesn't even penetrate his byrnie, but he'll be black and blue from my blows should he live through this. Which I can't allow him to do. I spare a glimpse at Oswy. He remains focused on our enemy, but even I can see the shield he holds threatens to fall. If our foeman steps aside, the shield Oswy's holding will take him to the ground, and then it'll be easy to pierce into his neck.

Frustrated, I step back into the shield wall, a kick preventing Cenred's opponent from taking my place.

I can't tell Oswy what to do. I'll have to do it. I can't warn Cenred, either. I flash a look along the shield wall. We're beating our enemy. There are fewer of them standing, and the cries of the wounded flood the air. Right now, my focus remains on Oswy.

Tensing my body, I thrust myself into Oswy, knocking his balance, so he stumbles sideways and backwards. His reactions are so slow he doesn't think to remove his hold on the shield as he goes. His cry of rage doesn't distract me as I watch our enemy pursuing Oswy down. When he lands, it's going to hurt Oswy, but better hurt than dead. Quickly, I pivot to follow the huge man, stabbing into the slither of the exposed neck that's finally revealed.

He fights on despite the burbling blood surging from his wounds, and me clinging to his back.

'Just bloody die,' I huff, straddling his flailing legs and digging my blade into and out of his neck. Oswy's screaming for help, but until our foeman dies, he'll have to wait.

I thrust and jab. Sweat drips into my mouth, blood as well, and still I stab because Oswy's foeman continues to fight him. I hope Cenred and the men to Oswy's left have closed the gap in the shield wall.

'Die, you bastard, die,' I shriek, and finally, the man stills. I thrust one more time, my blade slick with the gore of his body, and only then stand. I'm panting heavily but aware I need to pull Oswy free from the weight of the dead man and rejoin the shield wall.

Only I don't.

'I think he's bloody dead,' Cenred states, offering me his arm to right my balance, before trying to pull the corpse aside.

'I hope he is,' I huff, looking around me, sweat dripping down my face and stinging my new wound. Landwine's also aiding Oswy. I look upwards. The Wessex warriors that were up there are gone. I hope they're dead.

'Icel, you bastard.' Oswy's voice emerges from below the lump of the lifeless body.

'It was that, or you'd be bloody dead,' I huff, wishing my chest felt less tight and I could take a full breath.

Oswy's face appears first as the dead man is pulled away, furious, but so white it's almost blue.

'He needs to go back to the fort,' I announce. My fellow warriors pick over the dead to ensure they're little more than corpses. Wulfheard joins us, confusion in his eyes.

'What's this?' he questions, looking from me to Oswy, still on the ground.

'Oswy's sick. He needs to return to the fort. Look at the state of him.'

With the foeman finally removed, Oswy surges upwards, filled with wrath. But his words die on his lips as he sways alarmingly. Luckily, Landwine's there to ensure he stays upright. Wulfheard's lips twist.

'You look like crap. Ordlaf, take him back to the fort. Make sure he gets there. Right, the rest of you, we need to help Ealdorman Tidwulf's men.'

Oswy takes a staggering step towards me, no doubt to deny my words, but he wavers again. He offers me a tired smirk.

'My thanks, Icel. That was a bloody stupid thing to do, but he was going to beat me.'

'I know that. Now, go and see Wynflæd and Cuthred. They'll look after you.'

I hear my fellow warrior, Ordlaf, collect Oswy's weight over his shoulders, but my focus is on continuing the fight. We still need to beat the rest of the Wessex warriors attacking our Mercian allies. And then we need to free Lundenwic from the Wessex force. And then we can discover exactly what Lord Wigmund has been up to in his father's absence.

16

I amble to a run, mindful of my face and all the other hurts starting to make themselves known. Cenred's beside me as we dash through the Wessex campsite. We bend to check the temporary structures house no one else, and they don't. It's full light now; the mist from the river has retreated beneath the advance of the sun. I survey the Thames as I run, looking to see what's happening. I can't distinguish other ships on it. The enemy isn't about to be rescued. Neither do they seem to have any means of escape. I consider where the ships that brought them to Mercia have gone.

A stream of Wessex horses thunders to a run. I jump off their path, a wrathful look directed to Uor, who offers no apology for his actions in sending the Wessex horses into our path. The enemy won't be getting anywhere with them. I hope they don't spook the horses we've left behind. It might have been better to leave the Wessex ones in the camp for the time being. I'm not about to argue with Uor about that, though. I need to focus on breathing and running.

In a short time, we reach where the rest of the Wessex

warriors face the Mercians under the command of Ealdorman Tidwulf's man. I count the number of foemen still standing, and decide there are about thirty of them. A man at my feet gargles. I do him the honour of ending his life with a slash to his exposed throat. His belly is a riot of glistening innards. He's never going to survive that, my healer's eyes informs me. Not that a warrior would have reached a different conclusion.

'Shield wall,' Wulfheard growls. Once more, though missing Oswy to my left, we resume our attacking positions with groans and grunts. My hand hurts from where I leant over my shield, twisting it in the process. But it's my face that burns as though branded with fire. I lift my hand to run it over the seeping cut but stop myself. My gloves are fouled with the blood of our enemy. I don't want that on my face.

The Wessex warriors have made more effort with their defences here, digging a deeper trench and filling it with anything they could find rather than relying on Londinium's wall and some sharpened wooden stakes. Now that we're within the ditch, it doesn't hinder us.

'Let's finish this,' Wulfheard urges. I note a few frightened eyes looking at us from turned heads as we move forward. The Wessex warriors will be crushed between two Mercian forces. They stand no chance of escaping. Not now their horses are gone, and their allies no longer protect their backs.

The enemy shield wall concertinas as every other man turns to face us on a barked instruction. It also shrinks, and at either end Mercians find themselves facing one another, but not here, at the centre, where Cenred and I stand.

Cries of fury erupt from the Wessex warriors at finding themselves encircled. I brace myself in the churned mud and the slick entrails of the dead. I don't imagine this'll take very long, but it's best not to be too confident, even when it seems so easy to overpower them. I'm wary those attacking Lundenwic might suddenly attempt to reinforce their allies. Equally, while I couldn't see a ship on the Thames, it doesn't mean there might not be one waiting to disgorge more warriors from Wessex.

My shield slaps against one of the enemy ones. He has some strength in him as he huffs and puffs, his hot breath making me wrinkle my nose. I hope my breath doesn't stink as much, but then, my enemy has a mouth filled with more holes than teeth. He probably has a rich, sweet diet of berries and good bread to have such bad teeth – I again call on all Wynflæd taught me to reach that decision. He must be beloved of his oath-sworn lord, whomever that might be, to be rewarded with such fine food. I suspect it's Lord Æthelwulf. I imagine he's the one behind the attack and the efforts to capture the queen, or King Wiglaf, whichever proved easier to accomplish. As neither of those things have been achieved, his intentions have changed. It's all about overwhelming the Mercians now.

A blade impacts the edge of my shield, unbalancing my hold on it. I snarl and firm up my grip. With my seax, I repay the kindness, only my blade strikes a helm, not a shield. A rumble of fury resounds. I find a grin on my tight lips, even though it makes my cheek twinge in pain. There's no harm in enjoying this, I acknowledge.

I punch and stab, using the sharpened edge of the blade, as well as the hilt, turning my hand so that it hits his helm with a loud twang once more. I look at my foeman. His eyes are wide and unfocused. I reach across and clatter him on the head with the hilt of my seax. He tumbles to the ground, almost taking my shield with him, his war axe stuck to it. I bang against the axe handle in my foeman's hand with my shield. It comes free easily, and I collect it in my hand considering whether I want to use it or not.

Deciding I do, I grip the war axe tightly, returning my seax to my weapons belt. The back of one of my enemies greets me, unaware there's no longer one of his allies protecting him. Swinging as wide as I can in the confined space, I aim for his lower back. His byrnie rides up, revealing a flash of pink flesh. In a heartbeat, it shimmers redly instead. The man buckles to his knees. Again, I employ the axe and crash it into his helm, so that it wedges there. He falls forward. I look up to see the face of one of Ealdorman Tidwulf's warriors. He flashes me a grin and bends to slice open our foeman's neck. The man kicks out once before lying still.

I breathe in deeply because the fight's over before it's really started. I bend and check my first enemy is entirely dead, and satisfied he is, I survey the enemy camp for signs of other foemen.

'Icel, we're not taking our bloody ease,' Wulfheard roars. I swivel to him and appreciate the Mercians are on the move. Ambling to a run, we retrace our steps through the destroyed Wessex encampment. I'm reunited with Bicwide, where he and the rest of the horses wait. His nostrils are wide, eyes fear-crazed. I run my hand along his neck before mounting. We still have the beleaguered Mercians within Lundenwic to rescue.

I notice the Wessex horses milling amongst our mounts. Uor didn't take them far. We don't want them coming with us. But it seems those protecting Londinium have seen the problem. Ten Mercian warriors run towards us, down the steep hill, armoured but unencumbered with shields.

'We'll take them,' one huffs, reaching for reins and lead ropes, or adding them to the horses. The animals are docile with the smell of blood and death in the air. They don't make any attempt to escape.

'Right, arseholes,' Wulfheard huffs from the back of Bada. 'That was the easy bit. Let's kill these bastards and send them back to Wessex as little more than a jumble of bones.' With that, he kicks Bada, who lurches to a gallop, eager to be away from the stink of the dead. I cast a glance back that way. The enemy encampment's silent. Nothing moves but the flap of carrion crows, already come to explore, and one or two Mercians, picking through the dead. I grimace. There are many bodies to bury. I don't envy whoever gets that task. I hope it's not me.

The rumble of hooves over the wooden bridge that crests the River Fleet dividing Lundenwic from Londinium penetrates my hearing, and I encourage Bicwide to move faster. I don't want Wulfheard roaring my name to tell me to hurry up. Landwine rides beside me. His face is liberally splattered with blood and grime. He was tasked with stopping the Wessex warriors from throwing mud and stones at us from their perches on Londinium's walls. He was successful but at a cost.

'I stink,' he roars, offering me a toothy grin.

'As long as you don't smell yourself, you'll be fine,' I reply, wishing he was downwind of me. His chuckles reach me as he rushes onwards.

As Bicwide's hooves hit the wooden bridge, I focus not on what we've achieved but on what still needs to be done.

Lundenwic burns. Even now, someone has found something else to set ablaze. The enemy isn't firmly in command of Lundenwic, but they block the easiest route inside the defences, which runs between the two settlements. Ahead, the king's force under Commander Eahric already surges against the enemy warriors. We're not to reinforce them. Our task is to seek entrance from the north. Wulfheard leads the way. The ground's uneven, rising and falling, so that sometimes we can see the defences of ditch and rampart and sometimes not. The cries of the raging battle Commander Eahric's fighting flood the air.

I don't know who's winning. That's not what's important at the moment. Our orders are to relieve Lundenwic.

I consider what Lord Wigmund and Ealdorman Sigered might be doing, but I doubt it's anything other than sheltering behind others who have to fight in their name. If they set Lundenwic ablaze, they'll have long since regretted that. Admittedly, as they must know their plan to rescue the queen failed, they might also have fled. But, no, I suspect they'll be inside the hall, where the queen's trial began, and therefore safe in the centre of Lundenwic. I suspect it's Ealdorman Muca and his warriors who are protecting Lundenwic with the aid of those who didn't wish to leave their homes to seek shelter within Londinium, the traders and merchants.

I'm almost looking forward to the king getting his hands on Lord Wigmund. I know the king must take firm action against his son, as well as his wife. I appreciate the king is troubled by this, but there's only one solution to the problem, and we all know it. I understand Ealdormen Ælfstan and Tidwulf have already informed the king of their demands. They'll see justice served. I'm sure Ealdorman Muca will add his voice to those cries.

'Let us in.' Wulfheard's ahead, already demanding admittance at the northern gate. I see that some of the defences have been burnt, but the ditch remains intact.

A scurry of activity, with helmed heads popping over the top of the gate to ensure we're Mercians, and a board's lowered over the deep ditch by men and women who erupt from behind the closed gate.

'Are you well?' Wulfheard questions hurriedly.

'Yes, we are,' a man calls. His left eye is swollen shut. Black and purple bruises above it make it impossible for him to see well. He tilts his head back and looks down his fat nose at us. It looks like that's taken a mighty punch as well. 'The bastards are at the eastern gate and Ealdorman Muca and his men are holding them off,' he states, although that's obvious to us. 'But here, we've taken shelter inside the gatehouse.'

Wulfheard hastens over the ditch and we join him, the sound of hooves loud over the wooden boards. 'Bring up the boards and close the gate again. And then stay inside the gatehouse. We'll deal with the enemy. Don't take any risks,' Wulfheard calls, his words filled with command.

'My lord.' The man bows, almost overbalancing with his deference and relief at knowing he's not been abandoned by Mercia's warriors.

'I'm no lord,' Wulfheard calls over his shoulder. 'I'm a warrior of Mercia and we're here to protect you from the Wessex bastards, and those who mean to betray Mercia.'

17

I survey the immediate area. Here it's easy to see how far the enemy have penetrated within Lundenwic. Which isn't far. But, as we get closer and closer to the eastern gate, the number of smoking ruins increases dramatically. What vegetable gardens people had have been ransacked or plundered, even though it's too early for much that's edible to have grown and be ready to eat. I note with dismay the dead chickens and goats abandoned in the street and also the sight of Mercians lying dead and sightless.

'Bastard Wessex arseholes,' Landwine growls, speaking for all of us.

The smoke from the burning ruins obscures our view as we near the eastern gate, reminding me of the dank mist rising from the River Thames earlier.

'Halt,' Wulfheard commands. I note he speaks for all the Mercians, taking command of Ealdorman Tidwulf's men as well. Ealdorman Tidwulf has no part to play in this fight because of his wound, but that doesn't stop his warriors from seeking vengeance. The sound of the horses' hooves is muted by the curling smoke, but we can still hear the fighting taking place outside Lundenwic under Commander Eahric's instructions. Although, without the clear delineation of the street, I would think the noise came from behind, not in front. 'Leave the horses,' Wulfheard commands.

I slide from Bicwide, not wanting to abandon him here. The smell of the smoke has infected all of the animals. They move uneasily. We should have left them at the northern gate, I realise, and they'd have been better protected.

'We know where the enemy are. We overwhelm them as quickly as possible. Take prisoners if you want, but I'd prefer it if all of them were dead. Don't kill your fellow Mercians fighting under Ealdorman Muca. We don't know where they are, or how many of them have survived. Come on.' And with no further words or discussion of tactics, Wulfheard disappears into the smoke. I cough and spit aside the filth in my mouth. I was thirsty before. Now I fear I could drink the contents of the River Thames and still not be satisfied.

'Let's get this over and done with,' Landwine huffs.

I give Bicwide a parting pat on his nose. 'Stay here, my friend,' I urge him, and follow my fellow warriors into the smoking air.

Immediately, my eyes sting. Somewhere, something's blazing, fogging the air with the smell of blistering heat as well as dirty grey smoke. The closer we get to the sound of fighting, the more and more difficult it is to see. I lurch to the side, and stumble, seax extended, shield before me, but it's little more than a twirling column of smoke and not a man at all.

'Jumping at shadows,' Kyre chuckles, but I know I'm not the only one to have done so. My arms are tired, my legs as well. My chest feels tight because I can't inhale a deep breath without coughing or choking. My face throbs, and all of my old hurts gained fighting Eadweard and his cronies are making themselves felt.

This is the longest battle I've endured since they beat me. The fight outside Canterbury wasn't so protracted. Admittedly, some might argue we were fighting from the moment Brihthild revealed herself as the enemy, so maybe it was. All the same, I feel fatigued and we're far from done.

I peer into the gloom. I can pick out images now: the blackened ruins of a dwelling here, the smoking remains of a fire there. But it's still not easy as I collide with a standing piece of wood that almost impales my belly. I veer aside from it. Cenred's ahead, his tall shoulders giving me something to focus on, while Kyre's beside me. He's puffing heavily. We all are. We sound like we're afflicted with a winter cold.

A flash of something vivid catches my eye in the dull gloom. I peer closer. There's a figure lying low. I knock Kyre's arm, pointing.

'Go for it,' he commands. Pretending I walk in Cenred's footsteps, I only veer aside at the last moment. The enemy warrior surges upwards, his bright cloak a beacon in the smoke. He thought to trick me but needs to improve on his camouflage. Not that he'll have the opportunity now.

My shield smashes into his face before he's fully upright. Kyre's behind me, his weapons ready to assist if needed. My foeman's cry of fury ends in a wet crunch as his nose erupts beneath the force of my shield. His eyes shut at the onslaught of pain, and before he can defend himself further, my blade's through his open mouth, and he's dying.

'Arsehole,' I glower. My actions have alerted the rest of the Mercians to the possibility there are more of our enemies hiding. We thought Lundenwic would be filled with Mercians, not Wessex warriors, but everything is muddled. As the man slumps to the ground, the thud of iron on wood reverberates through the murkiness.

'How many of the bastards are there?' Kyre voices my thoughts. I'd reply, but another gaudy flash catches my eye. I surge around Kyre, skewering another Wessex foeman on my seax before he can impale my fellow warrior.

As the man's cry of pain echoes in the dulled light, it's as though a signal's been given. Abruptly, there are Wessex warriors everywhere. They cast aside whatever they've been using to hide, and rush into us. I meet the crash of a shield with my seax, and then thrust my shield against my foeman. He's strong. He's not already fought one battle. Resolve thrums through me. I won't allow him to win just because he's fresher than I am.

His shield deviates towards my face. I duck away, using my shield to hold him at bay. He thinks to hit my weeping cheek wound and pain me that way. It would be a good tactic, if I wasn't so bloody aware of it. My surroundings fill with the frantic bustle of men fighting one another. In the distance, the Mercians attempt to battle their way through to us from where they already skirmish with the enemy from outside the eastern gate, but for the time being, this is our fight.

I swing my shield aside, stamping towards my opponent, and almost land a blow to the side of his neck. At the last possible moment, he moves away. My blade hits his arm not his neck, and I'm breathing heavily from the effort, coughing as well. He's nimble on his feet, a grimace on his face. He takes no joy in this fight to the death.

His weapon swerves towards my left eye. My helm absorbs the heavy blow although my eyes close instinctively. I need to do better. I can't allow him to get so close again.

Holding my shield before me, I move nearer to him, so our shields are held between us. I take a deep breath and prepare for what I must do next. My foeman thrusts his blade towards me, but this time, I allow it. I'll take a slicing cut, provided I can get nearer to him. As his seax rips yet another hole in my face, this time on my chin, my blade finally connects with his neck. An *umph* of triumph quickly turns to a roar of pain, as blood sheets wetly over my gloved hand. He's not dead yet though. It wasn't a killing strike.

Sensing he only has one more chance, his attack becomes wilder, hitting me with lessening force but making it impossible for me to drop my shield. A cut is one thing, I'll not risk a deeper wound.

Instead, and even though it goes against every bone in my body, I hold my ground. He'll grow weaker much quicker than I will with the injury he's taken.

When the scrapes against my shield are little more than the touch of a feather, I lower it and stab him once more. His neck wound doubles in size. He falls to the floor with a groan.

I survey the battle while I try to suck air into my body. My fellow warriors are fighting well. But there are many more Wessex warriors than I expected. I thought Ealdorman Muca would be protecting the interior of Lundenwic, but perhaps he and his warriors have been overwhelmed. Two foemen rush at me, neither seeming to notice the dead body. Instead, they eye me appraisingly, looking at my weeping chin and blooded cheek. They sense victory.

Without pause, I lift my shield to counter the one while stepping closely into the reach of the other. Both men are similar in height, shorter than me, so I look over their heads, not meeting their eyes. With my range, I quickly land a blow against the first man, impacting his byrnie to drive the breath from him. He doubles over, but his ally rushes me, evading my shield to almost come around me.

The smoke billows blackly. For a moment, I see nothing but the shimmer of his helm while I blink to clear my vision. When I can see again, his blade is almost at my throat. I duck low and spin aside from it, hitting the gasping man in the process. He feebly defends himself, but he's not the problem. Not right now.

Coursing upright, I rush the man who thinks to kill me with subterfuge. I force him backwards and then backwards again. I'm mindful of the smouldering ruins of the burned dwellings. A spark erupts from the man's booted foot, the blast of heat making me close my eyes, even though I don't want to do so. I bat aside the heat on my chin, fearing what remains of my beard will catch alight.

When I focus again, both men leer at me. The winded man stands slightly crooked but with the sense to hold his shield before him. The other is stamping on the embers of the burning building, encouraging air beneath the wreckage, hoping to set it ablaze once more.

'Bollocks to this,' I glower. I rush him. At the last moment, I dart to the side to evade a single piece of upright wood and crash into his side. He tumbles beneath me in a welter of kicks and punches. Now he's at risk of burning as the crackle of resurrected flame reaches my ears.

I smell burning flesh. The man shrieks, desperate to stand, but my weight is on him. I rear up on my knees, ignoring the heat that works its way along them, and the slight smell of burning leather. I punch him. Behind me, the other warrior pummels my back with his fists, but I'll kill one of them and then the other.

The downed man's nose erupts in a flurry of blood, his eyes rolling backwards in his head. I reach for my seax and stab into his exposed neck. I surge to my feet then, aware the dead man's helm has come loose and threads of his hair are ablaze. The other shrieks in fear. I rush him, using my fists, the shield abandoned on the floor. My left hand punches while my right stabs, and my enemy quickly finds himself abutting the standing wooden post I was lucky to evade earlier.

His shriek of terror encourages me to continue to punch and stab. His hands are to either side of him. He doesn't even think of using his shield. Blood drips from a cut lip as I cuff him once more, knocking his helm to one side to jab my seax upwards into his chin. Mouth open, I see the blade on his impaled tongue.

I breathe deeply, glad the two bastards are dead, and only then appreciate the building is well and truly ablaze. My boots are on fire. Bending quickly, I reclaim my shield and hop onto the roadway, wincing. Behind me, a sudden flame ignites both men's bodies.

'Bloody hell,' I glower, bending to suck in much-needed air, trying to keep low below the layer of smoke. My fellow warriors are prevailing. I can't see any more obvious hidden enemies, but I'm not moving on until we're all together.

I eye Wulfheard. He fights one warrior with the ferocity of a wolf defending its cubs. His movements are precise, short and sharp. The man falls below him, and he doesn't even check he's dead, striding to me, face glowering in the yellow glow from the flames.

'Arseholes,' he roars in my face.

I swerve away from him. He reaches out, breath hot, to grip my forearm in an apology.

'You look like horse shit,' he mutters when there's the breath to speak.

'You don't look much better.' Wulfheard's helm is firmly held on his head, but I can see cuts and bruises forming on his right arm. A splash of blood covers his nose guard. I don't think it's his.

'Come on, warriors of Mercia,' he bellows. All around me, my allies stagger to join us, the enemy dead or dying. Some of our foemen are encased in flames, including the two men I killed.

The raging, choking black smoke makes it clear where we are to any who seek us.

Overhead, I hear the shriek of an eagle, and grimace. The bloody bird has been watching me for days.

'Come on,' Wulfheard huffs, ambling to a run as Kyre joins us. I look at my fellow warriors. In the greyness of the dense smoke, we look like creatures from the depths of hell. The only colour comes from the blood that coats us and the brief slashes of skin on display.

'Let's get this bloody over and done with,' Cenred gasps. His chin bleeds more violently than mine. I'd like to take the time to stop it, but the only thing to hand is the heat of the flames, and Cenred won't appreciate that.

On legs almost numb, I follow Wulfheard, streaming eyes peering all around me. We don't want to face an attack from the rear if there are more of them waiting to engage with us. But no one else emerges from the dankness. Instead, we stagger to a halt, eyeing the line of Wessex warriors defending against the might of Mercia. It's so bizarre. The Wessex warriors are suddenly the ones protecting Lundenwic while the Mercians are attacking it. Only that's not the case. The Mercians seek to reclaim what the Wessex warriors hold.

It's difficult to determine, but I believe the Mercians are prevailing. Bodies lie abandoned in what's visible of the recently cut ditch, and the cry of frightened horses, stabled close to another building threatening to burst into flame once more, adds a haunting feel to the surreal, smoke-infused, almost dark, scene.

'Pick one and kill the bastard,' Wulfheard instructs. While the others do just that, I hesitate. Wulfheard turns to look at me, offering me an appraising glance as though reading my thoughts. 'Release the trapped horses. I don't object to killing Wessex warriors, but the horses had no choice.'

With a grin of thanks, which reminds me of all the cuts on my face, I force myself to a quick run despite everything hurting, and the choking cloud of smoke. I leap over the dead, wincing at the sightless eyes and severed flesh on display. Some of the enemy have had poor deaths, taking a long time to die, if my knowledge of such wounds is accurate.

I hear a rumbling screech of fury as I'm about to reach the shrieking horses and realise the Mercians at the back of the Wessex warriors have been discovered. I must release the horses before the enemy can get to them.

The animals are inside a stable, the building long and relatively unscathed by the raging fire, but for a random snaking line of flame that has unfortunately found some abandoned hay on the floor.

I'd stamp it out if I could but the flames are already too violent, threatening to entirely block the entrance. There's not even a half-full bucket of water to aid me nearby.

'Bloody hell.' Without further thought, I dash through the flames and within the stables, hand raised above my head to try and help me see better. 'Now I just need to get out of here,' I mutter unhappily, already moving to release the trapped horses.

A neigh of terror and a shriek of pain ripples through the air as the first horse rushes through the flames, escaping the way I entered. I wince to see a flicker of flame catch in its white mane, driving it to even faster speed, its fear infectious and upsetting the already terrified horses.

'Bollocks.' I realise I'm doing this all wrong. The animals need a way to escape, and there isn't one now. A sudden whoosh of too-hot air and the beams above my head dance with the hungry flames. 'Bloody bollocks.' I rush to the far end of the stable, leaving the stabled horses for now. Their nickers of terror are overwhelming, my ears thudding with them. But I need a way for them to escape that isn't through the blazing doorway. I throw myself bodily against the wattle and daub walls, hoping they'll be old and need repair. I gasp in pain as I crash against the wall, realising I'm not to be so lucky. The wall holds firm. 'Arse,' I exclaim, bending low to recover my breath, and right my helm.

The smoke in the room's growing more intense, the harsh neighs and whinnies of the horses so loud I can't hear the fighting taking place outside. I know what I need to do. I open the remaining stable doors, slapping the animals' arses to have them facing me, and not the fire covering the exit. Eyes wide with terror, they struggle to obey me. One of the beasts could be a brother to Bicwide, with his wide shoulders and huge hooves. I haul myself onto his back, wincing at all my hurts, and coughing again now that I'm closer to the burning roof and the layer of thick smoke.

'Here goes nothing,' I offer him, choking. A sharp wail of protesting wood assures me I don't have long as another wave of heat ripples the air. I direct the horse at the wall that held firm against me. He runs at it, not needing my encouragement to escape through the blocked passage. He's not alone in being so terrified, rational thought has deserted him.

We'll either succeed or fail. I know what I bloody hope.

18

I close my eyes and, with tense shoulders, the horse races for the solid impeding wall. At the last moment, the animal stops, not trusting my frantic kicks to his haunches, but rather his eyes. I growl low in my throat, urging him onwards. I kick his sides, and the animal, with the shrill shrieks of the others behind us, rears backwards, hooves kicking out against the bloody wall.

I feel myself slipping and stop myself from grabbing tighter to his mane. A sharp blast of cold air ripples over my face. I thud to the ground, lucky to land on my feet, over his rear end, and rush to the two small open gaps he's opened. The heat's causing sweat to sheet down my grubby, smoke-stained face, stinging both of my cheek wounds, and the one on my chin. I use my gloved hands to widen the gaps in the wall, punching and kicking. For a moment, the wattle and daub hold firm. I cough from my exertions and the sudden blast of cool air is a welcome balm to my aching throat.

The horse rears again. I avoid a glancing blow to my right shoulder from a hoof, but between us we're making progress. Running back a few steps, I direct my right shoulder at the growing cavity, relief coursing through my body as I charge all the way through, closing my eyes so as to stop dust and splinters stinging them. The horse behind me bends its head to follow, increasing the size of the hole with his passage.

I look around, but I can't see an axe and wish I'd not left the one I had earlier in the enemy's helm. I rush against the wall again from the exterior, more and more of the flaking wattle and daub falling to the ground. I'm unsurprised the building has caught aflame so quickly. Even with the dank summer weather, it's dry as tinder. More and more of the horses force their way through the ever-growing gap. Some of them have no thought for the others, terror making them barge past one another.

I punch and kick, and then I yank and throw the bits of wattle and daub that shear away in my hands, and more and more of the wall falls away. Most of the animals are free now. I encourage the others onwards. The smoke belches whitely, obscuring my view. I think all the horses have escaped. I don't wish to run inside again. I hope the animal that first caught alight has managed to extinguish itself somehow.

Panting, hands on my knees once more, I take stock of what's happening. The sound of the ongoing fight can be heard, but there are more Mercian than Wessex voices. The Mercians will triumph. But then what? King Wiglaf will need to contend with his wife, and, it seems, his son, who's decided to lay claim to the kingship, assuming his father is dead.

The horses have run from the fires. Only the initial animal waits, panting softly, the one alike Bicwide. I walk towards him, nose wrinkling at the stink of burning hair and smoke that clings to my body.

'It's been one hell of a day,' I mutter, hand extended to run it along his neck. He shivers beneath my touch. 'All is well now,' I murmur, 'you're free from the flames.' I consider mounting and riding him to where my fellow warriors fight, but he's endured enough. 'Away with you,' I mutter, a gentle prod to encourage him further into the heart of Lundenwic, where I hope Mercians will find him.

A crash behind us heralds the fall of the buildings, the wooden struts giving way, the wattle and daub evaporating beneath the onslaught of the flames. I close my eyes, keen to avoid flying ash or more sparks. When I open them again, I have a clear line of sight to the battle. I try and make sense of what I'm seeing. Is the fighting finished? Do I need to hasten back to my fellow warriors? Are the Mercians victorious?

A shout reaches my ears, but I can't understand it. What does it mean? And then my eyes narrow, and I understand only too well as I peer, not towards the fighting, but instead into Lundenwic itself.

I turn to the horse, who seems much restored and has ignored my command, and offer him a smile.

'Sorry, my friend. I've need of you yet.' Launching onto the animal's back, mindful there's no saddle or reins, I encourage him around the smoking remains of the stable building, pleased to see the fire hasn't spread.

The horse takes my instructions to ride to my allies without argument. We hurry to a trot. I don't want to force him to a gallop when neither of us might see obstructions to our passage. I cough dryly. If I was thirsty before, I think I could drink two rivers now, but there's not the time. From my vantage, I gaze at my fellow warriors who are done fighting, none of them even looking to see who rides towards them, as they try to recover from all they've endured.

'Wulfheard,' I bellow above the thunder of the animal's hooves, loud enough it makes my head ache. 'Inside Lundenwic.' I point, and he turns, his expression curling in disgust.

'Bastards,' he expels. 'Men, to me. Leave the dead and dying. We've got another problem.'

From the heart of Lundenwic, a contingent of Wessex warriors surges towards us. Luckily, they're too late to help their fellows, but that leaves us with a problem.

This fight is far from done if more Wessex warriors are within Lundenwic. Again, I consider what Lord Wigmund has been doing while Ealdorman Muca's warriors have been labouring to protect the settlement.

I encourage my borrowed horse onwards. His hooves kick up ash, while the smoke swirls around them. I grimace as I realise there's more than just a contingent of enemy horsemen. There are also foot warriors, carrying shields and spears and wearing warrior helms. I look to the man seated on the first horse. He carries the Wessex banner of a white wyvern on a black background. I don't recognise him, but the man behind? Him I know only too well.

Lord Æthelwulf, the king of Wessex's son. But it's the man beside him that has my fists clenching inside my gloves.

Lord Wigmund, the son of the Mercian king. He rides in gleaming battle gear, including a helm crowned with the bristles of a boar or horse dyed red. Ealdorman Sigered is beside him, bedecked as though he might actually be able to lift the finely hilted sword at his side.

I kick the horse to a faster pace, conscious of my fellow warriors running beside me. I don't know where we left Bicwide and the other horses. I've been turned around in the smoke too many times. I don't miss that, despite the filth on my face and the sweat running down my back, I actually mirror the formation of the Wessex lord and Lord Wigmund, with their foot warriors trailing behind them. If I thought in such a way, I could be a king coming to reclaim my holdings. I'm grateful King Wiglaf lives.

'Ah, young Icel,' Lord Æthelwulf calls, a rictus smile on his familiar face with his dirty blonde hair, beard and moustache. I think his nose has grown even longer above his awful moustache. It's unfortunate he knows who I am. I look to Lord Wigmund, who rides as though the conquering king for all his slight build betrays him. 'It's good you're here. Now we can apprehend you.'

I eye him, mindful he instructs some of his warriors to come towards me.

'On what grounds?' I demand.

'For allowing King Wiglaf to be killed, of course.'

'But King Wiglaf isn't dead,' I shout, slowing the horse to allow Wulfheard and my fellow warriors to catch me.

'What?' Lord Æthelwulf demands, a sly look directed to Wigmund. I don't miss the self-important smirk slips from Wigmund's face.

'King Wiglaf isn't dead. All of these Mercian warriors will attest to that,' I repeat, indicating Wulfheard and the rest of my fellow warriors. Wulfheard growls low in his throat.

Ealdorman Sigered's delighted sneer slithers from his face. Now, he looks frantically behind him, and I know exactly what he intends to do.

'King Wiglaf lives. Indeed, he'll be here soon, I assure you. Your allies are all dead.' Now, it's Lord Æthelwulf's warriors who grumble with unease. They appear even more ill at ease than Lord Wigmund.

'But we have reports of his death.' Lord Æthelwulf isn't to be dissuaded, and thinks he can argue with me about it.

'Then they're false.' Wulfheard adds his voice to mine. 'Your men are dead. Your encampment's destroyed.'

A flicker of discomfort finally reveals itself on Lord Æthelwulf's face. I want to enjoy this moment and laugh in his face, but I'm astounded to find him here, with Lord Wigmund. I can't believe it. I've suspected it, but to see it happening with my eyes astonishes me.

'I've seen proof,' Lord Æthelwulf persists, as though I'm lying to him.

'Then it wasn't proof of my death.' And King Wiglaf emerges from behind us, appearing from the smoke. I smile broadly. This is going to get bloody interesting.

19

Quickly, Lord Wigmund's face reveals his panic, but not as much as Lord Æthelwulf's. Bloody arse.

'My lord king,' Lord Æthelwulf begins. Ealdorman Sigered's already turned his horse, showing more skill than I thought he had. Lord Wigmund attempts to do the same, but he's so ineffective, the horse refuses to obey his urgent commands. Other Mercians slip away as well. I note them with tight fury. The bastards tried to betray their kingdom. They sit here, safe inside Mercia, never having shed blood or lost friends to the menace of Wessex, and now they slink away as though there'll be no punishment for all they've unleashed.

'I'm not your lord king,' Wiglaf bellows. The rumble of more Mercian horses arriving can be heard. I don't move my eyes from watching the interplay over Lord Æthelwulf's face. I take some delight in seeing his elaborate scheming with Queen Cynethryth come to nothing.

'I...' Lord Æthelwulf begins.

'You're an enemy on Mercian land. You'll be hunted down and punished,' King Wiglaf announces.

With a grin on my dirty, singed, sweating and painful face, I knee my horse forward, Wulfheard, Kyre and Cenred standing beside me. Horror flickers over Lord Æthelwulf's face. He opens his mouth to shout, but whatever he means to say goes unheard.

'My son is mine,' King Wiglaf commands. I want to argue about that, but my focus is on Lord Æthelwulf. How I hate the pompous arse.

Lord Æthelwulf turns his horse quickly, a much better horseman than Wigmund, his warriors already streaming away, back through Lundenwic to the west, no doubt, towards the quayside, or perhaps along the banks of the River Thames. If they can reach the shallows upstream at Laleham Gulls they might make it back to Wessex unscathed. But I know our role in this. We must stop them.

With thundering hooves beneath me, I set my eyes on Lord Æthelwulf. I pull my seax to hand, but lacking a saddle, I quickly replace it. My fellow warriors can kill the foot warriors. I want Lord Æthelwulf and his meddling ways to end. I can well imagine the look on King Ecgberht's face when he hears a Mercian has killed his son.

Bending low, I grip my horse's mane, even as the mounted Wessex warriors, about fifty of them, surround Lord Æthelwulf to rush away. They're quickly up to speed, as I hurry to follow them.

We pass the main hall where all this began, which almost blurs with the swiftness of the horses. We're on the main road, heading to the west, but there are only a few mounted Mercians with me. I'd expect the ealdormen or the king to be beside us, but the horse is so fleet-footed, I'm entirely alone.

I recall when I chased King Ecgberht through Lundenwic six years before. He escaped on that occasion. I can't allow Lord Æthelwulf to do the same.

My breath is hot, my body thundering with rage as I focus on those ahead, my aches and pains forgotten about, as is my raging thirst. I focus only on the retreating back of Lord Æthelwulf.

I'm unsurprised when three riders stop and turn to face me. Beneath my helm and with the horse's uneven stride, it's impossible to focus on them all. My sweating face makes the helm bounce up and down, rubbing my multiple cuts every time.

For a moment, I think I'm going to escape through their feeble defence, but two of the horses move to cut me off. I'm funnelled between them. There's no time to change my horse's direction. The third warrior waits, a sneer of triumph on his face, holding his spear before him. He thinks to skewer me with it.

I hold my nerve. The horse is going too fast for me to stop him. I duck my head down, holding my body low, hopeful the spear will pass over me, even as my horse, making use of those giant hooves once more, thunders into the animal.

With a whoosh of air, the spear pings off my helm but doesn't do me any damage. At the last moment my horse manages to jump free from the three men. I've not managed to kill any of them, but right now, I only want to stop Lord Æthelwulf. Someone else will have to contend with these three.

Cries of fury meet my evasion. The rumble of hooves chasing me rings loud in my ears. I sit up again, a glance behind me assuring me they're chasing me down, and so are my fellow Mercians, now mounted.

This is all far too similar. I wish we'd realised Lord Æthelwulf would be here. We could have cut him off from the west instead of entering Lundenwic from the north, but now isn't the time to curse our poor planning. We could only work with what we knew.

I grip the mane of my horse as he leaps the ditched embankment. Outside Lundenwic, the ground's uneven. I remember it well from my last journey here. I need to stay in my seat, and that's not going to be easy now the reasonably flat surface of Lundenwic's road has been left far behind me.

'Hurry up, Icel.' Wulfheard roars past me, lying almost flat to Bada's neck, with the advantage of a saddle and reins.

Others quickly catch me, including Commander Eahric. For a tall man, he looks surprisingly small on his horse as he rushes to catch Wulfheard. I turn again. The three enemy warriors no longer chase us, but more and more Mercians are erupting into the countryside to the west of Lundenwic. I hear the shriek of distressed birds and the sharp thwack of wings rising high into the air as they're disturbed from where they rested on the ground. Ahead, more and more of Lord Æthelwulf's warriors have swerved aside to prevent us from catching their oath-sworn lord, but the majority of the Mercians pay them no heed, crashing through their feeble line of defence.

The sight of the River Thames, grey and forbidding, urges me onwards. Lord Æthelwulf isn't to reach the implied safety of its banks. I see no ship, so he'll have to swim it, but I know that can be accomplished, even if it's not easy.

Goðemon overtakes me; Uor, as well. I growl. I want to be the one to get to Lord Æthelwulf, but most of my warrior allies have forged on ahead. They've all taken the time to grab their horses. Only I ride the horse I rescued from the burning stables.

I curse my lack of forethought. In a race such as this, I needed the best animal and equipment possible to ensure I was part of the fight.

Even Ealdorman Ælfstan overtakes me. I glower and curse myself. If one of them doesn't stop the king of Kent, I'll be bloody furious with them.

And then my eyes see something that makes my heart sink. There's a ship. It has no sail, but the oars seem to hold it motionless in the water, almost in the middle of the River Thames.

Without the sail, I can't decide if it's Mercian or from Wessex. I hope it's not from bloody Wessex.

The ship isn't level with where Lord Æthelwulf has run. That gives me pause for thought. I can tell I'm not needed to continue chasing Lord Æthelwulf, and my horse is tiring rapidly beneath me. He's not had the best morning. I can feel where the fire singed his coat. I encourage him to stop. Another handful of Mercians sweep past me, but now I want to know what's happening with the ship.

Slowly, my horse panting, his chest rising and falling rapidly, I urge him in an almost direct line towards the riverbank. The ship remains where it is. I squint against the brightness of the daylight, but it's almost impossible. The craft is merely etched in black. I can't see people moving on it, although there must be some for the oars to be deployed and for the ship to hold steady in the middle of the River Thames.

Just before reaching the bank, I pull the horse to a halt, a small stream allowing him to bend his head and drink deeply. His coat is flecked in sweat, and a stink of burning causes me to cough away the acrid stench. He's foaming at the mouth. The animal has done enough.

I dismount, taking a few more steps towards the river, my gaze fixed on the ship. Now, I hear voices calling one to another, their cries far from filled with fear or angst.

'Who are you?' I demand to know.

'Who wants to bloody know?' a rough voice responds. It's still impossible to see more than a hint of who the other person is. They stand to answer me, but it doesn't help. My gaze turns westwards, but the horses are out of sight, both Mercians and Wessex warriors.

'Mercian?' I question.

'Who wants to bloody know?' the voice repeats.

'I'm a warrior of Mercia. Are you Mercian or not?' I ask hotly.

I can't see any weapons on display, but then, I can't see much of anything.

'No, we're not. But we're not from Wessex either,' another shouts. This one sounds like a woman. 'Ignore my arse of a brother,' the words continue. 'He'd sooner get himself embroiled in war than tell you who we are.'

'Who are you?'

'Traders, nothing more. We've been trying to come ashore for days but couldn't risk it with all the fires and warriors.'

I sigh at that. I thought this ship was from Wessex. But it's not. I need to get back to the real fight, although I doubt my horse will take me there.

'Then you should stay where you are – for now. It's not safe, not until the enemy has been sent back to Wessex.'

A murmur of conversation reaches my ears. One voice is sharp with fury, although I can't tell much else aside from it. The other one is softer and more cajoling.

'Where did you come from?'

I've turned aside to return to my horse, but the question perplexes me. They're to the west of Lundenwic. They should surely be to the east if they were traders from the continent. Unease ripples my spine once more.

'Icel?' a voice I recognise shouts.

'Lord Coenwulf?' I rejoin, startled.

'Icel,' another queries.

'Edwin?'

'What are you bloody doing here?' We all speak at the same time.

'Bloody hell,' I expel. 'You could have picked a better time to make your homecoming.'

'King Wiglaf sent word we should return,' Edwin speaks, and now the sound of oars moving through the water reaches my ears.

'How are my children?' Lord Coenwulf demands. Finally, I sight him and Edwin, and all the others on the ship. I smile to see those who followed Coenwulf into banishment.

'They're well. Your sister cares for them.' I hope I'm right when I say that. I realise I'm not entirely sure where they are.

'Take me to the bloody king,' Lord Coenwulf demands, almost falling from the ship in his eagerness.

'The king's a little preoccupied now,' I reply. 'The king of Kent.'

'Yes, yes, I know all that. But, as soon as I've seen the king, I can return to my children.'

'You might just want to wait a little longer.' I'm moving towards the ship, fearful he'll slide from it and into the water. I can see how he still favours one leg.

'I've waited long enough,' Lord Coenwulf expels. His face is tight with fury. He seems much restored to the man he once was. I catch Edwin's eye, and he offers me a wide smile.

'My lord.' I hold my hands out, trying to urge him back into the boat even as the water rises above my boots. 'There are no horses here. Wait. Go to the quayside. You'll be allowed entry now. The enemy's gone.'

Lord Coenwulf shakes his head and lifts his leg as though he'll climb into the water, only for a bellow of rage to come from further down the river. We all turn to look, Lord Coenwulf half in and half out of the ship. I'm shocked once more at what I can see.

There was a ship for the Wessex warriors after all, but now it blazes, the sails disappearing almost in a puff of smoke, as men hasten to jump into the River Thames to evade the flames.

The woman I spoke to shouts to her men.

'Come on, we can rescue them.' She calls snapped

commands, having the ship turn back into the river's flow before Lord Coenwulf can right himself. Edwin's quick to grab him from behind. I notice his well-groomed beard and moustache with a smirk. I never thought he'd manage to grow such as that.

'Only rescue them if they're Mercian,' I call, but I doubt that'll sway them. The shrieks and splashes of those abandoning the Wessex ship flood the air. My horse looks up from drinking, and then quickly returns to the task, but we're not alone any more. More and more Mercians race towards the river, many of them lacking a horse, which accounts for the delay, and for why they pant so heavily.

I stand and watch. I'm mindful Lord Æthelwulf might not be on the Wessex ship, and this could be a ploy to have us stop looking for him. And yet, I can't see how it's not connected.

The flames grow even higher on the ship, the harsh shrieks of men in the water running as a counterpart to the roar of the flames and the shouts of those trying to rescue those who might be sucked beneath the wet expanse.

To the far side of the river, people from Wessex have come to stand on the riverbank. They shout encouragement to those swimming towards them, which tells me all I need to know. If they were Mercians, they'd be coming this way. They must be the Wessex warriors.

I snarl, feeling ineffectual. I can't do anything to stop them reaching Wessex. I could risk swimming across, but I'd only arrive when they were all standing on the far shore, and then I'd be in danger of being killed by them.

No, I stay in place as my fellow Mercians join me. Then my eye is caught by a shimmer of silver and gold, by a flash of white horsehair, on the far bank, and my lips turn into a grimace.

King Ecgberht has come to witness his son's triumph. The

bastard. Instead, he'll watch his failure, or even better, his death as he's sucked into the watery depths of the River Thames.

The shouts of the Wessex warriors reach my ears, alongside the thunder of heavy hoofbeats. I turn aside and see Wulfheard and Ealdorman Ælfstan returning this way. Their faces are black with fury, and I know what they'll say even before they shout the news to me.

'Lord Æthelwulf escaped,' Wulfheard huffs, Commander Eahric arriving behind him.

'Was he in the ship?'

'Yes.'

'Then, it might be that he doesn't escape for long,' I suggest, watching Lord Coenwulf's ship and her crew hauling in men as though they're giant fish flopping onto dry land.

'Why?'

'That's Lord Coenwulf,' I counter. A slow smile spreads across Commander Eahric's face, while Wulfheard's gaze settles on me.

'Why's he back?' he muses, but I don't answer. It seems self-evident. King Wiglaf decided Lord Coenwulf could return as soon as he knew to doubt Eadbald's testimony. I confess I'm pleased the king has already made the decision. With all the half-truths and evasion of the queen and Brihthild, the king needed to be strong enough to act without waiting for someone to chisel the truth from them.

King Ecgberht, evidently realising his son's peril, must order his people into the river as the far bank erupts into activity. He's recognised the ship is Mercian or has Mercians on board rather than those from Wessex. Horses and warriors pant, and even some of the traders from Lundenwic hurry to us, bringing ropes to pull men free from the river. Against the smoking remains of the burnt parts of the settlement, I see more ships coming along the river towards us. I hope they're Mercian and not from Wessex.

King Wiglaf arrives, mounted and lacking the splendour of King Ecgberht, but then, Wiglaf's been fighting even though he was to stay within Londinium on the command of his ealdormen. Blood covers his byrnie, and his blades glisten wetly. We might have prevented him from fighting to begin with, but now he's working on taking vengeance against the Wessex warriors.

'What's this?' he demands.

'The Wessex ship floundered in the middle of the river. We believe Lord Æthelwulf was aboard. That ship there has Lord Coenwulf on it, returning from Frankia. They're pulling in those they can.'

King Wiglaf nods. Behind him, I see his son mounted on his fine horse. Lord Wigmund's face is mutinous. He's tied to the saddle, but only those close can see that. King Ecgberht, on the far side of the River Thames, won't know King Wiglaf has apprehended his son. Although, he might suspect it. I realise King Ecgberht must have known of Lord Wigmund and Lord Æthelwulf's intentions to be here now, waiting, no doubt, to be escorted into Lundenwic having used the ship now burning to cross into Mercian-held land.

A groping wet hand reaches for the riverbank. Cenred hastens to aid the man to his feet, uncaring of whether he's Mercian or not. Only when he stands do I recognise him.

'Bloody hell, Kyre,' Wulfheard explodes. 'I told you not to follow them into the river.'

'Did anyone else do so?' I ask quickly. I'd not considered it might be my friends drowning beneath the weight of their byrnies in the River Thames. I seek out my allies, but there are too many people watching to pick out my friends.

'Just me.' Kyre heaves breath into his chest. 'I was sure I had him, the bastard.'

I shake my head, hurrying to help him remove his byrnie,

which weighs more than four sacks of flour, even as someone steps forward to offer their cloak for his shoulders. I murmur my thanks to the woman. She offers me an appraising smile with a glint in her eyes. I swallow nervously away from such rampant attention and move aside. I hear Wulfheard's chuckle. That man misses nothing.

Finally, the work of those on the trading ship comes to an end. There's no more splashing. A few others have been hauled ashore using hempen ropes. Wessex warriors stand and shiver on Mercian land. No one offers them a cloak, or even aids them in removing their equipment. One of the ships coming towards us arrives.

'We've found three bodies,' a voice calls. I shudder at the news, although I hope they're all from Wessex.

'I think we've seen enough,' King Wiglaf responds, turning his horse to ride back towards the smoking remains of Lundenwic. The entire settlement hasn't burned, although it certainly feels like it has. I look for my horse. The animal still drinks, as do others. Overhead, the sun's riding high. Has this all occurred in only one morning? I shake my head in amazement.

On the far bank, King Ecgberht slinks away.

'Did he find his son?'

Wulfheard shrugs. 'No idea. But, he's decided he's seen enough.'

Lord Coenwulf's trading ship turns to head towards Lundenwic.

'How many?' Commander Eahric demands.

'Eight, two dead,' a voice responds. It's the woman again. 'We'll bring them ashore at the quayside,' she calls. Already oars are being used, although the current seems strong.

With a parting glance towards King Ecgberht and his men, I move to my horse. I'm not riding him back, but I must return him.

I don't know who he belongs to, but he's a fine animal. I clamp down on my desire to buy another horse. One man has only so many arses that need to sit on a saddle.

'Come on,' I murmur. I'm already thinking of Oswy. I need to ensure he's being looked after. I could also do with some of my wounds being looked at. I'm itchy from sweat and smoke. My lips are drier than a body that's been long interred beneath the soil, and I'd welcome something to eat.

'Five of you remain here,' I hear Commander Eahric order. 'Ensure no one else comes ashore. Return when it's time to eat once more.' I'm grateful not to be included in that.

King Wiglaf's slowed. He speaks to his son. His shoulders are tense. Lord Wigmund's face is red with fury while his lips open and shut rapidly. Perhaps they shouldn't be having this argument here. I don't know where Ealdorman Sigered is. Did he try to escape to Wessex? I hope he's one of those who's drowned. I doubt I'll get my wish.

The men and women from Lundenwic stream back towards the settlement. Kyre's pressed onto Wulfheard's horse because we can't find his animal. It'll be somewhere close, I'm sure. Wulfheard walks with Commander Eahric.

I turn to see Cenred and Uor. The two men are too tired to talk, shoulders sagging as they walk with their horses.

We're all knackered. But Mercia is once more safe. Or so I hope.

Only then, it isn't.

20

We're not expecting it. We're not prepared for it. I don't even know how they've done it. One moment, we're all walking back towards Lundenwic, heads bowed, exhausted. The next, Lord Wigmund's horse rears. He scrabbles to hold on, only his bindings keeping him mounted.

'What?' King Wiglaf calls, his hand already reaching for a weapon. I do the same, abandoning my horse to rush closer. The king and his son are only just ahead.

'Wulfheard,' I bellow. Ealdorman Ælfstan's already alert to the danger. The horse hasn't been startled by a small creature or a bird taking flight. No, a Wessex warrior stands there. In fact, about ten of them.

Their eyes are hooded, grimaces revealing a collection of yellow teeth. Their faces are filthy.

'Bastards,' I growl, running even faster, legs pumping beneath me, cheek and chin wounds pulsing and stinging with sweat and exertion.

A sharp movement, and suddenly, one of the men is mounted behind Lord Wigmund, a seax blade held at his captive's throat.

'Stay away,' he growls, voice guttural and filled with loathing, the Wessex accent impossible to ignore. 'Stay away, you bastards, or he dies. Let us through. We've business with Lord Wigmund that can only be conducted in Wessex.'

These ten men face over a hundred Mercian warriors. Knackered we might be, but we'll still fight. The howls of those without byrnies and weapons flood the air. I can't see King Wiglaf's face, but I imagine his expression only too well. The enemy need to pay.

'Release my son,' King Wiglaf commands stridently.

'No.' The man doesn't even consider it.

'Release my son, and your death will be swift,' King Wiglaf tries to cajole.

'No. Lord Wigmund is ours. Allow us through.' The other nine men surround Lord Wigmund and his horse. King Wiglaf remains close. The enemy have blades to hand, and four of them have spears, held menacingly outwards, daring us to get nearer.

The horse is uneasy, moving forwards and backwards, and emitting a shrill whinny of unhappiness. It won't like having two riders.

'Don't injure my son.' King Wiglaf tries a different tack. My eyes are everywhere, trying to decide what to do. Beside me, Wulfheard's wound tighter than loom-weighted thread. He's itching to kill the Wessex warriors.

'Don't get any closer,' the man holding Lord Wigmund retorts. He seems very confident for someone who's outnumbered and far from home.

'We won't,' King Wiglaf answers, his hands to either side, showing we shouldn't approach.

'Now, escort us to the river. There's a ship on the way.'

I turn. There can't be another one. But sure enough, one wallows in the centre of the River Thames. It's not the one which has brought Lord Coenwulf back to Mercia. That's almost returned to Lundenwic. I can see it in the distance through the haze of clinging smoke. It's not the one that sank. This then is another one. How, I consider, do we keep missing them?

'Do as he says,' King Wiglaf directs. I'm not alone in growling, even as I step aside to allow the horse and the Wessex warriors through.

'Father,' Lord Wigmund manages to cry. I see how he holds himself steady against the horse's gait and the blade at his throat. Tears stream from his eyes.

'Shut up,' the guttural voice orders. Lord Wigmund bites his lip. Already, a thin line of blood shows on his neck. I don't see how he's going to survive this. Lady Ælflæd's image appears in my mind. It's inopportune, but perhaps if her husband were dead, we could resume our friendship. I'd like that.

But no. Lord Wigmund's the future of Mercia. It's him, or one of three small children. Or me. I don't bloody want it. We must rescue him, even if he is a snivelling traitor who's tried to betray Mercia to the Wessex king. Now, it seems, they'll betray him in return.

The Wessex men walk through our guard, back where we've just come from, towards the river. I can smell their foulness. How long have they been hiding? How could they even predict this would happen, or have they simply taken advantage of our momentary relief at banishing the rest of the enemy?

King Wiglaf follows the unruly procession, Commander Eahric at his side, hastily ordering the Mercians to stay close, but not too close.

Lord Wigmund shrieks again, a sound filled with terror, as the horse missteps. No doubt the cut on his neck has grown ever wider as his captor's knife slips. I hate that man. I know what it is to be held in the thrall of someone else. I know what it is to feel useless, terrified and bloody, bloody scared.

I look up. King Ecgberht and his distinctive white-crested helm have returned to the far bank of the river. Why would they want Lord Wigmund? If they wished to rule Mercia, surely they'd sooner Lord Wigmund was dead. Just another one of the many Mercian æthelings to be disposed of. Perhaps they think to take advantage of King Wiglaf's love for his son, not that I'm sure there's a great deal there. But what do I know? I had no mother. My father didn't recognise me as his son. I've been raised by Edwin's mother, Wynflæd and my uncle. I don't know what it is to be loved by a father.

We draw closer and closer, the figures on the boat slowly coming into focus. I'm convinced one of them is Lord Æthelwulf. If only I had a bow and arrow or a spear, I'd direct it at the bastard.

No one speaks. There's no sound. It's too quiet. Even the birds have fled. I look upwards, seeking out the sun's placement, and see a darkened shape against its brightness. I look away and then look again. I know what it is even before the harsh shriek of its cry reaches my ears.

It's another eagle, the emblem of Mercia, and I know what I need to do.

I reach out and grip Wulfheard's arm, showing him my intentions. He shakes his head frantically, but it doesn't stop me and my plans, which are forming quickly, reacting to every step the horse takes closer to the River Thames, the waiting ship and fresh catastrophe for Mercia.

I wait, bide my time, and then begin to move closer to the enemy when their eyes are elsewhere. They can sense their triumph, which will make them too confident.

Any moment now, the time will come. I must be ready.

Abruptly, the ground clears before us, the green of the grasses and fields under cultivation giving way to the brown muck of the riverbank. The ship's almost ashore or as close to shore as possible. The men will have to wade waist-deep into the river. And that's when the eagle overhead shrieks, the cry loud, elongated and coming from far too close.

Everyone looks up. Everyone. Some even duck aside as though the bird will attack them. It's the cry of a bird on the hunt.

Now is my chance.

I'll be the hunter.

On legs that should ache and throb with tiredness, I flee over the uneven ground. I absorb the dips and crests easily, not even seeming to need to breathe. I focus only on the horse, on Lord Wigmund, and on the enemy.

Beside the horse, one of the spearmen looks upward, mouth hanging open so far drool fills his beard.

He's mine.

I leap at him, stabbing down, and using his collapsing body to jump as high as possible. Lord Wigmund doesn't see me coming. Neither does the man who holds him captive. Or any of the bastards.

Time slows. I hear little but the wind, as if I'm the bird and not the eagle overhead. I kick in the air as though there's something there to give me the added impetus.

The cry of my name ripping from Wulfheard's lips is filled with fear and worry.

And my shoulder crashes into Lord Wigmund. I feel him slipping, along with me. I can smell his fear and only then do I remember he was bound to the horse. Before we hit the ground, I reach for the bindings, desperate to release him before the horse bolts with the unexpected action. The rope severs with the sharp slice from my seax. We land, the air expelled from my body, in a

Betrayal of Mercia 241

tangle of arms and legs, backs and arses. I roll to my feet, mindful this is far from over. There are enemies all around.

The horse shrieks. It rolls, taking the man on its back with it, although Lord Wigmund surprises me by managing to scrabble clear alongside me. I succeeded in severing the rope that tied him to the horse, but his hands remain bound, and now the surviving enemy is advancing.

They move slowly, hesitantly, caught entirely unprepared, assessing what their chances of success are now.

'Go,' I huff, pushing Lord Wigmund behind me. 'Go,' I cry, hoping Wulfheard, the king, or Commander Eahric or any of the damn Mercians might have been alert to my intentions. The horse kicks its long legs as it tries to stand, booting the man to the left of it for good measure. He falls, legs collapsing beneath him.

The rider's trapped beneath the horse. I hear his bones crunching as the horse fights to stand. I'd wince, but three enemies are coming nearer, and Lord Wigmund remains behind me. I need him to go. While he stays, he risks being cut by our foemen or kicked by the terrified horse. I lash out with my seax, mindful of the two men with the spears. I can't see what's happening at the river, but there's a loud crash. Are the Wessex warriors such fools they'll risk coming ashore when the king and half of his oath-sworn warriors are here to kill them?

The spear holders are slow. Instead, a man with a dour expression and sharp eyes rushes me with a seax. I hold it aside, moving my other arm as though it, too, has a blade. But it's just a means of distracting my enemy. I can fend him off with my arm if I must. It won't be bloody pretty, though.

All hell has broken loose. The Mercians shout, Wulfheard's voice above all others. I need them to hurry up. Three men threaten me, and Lord Wigmund still hasn't moved. He didn't go when I ordered him to do so. I don't know what he's bloody doing.

I hear a shriek and a gargle of a cut-off cry even as I counter the rushing attack of others. I risk glancing behind and see Mercians rushing to aid me. Cenred and Kyre lead them. Their faces are flecked with rage and fury. How dare the Wessex warriors try something like this?

I share their anger. It's not helping me. A spear comes towards my head. I duck low, but there's another one, and the seax wielder. They look like mean warriors but that might be the mud stuck to their faces and clothes.

I can't fight them alone. Wulfheard's not near enough to help me. I still fear for the king's son, although he's little use to anyone. But it's how it looks. Enough of Mercia's kings have fallen on the blades of their enemies. We can't allow the king's son to join that number. I can't countenance it, even though I hate him and wish he were dead.

I lift my shoulder to redirect the spear. It goes wildly high, the man's hands coming too close to me. I'd attack him, but the spear and the seax make it impossible.

I'm aware of the horse finally regaining its feet. I eye my enemy. The spear remains in the air. If the spearman takes it back and jabs again, I won't be able to evade it, not the spears and the seax. This is going very wrong.

None of my allies are close enough to be of any use.

I turn into the seax strike, allowing the spear to fall, mindful I only store problems for later. Maybe there's time for another to reach us. I'm not sure. Where before everything was happening too slowly, now it's happening too fast.

I lash out with my blade but meet nothing but air.

'Go,' I huff to Lord Wigmund once more, but I know he doesn't do so. Instead, and I confess I turn a furrowed brow his way, he stands beside me, stance wide, prepared to meet the enemy's onslaught with a seax in his hand. Did he have that all along? Why didn't he fight himself free? I banish the thought. I'll think about that later.

I stab out, and then punch with my other hand, landing a blow on both of my foemen, while Lord Wigmund almost runs down one of the spearmen, getting close enough to him the spear's useless. Lord Wigmund jabs and slashes at our enemy. He's not in danger of hurting anyone but himself with such wild strikes, but the enemy don't know that.

And then Cenred's there, his rapid steps taking him to aid Lord Wigmund.

'Bastard,' the Wessex seax holder glowers at me. I lift my elbow and jab into the spear holder I face. His nose erupts in a flood of bright blood as he buckles and falls.

'Same,' I counter, bending to wrench the spear from my enemy's limp hand and then using it to scythe my way closer to the seax wielder.

My exertions have caught up with me. My face is pulsing. My legs are trembling. My breath is coming too rapidly in and out of my chest. My throat's tight.

I fear no one need strike me, and I'll still take to my knees. It's been a bloody long day.

A spear thrusts its way through the seax man, his eyes rotating from glowering at me to looking at the weapon as though he doesn't know what it is.

Blood splatter hits my nose and mouth. I spit it aside, a nod to Kyre to show my thanks. The man on the ground holds his nose, howling against the pain. With my seax, I slice across his neck and then stab into his chest as well, just to assure myself he's dead.

I bend, suck in much-needed air, and gaze around me frantically. Lord Wigmund remains at my side, but Cenred stands with him, more able to defend him than Wigmund can himself. Kyre's moved to the other Wessex warriors who remain, but only one continues to fight. Two of them, I see, have rushed into the water. Not that they'll get far. Goðemon and Ealdorman Ælfstan are after them like rats running from a blazing barn.

Behind me, I see the man who began all this, staring sightlessly, his one leg at a terrible angle, revealing white bone beneath the severed flesh. But what killed him was a weeping and savage cut on his chest. I wince to see the savagery, turning to face Lord Wigmund. His pale face is flushed red, spattered with blood, and I know who killed our foeman. I confess I'm impressed. Here, when his life depended on it, he killed one of our enemies. I didn't believe Lord Wigmund even knew how to kill.

'My thanks,' he pants. King Wiglaf rides closer. He eyes me, with an incline of his head and I can well imagine the conversation we're going to share about this when we're next alone.

'Bring my son another horse,' the king commands. The original horse is wild-eyed and won't take to being ridden. The splashing and cries from the waterfront have quietened. Ealdorman Ælfstan stamps from the water, dragging a lifeless form behind him. The ship's already made a hasty departure towards the Wessex side of the river. King Ecgberht has disappeared once more. His white-horsehair helm is no longer visible. His son has failed him. That brings me some pleasure. I hate bloody Lord Æthelwulf, but I'm angry he's lived through this.

Goðemon appears next, dragging a flailing figure from the water by his hair. I'm still breathing deeply, trying to catch my breath even as King Wiglaf reaches the figure, who's quickly trussed and tied with a strip of cloth Goðemon rips from his tunic. The wet fabric binds the prisoner tightly.

King Wiglaf looks down from his horse and jerks the chin upwards.

I gasp. I've seen the man before. He was the messenger who

came to take back Brihthild, supposedly on the orders of the archbishop, Lanfrac was his name. As I suspected, he must be one of Lord Æthelwulf's creatures.

Lord Wigmund's been brought a horse. He's shoved onto the animal, and bound to it again by Commander Eahric. He's a brave man. But he also knows the mind of the king he serves. Lord Wigmund is a traitor, but he's to face Mercian not Wessex justice. And he must live to do so.

The soft whimper from one of the dying men has Wulfheard bending to end his life. He looks at me with an appraising glance.

'Bloody hell, Icel,' he huffs. 'That was dangerous.' There's respect and also fear in his voice, which surprises me. King Wiglaf turns his horse, an assessing look on his face. He brings the horse to a stop beside me.

'Icel, no one else would have risked that,' he admonishes. His words are breathless, ripe with shock.

'I doubt that, my lord king,' I pant. 'It was just a matter of waiting for the right time.'

Overhead, the cry of the eagle rings loudly once more. Again, everyone looks upwards unbidden – well, all apart from me and the king. He nods slowly, acknowledging my words. I hold his gaze. Much passes between us, but all of it remains unsaid. Perhaps no one else would have done what I did. Maybe he questions why I risked so much. But that's my secret to keep. He need never know how much of Mercia runs in my blood, and what I'll do to protect her, and me from having to claim the kingship.

21

I take the horse I took from the burning stables to find Bicwide. Commander Eahric's orders ring throughout Lundenwic, as do Ealdorman Muca's. He limps from within the hall, his face bloodied and dirty with ash. People slowly start to reappear from where they've been hiding. I swallow my grief at the dead I see. The Wessex warriors have stolen the lives of Mercians who were never even fighting.

They're no better than the bastard Viking raiders.

The king has taken his son and Ealdorman Ælfstan and ridden towards Londinium. If I were him, I'd welcome the comfort of knowing firm walls protected me as well. And the knowledge of firm locks and doors to keep Lord Wigmund controlled are no doubt also appealing.

Weeping and wailing haunts the streets, as do strange, wraith-like creatures stained with the smoke and ash of the many fires. The west of Lundenwic is largely undamaged. The same can't be said for the east. Horses and animals mill in the streets, unsure where to go. Those with their wits about them hurry to retrieve them and take them to a temporary enclosure that's sprung up close to the northern gate. That's where I find Bicwide.

I smile to see my horse, unleashing a torrent of pain from my cheek and chin wounds, reminding myself in the process that I'm caked in mud, sweat and blood. Bicwide's unharmed. That pleases me. I confess, exhaustion weighs me down, and I'm not alone.

Wulfheard eyes me with some concern. Others of our men look at me with a new-found respect.

'Bloody hell, Icel.' Cenred's the only one to give voice to what they're all thinking. 'You're a lucky sod the king's son didn't get killed. I don't think many of us would have taken that gamble.'

I nod mutely, gratefully accepting a beaker of water brought to me by someone with the wherewithal to realise we all need food and water. The taste isn't the most pleasant, but it feels like heaven as my lips finally have some moisture on them. I cough away the reek of the smoke.

The many fires are out. Now, there's just the swirl of smoke flooding the air. I'd welcome a stiff breeze to drive it from the streets.

'Someone had to do something.' I cough once more, and shrug, handing the water back, although I'd sooner drink it all. Uor eyes me with something like wonder in his eyes. 'I'm sure you'd all have thought of something similar,' I deflect. I don't want to be thought of as anything special. I did what had to be done. 'If anything, thank the eagle, not me.' Now Wulfheard's dusty eyebrows furrow while Cenred tips his head towards me, a smirk playing on his lips as he shakes his head at my denial.

'We're to follow the king back to Londinium,' Wulfheard announces. I'm not alone in groaning.

'Can't we pick the dead clean first?' Landwine requests, a

gleam in his eyes. There were some mighty fine seaxes and swords on display.

'The people of Lundenwic will have beaten us to it,' Wulfheard comments. I'd ask him why, but a young girl, perhaps no older than ten summers, runs into our line of sight, brandishing a shimmering sword in her hand that's almost taller than she is – the patina of blood flashes in the dull glow permeating the smoke.

'Ah,' Landwine acknowledges. I imagine I'm not alone in hoping the girl doesn't trip and hurt herself on such a blade.

'We'll retrieve them at some point,' Wulfheard announces. 'Or perhaps the king will determine all weapons should be surrendered in exchange for recompense.'

My thoughts turn to Oswy. I hope he's well.

'What of Lord Coenwulf?' Goðemon questions.

'He'll be welcomed by the king, and will be reunited with his sister and his children as well,' Wulfheard speaks confidently. I'm sure he will too.

'Did you see that bastard?' Kyre questions, his eyes still wild with battle rage where he rests with his horse. 'That bastard king of Wessex. He's a greedy arsehole.'

Murmurs of agreement greet his words.

'He made it very clear he was involved,' Wulfheard muses. 'I can't see friendly relations being restored between Mercia and Wessex anytime soon.'

'What of the queen and the ætheling?' Waldhere asks. He's removed his helm. His eyes and nose remain their usual colour, although sweat-soaked. With the ash from the fires, he looks strange. White eyes on a grey face. I'd laugh at him, but I imagine we all look identical.

Wulfheard shrugs once more. 'It's not for us to decide. The men of the witan and the king will resolve the issue. They're both in it up to their necks. The king would be a fool to think their actions can be forgiven.'

Murmurs of agreement and resignation ripple through us. There's suddenly a great deal of activity nearby, but thankfully, we can be still for the first time since before daybreak. It's been an unusual few days. Men and women call for one another, names floating strangely in the grey half-light.

'Come on,' Wulfheard cajoles. I'm almost asleep standing up. His words startle me to wakefulness, my hand reaching for my grimy seax. Wulfheard catches the movement and shakes his head, an amused smirk on his lips. 'Come on, you lazy lot,' he instructs, swinging into his saddle with an ease I envy. It takes me much longer to haul myself into Bicwide's wide saddle. When I first bought him, a mere few months ago, his saddle was uncomfortable and too large for me. In the intervening time, it's become more comfortable. Now I welcome it as a means of not having to walk any further.

With straining doors and complaints from the gate guards, we're allowed to exit Lundenwic, taking our horses with us. I maintain a hold on the horse I rode out of the stable. I don't know whom he belongs to, and I want to ask Cuthred, for Wynflæd won't do it, to tend to his burns.

It feels like another world outside the defences. The smoke doesn't drift beyond the gateway. Overhead, the sun's bright, holding a promise of much-delayed warmth. I look for the eagle, but the bird's abandoned me. Still, I muse on its significance. How often, I think, has an eagle aided me or been sighted just before a momentous event? I wish I could recall. I know it's more often than I realise. I'd ask my fellow warriors, but they're slumped in their saddles. With fatigue showing in the way they ride, they'd not take kindly to such a strange question. I don't want to face the ridicule. I'll consider it myself, instead.

Here, everything feels benign and not at all as though we've just fought for the future of Mercia and to protect the life of the king. Even the River Thames, in the near distance, sparkles blue and no longer menacingly grey. I peer at Wessex, but it's too far away to see if the Wessex warriors remain on alert. I imagine they're slinking their way home. I hope King Ecgberht finally relinquishes his dreams of taking Mercia. I anticipate the king will finally quiet his wife and the conspiracy around her which has endangered so many Mercians.

The gates to Londinium are shut tight. A shout from those on guard duty on the battlements has them creaking open. We enter and immediately my eyes rest on Cuthred. He offers me an uncertain smile. I consider why Wynflæd isn't there, and feel a stirring of worry for Oswy. I knew he was too ill to be fighting. I should have been firmer. I should have forced him to remain behind.

Dismounting is an agony. I call Cuthred to me. He comes quickly, dodging the horses and exhausted warriors. There's a flurry of activity as others come to take our animals. A dull cheer echoes, and the voices of those who didn't fight and still have the strength to speak are too sharp and bright.

'How's Oswy?' I demand, mindful of the two horses trying to reach the water trough.

'Oswy's fine. He'll be well. Bloody fool should have stayed within. He has a fever. I've given him herbs and a healing pottage. He needs to rest, which is like asking you lot to cut off a damn limb.' He tries to be humorous, but I detect something else.

'What is it?' I demand, watching him over Bicwide's high back.

'The king's son,' he whispers, having checked no one can overhear him. 'Wynflæd's with him now.'

My forehead furrows. This isn't what I was expecting. 'What's the matter with him? I thought he only took a cut to the neck?'

'It's not that. The neck wound will heal easily enough. But he took another blow. I doubt anyone noticed. He's been skewered through the back as well. It bleeds a great deal.'

I shudder, reminded too easily of the wound that killed Brihthild's brother within Canterbury. 'Will he be well?'

'I don't know. Wynflæd's worried, and when she's concerned, I know to be worried as well.'

'Bollocks,' explodes from my mouth. 'I thought he'd escaped almost unscathed.'

'So did he and the king. It was only noticed when he dismounted, leaving a pool of blood behind.'

'Arse,' I say more softly, removing Bicwide's saddle, and then wondering where I can leave it in the press of men and boys close to the stables. I'm fearful I'll get the blame for this. 'I hope she can help him,' I murmur, even as Cuthred manages to distract himself with a wince of sympathy for the additional horse's wounds.

He eyes me with confusion.

'The stable was burning to the ground. The entrance was blocked. I had him escape through the wall. Have you got anything to ease the soreness?'

'I'll slather some ointment on it,' Cuthred murmurs, his eyes prodding at the collection of burn marks around the animal's neck and down its forelegs. 'It could have been a lot worse,' he announces.

'It could, yes,' I agree. 'Lord Coenwulf's returned. He was on a ship in the River Thames.'

'So King Wiglaf recalled him regardless of our journey to Wessex?'

I nod, as we move aside, leaving Bicwide and the other horse to fight over a hay net. I'm impressed they have the energy to do so. If I had to fight for my food now, I'd roll over and sleep. At the thought, my belly growls. Cuthred smirks at me.

'Oswy's asleep in one of the rooms away from the main hall. Wynflæd thought it was best for him there. They're cooking pottage. Get some, and I'll tend to the horse. And then I'll go and find out how Lord Wigmund's faring, and then I'll sort out your face. Again.'

I nod. My legs feel leaden. I turn and see my fellow warriors look no better than me. We're all dusted with the grey of ash and the blood of others. We look as though we've risen from a grave.

Murmurs reach my ears, but I pay them no heed. I take up space on one of the few benches within the hall, and when Cenred nudges me, I welcome a bowl of pottage. I eat it too quickly, burning my mouth, barely aware of the meaty taste. I sense the bowl and spoon being taken from my unmoving hands. Cenred begins his ministrations, but even they don't rouse me, despite the pain. My eyes close in sleep. I don't think I'll notice if the world set on fire. I need some sleep, desperately.

Wynflæd's waspish voice jolts me awake, as I blink the grit from my eyes. I can't tell if it's morning or night. 'How long have I been asleep?' I question, astounded to find myself still sitting on the bench.

'All night. Now, come with me,' she instructs. Standing is agony. Walking is even worse, while the pottage I ate yesterday is like a leaden lump in my belly. What does she want me for?

22

I'm led to a small room on the far side of the fort. I bend my head to enter, although Wynflæd needs to do no such thing. It takes me a moment for my eyes to adjust to the dull light, and when it does, I'm startled by who's within.

Somehow, I expected it to be Lord Wigmund's room, and it is, but the king and queen are also there. Ealdormen Ælfstan and Tidwulf are in attendance, Tidwulf looking frail from his wound, but risen from his sickbed. Ealdorman Ælfstan acknowledges me with a tip of his head. I notice his hand isn't far from his weapons belt. The presence of the queen explains the many guards we had to pass through to gain entry. There's no window. The only way in or out is through the door we've used.

I bow.

'My lord king, my lady queen, my Lord Wigmund.' Of them all, only Wigmund doesn't hear me. He's sleeping, face sheeted with sweat. Despite the few tallow candles lighting the space oddly yellow, the livid red mark running across his neck is easy to see. I wince. It looks bloody painful.

'This is your fault,' Queen Cynethryth hisses, hands bound

before her, but her fingers curled as though she means to scrape them down my face. Her features are white with fury. Her eyes appear bloodshot and, while she's been given new clothes to wear since her trip along the rocky foreshore of Londinium, she remains a prisoner.

'Be quiet,' King Wiglaf snaps angrily from the other side of his son's bed. He's not changed his clothes since the battle. Indeed, the scent of smoke hangs heavy in the air. I doubt any of us have changed. 'You're here on sufferance because I'm not a heartless man. If you don't keep your mouth shut, I'll have you returned to your prison.'

I look at the queen. I can see how much it pains her to keep quiet as she bites her lower lip to stop complaints pouring from her mouth.

'Icel, as you can see,' King Wiglaf begins in a softer tone, 'my son is wounded. Wynflæd's doing all she can for him. My thanks. She assures me he'll recover, given time.'

I nod along. 'Wynflæd knows her craft,' I offer, unsure why I might be asked to vouch for her. King Wiglaf knows her. He trusts her. Even the queen does.

'My thanks,' Wynflæd offers waspishly. I expect her to smile, but she doesn't, concern etched onto her face, which I know intimately. If I closed my eyes, I could still say where every laughter line can be found. She's as familiar to me as my seax handle, and the burn emblazoned on my palm.

'You're here at the request of Lady Ælflæd.'

I feel my lips opening at this, but clamp them shut thanks to a warning glance from Ealdorman Ælfstan. He seems tired. He looks how I feel. This has been a hellish few days.

'She says you've saved her nephews, and the woman who cared for them. You helped her brother and ensured he walked again, even if with a limp. She requests you tend to her husband in his time of need. Admittedly, there was also a mention of a horse or two.' The king's face furrows as he mutters the addition, showing how perplexed he is to have horses mentioned in the same breath as the young boys.

I stand, mystified, looking from Wynflæd to the king and then to Lord Wigmund.

'My lord king,' I stutter, entirely confounded. 'I'm no longer a healer, as you know. I'm a warrior of Mercia.'

'All the same. You and Wynflæd will tend to his every need. Alongside your young friend, Cuthred. You'll ask for anything and everything you need. Until Lord Wigmund's once more on his feet and able to resume his duties, you're to be at his side. This is Lady Ælflæd's wish, and it's also mine. The queen will be allowed to see him once a day. That time will be arranged by me, and she'll be escorted here and taken away by my guards. During her visits, you must listen to everything she says and report back information that's pertinent to this current calamity. Is that understood?'

I nod, because I've no choice in this, but then I do think of one question. 'Lady Ælflæd and her son and nephews, they're safe?' I know they didn't make it to Londinium during the attack. I've been fearful for them, despite assurances they were well.

'Of course. They escaped the Wessex attack and have been sheltering away from Londonia. A message was sent to them asking them to return. They'll shortly be reunited with her brother and the children's father. She doesn't wish to risk her son and so will remain distant from her husband, within Lundenwic.' The king's words show no emotion, but they astound me. I knew the pair to be estranged, and living separate lives after his potential involvement in the plot to kill her nephews was discovered. Surely, she'd welcome Lord Wigmund's death. 'When he's well once more, the queen and he will face the king's justice and explain their role in what's befallen Mercia in the last few days. I command you, Wynflæd and Icel, to ensure my son is able to stand unaided. I'll not have men and women sympathetic to him just because of his wounds. He's a man. He'll account for his actions as a man.'

I nod and look away as the king bows to sweep his son's hair clear from his forehead. I don't wish to see the compassion in the action, or the love that's evident on his face. Lord Wigmund's an embarrassment to his father, but it seems that doesn't stop him from caring for him. The love for a child and lack of loyalty to a king makes for an uneasy combination.

'Now, the queen is to be returned to her imprisonment.' Ealdormen Ælfstan moves towards her, no doubt to escort her away. I think she'll argue. After all, this is a perfect excuse to evade the dankness of the cell she's being kept in. But she continues to hold her tongue. With his hand on the queen's bound hands, the ealdorman calls to be allowed to leave.

When she's gone, the king looks at me.

'This isn't what I wanted to happen,' King Wiglaf mutters. 'Not at all. Know this, Icel. There's no blame attached to you. The stupid boy is responsible.' And with that, King Wiglaf exits the room, alongside Ealdorman Tidwulf who moves more slowly than the king, leaving me and Wynflæd to stand and stare at one another, until Cuthred slips back inside, relief showing on his face.

'Bloody hell,' he huffs.

'Bloody hell, indeed,' I murmur.

Wynflæd fixes me with an almost furious look.

'I was angry, and now I'm enraged at your involvement,' she directs at me. 'But the king doesn't wish to argue with Lady Ælflæd, and I suppose, if you're here, you can at least relieve Cuthred from the drudge work of getting water and taking away the shit and piss.' So spoken, she settles on a stool close to Lord Wigmund and retrieves something hanging from her dress cord.

When Cuthred and I stand there, unsure what to do, she huffs again.

'Find something to do. Looking at him won't make his wound heal any quicker.'

There's not much space in the small cell-like room. I have to hunch my shoulders, because it's not high enough for me to stand upright. Cuthred's struggling as well. I feel itchy and need to piss. I look at the empty buckets used to collect water close to the door, and immediately stride to collect them. Cuthred hurries to do the same. I think Wynflæd will hold her tongue, but she could never do that.

'The king will hear of it if you're not doing something useful.'

I grimace, but hasten to escape all the same. I can't do much for Lord Wigmund while he's sleeping. I know Wynflæd will have tended to the injuries. What he needs now is rest and a healing pottage. There's no hearth in the room to produce what's required.

'Where are you working?' I question Cuthred, nodding to the guards as they allow us to leave. I recognise them as Commander Eahric's most trusted men. They're so big they almost block the entire doorway just standing there.

'There's a hearth in the great hall and also another one in the kitchen, where most of the food's being prepared.'

'And what has Wynflæd bid you concoct?'

'A healing poultice and a pottage as well.' Cuthred's face flickers with relief as the guards allow him to walk past without comment. I'd be intimidated as well if I didn't wear as much leather and iron as them.

'So, we need water, and I need to piss, and then I'll help you,' I offer.

He nods, pleased with the resolution. I sense he wants to ask me a great deal, but instead, he leads me to the well within the fort. I leave him to haul up more water and make my way to the latrines.

I greet those I know while walking, noting bruises and cuts. It's only just light enough to see. No one seems to be wailing in agony, but they're probably elsewhere, like Oswy. Or, if they're lucky, being allowed to sleep off yesterday's exertions.

I consider why Lady Ælflæd has specifically asked me to tend to her husband. She knows I hate him. I thought she hated him. Why, then, is she so keen for him to live? Or isn't she? By some unspoken agreement, am I meant to ensure he doesn't recover? I'm sure she wouldn't place that responsibility on me. Would she? I dismiss the suggestion as I make myself presentable with the aid of a barrel used to collect rainwater thrown over my body after I've finished at the latrine ditch. The smell of so many people in one place is overwhelming. I look at the gateway, noting it remains locked against any threat from Wessex, even though the enemy warriors have been killed or have escaped across the River Thames.

Returning to Cuthred, I reach for one of the buckets of water, surprised by how hard it is to carry. My arms are weak from all the fighting I've been doing. He notes it with a wry smile as water slops over my feet on the way to the hearth fire.

'You need to walk with it away from your legs, or there'll be nothing left in it.'

I smile. I remember learning that lesson well.

In the kitchen area, food's being arranged, but the huge pots suspended over the fire are burbling away with little need for others to attend to them. The wooden boards are loaded with what fresh produce there is, but only two people occupy the kitchen, one of them asleep, the other almost asleep.

The one who's awake looks at Cuthred, but says nothing. It's clear he's a familiar face here. There's a small table filled with his supplies.

I lower the water buckets and take a good look around.

As expected, Cuthred and Wynflæd know what they're doing. I really don't understand why I've been forced to become involved.

'Here, make yourself useful,' Cuthred offers. 'Get these roots chopped and added to that pot over there.' He inclines his head towards the hearth fire. There are two small pots. One nestles in the flames, and one is held higher above it.

I set to work, using the knife lying there.

I find the action strangely soothing. My arms and legs feel tight, but the movement is as familiar to me as defending myself with a seax or shield. Cuthred and I don't speak as we labour. He's busy with some butter. I smirk at the sight of it. It's evidence we're in the king's kitchen. If I were anywhere else within Mercia, on one of the many roads or trackways, I'd not have butter to hand.

Cuthred passes me more and more items to prepare. Wild carrots to shred. Garlic to cut and crush. The smell of the pottage makes my belly growl, but I don't help myself to it. I'll eat when everyone else does.

Cuthred pulls something else towards me.

'Seaweed?' I question.

'Yes, it's a good month for it,' he offers without looking up. I consider from where it's come.

I notice he also has fresh yarrow, fennel, water mint, horse-radish, dandelion flowers, woodruff and onions. Lord Wigmund's wound might be unfortunate, but he's certainly picked the best time of year to be treated. Having this year's harvest almost at hand, even with the poor weather, will aid his recovery.

We work in companionable silence. I know if Wynflæd needs

us, she'll ensure we know. Some spare guards could do her bidding and would want to do so willingly. I consider Oswy. I'd like to check he's recovering, although I accept Cuthred's determination about his illness. I'm also curious about where Lord Coenwulf might be. Not that I have long to discover the answer to that.

'Icel,' a familiar voice calls to me. Startled, I find Edwin before me.

'Bloody hell,' I gasp. Cuthred's taken the opportunity to stop his labours as well.

'I thought you were a great warrior,' he calls, striding forward to engulf me in his arms. I return the embrace. I've never known Edwin feel so solid before. Has he, finally, become the warrior he always dreamed of being? 'Why are you in the damn kitchen?' he huffs into my ear, tickling it with his thick beard.

I step back and examine him.

'You've changed,' I accuse.

'You haven't,' he counters.

'Have you grown taller?' I question.

'Perhaps.' He smiles. 'Who's this?'

'Cuthred. You must have met him.'

'If I have, I've forgotten, apologies.' He reaches over and grips Cuthred's arm. I wince as Cuthred almost loses his balance.

'I'm Wynflæd's assistant,' Cuthred squeaks.

'No, you're not. He was a little shit, more likely to be falling from a tree than looking all serious in the kitchen.' His gaze sweeps from me to Cuthred, his mouth opening in an O of shock. 'It really is you?' he grumbles. 'Bloody hell fire.'

Edwin wears fine clothes, tall leather boots encasing his calves. He looks almost like a king.

'I see Frankia has treated you well.'

'It has, yes. I didn't want to go, and neither did Lord Coenwulf, but we've taken advantage of it. I trained with the king's warriors. They taught me a thing or two, I can tell you.'

'Why are you back?'

'The king ordered his return, saying his exile was at an end.'

'Has Lord Coenwulf seen the children?'

Edwin waves his hands as though it's not important, but he nods. 'Yes, he and his sister are together, speaking of all that's happened in our absence. I can scarcely believe it's only been a year.'

'And Eadburg?'

'Never fear, my friend. Eadburg and I are as besotted with each other as we were before everything happened.'

I nod, pleased with Edwin's response. He doesn't hesitate. I believe his words. I hope Eadburg will as well. She feared her scars would make him unwilling to resume their relationship. I trusted Edwin enough to know it would make no difference.

'We'll marry and live at Kingsholm.' That delights me. 'Frankia's an astounding place, but it's too bloody big.' I laugh at his jubilant tone.

'Your mother will be pleased to see you.'

'And I her. Now, what are you doing in here?'

'You don't know everything, then,' I counter. 'Lady Ælflæd has bid me tend to her husband.'

'But you're in the kitchen?'

'There are always remedies to prepare.'

'Hum.' Edwin's gaze is searching. I don't welcome it. 'I'll leave you to your task. When you're free from your duties, seek me out. I've much to teach you, Icel. Much indeed.'

His laughter echoes back through the room as he strides out. I turn back to the board and pile of herbs, while Cuthred and I share a glance. Both of us would rather be somewhere else.

'I'll go and see if Wynflæd needs anything,' I murmur, keen to have some time to myself.

'Tell her everything is being organised as she requested,' he mutters. I see we're both a little sulky after Edwin's larger-than-life return. It makes me wonder what I've been doing for the last year. Evidently, not enough.

I'm allowed through the ring of guards and walk into the room to find Wynflæd on her feet, bustling around the room. She looks up at my arrival.

'About bloody time,' she snaps. 'Help me.'

I see what she's trying to do and leap forwards. Lord Wigmund is a motionless lump, and still, she's trying to turn him on her own. I manage the action easily, holding him steady on his side so she can inspect the wound. I wince to see the blood-drenched linen he lies upon, and Wynflæd's breath whistles through her tight lips.

'This isn't bloody good,' she informs me, not that I needed her to tell me that. It's evident. 'I thought I'd bound the wound well enough, but it still bleeds, and listen to his breathing.' I realise then the whistly sound in the room is the air pumping in and out of Lord Wigmund's body.

'That's unwelcome,' I mutter.

'The blade has penetrated deeply,' she states.

I look at his face, noticing the blue of his lips.

'I fear he's wounded inside, and I won't be able to heal that.'

'What should we do?'

For the first time, I see a flicker of fear on Wynflæd's face. 'We need Theodore and Gaya.'

'I'm surprised the king hasn't already sent for them.'

'He has. I told him immediately the wound was severe. He took my caution seriously, but it'll be days before they arrive.'

'Should we turn him on his front? Would that ease him?'

'No, it'll do more harm. I'll layer a poultice over the wound. It'll seal it, I hope. In the meantime, we must think of another means of ensuring he keeps breathing.'

Lord Wigmund hasn't stirred despite what we've been doing to him. Indeed, he lies so still I could think him dead if not for the fierce heat coming from his skin.

'He's burning up.'

'He has a fever as well,' Wynflæd mutters unhappily.

Silence falls between us. I wait for Wynflæd to tell me what to do next. I sense her unease. She's been tasked with restoring the king's son to full health. He'll not accept failure.

'We'll heat the room with good vapours,' she announces, busily applying the poultice to Lord Wigmund's wound. I'm frustrated his neck wound is clean and seems to be healing nicely. 'We'll ask for incense from the bishop. You'll also bring me wax and have a brazier, no, two of them, brought to the room. We'll make it hot and easier for him to breathe,' she announces. But she's not finished. 'We'll also boil horehound, radish, celandine, catmint, marshmallow in honey and butter. Inform Cuthred he's to make that as well. He'll know how to do it.'

I stop myself from reminding her I know how to do it, as well.

'We'll also prepare the cure for lung disease. Tell Cuthred I want it boiled to the precise requirements, and if he can't remember, he's to be honest and tell me.'

'Isn't that too much?' I murmur. 'Shouldn't we wait for one treatment to work before beginning another?'

'Do you wish to tell the king his son died because we were unsure what would work?' Her words are edged.

'I—' I begin, but she talks over me.

'The king expects us to ensure his son's life. At the moment, that's looking increasingly unlikely. Now, Icel, go and send for the bishop and inform Cuthred of what I want him to do. Return when the braziers are ready, and we'll apply the incense to them and hopefully, help him breathe. Hurry.'

Before I leave, I gently lay him back down. Wynflæd has spread the poultice over the wound. It's a small scratch, little more, but it's done a great deal of damage. I always thought Lord Wigmund was useless, but he didn't deserve this. No one does.

'Go,' she hisses at me. I cast one more look at him, noting the blue on his lips and wishing there was more to be done.

Outside, I see Ealdorman Ælfstan and hurry to him. He watches me with alarm.

'I need incense from the bishop.'

'I'll go myself,' he assures me, already hastening to a run.

Next, I return to the kitchen. 'Cuthred, Wynflæd wants you to make the lung disease cure. She's adamant you're to speak now if you don't know the correct amount to be used of each item. I also need two braziers.' This I direct to the servants in the room. They bow quickly and hurry on their way. 'Take them to Wynflæd,' I shout after them. Alone with Cuthred, I speak quietly. 'She's really worried,' I mutter. 'She's throwing everything at it and has demanded the king send for Theodore and Gaya.'

Cuthred shows no concern. He nods wisely. 'She knows what she's doing. As do Theodore and Gaya. She won't allow the worst to befall him.'

'She'll try not to, but his lips are blue.'

'Has she sent for incense?'

'Yes,' I confirm. 'Ealdorman Ælfstan has gone himself.'

'Then, Icel, you need to stop worrying and go and find me some bog myrtle.'

'Where am I going to get that from?' I growl.

'I suggest you start with the bog,' Cuthred answers unhelpfully. I've half a mind to tell him to go and find it, but I'm better suited to that than concocting the lung cure Wynflæd requests.

'I'll go then,' I murmur, mind busy trying to decide the best place to find what he wants. It's the right time of the year, I know to collect the leaves; but where it might be, I'm unsure. 'Did she not give you any when we went to Winchester?'

'If she had, Icel, I wouldn't be asking you for some now, would I?'

'Fine,' I growl. The smell of cooking food has my belly rumbling once more, but I know better than to stop and eat. Instead, I help myself to a crust of bread and a chunk of cheese before leaving the kitchen to eat while I seek out the bog myrtle. I look up, surprised to see the sun still shining overhead. In my mind, it's much closer to dusk. Instead, the sunlight is bright, and I have time to find what's needed. All I need to do is decide where to look.

23

The stink of the wet ground's overwhelming. I'm close to the River Walbrook, which flows through the centre of Londinium. The ground's also marshy, although I'm unsure whether it's the right sort of boggy. There are an abundance of plants bursting to life along the banks. So far, I've not seen any bog myrtle. I wouldn't be surprised to discover there's none. It's hardly the correct location. I know it's a more common plant north of Mercia. In the past, Wynflæd has traded for it with those from the northern lands of Northumbria. But now we need some, and I have to look within Londinium. I'm not very hopeful I'll be successful.

I planned to come alone, but Cenred's followed me. His face is bruised and battered, and he's walking with a slight limp. He looks tired, but has decided to keep me company. I'd thank him if he'd only stop moaning.

'This place is bloody stinking,' he mutters. He's not even down by the river. Instead, he walks along the riverbank, trying to avoid stepping in mud and getting stung by the many nettles that have started to become vicious.

'You want to be down here,' I call to him, eyes taking in all around me. There's an abundance of nettles and dandelions. The buzz of summer insects is loud in my ears, adding to the feeling of itchiness my healing wounds are already causing.

'No thanks, it's bad enough up here. What are you looking for?'

'Bog myrtle,' I hiss for about the tenth time.

'What's it used for?'

'Healing,' I mutter. I wish he'd go away.

'And what does it look like?'

I stand and place my hands on my hips. I may as well answer him. 'It grows to about this high,' I direct, standing with my hand above my knee but lower than my arse. 'It smells like, well, it smells like the outdoors, and it's sweet.'

'Unlike you,' Cenred offers almost so softly I don't hear him.

'Unlike you,' I counter, feeling childish. After all I've done, I sense I'm being punished. Surely this task should have fallen to someone else. Shouldn't I be tending to Lord Wigmund? Although, no, I retract that. I'm aware Lady Ælflæd and the king have bid me care for Lord Wigmund, but I'd sooner not. I don't think I feel guilt for his injury. If anything, I remain angry with him. This is all his fault. All of it. He and his bloody treasonous mother.

'Is this it?' Cenred calls. I glance up, realising in my fury I'm walking without truly looking. I gaze where Cenred points, and then I look at him. I feel a smirk on my face. He points not at bog myrtle but at a small, spreading crab-apple tree. The two couldn't be less alike.

'No,' I mutter, trying not to laugh aloud. I realise then that perhaps I'm well suited to the endeavour. If we'd sent men like Cenred to complete the task, we might end up with a handful of weeds or a bowlful of dead leaves.

'Is this it?' Cenred tries again. I've been concentrating and looking more carefully at the plants nearby. I sense we're getting closer to finding what we want. I consider just shouting a negative to Cenred, but he is here, and none of the others are. I glance up and my eyes widen.

'That might be it,' I announce joyfully, surging up the steep bank, feeling a hundred hurts in my body, to look down at what Cenred's found, clenching my fists to stop myself from scratching my two cheek wounds and the cut on my chin.

The plant's low to the ground. If anything, it looks nothing like I described, but the aroma is right. Here, with the sun overhead and the dank conditions underfoot, it smells as though I'm walking through a woodland thick with year-round growth.

'That's it,' I cry, delighted. Cenred grins like a child. I slap him on the back in thanks, and he winces. I ignore that and bend to remove some of the catkins, as well as some of the early growths. I ensure I have a bowlful. 'Remember where this is,' I urge him, looking around to find something to mark this place in case I need to return for more.

'Here,' he offers, pulling a thin strip of linen from his arm and tying it around a single stick he wedges into the ground. I eye it and then nod. It's as good as anything.

Returning to the ruins of the stone path that once ran through Londinium, I straighten my back and peer around. There's little to see. The Mercians are either inside the fort itself or down by the quayside. The rest of Londinium is as abandoned as it has been for many summers, too many to count.

'Why don't those who dwell within Lundenwic just come here? It would save the need to build defences.'

Cenred chuckles. 'They say the ghosts of the past haunt this place. Some say they hear the shrieks of the long dead. Some even say the Roman gods still roam this place, vying for the veneration they once had. The bishop is determined to build within the walls, but so far, he hasn't.'

I shake my head. 'I never heard such horse shit.'

'Are you one to discount the religions of others so easily? I'm not,' he announces with a grin on his fat lips.

'Have you put something on those?' I point.

He licks them while shrugging his shoulders. 'There's a lot going on at the moment. Better to stay out of the way of the healers and Wynflæd in particular.'

'Perhaps, but don't they hurt?'

'Not really. Can't feel them at all, so they can't hurt.'

I grin, pleased now he's come to find me.

'No one blames you, Icel. I thought you should know that.'

My good mood evaporates. Cenred voices my feelings too closely, even as I've been denying them.

'If the bastard dies, he has only himself to blame. Even the king knows it. He made it clear the guilt lies with his wife, and son.'

'What will happen to the queen?' I question, watching the stones beneath my feet. In some places, there's more soil than stone. If I'm not careful, I'll stub my toe. I can't imagine a cart ever using the path. It would have become stuck far too easily in the many pot holes.

'The king will divorce her and lock her up in a nunnery under a heavy guard.'

'He won't have her exiled?'

'No, he won't risk it. The queen's best kept where all can see her. He knows that. She knows that. That's why she tried so bloody hard to escape.'

'And Lord Wigmund?'

'It'll all depend on whether he lives or not, and if he does live, whether he's capable of ruling after his father.'

I nod again. Cenred's words are comforting, but they're also not. I look at the herbs in my bowl. Even with all my knowledge, I don't think it'll be enough to cure the king's son. Then, everything we've been fighting for will need to be reconsidered. At least there are the three young boys. Provided King Wiglaf lives long enough, one of them can be king in his place. We just need to ensure that happens should Lord Wigmund die.

24

Theodore and Gaya arrive five days later. Lord Wigmund has woken on occasion. Wynflæd's slept for less time than he's been awake, and while Oswy and Ealdorman Tidwulf are both on their feet once more, there's a deep sense of foreboding within Londinium.

I've not seen Lord Coenwulf or Lady Ælflæd in all that time. I've seen the king only from a distance. I've managed to bathe, and my cheek wounds are healing, and I'm plagued by the scab on my chin. It's so itchy now the summer heat has belatedly arrived.

'Theodore, Gaya.' I look up from my tasks in the kitchen to see them entering, followed by servants who carry boxes and sacks. I wonder what they contain.

'Ah, young Icel.' Gaya appraises me, running her eyes up and down my long body. I overtop her by almost two of her heads. 'You're much recovered from some of your wounds,' she announces with satisfaction. I smile, pleased to see them. Wynflæd's making herself ill with such non-stop care for Lord

Wigmund. She seems to take his festering wound as a slight against her skills.

Theodore comes to me next, embracing me so I feel the strength in him. If either of them are worried about being once more inside Londinium, they don't show it. The ghost of their master has long been banished. They've been free for many years.

'The king's son is still failing?' Theodore murmurs so all those in the kitchen don't hear him.

'Yes. The incense has aided but not healed.'

He nods. A distant look in his eyes assures me he's considering another treatment. 'We will go and see him, and Wynflæd. Stay here. We might need you. Ensure our supplies are placed away from the heat of the hearth in our absence.'

I nod, mindful Cuthred and I suddenly have six other people looking at us. All of them carry something. The only advantage is none of their loads seems heavy, only bulky. I catch a withering look from the men and women who feed the garrison and gesture for the six to come closer to me.

I don't think I know them, but Cuthred chatters on with animation as wooden chests are placed on the ground, and the sacks are laid beside them. It seems everything might require access. The smells of heat and spice wash over me. Outside, it's a hot summer day. In the kitchen, it's hotter than a furnace.

'You know these men and women?' I ask Cuthred as they turn to leave.

'Yes, they're Ealdorman Tidwulf's people. They work with Theodore and Gaya. They're all involved in the task of recording the cures from the kingdom of Mercia and further afield.'

I nod, wondering why they get to leave the kitchen when I've been bid to remain inside it, but they've only just arrived. No doubt they need food and rest. I amuse myself by examining the chests and sacks, eyeing everything inside. I don't recognise all of the herbs or ointments. Some are noxious, and I jolt away from the acrid stink. Some gleam with bright colour, and yet others are things I know only too well, jars of precious honey and bundles of finely woven flax linen to be used as bandages.

I fear I didn't really rescue Lord Wigmund from being captured. I should have allowed him to be led on to the Wessex ship because at least then he'd be more alive than he is now. Cenred's words when I was seeking the bog myrtle reassure me, as do the king's, and yet I can't help feeling I'm to blame now I've had time to consider it. I was hasty. I should have thought more before I acted.

King Wiglaf visits his son at least once a day. I've started to shun those visits to avoid the fervent hope showing on his face. Despite everything Lord Wigmund has done, the king still wishes his son to heal.

The incense and damp warmth of the room, created by having water close to the braziers, does seem to have made it easier for Wigmund to breathe. His lips have lost the blue tinge, but his breathing is far from restored to normal. I hope, like the king, Theodore and Gaya will know some other restorative, taught to them when they lived in their hot homelands far to the south.

'Ah, Icel, there you are.' Wynflæd's words are flecked with exhaustion. Her black stick props her up, her thin hand gripping it for fear she might fall. Without it, I doubt she'd be able to stand, let alone walk. Her arm quivers. I don't like to see her expend so much of her vitality helping Lord Wigmund. 'I see Theodore and Gaya have arrived.' She eyes the chests and sacks keenly.

'Yes, Wynflæd. I've done as they requested.'

'They bid me rest,' she offers with a small bark of laughter. 'For once, I'm inclined to do so. Come and find me if Lord

Wigmund falters.' I'm astounded she's taking orders now. She's more likely to be giving them. The sound of her walking stick over the stone floor is painful to hear, and it goes on for a long time. Only when I know she's gone do I meet Cuthred's fearful gaze.

'She just needs to sleep,' I offer, but I'm as worried as he is. A hard lump of anxiety such that I've not known for a long time seems to sit in my throat. She's unimaginably old.

'And perhaps we could offer her a pottage to aid her,' he suggests. I see it's an effort for him to bite back his worries. I nod. It's good to have something to focus on.

Together, we begin the task with more willing than we have any of those which we've been set by Wynflæd for Lord Wigmund.

My world has become very small. The kitchen. Wigmund's sickroom. The main hall where I sleep each night. Sometimes the stables, when I manage to sneak outside for some time with Bicwide and the other horse. No one's claimed him. Most seem to think he belongs to me now. I really don't need another bloody horse. But I do like him. He's an intelligent animal, healing well from the burn marks.

But outside my world, the ruling of Mercia is continuing apace. Lundenwic's destroyed and burned defences are already being rebuilt, the sound of wood being cut and shaped ringing through the air each morning. The king has summoned the witan to convene in five days' time. The matter of the queen, Wessex and his son will be discussed. Lord Coenwulf's return to Mercia will be formalised, as will the alliances he hopes to forge between Frankia and Mercia. Brihthild's future also needs to be discussed. The matter of Ealdorman Sigered will be reviewed, as will the future of the men who tried to help the queen escape from her imprisonment, including Eadbald. The wergild due for the dead woman must still be paid.

No doubt the king will likewise need to debate the involvement of the archbishop of Canterbury as well. The bishops have been vocal in being uneasy their superior is essentially in enemy-held territory. The king's informed them they'll never again be allowed to venture to Wessex. There's an impasse, which can't continue for much longer.

But for me, there's nothing so huge to contemplate. Oswy's well. Cenred has also recovered and even Kyre's fully healed, despite his involvement in defeating the Wessex invasion. With Lord Coenwulf returned I don't need to worry about the children any more. Edwin and Eadburg have already wed. I seem to be sitting still while events whirl around me.

I've seen Ealdorman Ælfstan infrequently. He procured the incense from the bishop but has been busy on tasks for the king, and taking over Ealdorman Tidwulf's responsibilities while he healed. Wulfheard's rarely to be seen either. The men of the war band have taken it upon themselves to spend their time in the training ground. They use anything they can find to build on their strength. I'm not alone in fearing something else will happen.

The news from the east is that the Viking raiders are once more confirmed to hold the Isle of Sheppey. I hope the men and women who live close by aren't being held captive. Admittedly, the island is all but bereft of any inhabitants. People would do well to stay away from that place. King Ecgberht should be defending the land he claims as opposed to pursuing that which he doesn't.

I've only seen the queen twice. She sits ramrod straight before her son, not even holding his hand, or speaking to him, as Wynflæd has ordered everyone to do. The queen's a hard bitch. I'm grateful I'm not her son. If Lord Wigmund never wakes, then the future of Mercia will be precarious. The queen will have no place at all. She's too old to carry another child, or so Wynflæd assures me. But the king could marry again. Or he could simply ensure the kingdom passes to his grandson, provided he lives for many more winters.

'Icel.' Having helped Cuthred, I've escaped outside, keen to feel the heat of the sun on my face. Edwin calls to me. I turn to greet him, with a smile. Only he's not smiling. 'Come with me,' he urges, indicating I should follow him deeper into Londinium. A shiver of worry worms its way into my belly. What's this about then?

The last time I saw him, he was all smiles and cheers, enjoying being back in Mercia. Something has changed.

'I've been attending upon Lord Coenwulf, and his sister.'

I nod. I know that.

'And there have been many courting the pair of them. The ealdormen are keen to be associated with them.'

'I expected as much,' I offer, still unsure why Edwin has brought me here to inform me of this.

'I've also heard Ealdorman Sigered intends to charge you with the murder of the king's son as a means of winning favour for himself.'

'But Lord Wigmund lives.'

'For now he does, yes. Ealdorman Sigered means to draw allies to him ahead of what all believe will be Lord Wigmund's oncoming death.'

'Theodore and Gaya are here. They won't allow him to die.' I should have suspected something like this from the pestilent boil that is Ealdorman Sigered. He wasn't likely to accept punishment easily so now he tries to turn it on someone else. He should have been apprehended after allying with Lord Æthelwulf, but the king is waiting for the witan to do anything. 'He should be the one accused of treason.'

'He says he was only doing as his king commanded.'

'Lord Wigmund wasn't king,' I hiss, my joy in the bright sunshine fading. Instead, I feel exposed. It's all well and good Cenred and the king assuring me no one blames me apart from myself, but where politics and kingdoms are concerned, it's a very different matter. 'And what, Lord Coenwulf intends to press the accusations?'

'No, no, he doesn't. And nor, I think, does Lady Ælflæd, and of them all, I'd expect her to have the most to complain about if her husband dies.'

I don't agree with that, but I don't say so. 'Why are you telling me this?'

'You need to try even harder to ensure Lord Wigmund lives. If he lives, Ealdorman Sigered won't be able to press the issue, and instead, he'll be the one risking his future.'

'I can't do anything else. Wynflæd, Theodore and Gaya will be the ones to heal him.'

Edwin nods, but then his face darkens. He coughs to clear his throat, fiddling with a loose thread on his tunic. He looks like a child who knows he's about to say something which will be poorly received. 'I fear if Lord Wigmund wakes up, some will move to kill him.' I gasp at that, eyes turning towards the fort, where Lord Wigmund is under the care of Theodore and Gaya. 'I wouldn't leave him unattended,' Edwin muses. 'I'd tell Ealdorman Ælfstan to set a guard from amongst his own men. The king's warriors might harbour an enemy amongst them, who could kill Lord Wigmund when no one's looking.'

The words are far from comforting, but I don't doubt their sincerity. Edwin means me no harm. But he's only one. There are many who see me as a threat. If only they knew the truth of who I am, they'd perhaps fear me more.

'My thanks,' I murmur to Edwin, turning to walk back to the fort. I thought to relax. Instead, I need to find my byrnie and seax. If I can't heal Wigmund with my declining knowledge of herb lore, then I can certainly ensure no Mercian can get close to him with a blade. Or poison.

25

Wulfheard listens to my concerns, and immediately arranges with Ealdorman Ælfstan for us all to stand guard duty. I'm surprised when not even Oswy complains about the new arrangement.

If the king notices the change on his daily visit, he makes no comment. And, by the third day, when Wynflæd has slept an entire day away, Lord Wigmund finally stirs for longer than a momentary opening of his eyes.

I'm on guard duty when it happens. There's a flurry of voices, and then Theodore calls through the doorway.

'Summon the king. Lord Wigmund's awake and sensible of his surroundings.'

I turn to Cenred, with whom I'm on guard duty. He shakes his head. We need to remain where we are.

I call to another servant, a woman washing the filth of a thousand pairs of feet from the flagstones within the fort. She bobs a curtsey and hastens to find King Wiglaf.

I turn towards the doorway, behind which Theodore can be heard speaking. I listen carefully, but he murmurs, making it impossible.

'Wynflæd will be pleased,' Cenred offers. I nod. She will. And then the king's hurrying towards us, a tight smile of joy on his face. Now his son is awake, everything will change. I just hope it means he's on the mend, and not likely to suffer a relapse.

All is activity and the palpable sense of dread lifts from the fort. The witan will convene in two days. It'll be good to have Lord Wigmund in attendance. Injured or not, he and his mother have much to account for.

Brihthild, who also remains in captivity but under a much lighter guard than the queen and within Lundenwic, will also discover her fate. My rage towards her has dimmed. Within Canterbury, I could have happily ended her life. Now, though, I think she's as much a feather blowing in the breeze of politicking and posturing as I am. Ealdorman Muca did a fine job of holding Lundenwic when it was besieged. He kept many people safe, including the bishops and Brihthild while Lord Wigmund and Ealdorman Sigered worked only to reach an accord with Lord Æthelwulf.

As soon as the king has left his son, his steps firm, nodding with pleasure as he greets me, the queen is brought up from her incarceration. While she remains under a tight guard, the king has ordered she be allowed her finest clothes. Her hair might be in disarray, but the shimmer of her jewelled gown is impossible to ignore. She walks with less confidence than the king. But then, her son being alive makes things more difficult for her, not less.

'What a tangled web,' Cenred muses, watching her as she's brought inside by Maneca and Kyre. They're armed; the queen isn't. She doesn't even have her girdle. Ealdorman Ælfstan's warriors are taking no chances Lord Wigmund might still be threatened.

I try and release the tightness in my shoulders, but it's impossible.

It was uncomfortable when Lord Wigmund was senseless to the world. Now it's even more intolerable.

'The witan will decide what's to be done with her and Lord Wigmund,' Cenred murmurs, sensing my unease. 'King Wiglaf will listen to his councillors, although hopefully not Ealdorman Sigered.'

When the queen leaves, sometime later, having never been left alone with her son, Kyre grimaces. I'd like to know all he's heard, but he shakes his head. The queen remains tight-lipped.

* * *

The witan is convened within Lundenwic two days later. I don't like the risk King Wiglaf's taking, not again, but as we ride through the burned remnants of the eastern gateway, I see the shimmer of iron along the quayside, and also surrounding Lundenwic. The king's taking no chances, after all. Ealdorman Ælfstan's warriors are to keep guard over Lord Wigmund, his mother, Brihthild and the others who must account for their actions. Ealdorman Muca and his men are to watch Lundenwic. If Wessex should attack, we'll be ready.

Lord Wigmund's hunched on his saddle. He remains in discomfort, but refuses to walk, or be carried on a cart. So he's ridden, with me, Cenred, Oswy and Ealdorman Ælfstan accompanying him. There's no fanfare. When we passed below the protective gateway of Londinium, I felt a shiver of dread. I don't know what the day will bring. It seems impossible that, by the end of it, the queen will be sent to live her life in a nunnery, under heavy guard, tarnished with the crimes of attempted murder, murder and treason, while Lord Wigmund will be held accountable for his part in it. Or that Ealdorman Sigered will be banished, but Edwin assures me this is being discussed. It seems impossible. I suspect they'll all try and wriggle out of facing justice for their crimes.

Queen Cynethryth has been allowed to bathe and dress appropriately. I'm not sure what 'appropriate' is for a woman who conspired against the king, but Wynflæd, now she's restored to her usual ill humour and no longer fearful for the king's son, has taken great delight in telling me of previous queens of Mercia. It's astounded me.

'Come here, Icel,' she called, pulling me with her to walk outside, her hand clamped to my right arm, her left arm holding her stick. 'I'll tell you of events I never told you before.'

Cuthred, with his usual ability to listen in, sidled up behind me. Wynflæd knew he was there. She made no comment.

'Mercia hasn't fared well with the women wed to their kings.' A soft cackle. 'Or the children born between a king and a queen. Wigmund's merely the most current of many disappointments.'

I shook my head, perplexed to hear her speak in such a way, when she'd worn herself ragged caring for him.

'Lord Coenwulf there, his father became king because his brother's daughter killed her brother.'

'I thought that was a lie,' I countered.

'That's how King Coenwulf had it reported. It was all true though. I didn't witness it, but I know of others who did.'

'What, watched her kill her brother?'

'No, witnessed the king speak of it, to a select few. And before her, Offa's wife also had blood on her hands, as did Offa's sister.'

I shuddered at the thought. 'Why?'

'A woman must live by her wits, and safeguard her future, for fear she'll be locked up tight in a nunnery, with no means of engaging with the world at large. Think of Lady Cynehild.' Wynflæd met my searching gaze then. 'She remarried, and meddled where she shouldn't have done. Admittedly, she stopped far short of murdering anyone.'

'So, the king should have expected this then?' I was astounded.

'Maybe. He married her.' Wynflæd cackled softly. 'A man may wed a woman for her title, and lands. A woman may divorce a man. But better to have him dead, and then take his place. A grieving woman will have the sympathy of others. A widow has more freedom than a wife.'

'You almost sound like you approve.'

'I do not,' she countered, but her eyes glittered.

'Were you ever wed?' I found the words pouring from my mouth before I could stop them. A sharp slap on my face from her thin hand assured me I should have tried harder not to speak.

Now, as we parade through Lundenwic, the populace glower at Lord Wigmund, as he sits awkwardly in his saddle. Their eyes pass over us warriors as though we're not really there. I'd complain about that, but it's better not to be seen. I labour for the Mercians. I don't do it for the glory of being recognised.

The hall's relatively unscathed from the attack of the Wessex warriors. I can see where some of the thatch has perhaps burned, but other than that, it's been cleaned well.

We dismount, and I aid Lord Wigmund. He doesn't like it, but he can either accept our help, or land on his face. He really is very weak, despite the healing pottages and vast quantity of fresh food with which he's been fed. He's even been given the best cuts of meat to feast upon. I could be jealous, but I don't envy him what he needs to endure now. I'd never wish to be in his position.

As Lord Wigmund stands, he attempts to do so proudly. I hear the hiss of pain. The wound in his back is healing well. The scar on his neck will never leave him. But he's been abed for nearly two weeks.

Together, we walk into the hall, Ealdorman Ælfstan's warriors keeping step with us. The men and women of the witan turn to watch our approach. Here, as opposed to outside, I do feel seen, and I don't like the unease that prickles along my back. This is too much to endure.

Ealdorman Ælfstan escorts Lord Wigmund to his place beside where his father will sit on the dais. His mother is already there, sitting under heavy guard, away from the king. I catch sight of Brihthild. I've not seen her for many days. She offers me a tight smile. The change in her demeanour is amazing. She sits proudly, wearing good clothes and evidently in excellent keeping for a woman who's deemed as lacking all oath-helpers because she's from Wessex.

I consider what she's been offered by the king to speak, or whether she's simply decided it's better to reveal what she knows, as I take my place behind where the king will sit on the dais. King Wiglaf requires a display of power. It might mean standing for much of the day. I hope I can do it without fidgeting. I try not to consider the wounds on my face. If I think about them, I'll want to scratch at them. Why wounds have to itch as they heal, I'll never know.

I also see Lady Ælflæd and Lord Coenwulf. I've not spoken with Lord Coenwulf since the day of his return. He inclines his head towards me; Lady Ælflæd doesn't notice me. I've not communicated with her about the demand she placed on me to tend to her husband. I wish I knew whether she was pleased he yet lived. Admittedly, I did little to aid Lord Wigmund. It was Wynflæd, Theodore and Gaya who ensured he's here today, waiting to hear what his father, and the witan, will decree. I see Lady Ælflæd's son is with her, or rather, in the arms of Eadburg. Lord Coenwulf's sons are also there. I pity them having to listen to this, but perhaps it's better they do. They need to know, however young they are, that those who hurt them will be punished.

Wynflæd and Cuthred have been accorded places on the few benches that are available to sit upon, as in the original gathering. Many will have to stand to witness today's trial in order to cram more people within the buildings.

Once more Bishop Ceolbeorht will preside over much of what's said. I eye Bishop Æthelweald with a low growl. I still hate him, and distrust him, although he doesn't seem to have allied himself with Lord Wigmund's attempt to become king. I consider where he was during the attacks on Lundenwic. I notice Ealdorman Sigered sitting regally with the rest of the ealdormen, even while his grandson is seated with the others accused of treason. I glower at that. Hopefully, Ealdorman Sigered will soon face justice for his actions as well.

King Wiglaf arrives with little fanfare. He keeps his gaze on something none of us can see. He doesn't seek out the eyes of any of his ealdormen, and certainly not his wife, as he seats himself before me. His expression is pensive as he acknowledges me and then sweeps his cloak aside to settle in his chair.

'My lord king, lord prince, lady queen, ealdormen, bishops, abbots, abbesses and men and women of the witan.' Bishop Ceolbeorht bows towards the king and his son, and then slightly inclines his head towards the queen, and the room at large. 'We're pleased to see Lord Wigmund much restored, and also the return of Lord Coenwulf of Kingsholm from his exile.'

After those niceties are completed, Bishop Ceolbeorht clears his throat. He offers no prayers. Perhaps they'll come later. Maybe, in what will transpire, he thinks his God will play no part.

'When we parted some weeks ago, we'd heard compelling evidence spoken against a lady of Mercia that we suspect to be the queen, and others who were implicated in the conspiracy against Mercia. Alas, we didn't have reports that certainly proved Queen Cynethryth's involvement. Now, we find ourselves with overwhelming evidence of the complicity of more people. And we must also decide on the queen's violent attack against Brihthild, here, before us all, in which Lord Budworth was wounded, although, thankfully, not mortally. And also, seek justice for the murder of one of the queen's loyal attendants. First, I will question Brihthild again. I hope you remember that none would be her oath-helper, but she has assured me she'll faithfully recount all she has heard and seen in this troubling matter.'

Brihthild isn't bound this time. She's allowed to walk before the king without guards dogging her movements, and even inclines her head respectfully as she directs her steps towards a waiting seat. When her gaze flashes towards the queen, I see her lips curl with disgust.

'Now, Brihthild of Wessex, you spoke of the involvement of a lady of Mercia with Lord Æthelwulf, the king of Wessex's son. We have, I think everyone here can agree, seen compelling evidence of Lord Æthelwulf's desire to meddle in Mercia's affairs. Is there anything else you would tell us?'

Brihthild pauses and then nods. From where I'm standing, I see a side-on view of her face. She's fierce, but calm. 'I would speak honestly of the contract between Mercia's queen and Lord Æthelwulf. I also know the names of others who were involved. I would speak them now.'

Silence booms throughout the hall. No one dares breathe. No one, it seems, even risks moving for fear they might miss what she'll say next.

'Eadbald, as you know. Wulfnoth of Eamont, as you know. Queen Cynethryth, as you suspected but I didn't name but now do. Bishop Æthelweald, as you do not know.'

All eyes flicker towards the bishop of Lichfield. I don't look at him. Instead, I watch Brihthild, desperate to reassure myself, this time, she speaks the truth. I'm frantic for the bishop to be involved in this. Bishop Ceolbeorht shows no surprise either. Did he already know Bishop Æthelweald would be named by Brihthild? It seems while we needed Brihthild to name the queen, it's Bishop Æthelweald's complicity that astounds the audience.

'Lord Wigmund, as you do not know,' Brihthild continues.

At this, I hear a hiss of outrage, and witness a flicker of unease on Lord Wigmund's face.

'Although, my lord bishop, my lord king, I've long suspected his name was merely employed, perhaps without him even knowing.'

I admire her for admitting to this. I hope the king hasn't interfered to stop his son being accused.

'In Wessex, Lord Æthelwulf, and his father were involved. As were the men that are now dead, Heardlulf and others of his ilk, who acted as messengers between Wessex and Mercia. And the man who came here from the archbishop just before the queen attacked me, Lanfrac.' Her words are clear. I wish I could see the queen's reaction, but equally, I don't wish to, as she faces the assembly and not the king. She's fallen low indeed. Her ambitions have become as dust in the wind.

'And the intention?'

'To remove King Wiglaf, and place Lord Wigmund in his father's place, having... dispatched' – her words falter before choosing that word, her careful pose slightly crumbling when faced with the earnest faces of young Coenwulf and Coelwulf – 'any others who might have a claim to the kingship, other than his small son.' I watch her swallow heavily. Bishop Ceolbeorht's face remains bland. I'm impressed he can be so calm.

I note she's not mentioned Ealdorman Sigered, which worries me. I hoped she would.

I see two of Ealdorman Muca's warriors have moved close to Bishop Æthelweald. He won't be escaping anytime soon, even if the current focus remains on the queen and her son.

'Eadbald will speak for himself to these charges, as we have him here before us. Now, Brihthild, you freely offer this information, and no one has forced you to say these names.'

'No, my lord bishop.'

'Perhaps the unwarranted attack on you might have made you turn on the queen?' He questions what many must be thinking.

'No, my lord bishop. I assure you I share freely and with no malice towards the queen for what she did to me.' The bite of her words somewhat belies that statement.

'Indeed,' he offers with a wry smile. 'Did you know, out of interest, that your master, Lord Æthelwulf, intended to abduct Mercia's queen to prevent her from facing justice for her crimes?'

'No, my lord bishop. I didn't.'

'Thank you,' he replies, already busy on the next order of business.

'What will happen to me?' Brihthild questions. 'I asked not to be returned to Wessex, for Lord Æthelwulf will have me killed.'

'That will be for the king and his witan to decide. We're assured of your guilt in this matter, but that doesn't mean we'll condemn you to death, despite the murder of your brother.' Bishop Ceolbeorht's voice is surprisingly reassuring, although the final phrase is filled with censure. 'Now, I'll ask Bishop Æthelweald to account for his involvement,' the bishop resumes, dismissing Brihthild, who stands and returns to her chair.

Bishop Æthelweald's face is fiery. He tries not to struggle at the bishop's command, but I don't miss his gaze sweeping towards the open doorway, which is far from inviting with all those standing or sitting here to witness the trial. From the roadway, there's no sound. Instead, the doors are open because many wish to witness this, and if they can't see it, then they wish to listen so they can say they were there when the guilt of Mercia's queen, and others of her noblemen, were announced.

While his robes flash with rich gems, Bishop Æthelweald takes his seat before the bishop, shrugging off the helping hands of those who keep him under watchful guard. Again, at a command from the king, the two warriors step away from the bishop. I can tell they don't want to do so, but it seems unlikely Bishop Æthelweald is armed.

'Bishop Æthelweald,' Bishop Ceolbeorht begins, no trace of warmth in his forbidding tone. 'I would, as others before you, announce you have people who are your oath-helpers but, despite your position as one of Mercia's bishops, no one will vouch for your integrity until we've heard what you have to say about these serious allegations. It seems unfortunate you've been named as a part of the conspiracy. We have one woman's word. Admittedly, a Wessex woman who hates Mercia. What would you say in reply?'

'I would call upon many oath-helpers who would speak for my integrity and assure everyone I would never be involved in such a movement against our ordained king.' Bishop Æthelweald raises his voice to ensure all hear him as he sidesteps Bishop Ceolbeorht's question.

'That may be, but only holy men and women may be your oath-helpers here, and we all wish to know how you answer for the explicit charge laid against you. Others can't tell us all that unfolds within your mind. They can only speak to your actions.'

'I'm a holy bishop, subject only to the archbishop of Canterbury, the pope and our Lord God.' His fierce rebuttal sounds desperate.

'And you've been named by one of those we know was involved in this terrible conspiracy. Why would she even know your name, if she's not heard it whispered on the lips of the other implicated?'

'She knows me from Canterbury?' Bishop Æthelweald retorts hotly.

'So, your name is just one of many she might have chosen? It could easily have been one of the other bishops of Mercia, is that what you're saying?' As he speaks, Bishop Ceolbeorht uses his hands to indicate those seated behind him.

'It could, yes,' Bishop Æthelweald replies, as though that's a suitable answer.

Oswy snarls. I fix him with a firm look. He tries to release the tightness of his neck and shoulders, but it doesn't work. His eyes are fixed and fiery, unable to look away from the squirming bishop.

'Your scribe, Brother Sampson, or Heca as he's also known.'

'What of him? He's denied any involvement in this terrible conspiracy, just as I do.'

'He has, yes. And we do believe his words.' The implication is clear for all to hear. 'But, he has a most distinctive style of writing, would you not say?'

'Perhaps. I don't examine his writing. It's good enough for the scriptorium and the king's official transactions which must be recorded to ensure none misremember facts or call them into question, especially in land transactions.'

Bishop Ceolbeorht's dismayed gaze is telling as he looks down before resuming his questioning. 'We believe his hand wrote the message discovered by Lord Budworth in Wessex. And yet, Brother Sampson denies it, and we're minded to believe him. He has many oath-helpers and has always been a man of firm convictions and loyalty to Mercia. But, it is a fair copy of his distinctive writing style, is it not? It speaks of someone who knows how to obscure his own writing and one who's able to copy another's well.' Here Bishop Ceolbeorht pauses once more, and I suspect it is to allow Bishop Æthelweald to pronounce his guilt. When he doesn't, Bishop Ceolbeorht continues, with a soft sigh. 'The vellum this message is written on has a particular thickness to it. I understand you utilise such vellums for personal use. It's quite specific in the way the hide's scraped clear of animal hair. A particular angle is used, towards the right, and not straight down. Do you recognise it?'

Unable to help myself, I glance at Bishop Æthelweald, dropping my impassive gaze towards those facing the bishop and those implicated. His mouth opens and closes like a fish out of water. All of his fine words of denial have deserted him. It seems then Bishop Ceolbeorht was prepared for Brihthild to name the erstwhile bishop.

'And indeed, we have this sheet here,' and Bishop Ceolbeorht holds it before him. 'There have been attempts to scrub away the writing, but it's poorly done. I believe you'll recognise the top of this sheet as certainly in your hand, as confirmed by Brother Sampson and many others in receipt of your correspondence. And the bottom? Well, that reveals where you endeavoured to write in the style of another.' Bishop Ceolbeorht has one of his scribes bring the vellum sheet close to Bishop Æthelweald. Even though I won't be able to see anything from such a distance, I find myself craning to look. I'm not alone in that.

Bishop Æthelweald visibly shudders on seeing the evidence presented before him. The scribe continues to reveal all to King Wiglaf. King Wiglaf doesn't ask to hold the vellum, but he does peer at it. As he does so, I finally get a good look. It's easy to see where some of the words have been scraped away, but enough of the dark ink remains for me to determine the evolution of the handwriting. I recognise it as that found on the message inside Bicwide's saddle.

As the scribe returns to Bishop Ceolbeorht, the king appraises Bishop Æthelweald. I imagine he's disappointed in him. But there's much more the bishop can tell us.

'Now, Bishop Æthelweald, your involvement is proved, and not just in the words of Brihthild. In the matter of your punishment, crimes such as these should be referred to the archbishop of Canterbury, but he's too close to your real masters in Kent and Wessex. Instead, the bishops will convene and discuss your banishment. Your punishment can be somewhat modified to perhaps include passage to Rome, and the means to seek absolution, if you speak of those you know were also involved. After all, as a bishop, you should speak with an integrity similar to that of an ealdorman.'

I don't know whom to look at, so attempt to keep my gaze on the open doorway, alert to any possible danger. The silence drags. I don't think any of us believe Bishop Æthelweald would be self-serving enough to hold his tongue. He might lose Lichfield, but the promise of a new home, far from Mercia, is sure to appeal.

'If you decide to keep quiet, you'll leave Mercia with nothing but the clothes on your back. The crime you've committed is one of treason, although, in effect, it's a crime against our Heavenly Father, who ordained King Wiglaf and placed him as king over the kingdom of Mercia. You've sinned against your church, and against the king's *mund*.'

I suspect Bishop Æthelweald's torn. His guilt is proven. But should he compound that culpability by remaining silent, or should he speak out? Either way, it appears he's going to make us wait.

'I acted with good intentions,' Bishop Æthelweald finally concedes, still trying to wheedle his way out of a terrible punishment. 'It was on the instructions of my queen. I understood it was a political act, agreed upon with the king and Ealdorman Sigered to determine how deep the conspiracy within Wessex went, and how far Lord Æthelwulf would take it.'

I feel my eyes boggle at the admission. He names Ealdorman Sigered, already labouring to his feet, words of denial on his lips, as well as the queen. This gives me as much pleasure as Bishop Æthelweald's own denouncement.

'Silence,' King Wiglaf eventually booms when the crescendo of outrage has grown almost hysterical. 'Silence in the king's hall.' Not that everyone obeys the king immediately. Instead, Ealdorman Sigered decries the charge, even as the king orders two of his guards to stand with the interfering old man.

Bishop Ceolbeorht waits for silence to be restored and then begins to speak.

'Bishop Æthelweald, as previously agreed with my fellow bishops, abbots and abbesses, you'll be escorted from these shores, given enough wealth and the resources to journey to Rome. Once there, we suggest you throw yourself on the Holy Father's mercy, and he'll aid you in finding the path to righteousness once more, because it is clear you've strayed far from the true path of those beholden to our Lord God, and our king.'

So spoken, Bishop Ceolbeorht reclaims his seat. Four of the king's guard, led by Commander Eahric, walk to remove Bishop Æthelweald. He stands, a once proud man cast low, and turns to the king. For a moment, I think he'll attack the man he's tried to displace. Instead, and I'd love to know how much it pains him, he lowers himself and prostrates himself on the ground. I find myself wincing at the sounds of his knees popping and the creak of his back.

'Help him to his feet,' King Wiglaf eventually commands. He's allowed the moment to elongate. I'm finding it hard to stay still.

As Bishop Æthelweald regains his feet, I sense the queen appraising him and Ealdorman Sigered. I feel my hand reaching for my seax. I won't allow the queen to wound anyone else. But the moment passes. Bishop Æthelweald leaves the hall, a path forged amongst everyone there by Commander Eahric using his battlefield voice. It thrums in the enclosed space, echoing too loudly in my ears.

From outside, those who didn't witness Bishop Æthelweald's downfall shout abuse his way. I'd smile at some of the choice terminology, but perhaps now isn't the time.

'To return to immediate matters,' Bishop Ceolbeorht resumes when silence has been restored once more. 'Lord Wigmund.' The bishop inclines his head towards the king's son. 'Your named part in the treason against the king is unfortunate. Would you like to defend yourself?'

I eye Lord Wigmund, where his frantic gaze rests on his father. His face was already pale from his wounds. Now it's bleached, almost blue. Finding nothing there, his head turns towards where his mother sits, impassively. Does he hope she'll speak for him? The pair have always been so close. They must both be implicated. She can't have acted without him, not when she hoped to make him king in place of his father.

'I would speak,' the queen announces. No doubt this was Bishop Ceolbeorht's intention in accusing Lord Wigmund first. A woman who would kill children, one of her most intimate servants and involve another kingdom in trying to make her son king, must surely want to protect him now all has fallen to ruin. 'My son was not in any way involved in my attempts to make him king of Mercia.'

'What of him being declared Mercia's king by Lord Æthelwulf of Wessex when King Wiglaf was believed dead?'

'That was Lord Æthelwulf, fulfilling the agreement.'

'But you were under lock and key within Londinium?'

'It was all decided before that,' the queen snaps. I'm unsure whether to admire her bravery, or think her an even bigger fool than I already did. I'm not convinced, despite everything, it's worth defending Lord Wigmund, who seems to be in this up to his royal neck. Almost dying doesn't mean he can be forgiven for his actions.

'So, you knew there would be an attack from Wessex during the first day of your trial?'

'I did, yes. I was informed of this by those who knew of my predicament once she,' and it's clear from the queen's sneer she means Brihthild, 'was brought to Mercia.'

'So, aside from the man who died in Wessex, there were also others acting as go-betweens between you and the alleged son of your friend, as Brihthild suggested?'

'At the very beginning Eadweard acted as a messenger, before he was given a different task, to take control of the small children. Then, other arrangements were made.'

'Eadweard is the man who tried to kill Lord Budworth?'

'He is, yes.'

I shudder at the coldness of her tone. She really doesn't bloody like me.

'And was the man who died in Wessex, Heardlulf, and whose horse Lord Budworth found, the immediate and only successor to Eadweard?'

'Yes,' she pronounces quickly. I'm not sure I believe her.

'And since Heardlulf's death?'

Here, she hesitates. I feel my eyes narrow. And then my eyes are drawn to her as she sits straighter, not meeting her husband's eyes, but gazing at Bishop Ceolbeorht.

'When I heard nothing further last winter, I believed my Wessex allies had taken my valuable gem and decided to keep it, and stay far away from Mercia. I took it to mean everything was over and nothing would ever happen. When the king sent Lord

Budworth to Winchester, he stirred up the hornets' nest once more, and everything began to proceed as we'd agreed.'

I gasp at the implication that, somehow, this was the king's fault. I hear Wiglaf's bark of laughter. I witness Bishop Ceolbeorht's eyes open wide in shock, and even Ealdorman Sigered looks aghast.

'So, Eadbald, the man who spoke against Lord Coenwulf, and then tried to help you escape, wasn't one of your messengers? Or Ealdorman Sigered's grandson, who also tried to rescue you from Londinium?'

'No, Ealdorman Sigered's grandson and his allies were fools who were only useful for breaking me out of my prison. They couldn't even manage that, could they?' Her words thrum with disgust.

Bishop Ceolbeorht eventually recovers himself, with a nudge from Bishop Heahbeorht of Hereford beside him, only King Wiglaf interjects, recovering from his shock as quickly as the bishop.

'I think we've heard enough,' King Wiglaf announces, his words tinged with resolve. 'I assume, bishops, abbesses and abbots, there'll be no difficulties in me obtaining a separation from my wife? Not that I intend to wed again, but Mercia must not have a treasonous queen.'

The holy men and women look sagely at their spokesperson, Bishop Ceolbeorht, and nod.

'We agree to your request,' Bishop Ceolbeorht intones solemnly. 'And now we must decide if the queen is guilty of involvement in the conspiracy against Mercia's kingship. Do we need to convene and discuss this further?' the bishop asks his holy men and women. I can't see anyone needs to discuss anything. It's clear to me the queen carries as much guilt as Bishop Æthelweald, already banished from Mercia.

'I don't believe that will be necessary,' Bishop Heahbeorht of Hereford states quickly. 'I think all that remains is for a just punishment to be determined upon. One that will not imperil the souls of those forced to listen to the terrible things that have been done.'

'Then, we'll have Lady Cynethryth escorted to confinement. It'll be no secret that she's to go to a nunnery. Which one, will be kept secret. Mercia can't endure another of her scheming plots,' Bishop Ceolbeorht announces. 'Now, my lord king, it falls to you to decide what must be done about Lord Wigmund?' Bishop Ceolbeorht concedes.

'He'll be watched carefully, and re-educated in what it means to be an ætheling of Mercia. He's paid dearly with his injury. He'll have a guard at all times, and his wife need not live with him until he's deemed rehabilitated,' King Wiglaf announces quickly. I fear he errs in not punishing his son further. Lord Wigmund, allowed to move around at will, could bring miscreants to his side. But, I confess, as much as I hate him, I've always been surprised he was involved in the plot. It makes much more sense to think his mother was pulling his strings.

'Then, I believe today's trial is concluded. Brihthild will also be escorted away from Mercia. The matter of Ealdorman Sigered, my lord king, will need further investigation, as will that of his grandson. But, for today, the main conspirators have been found guilty. We'll decide on a suitable punishment for Brihthild of Wessex and see it done. It will not, as I said, be her death, or her return to Wessex.'

'Until such time as we have all the answers, the ealdorman will be guarded in Londinium, as well as the others. It seems while my warriors should be protecting Mercia from Wessex and the Viking raiders, they'll instead be inside Londinium, or in a nunnery.' King Wiglaf sounds displeased. I hope he doesn't mean us when he says that. I've no desire to be anywhere near any of the treasonous fools. 'In light of all this,' King Wiglaf continues, 'I wish to extend a heartfelt and genuine apology to Lord Coenwulf. No man should be kept from his children, or banished from his homeland when he's been as much a victim as Mercia's kingship has been. While young Lord Wigstan is the son of my son, and an ætheling, I also make it known, here and now, that young Coenwulf and Coelwulf are to be considered as æthelings and protected carefully from any who might think to harm them. They'll be raised with their cousin, I hope, and will support one another. Only then will this fighting over control of the kingship finally come to an end. What began with King Beornwulf's usurpation of King Coelwulf must end. The two ruling lines of Mercia are now united in the person of young Wigstan. May he live a long and happy life.'

I feel my traitorous eyes seeking out Lord Beorhtwulf in the crowd. So far, he's not been implicated in the queen's plot but the king's words dismiss his claim as any sort of ætheling. I consider if the king suspects him, or whether it's an oversight.

'I extend my thanks to the people of Mercia and those who assist me in ruling and protecting her that we've survived these terrible events. We'll move forward as one. We'll be wary of the Wessex kingship and the Viking raiders, and we'll not allow conspiracy to make Mercia bow down to anyone.'

Cheers greet his words, mine alongside the others.

I sense a weight lift from my shoulders.

The children are safe. Mercia is safe.

I join in the cry of 'Long live the king' as King Wiglaf strides from the hall, confident and assured, despite all he's endured. He's a brave man. I admire him all the more when his fights are within the witan and not the slaughter field.

26

I see Brihthild before she and Bishop Æthelweald are led to the ship, waiting to take them far from Mercia, as the holy men and women determined should be her punishment. She might have killed her brother, but that crime occurred outside Mercia. She's only being punished for her part in the conspiracy against the æthelings. Whether she warrants such regard is not for me to say.

Lord Coenwulf has offered some of his contacts in Frankia as a place for them to start their lives afresh. I don't think Bishop Æthelweald deserves that much help.

'Icel, Cuthred.' Brihthild greets us both keenly. She's pleased to be leaving Mercia. Perhaps that shouldn't surprise me. 'I wanted to apologise for the deceit. Equally, Icel, I think you owe me an apology.' She arches an eyebrow, but I shake my head.

'I didn't kill your brother.'

'No, I realise that, but you deceived him.'

'Perhaps, but I helped him and his friend as well. As you now know, there are always degrees of guilt.'

Her lips purse, and she inclines her head from side to side. 'Then we'll part as friends.'

'Who'll never see each other again,' I affirm. I never wish to encounter her in this life.

'I'll be grateful never to step foot in Mercia or Wessex during my life.'

I don't share her enthusiasm for the unknown. My face must reveal it because she laughs, a sound I've never heard before, and stands on tiptoes to place a kiss on my scarred cheek and also on Cuthred's.

'Stay safe,' she mutters and then boards the waiting ship. It's not the one that will take her across the Narrow Sea. This one is the rowing boat that was used to try and rescue the queen. It'll take her to the ship which returned Lord Coenwulf to Mercia where the water runs much deeper.

It's not rained for many days. Summer is in the ascendant, and the River Thames runs too shallow for the larger craft to wait on the quayside for them.

For now, King Wiglaf holds his position, but it remains precarious after the treason of his wife and bishop.

'And you,' Cuthred calls. He watches Brihthild with a fascination all young men have for women they like. With her, it's tinged with the thrill of the danger she embodies. I know to be wary. I'm not sure Cuthred does.

I say nothing to Bishop Æthelweald, but it pleases me to watch him entering the boat and trying to stay balanced. He has more than the clothes on his back, but not much. I assume much of his wealth and belongings remain in Lichfield. And they'll stay there for the next man to be proclaimed as Lichfield's bishop. I hope he's less tricky than Æthelweald. I always knew I hated the man.

Finally, Eadbald and Sigegar are also loaded on to the boat. The holy men and women took little time to decide on their guilt. Exile is a small price for them to pay for all they've done.

We're joined by Oswy, Cenred and Wulfheard. The five of us stand and watch as the boatmen manoeuvre the small craft towards the bigger one, waiting in the middle of the river. None of us speaks.

This has been a long-running difficulty for Mercia. I confess, I'm still not entirely comfortable with the outcome. But then, I'm not the king or one of the bishops. Once more, I'm glad I'm not.

'Lord Beorhtwulf has buggered off back to his estates with his tail between his legs.' Wulfheard eventually breaks the silence.

'And what of Ealdorman Sigered?'

'Ealdorman Ælfstan believes he'll survive on this occasion. He's a slippery worm, and one the king needs, although no one else sees that.'

'So, he'll make the same mistake again?' Cenred questions angrily.

'No, the king's alert to the problem. Ealdorman Sigered will be kept close. Much closer than any other. He might never see his hall again. He'll be tied to the king. He might even have to ride into battle beside him.'

My lips turn down. I'd much sooner Ealdorman Sigered was on the boat that's just sailed out of view.

'Remember, Icel, keep your friends close and your enemies even closer.' Wulfheard laughs.

I sense them moving away now that the boat's gone, but I linger. The sun's bright, making it difficult to see across the river towards Wessex, or indeed, along it, to where I know the river meets the sea.

I feel a shudder of foreboding. We have peace, but how long will it last for?

'Come on, Icel. We've got things to do. We can't stand around all day.'

I huff softly and, with a lingering glance, turn my back on the river, the border, and the problem of Wessex and, indeed, the Viking raiders.

Perhaps, I realise, I should enjoy it while I can.

* * *

'Lord Icel.'

I glance up later that afternoon as my name is called into the kitchen. Theodore and Gaya are busy tallying up their supplies and seeing what they need to replace. They're not leaving Lord Wigmund yet, neither are Wynflæd or Cuthred. I'm taking my ease with them, surrounding myself with the familiar smells of my childhood, even as I realise I know much less than I once thought I did.

'My Lord Coenwulf.'

He offers me a lopsided smile and beckons me to him. 'Come, the children wish to see you, and we've much to discuss.'

I hurry to stand and join him. The sun remains high in the sky, and outside, it's warmer than inside where the thick walls keep the kitchen cool. Lord Coenwulf directs me to the stables, where I hear the voices of the children. I also detect the rumble of Edwin's voice, and that of Eadburg's as she cautions the children.

'We've not had time to talk,' Lord Coenwulf announces. 'We'll be travelling to Kingsholm. I thought now would be a good time to extend my grateful thanks for all you've done for me and my sons.'

I swallow. While he smiles at me, I feel uncomfortable. Mostly because I realise I didn't do it for him. Lord Coenwulf still walks with a limp. He's far from a commanding presence, but he's a loving father. Maybe that's enough for him.

'The king has gifted me great treasures in recompense, but

really, all I need are my children, and that they still live, I understand, is entirely down to you.'

I watch Coenwulf and Coelwulf, unable to keep a smile from my face. Coenwulf walks towards me, and slips his hand briefly into mine. It's warm, and a little damp. I try not to think about that.

'Children should never be involved in these terrible games,' I offer, unsure what else to say.

'Whatever accord you forged with my wife, because I'm not blind enough to believe there wasn't one, is now fulfilled. I'll care for my children, as will my sister, and all will be well.'

I incline my head. I appreciate what he's saying to me, but it's untrue. Lady Cynehild's request to me cannot be dispended with so easily. Not that Lord Coenwulf needs to know that. While peace reigns, it's impossible to think of future difficulties, but I'm sure they'll come.

'I would also reward you, as the king did me.'

'My lord,' I start to deny.

'This isn't something about which you can bargain with me.' Lord Coenwulf smirks. 'And anyway, I think it really belongs to you anyway.'

I'm unsure what he means until he places the original piece of amber into my hand. I'd forgotten how heavy it was.

'You bought the horse fairly. To the purchaser goes the prize. I'll leave it with you to decide what to do with it.'

'Doesn't it belong to the queen?' I counter, marvelling at the colours shimmering on the surface of the glowing stone.

'We have no queen, Lord Icel. All she had was taken from her. You're not alone in benefitting from her downfall.'

I swallow. I'm unsure how I feel about all this. But it seems I'm not allowed to argue about it. Lord Coenwulf sounds severe about that.

'I learned a great deal while I was in Frankia. The Viking raiders are not going away anytime soon. Neither is the power of Wessex and her ambitions to be easily dispensed with. I fear there'll be many fights in the future, and that, my friend, will ensure you can buy your way out of some uncomfortable situations.'

'Then you have my thanks, Lord Coenwulf. I'll keep it safe.'

'And, of course, you'll probably need to use some of it to recompense the innkeeper in Worcester. Rumour has it Brute made quite a mess of the place before Pega collected him.'

I groan at that, not that it comes as a surprise. 'And Lady Ælflæd? What is she to do now?'

'She'll be with me, at Kingsholm, with my younger sister as well. Our family might not be Mercia's ruling line any more, but the latent power of our bloodline will be remembered. I'll be employing more guards, and reinforcing the defences. I'll protect my sisters, my sons and my nephew.'

'And King Wiglaf?'

'Is content with that. We made an accord. I married and had two sons with my wife before she died. I'll stand by that agreement.'

I nod. I'm not sure what I'm expecting to hear. I don't think this is it. Lord Coenwulf implies a peaceful future, even while building his walls high and speaking of the Viking raiders and Wessex. Perhaps, then, I should feel unease. Is this the calm before the storm?

I look to Edwin and Eadburg. They talk to the children and laugh at their antics. They seem wholly reconciled to one another, which pleases me.

'I know you had questions about Wulfnoth,' Lord Coenwulf continues. I startle. He inclines his head, noticing the movement. 'He was once a friend, but really, he was an enemy. My father was foolish enough to allow him unfettered access to him and his court. Wulfnoth turned it against him, allying with the future King Beornwulf. Not, I think, that my father died hating Beornwulf. My father wasn't a young man. The kingship never rested easily on his shoulders. All the same. King Beornwulf plunged Mercia into a decade of unease. I won't forgive him, or Wulfnoth for that, or indeed, your uncle. Cenred was a good man, in the end. But he was foolish. Remember, Icel, as you become a lord of Mercia, as well as one of her warriors, it's impossible to see the future. But, we can always repent of our decisions, provided we have the means to do so. Tread carefully. I'll watch what you become with eagerness, as will others who are your friends and allies, even your enemies. I wish you a good, long life and an assurance that, no matter what, you'll always be welcome at Kingsholm.'

I find myself unable to answer his strangely emotional speech. I look only at the boys, seeing in them the future of Mercia.

And then Lord Coenwulf speaks again. 'Mind, Brute might not be as bloody welcome,' and his rich laughter fills the stables.

HISTORICAL NOTES

In trying to stage a trial set in the Saxon period (which I now realise was a bit bonkers), I've relied heavily on a very short book, *Crime and Punishment in Anglo-Saxon England* by Andrew Rabin, and also his translations of the *Old English Legal Writings* by (Archbishop) Wulfstan (from the 1000s), from which I've determined how many oath-helpers people must have based on the Mercian Wergild listed within the source documents. This suggests the value placed on individuals – the king, of course, being at the top – although I've had to do some additional calculations, which I lay no claim to being entirely correct.

It's very difficult (for me) to understand what the kings and bishops were hoping to achieve at the time in terms of justice. This idea of forcing a reconciliation between the wounded parties somewhat does away with our current idea of right and wrong. Rabin attempts to explain this and is very largely successful (provided I've understood him correctly). Of course, many of these trials would have been concerned with arguments over land ownership, which were very tricky. In the famous case of Lady Eadgifu of Wessex (recorded in charter S1211), the mother of Kings Edmund and

Eadwig (who features in the *Brunanburh* series), her landholdings at Cooling required the intervention of her husband, stepson, son and grandson, in a long-running debacle which was never really resolved until the intervention of her grandson close to the end of her life. Even though she appears to have held the 'landboc' – the title deed for the land – and was a highly regarded member of the royal family, this wasn't enough to stop counterclaims. In the end, she assigned the land to the Christ Church religious community.

The phrasing 'thereafter there would be no friendship' is from another preserved charter detailing a land dispute in the later tenth century – between Wynflæd and Leofwine (S1454 dates from 990 to 992). In this, despite whoever was in the wrong or the right, the decision was made which was something of a compromise – both injured parties had to make concessions. No one truly 'won', even though Wynflæd had many who would speak on her behalf, including the king's mother, and the archbishop of York, and appealed directly to the king, Æthelred II, only for Leofwine to refuse to attend his summons saying that royal appeals couldn't precede a regional judgement on the matter.

The law codes from the Saxon period have survived from a number of different kings, the earliest dating to Wessex in the seventh century and known as the Laws of Ine. There are many others as well, the closer in time to us seemingly the more likely to have survived, and perhaps because they are believed to have been heavily influenced by Archbishop Wulfstan II (named above), whose writings have survived. There are many from the last century of Saxon England. While these detail many crimes and the necessary restitution, it's unknown how much these laws were applied and how much this was a lofty ideal of how justice should be enacted. Interestingly, there does seem to have been an aversion to capital punishment (as Rabin details). There was also a concern that the right sentence was handed to individuals – it was as bad to incorrectly punish as it was to have committed the crime.

Historically, there is no record that Queen Cynethryth ever conspired against her husband and Mercia either alone or with Wessex. Her conspiracy is born from the knowledge that Mercia's queens were powerful women who did like to meddle. She does also disappear from the historical record at about this time, as does Bishop Æthelweald. Whether the daughter of King Coenwulf (796–821) killed his son is unknown for sure. It seems highly suspicious, and some doubt the existence of young Kenelm/Cynehelm. However, a cult based at Winchcombe grew up around him and persisted for many years – this is the story that Wynflæd tells Icel.

I'm indebted to *The Forager's Calendar* by John Wright for helping me decide what plants would have been available at this time of year – summer, but a very wet one (similar to that experienced in 2024, although I wrote these scenes in January 2024). I've included gooseberries, a fruit I despise, and admittedly it might be a little too early for the berries to appear (and I am somewhat concerned they aren't a native species). As a sixteen-year-old student, I once spent one whole day working as a gooseberry picker and hated it. I earned the grand total of £5.00 for an entire day's work (it was the 1990s) and have never been able to look at a gooseberry since. I still recall how sore my fingers were afterwards.

I've written before, I think, of the fact that it's believed the River Thames was more easily navigated during the winter months when water levels were higher. For information on this, please access 'Connections and Obstructions: The Thames in Anglo-Saxon Military Strategy' by John Baker and Stuart

Brookes, available online, although you do have to purchase the article or the book it's in, which is *Beyond the Burghal Hidage*.

It's not believed there was a bridge over the Thames close to London at this time. The stark demarcation of Londonia into Londinium and Lundenwic is somewhat artificially applied by me. It's not known for sure that the settlements were quite so separate. I will continue to investigate in future books. I do seem to spend a lot of time trying to determine how to transport warriors and horses over the River Thames.

ACKNOWLEDGEMENTS

As ever, huge thanks to my editor, Caroline, for steering me right through another adventure for Icel. I wish I could make it easier on both of us, but alas, that's not the way my creative process works.

Thanks also to my copy editor, Ross, and proofreader, Shirley, and to all the Boldwood boys and girls, with a special shout out to Claire, Nia, Wendy, Ben and Hayley. I'd also like to express my warm thanks towards the narrator of this series, Sean Barrett. Thank you.

To my family, thank you for supporting me in your own special ways (and they can be very special sometimes).

To my support authors, Elizabeth R Andersen, Kelly Evans, Eilis Quinn, Donovan Cook, JC Duncan, Peter Gibbons, Adam Lofthouse and Richard Cullen, thank you for keeping me sane.

To my Street Team and other advanced readers, including the bloggers who support my book launches and Rachel who organises them, thank you, thank you, thank you.

And to my readers. Wow. Icel has taken us on a bit of journey in recent books. I've gone to places I never thought I would, and I want to thank you for sticking it out with me. We're going to get back to those pesky Viking raiders in Book 8. I hope you'll join Icel (and me).

ABOUT THE AUTHOR

MJ Porter is the author of many historical novels set predominantly in Seventh to Eleventh-Century England, and in Viking Age Denmark. Raised in the shadow of a building that was believed to house the bones of long-dead Kings of Mercia, meant that the author's writing destiny was set.

Sign up to MJ Porter's mailing list here for news, competitions and updates on future books.

Visit MJ's website: www.mjporterauthor.com

Follow MJ on social media:

x.com/coloursofunison
instagram.com/m_j_porter
bookbub.com/authors/mj-porter

ALSO BY MJ PORTER

The Eagle of Mercia Chronicles

Son of Mercia

Wolf of Mercia

Warrior of Mercia

Eagle of Mercia

Protector of Mercia

Enemies of Mercia

Betrayal of Mercia

The Brunanburh Series

King of Kings

Kings of War

Clash of Kings

Kings of Conflict

WARRIOR CHRONICLES

WELCOME TO THE CLAN ✕

THE HOME OF
BESTSELLING HISTORICAL
ADVENTURE FICTION!

WARNING:
MAY CONTAIN VIKINGS!

SIGN UP TO OUR
NEWSLETTER

BIT.LY/WARRIORCHRONICLES

Boldwood

Boldwood Books is an award-winning fiction publishing company seeking out the best stories from around the world.

Find out more at www.boldwoodbooks.com

Join our reader community for brilliant books, competitions and offers!

Follow us
@BoldwoodBooks
@TheBoldBookClub

Sign up to our weekly deals newsletter

https://bit.ly/BoldwoodBNewsletter

Printed in Great Britain
by Amazon